THE LINCOLN LOGS:

A DETECTIVE HARRY LINCOLN TRILOGY

HAROLD B. GOLDHAGEN

BOOKLOGIX˙
Alpharetta, GA

ISBN: 978-1-6653-0503-7

Library of Congress Control Number: 2022912720

∞This paper meets the requirements of ANSI/NISO Z39.48-1992
(Permanence of Paper)

0 7 1 3 2 2

ACKNOWLEDGEMENTS

My name appears on the cover of this book as the author. However, without the assistance of several imaginative and thoughtful people, this project might not have been completed. In detective stories such as these, no hair can be out of place. Two plus two must always equal four.

Primary recognition goes to my wife Betty Goldhagen for her patience in reading and re-reading these stories, tweaking here and there, improving each time. She contributed several twists and turns, adding to the suspense. Heartfelt thanks go to Alex Goldhagen, Mary Burke, Hannah Silvers, and Linda Tucker for keeping me focused and filtering the ideas that eventually developed into these stories. Thankfully, Ben Silvers was there to guide me through the foreign world of computers, for without his help, my manuscript would have been written in longhand on a legal pad.

To my old pal Michael Elia, who once again gave me the benefit of his professional editing talents, many thanks. Mike worked countless hours on each draft, illustrating to me how his edits made the stories better. This is the third manuscript that he's salvaged for me. I owe him my deepest and most sincere gratitude.

Finally, it would be remiss of me to not acknowledge my years with the police department. Without the experiences of those years, from the humorous to the brutally tragic, I could not have written this book, but despite their roots in actual occurrences, these stories, the characters, and the events are works of fiction developed exclusively between my ears.

DEDICATION

To my grandchildren Hannah and Benjamin Silvers, along with their Australian cousins, Mitchell and Joel Goldhagen. They represent a solid start for the next "Greatest Generation." Hopefully, this time it will be in a more peaceful and prosperous world.

A writer needs three things: Experience, observation and imagination. Any two of which at times can supply the lack of the third…

—*William Faulkner*

BOOK ONE

"RETRIBUTION"

CHAPTER 1

The telephone rang—never good news at this time of night.

Harry Lincoln answered on the fifth ring, expecting Detective Radio 199 to send him to the scene of another of the many homicides that occurred in the city.

Instead, it was the voice of his partner and good friend, Jim Conte. Harry was relieved.

"Harry," asked Jim. "Did I wake you?"

"No, Jim, I'm up. I've been sitting in my living room staring out of the window at the lights of the city's skyline, instead of lying in my bedroom asleep. Keep thinking about this case that's had us baffled for over a week."

"Me, too, Harry, and if I'm losing sleep over it, you should, also."

♦

Homicide detectives Harry Lincoln and Jim Conte were currently investigating the vicious rape and murder of a twenty-eight-year-old woman found by her husband on the living room floor of their upper middle-class home. Both veteran detectives were stunned by the terrible nature of the crime and the brutality of the attack.

It appeared that she had put up a fierce fight, but she had been horribly beaten. Three teeth had been knocked out, her nose had been broken, her jaw dislocated, and both eyes were swollen shut. April Scott lay in a pool of blood with her legs spread wide, skirt pushed up to her waist and her panties bunched around one ankle. The buttons of her blouse had been ripped off and her bra pushed up, exposing her breasts. Her pantyhose had been knotted tightly around her throat.

Neither cop would soon forget this crime scene.

♦

Detective Harry Lincoln had worked homicide for a decade, slopping through the blood and guts, and putrid odor of decaying corpses day after day, night after night. His job was to sort out the carnage left when one member of the human species inflicted the ultimate act of violence upon another.

Harry lived alone in a loft on the fringe of downtown, in an area that had been blighted for a number of years, but which was now being rejuvenated. He had received financial assistance from the city to purchase the loft, since the mayor wanted cops to live in the city. It benefitted the city to have added police visibility and cops coming and going at all hours in the different neighborhoods around town. It was a mutually beneficial arrangement; it was the only way most cops could afford decent, convenient housing.

Thirty-five years old and never married, Harry Lincoln believed the only way to be a successful homicide detective was to have no family obligations, no social plans to cancel, no dinners ruined, and no little league games and dance recitals to miss. When assigned to a homicide, a great deal had to be done, and done right then, for as long as it took. There is an axiom accepted in homicide squad rooms across the United States and throughout the civilized world:

"The first forty-eight hours of a homicide investigation are the most critical. Cases are most likely to be solved within that time frame. A successful outcome diminishes rapidly beyond that."

There was no such thing as punching a time clock at the end of an eight-hour day and hurrying home for dinner or a kid's event. In Harry's mind, a good homicide detective was married to the job. If you wanted a steady eight-hour shift, you got yourself re-assigned to the larceny squad or auto theft, maybe burglary.

After a moment or two, Jim asked, "Harry, why don't we have lunch with your dad tomorrow, if he's free? He can look at it with a fresh pair of eyes. It can't hurt."

"Good idea. I'll see if I can set it up."

♦

Partners for the past seven years, Harry and Jim were products of the city in which they now enforced the law. It was comparable in size and importance to other major cities. Its police department was comprised of 2,800 sworn police officers and several hundred civilian personnel. Its warts were absent from the Chamber of Commerce brochures. Warts were common to cities of any size, but the larger the city, the more warts it had. In major cities, warts become tumors, and some turned malignant.

Detectives Harry Lincoln and Jim Conte were two of the twenty-two homicide detectives responsible for eliminating those malignant tumors from an otherwise healthy society. They knew their way around and knew the streets. Jim Conte was Harry's senior by fifteen years, but each benefitted from the other's strengths. It was a good fit. After seven years, they had established a strong bond and a reputation as two of the best homicide detectives in the past twenty years, and they had a track record to prove it. Because their colleagues sometimes referred to them as "Heckle and Jeckle" (for the first initials of their names), and after extensive coverage in the media, they also had a following with the public.

◆

The three met the following day for lunch at Mike's Tavern, a landmark since the mid-1950s in a laid-back area of midtown. It was a favorite off-duty hangout for cops and firefighters. It was also popular with lawyers, courthouse employees, media types, white- and blue-collar workers, college kids, and neighborhood regulars. Photos and memorabilia honoring the city's first responders hung on one of the main dining room's walls. A red shirt with large white letters FDNY, donated by a group of New York City firefighters visiting the city after 9/11, was also displayed, enclosed in a large glass case. A sign named Mike's Tavern "the 10th Precinct." (The city had nine police precincts.)

The elder Lincoln, a retired cop, had spent most of his career working homicide. Ben Lincoln was the main reason Harry opted for the homicide squad when it was offered. Harry was very close to his father, a man he loved and respected.

When Harry's mother died ten years earlier, Ben sold the house where Harry had grown up and bought a small, one-bedroom townhouse. He had lived there alone ever since, playing his violin for pleasure. Ben and Harry, father and son, spent as much time together as they could, though Harry's job demanded most of his time. When possible, they attended the symphony or had epic battles over a chessboard. Ben taught Harry the game when he was a young boy. They since had played some close games, but Ben was still the master.

Now sixty years old, Ben was Harry's muse, advisor, and confidant. Whenever Harry had a problem, personal or professional, he went to his dad for advice. Jim Conte, a reliable and experienced source of advice, was Harry's "Plan B."

Mike's Tavern was the natural place to meet any time after the doors opened at eleven a.m. for a good lunch, a quick cup of coffee, or a couple of cold ones after the watch. One could usually find a friendly face there. Ben Lincoln went often and maintained contact with other retired cops from his era. He also liked to stay connected with some of the active duty cops. Mike's was a meeting place, a hangout.

As they settled into the restaurant, the subject was sports: baseball, football, basketball, and hockey. The three seemed to agree that they might be well suited to running the teams. Their criticism focused on anything from the bone-headed decisions made by management to the obscene amounts of money paid to professional athletes.

"Joe DiMaggio of the New York Yankees was the first Major League baseball player to make $100,000 a season," said Ben, reminiscing, "followed by Ted Williams, of the Boston Red Sox. Both played in the majors for several years and established themselves as the top baseball players of that era. Many people raised their eyebrows then. Today, rookies just up from the minors make nearly $500,000 for the six-month season before they've hit, caught, or thrown a baseball in a Major League game. Currently, most established professional athletes sign contracts worth millions of dollars, while cops and firefighters work two and sometimes three jobs to maintain a modest middle-class life. Something is seriously out of balance."

That led to issues closer to home: police salaries, promotions, health benefits, pensions, and some of the bone-headed decisions made by management.

When the waiter came for their order, they were ready. Ben requested the chicken quesadillas with a draft Harp beer, Harry had the fish and chips, and Jim ordered a hamburger. Both on-duty cops had to settle for a couple of glasses of iced tea. The tone of the conversation changed as they got down to business. Ben Lincoln listened intently as Harry briefed him on the Scott case.

"April Scott, a white female, age twenty-eight, was home alone because her husband was out of town for a few days attending a conference almost three thousand miles away in Oakland, California," Harry summarized for his dad. "The killer or killers apparently entered through an unlocked basement door; however, the front door was also unlocked. It's likely that he—and we'll keep it singular, for now—came in through the basement and left by the front door. Both doors were closed but unlocked, and there were no signs of forced entry in the house.

"Her husband, Jeff Scott, came home on Thursday after being away for five days—he'd left home on the previous Sunday—and found her on the living room floor. The medical examiner puts the time of death as sometime on Tuesday evening. Scott said in his initial statement that the front door was not locked, which he thought was unusual. Then he stepped into the living room and saw his wife on the floor. He went to her, realized she was dead, and called 911 from his cell phone as he was down on the floor with her. He said when he saw her clothing all disheveled he ran into the bedroom and got a blanket to cover her nakedness.

"He said he doesn't think he disturbed anything, except that he realized when the first police officer arrived he was cradling her head and crying. When we got there, Mr. Scott was on the verge of hysteria and barely able to tell us what little he did, which was enough for us to get started.

"His alibi is tight. We've checked. He was in California for the entire five days. The medical examiner said the cause of death was asphyxiation or suffocation due to strangulation by the pantyhose around her throat. This was confirmed in the autopsy."

Ben inquired about the rudimentary elements completed at the beginning of every homicide: witnesses, written statements, canvasing of neighbors, physical evidence, forensic evidence, crime lab reports, autopsy reports, and crime scene photos with measurements.

"Dad, the neighbors did not see or hear anything unusual; because of the cold weather, the doors and windows were all closed, and in each house the TVs were on. There is a vacant lot on the living room side of the house, and we haven't found any witnesses," said Harry, frustrated.

Jim spoke up, reading from a notebook. "It's not all gloom, though—lots of fingerprints and a bit of DNA. However, most of the prints belonged to the Scotts themselves and a few neighbors, relatives, and friends that have recently been in the house. A plumber did some repair work the week before and left his prints. We hammered him pretty good, and we feel that he was not involved. We have some decent unidentified prints that have been run through the FBI database with negative results so far. Now all we need is a suspect."

"We usually depend heavily on DNA evidence, a great tool that unfortunately you didn't have in your day, and like fingerprints it's indisputable, but this time it's pretty lean," Harry said as he pulled a sheet from the folder. "There was no trace of semen on her or in any of her orifices, indicating that he did not ejaculate or that he used a condom. Foreign pubic hair was found around her vaginal area and in the rug on the living room floor. The autopsy report showed traces of wood and paint particles and major injury to both her vagina and rectum, with a significant amount of blood from both, indicating forcible vaginal and anal rape. A foreign object may have been used; also, lubricant was present. Foreign skin and blood were found under her fingernails—minuscule traces, along with some skin particles, apparently, from when she was trying to fight him off her. There's a good chance he's been scratched up some."

Jim added that the only thing Mr. Scott said was not accounted for was her engagement ring, a one-carat round-cut diamond in a 14-carat white gold setting. "It was not on her finger or in the jewelry box where it was kept when she was not wearing it. In the autopsy report, there were marks on her ring finger consistent with a ring being forcibly removed."

Ben finished the last bits of quesadilla with the remaining salsa, took a long swallow of his beer, and asked the question he had been pondering since reviewing the crime scene photos. "The way he left her, without any dignity, even in death—which I've seen dozens of times—makes me wonder. Did he just not care, was he in a hurry to get the hell out of there, or was it on purpose? Maybe he was leaving some sort of message."

"Harry and I thought about that, Ben. If so, we figured the message was for us. So maybe before we clear this case, we'll have to solve a riddle."

They paid their bills, and as they left, Jim thanked Ben for his interest and insight.

"So long, Dad," Harry waved as he walked to his car. "I'll talk with you soon."

CHAPTER 2

A̶rnold Krebbs couldn't get her out of his mind and still tingled when he thought about the other night. There had been others, but she was special. He had watched her when she was fully dressed, then when she was oh, so completely naked, and each tantalizing step in between. She brought out something in him that he had not known was there. That night, they had taken it to the limit. It was better than a wet dream. It was real!

Arnold Krebbs lived in a small, shabby basement apartment of an old six-story building in one of the run-down areas of the city. Arnold was an unremarkable thirty-nine-year-old white male without family, friends, or acquaintances, not even a dog or cat—a loner. He was forgettable. People passing him on the street or eating in the same restaurant did not notice him; he blended into the cityscape. Arnold Krebbs was vanilla.

Arnold washed dishes for minimum wage in the Sandwich Shop, a small cafe eight blocks from his apartment. He earned extra money delivering orders for a nearby farmer's market. His bicycle, an ancient Schwinn with fat balloon tires—the difference between it and a ten-speed was like a lumbering draft horse compared to a sleek race horse—was equipped with a large wire basket on the front handle bars to carry the orders being delivered.

Arnold Krebbs was a window peeper—a peeping Tom. He rode his bicycle through the different neighborhoods late in the evenings, looking for lit ground floor windows with blinds or shades not closed properly. He was thrilled and amazed at the careless women who unintentionally offered him plenty to look at. At one house, a very attractive young woman worked out on a treadmill for about thirty minutes three times a week. She did her workouts wearing nothing but a bra and panties. He imagined her small breasts jiggling to the beat of the music, and when she finished her workout, she took off her bra and walked around to cool off, her nipples hard as diamonds.

Once again, while watching her, Arnold developed a demanding erection as hard as those diamond nipples and had to masturbate right then and there. Relief quickly spread through his arteries, and he pedaled home and popped open a bottle of beer from a six-pack he'd stolen from the market earlier that day.

He turned on his 16-inch black and white TV; it would stay on for the remainder of the night, showing mostly commercials or infomercials. The majority of them interested and intrigued him, but he lacked the money. Arnold relaxed now, thinking about those jiggling breasts that he could almost touch, and then he fell asleep.

CHAPTER 3

Had only one perpetrator beaten, raped, and murdered April Scott? The forensic trace evidence was from a lone male. Harry and Jim could now concentrate on just one murderer. Was there a connection between April Scott and her killer? Was it a random crime? Was there a motive other than rape? Was it a burglary? If so, why was the only item taken her engagement ring? Why was she so viciously tortured? These questions had to be answered before any progress could be made. They needed background information, so hard and embarrassing questions had to be asked of those who knew April Scott personally and professionally, but first, they had a meeting with Lieutenant James McGee, the homicide squad commander.

"Okay, hot shots; it's been a week now. Who killed April Scott?" McGee, not known for pleasantries or social niceties, wanted a briefing on the case.

"Well, Lieu, in a word—or rather, three words—we don't know."

This brought a barrage of sarcastic barks from the lieutenant about how the famous team of Lincoln and Conte were, according to the media, the "Chosen Ones."

"I'm sick and tired of reading your names every time I open a goddamn newspaper and looking at your faces when I turn on the fucking news. This is not Hollywood, and you're not fucking movie stars. You are detectives, and your job is to solve crimes, so do your goddamn jobs. Now, tell me what you do know."

The briefing did not take long—from the crime scene, the evidence, the autopsy report, the husband's statement to no witnesses, no motive, and no suspects.

"Okay, detectives, I want this cleared up fast. It's getting too much media attention. The heat is on, and you know that shit travels downhill. My phone has been ringing for the past couple of days, from the fucking media demanding a press conference to the chief of detectives and the chief of police. The next call will probably be from the goddamn mayor." McGee's bulldog Irish face had turned a rosy red. "And you know the shit is not going to stop with me. The both of you are next in line, so the next time you come in here, and I ask you who killed April Scott, you better not tell me that you don't know!"

◆

A couple of neighbors had to be interviewed in the Scott case that had not been available until now. Jim told Harry that he would handle them. Harry's girlfriend, Ellen Bainbridge, came over most Sundays, and she and Harry went out to dinner. Partners did those kinds of things for each other; it's what made them click.

"Anyway," Jim thought, "I'm not doing a damn thing except watching some mindless shit on TV."

Jim Conte lived alone since his divorce, which cost him his house, alimony, and support for his two sons' college expenses. He now lived within his means in a very modest apartment, which if Jim admitted the truth, was a dump. He was depressed and angry with his ex-wife, Doris, for taking it all from him. He had once confided to Harry, "Yeah, I fucked around some, but all men do. She caught me with one after twenty-five years of marriage, and you would have thought the world was ending. She turned it into World War III. The bitch took everything I had, but one day, I'll get even."

Sunday was date night. Harry and Ellen tried to have one night a week for themselves. Usually, Sundays were slow for Harry, and this Sunday, Jim was covering for him at work. The weekends were always good for Ellen, the twenty-nine-year-old who, like Harry, was married to her job. She was owner and CEO of Bainbridge Consultants, a human resources firm. The two of them were enjoying dinner at their favorite restaurant, Alex's at the River. It had the best view of the skyline from anywhere in the city and overlooked the river. It was a bit pricy, but worth it for the value received. Ellen loved the salmon Oscar, which she almost always had, but Harry was a steak and potatoes guy.

Ellen and Harry, satisfied—but not stuffed—from a wonderful dinner, returned to the loft, where Harry got the music going, the lush music they both liked. It was turned on low, just drifting through the loft, adding to the ambience. On Ellen's first visit to the loft, she was struck by its austerity. There were no pictures on the walls and not a plant anywhere. Since then, Ellen had added what she thought was missing, creating a warmer, more lived-in atmosphere. Ellen, Harry knew, was everything a man could want: gorgeous, bright, sexy, successful, and she could cook. Ellen brought Harry a beer and poured herself a glass of white wine, a California chardonnay, her favorite. They sat on the couch not saying much, just soaking it all in—two content people, glad to be together on a Sunday evening.

After a while, Ellen got up from the couch and went to the bedroom to change; the change was meant to please him. When she returned, it pleased him very much. Ellen was wearing one of his sport shirts, the top half-unbuttoned, with just enough cleavage showing to want to see more, the hem of the shirt not quite covering her panties. Those were the only two pieces of clothing she wore. Harry felt he could gaze at her for a very long time.

His natural inclination was to pull her down on the couch with him. His lust for her was just about out of control, but Ellen took him by the hand and led his five-foot, eleven-inch, one hundred-eighty-pound frame into the bedroom. Men were visual animals; hence, *Playboy* magazine and strip clubs. Harry's equilibrium tilted somewhat as Ellen let the shirt fall to the floor. There she stood, Harry thought, "the perfect figure on the perfect woman." Ellen helped him fumble out of his clothes, and then both became lost in each other for an exciting climax to a perfect evening.

CHAPTER 4

Arnold liked his job at the market, where sometimes the tips were more than he expected. The best part, though, was when he delivered an order and saw that an attractive woman lived at the address. He liked to return later in the evening to see if he could watch her. If she were like the others Arnold had watched, careless with the blinds or shades, he would see enough to satisfy him for the night.

As he roamed the neighborhoods, Arnold figured his chance of finding the right window at the right time was pretty good. To his delight, he almost always found the perfect window, and through it fulfilled fantasies, of which Arnold had many.

His biggest fears were dogs, husbands, boyfriends, and neighbors. He'd been scared off a few times, and he had been caught once. For that, he received a thirty-day suspended sentence, and he was ordered to go to counseling. He was never concerned about the police catching him. The few times he'd seen a patrol car, the cops were just driving through the neighborhood and not paying attention.

There were very few beauties of Playboy caliber. Most were average, and if they were not too fat, too skinny, or too old, Arnold Krebbs got pleasure watching them in their most private moments, never knowing they were being watched. He liked to return to some he had watched before; he had his favorites, and one of the best was the girl on the treadmill, but the other night was different. No, different wasn't strong enough; bizarre was the better word. It was like something out of a wet dream. He told himself to stop thinking about it before he slipped and said the wrong thing at the wrong time; it was a secret that he had to keep. He still couldn't believe it was real.

The Sandwich Shop, and the drudgery of washing the never-ending stacks of dishes, pots, and pans, didn't bother Arnold. He tried to do a good job; he didn't want the cook to complain to the boss about crud or grease left on something he had just washed. It wasn't that he liked washing dishes, or that the minimum wage salary improved his standard of living. Arnold's job included going down to the basement of the restaurant to bring up supplies. He had found an alcove halfway down with a grate that looked out to the restaurant at floor level. Most of the diners were from the office buildings close by; a lot were women. From his vantage point in that alcove, Arnold could look up their skirts and dresses. On his lunch break, he would grab a sandwich and a drink and then rush to the alcove. Whenever he was sent down to the basement for something, he would stop in the alcove for a quick peek. Arnold Krebbs did not want to lose this job.

Later that evening, Arnold rode his bicycle past the house, the house that was disturbing his dreams and unsettling him during waking hours. A portion of the yellow tape was still on the ground in the front yard, and he saw what looked like a detective car in the driveway. He kept going, riding through other neighborhoods, looking for a likely window where an unsuspecting woman might put on a show for him. As he rode and looked, he realized he did not have the same feeling of anticipation that had gripped him in the past. He should not have ridden past that house. Arnold decided to ride home. He was having flash backs to scenes he would never get out of his mind.

♦

Detectives Lincoln and Conte were at the Scott residence re-interviewing Jeff Scott, who was worn out and haggard looking two days after the funeral. "We know this is painful for you, but the more we know and the quicker we learn it, the more likely we'll find who did this."

Jeff gave them a vacant stare. "I was always gone. It was the job. If I had been home more, this terrible thing might not have happened."

Conte was sympathetic, but he had to press on. "Are you aware of anyone with whom she might have been more than friendly? Had she mentioned someone who made her uncomfortable or paid more than normal attention to her?"

"No," Jeff replied with a shake of his head. "April never seemed concerned or worried about anything."

For the past year, April Scott had been the assistant office manager at a medium-sized advertising agency located downtown.

Harry said, "We are about to interview some of her co-workers. Is there anyone who might be a good starting place? Is there any person she might have mentioned to you or someone who gave you an uneasy feeling? Are you aware of any enemies that she might have had? These questions and more have to be answered, so please help us."

They were discouraged when Jeff said, "I don't know any of her co-workers. I've never been to her office, and I am not aware of any enemies."

"We'll leave now, but should you have any thoughts about what we've talked about, please contact either of us at any hour, night or day. You have our contact information." Then Jim assured the grieving husband, "We are very sorry for what happened, and we'll do everything in our considerable power to catch the one who did this to April. We'll be in touch."

◆

The following afternoon, the two detectives visited the office where April Scott had worked. They learned quickly that April was not popular with her women co-workers, or even well liked.

"She dressed like a slut," said one direct woman. "Her hemlines were way too short. She couldn't sit down without showing the world everything she had, and her necklines were much too revealing."

A second woman added, "Several times when I was engaged in a business conversation with one of the men, April would sashay by in a tight skirt, like she was a fashion model on a runway, and the conversation would stop. The guy would just sit there, not moving, and gawk at her with his mouth open."

Ms. Evelyn Black, the office manager said, "She was a good worker, and she handled her responsibilities as my assistant well. I'm shocked and saddened by the terrible thing that happened to her, but in all honesty, her dress style was inappropriate for the office and did not set the right example. The women were constantly buzzing about her appearance, and the men were distracted, to say the least."

Jim said, "We understand that she wasn't liked by the women, but do you think anyone in this office disliked her enough to want her to be killed?"

"Oh, no," gasped Ms. Black, her hand over her mouth. "That's absurd!"

"Do you know of anyone, male or female, that she was friendly with, had a rapport with—you know, someone she might have gone to lunch with most every day?"

"No, I'm not aware of anyone," Ms. Black said. "April kept mostly to herself, but I'll ask around the office."

"One more thing," asked Jim. "How about the men? Do you think any of the men were misled by her appearance and actions to the point of wanting to fulfill a fantasy and showing up at her home?"

"There again, I have to say no," said a shocked Ms. Black. "I don't think any of the men in this office would be capable of anything like that."

♦

They left April Scott's office at the height of the afternoon rush, and Harry agreed to drop Jim at his apartment. Jim said that when he got to the office in the morning he would transcribe a summary of the afternoon's interviews on a supplemental form for the file.

Harry changed the conversation and casually said, "By the way, 'Inspector Clouseau,' we got a hit from the FBI fingerprint database. One of the unidentified prints from the Scott crime scene was a perfect palm print, and it belonged to one James William Conte. It was left on the glass top coffee table in the living room." Harry wanted to keep it light, but thought this might be a good time to tell his partner what had been on his mind for the past several weeks.

"First of all, it looks like you failed Crime Scene 101. Jim, you have been investigating homicides too long for you to touch anything before the scene has been processed. You're getting sloppy and careless—not only in leaving that print, but in your appearance. Some days you come in all rumpled, your clothes looking like you slept under a freeway bridge, and you needing a shave. When you are clean-shaven, you've nicked yourself up to where it's been noticed around the office. Maybe it's time to buy a new razor."

"Look, Harry... Yes, I fucked up once in all these years and touched something at a scene before it was processed. Tell me that you've never contaminated a crime scene. As for what I wear to work and how I shave or don't, that's my fucking business, so leave it right there, Harry."

"I know it's your business, Jim, but as your partner and friend, I want to help you, if I can, if you'll let me. I think you'd rather have this conversation with me than with Lieutenant McGee, who by the way, is going to go ape-shit when he learns about that print. It goes deeper than the print, Jim. Ever since your divorce, you've been a different guy. I think you need professional help."

Jim turned in his seat to face Harry and said in a menacing voice, "Stop the car, Harry." Then louder, "Harry, I said stop the fucking car." Harry pulled to the curb and stopped.

"Jim, it's ten, twelve more blocks to your apartment."

"I'll walk the rest of the way, Harry. Thanks for the ride."

Harry sat in the car and watched as Jim got out and walked away. He had never seen his partner like this. He seemed to be in a downward spiral.

Chapter 5

April Scott had not been happy for the last year of her six-year marriage. Jeff was a good husband and provider; they both had better than average incomes. They were young when they married—April twenty-two, Jeff twenty-five. Early in their marriage, they had agreed on careers rather than children. For vacations, they flew to different exotic destinations. The Caribbean was a favorite: St. Martin, St. Thomas, and Aruba, in particular. They enjoyed Europe, touring Paris one year and Rome, with a few days in Venice, the next. He had never physically or verbally abused her; they hardly ever quarreled. They were a normal, happy couple for five years, and then something happened; they just fizzled, or rather, he did.

Jeff's libido was all but gone; he had no desire for sex with April or anyone else. He had gone through a battery of doctors and specialists in different fields with no success. Whether physical or mental, he had a major case of erectile dysfunction.

April, however, was a different animal, with a strong sex drive and a healthy libido. She tried everything to bring him back, to interest him again. She tried kissing, caressing, fondling, and stroking until she was worn out. He had always liked seeing her in sexy lingerie, and he enjoyed it when she undressed for him slowly and provocatively. Some evenings, when the two of them were quietly watching TV, she gave him a quick, unexpected flash of her sexy panties, which served as a signal that they were headed for the bedroom. None of these things worked anymore; her husband was no longer her lover. Jeff Scott was impotent.

During all this, April had discovered something about herself; she enjoyed exposing and displaying herself. She got a perverse sexual satisfaction from it, a narcotic high. She knew she was attractive; enough people had told her how attractive she was. Standing naked before the full-length bedroom mirror, admiring herself, she thought her breasts were just the right size—nice and firm, not too big or too small, with hardly any droop. Her stomach was taut and flat, the trade-off for not having children. No one had to tell her that her legs were gorgeous; anytime she wore a close fitting skirt, dress, or tight pants and walked slowly through the office men stopped what they were doing and stared. She liked being looked at and admired.

As the vice-president for marketing at a software company, Jeff Scott spent nearly eighty percent of his time traveling around the country calling on vendors or attending conferences. He spent very little time at home, which April was not happy about, and she told him so. Jeff tried to placate her with the likelihood of a promotion to a top management position within a year or two, but she could not be appeased. This issue caused friction between them for the first time since they were married.

Disaster struck when Jeff's libido plummeted and he was no longer able to perform in their bedroom. Jeff continued to travel and work hard, and although April also worked hard, she was alone in the evenings and occasionally over a weekend. After a while, to amuse and entertain herself, she had an affair with a married man. She also flirted with the men at the office. Then a different kind of entertainment appeared. It started quite by accident, several weeks before her murder.

April had come home from work, collected the mail from the mailbox, and fixed herself a salad and a tall glass of iced tea. She brought them into the living room, kicked off her shoes, and turned on the TV to watch the news. After she ate, she made some coffee. She returned to the living room and settled down to watch her favorite sit-coms. Halfway through the second show, she heard a noise, kind of a thump outside the house against the wall. She turned quickly and saw movement at the window, and for an instant, thought she had seen the face of a man. The blinds were down, but open.

Is he an intruder? Or maybe a peeping Tom. Should I call the police? I'll just wait a few minutes holding my cell and see. I can always call 911, and I do have my gun. She had another thought. *If it's a peeping Tom, there's no need to involve the police. I can handle him myself, and maybe have some fun at the same time.*

She continued to watch TV, her peripheral vision tuned to the window. Within ten minutes, he appeared again. For the next fifteen minutes, she watched him out of the corner of her eye, watching her. *Okay, Mr. Peeping Tom, I'll give you something to look at.*

18

She stood up and slowly pulled her sweater over her head. The shirt came off next, and then her pants, all very slowly. Now in her bra and panties, she walked around the living room, deliberately folding her clothes, straightening up, and removing the dirty dishes to the kitchen. She then turned out the lights, changed into her pajamas in the darkened bedroom, and got into bed. She waited for almost an hour to make sure that he was not attempting to come in.

"That was fun," she thought to herself as she started to drift off. "He'll be back, and then I'll give him plenty to look at."

Then April Scott went to sleep.

CHAPTER 6

"Homicide. Lincoln," Harry answered.

"Detective Lincoln, I am—or was—April Scott's co-worker. I was the only woman she talked with; the others shunned her. I have some information that you might be interested in."

"Yes," said Harry. "I'm interested in anything concerning April Scott. Who am I talking with?"

"I'd rather not give my name, but I thought you'd like to know she was seeing someone. She told me that she slept with this guy on two different occasions. The problem was the man is married."

"Do you know his name or how I can contact him?" Harry asked, a bit skeptical, wondering if she just wanted to create a scandal.

"The only thing I know is that she referred to him as Bart, and he worked for Arkwright Aluminum, a client of ours here in the city."

She hung up abruptly, and the caller I.D. showed only "Unknown Name."

"Conte, get in here!" Lieutenant McGee bellowed into the squad room from his office doorway. As soon as Jim entered, the lieutenant slammed the door behind him. "What the hell is this?"

McGee waved the report from the FBI fingerprint database under Jim's nose.

"A palm print? You left your goddamn palm print at the scene of a homicide that you are investigating? What the hell were you doing, leaning on the coffee table so you could reach down and kiss your dead victim?"

"I must have touched the table when I leaned down to get a better look at how those pantyhose were knotted around her throat," answered a subdued Detective Conte.

"I must have touched the table," mimicked the lieutenant in a singsong fashion, still agitated. "You're damn right you touched the table, but you fucked up when you touched it before the room was processed. You, of all people, Conte, with all of your years of experience, the elder statesman of the homicide squad, the14-carat gold homicide detective, one of the chosen ones—you?"

Jim was humbled and apologetic. "I'm sorry, Lieutenant. It won't happen again."

"You're goddamn right it won't happen again, Conte, because if it does, your ass will be in uniform working traffic in some busy intersection in a shitty part of town, no matter how long you've been around. Now get out of here. Get to work and bring me the guy who killed April Scott."

Jim Conte picked up a set of keys to a car and a portable radio and left the squad room without a word to Harry, who was on the phone. Outside, at the rear of the building, was the detective car parking lot, a sea of unmarked cars, all the same make and model. The colors—grey, black, beige, white, and brown—and the license tags were the only differences. Jim took the grey car assigned to Harry and him.

He drove aimlessly, with no destination in mind, and finally entered the interstate freeway that circled the city. He wanted to calm down and collect his thoughts after the ass-chewing McGee had given him. *How utterly stupid and unforgivable to leave that print.*

His cell phone rang. It was Harry, but Jim did not answer it. He was not ready to speak to anyone right now, especially Harry. As he drove, his mind raced faster than did some of the morons passing him in their huge pick-up trucks.

His mood darkened when he thought of his ex-wife Doris. *You did this to me, Doris, you no-good, fucking bitch. We stopped having sex almost a year before the divorce. I'm not a monk, and I needed to get a little on the side, because after a while, sex with you wasn't worth the trouble. Now, after all these years, my life has turned to shit because of you, but maybe, just maybe, I'll have the last laugh.*

Jim drove the entire sixty-two mile circumference of the freeway and got off where he had entered. On the surface streets again, he drove to a pub where he and Harry sometimes grabbed a bite. His cell phone rang again. It was Harry for the third time, and this time, he answered. "Yeah, Harry. I'm at the pub for some lunch."

In less than fifteen minutes, Harry was sitting across from Jim, who was drinking what Harry guessed to be Scotch on the rocks, Jim's favorite. From the empty glass on the table, it wasn't his first.

21

"Partner, what the hell are you doing? It's lunchtime, and you never drank your lunch before. You are on duty now. You could be suspended for that, and you're going to leave here, get in that city car, and drive. That can get you locked up. Maybe fired!"

Harry ordered a couple of hamburgers and two glasses of iced tea for them. Jim left what remained in his glass and started to eat.

"Jim, what the hell happened in the lieutenant's office earlier? I heard him bellowing, but he always bellows. He doesn't know how to talk like a normal person. The next thing I know, you're gone."

"You were right, Harry. He got all over my ass about that palm print at the Scott murder scene, and I just wanted to be alone. I think I'll just cool it for the rest of the afternoon, take the car back to the office later, and then go home. We've been here long enough now, Harry. I'm okay to drive."

Harry told him about the woman's phone call. "I'll go by Arkwright Aluminum. See if I can locate this guy, if he exists. See you in the morning, partner."

◆

"Yes, detective, that would be Bart Russell. I'll ring him."

Harry stood before the reception desk at Arkwright Aluminum Company. "Mr. Russell will be right out. Please have a seat."

Within a minute, Russell appeared. Harry identified himself and asked where they could talk privately.

Sitting in Russell's office with the door closed, Harry began. "Mr. Russell, tell me about April Scott."

Bart Russell hesitated. "I'll tell you what I know about her and hope it will remain confidential. April and I met when her agency won the advertising contract with us. I was the contact person, and we worked closely together. There was a mutual attraction; lunches during the day became drinks after work, then dinners, ultimately leading us to a hotel room for sex on two occasions. The relationship ended by mutual agreement. I was admitted to the hospital and had hernia surgery on Tuesday morning, the same day she was murdered. I read about it in the paper two days later on Thursday, when I was released."

"Mr. Russell, if your alibi checks out okay, you won't be hearing from me; if not, I'll be back with an arrest warrant." He turned to leave, and then stopped with his hand on the doorknob. "If you had no involvement with her murder, our conversation will remain confidential."

◆

The next morning, the squad room had the usual buzz of activity. Some of the day watch, less than half of the detectives assigned to homicide, were at their desks working the phones, researching, and trying to keep up with the piles of paperwork. Of course, there was the inevitable banter and good-natured kidding laced with dark humor and profanity, and the never-ending war stories.

"Lincoln, Conte, come on in here," Lieutenant McGee called, motioning them into his office. "I think we might have another one. We just got a request from a patrol sergeant in the 7th Precinct for homicide detectives at 422 Greene Street. A woman was found dead in her house, and he said it appeared to be a homicide."

Harry and Jim had only been in the office for about an hour. They grabbed car keys and radios and were out the door.

When they arrived at the Greene Street address, they met with the sergeant. "The woman is a real estate agent. She did not show up at work this morning. She had a big closing on a house first thing this morning, and when she did not come in, they tried calling her. They called her house and cell phones and got no answer. She lives alone, and the boss got concerned and sent a young agent to her house.

"He told us that her car was in the driveway, and when he rang the bell and knocked on the door, he got no response. He said he started looking in windows, and when he got to the living room window, he saw her on the floor. He called 911 from his cell phone, and when we got here, I called for homicide. He's still here, and we'll hold on to him until you want to talk to him. The fire department broke in, and the EMTs confirmed that she was dead. The medical examiner is on the way."

Harry entered all the information into a notebook. Jim thanked the sergeant for his help and asked if a couple of his cars could stick around to keep the curious away from the house. "No one goes near the house unless they get clearance from Detective Lincoln or me, and whoever does get the okay needs to have one of your officers log them in. One more thing, sergeant—we'll need a list of all personnel who've been in the house before we arrived. That includes police, fire, and EMTs, and anyone else."

Harry and Jim approached the front door. "Let's step in very carefully and take a look, and Jim, this time keep your hands in your pockets," Harry said, trying to humor Jim into a better frame of mind.

"Not funny, Harry. I've heard about enough of that shit. When the crime scene techs get here, we'll tell them what we want from them, and then we'll wait outside." They went in and were stunned at what they saw.

The victim appeared to have been badly beaten around her face, but what shocked them was her clothing. The scene was a carbon copy of April Scott's murder: legs spread wide, skirt pushed up to her waist, blouse ripped open, and her bra pushed up, exposing her breasts. The only difference was the panties on the floor next to her, instead of around one ankle. There were pantyhose tied tightly around her throat.

As they stood in the foyer and looked into the living room, they observed that both rooms were orderly and without clutter. Everything seemed to be in its place, except for an overturned living room chair, and a book, eyeglasses, and some papers scattered on the floor.

"It was," Harry explained later to Ellen, "like those magazines we looked at when you showed me how to decorate the loft."

The crime scene techs moved into the house collecting forensic and physical evidence, taking photos and measurements, then tagging and bagging, and doing all the things that needed to be done before the crime scene was contaminated. Harry and Jim waited outside while Jim questioned Roy Harrison, the real estate agent who found the victim. He didn't add anything to what the sergeant had already told them.

"Roy, your written statement will be taken down at police headquarters. I'll have a patrol car take you there."

"If I do that, I'll have to come back here for my car. Why don't I just drive my car down?" replied Roy.

Jim agreed and instructed Roy Harrison to ask for Lieutenant McGee when he arrived. "Tell him you are there to give a written statement on the Greene Street homicide, and he'll fix you up."

The medical examiner arrived just as the techs finished processing the house. Harry and Jim went into the house with him. With the crime scene done, anything could be moved and touched. When the medical examiner was through poking, prodding, and turning the victim over, he made the time of death between seven and ten the night before. The cause of death was asphyxiation or suffocation by strangulation, and the pantyhose was the murder weapon.

"It appears that most of the blood is from her vagina and rectum and probably caused by something other than a penis. The autopsy will tell us more."

Before they left, Harry and Jim walked through the other rooms of the house and found them neat, clean, and orderly. Clothes hung in the closets with military precision, shoes stood in matched pairs, not one flopped on its side, all the items in the medicine cabinet had their labels facing out, and there were no dirty dishes in the kitchen sink. "I have nothing but admiration for anyone who keeps everything in the house so spotless and perfect," commented Harry. "I'm no slob, Jim, but I wouldn't be comfortable living in a place where nothing is ever out of place."

"Me, too, Harry. All you have to do is take a look at my joint."

♦

"Yes, Lieutenant," said Harry into his cell phone. "It certainly looks like a serial killer or a diabolical copycat. Everything done to the victim was done to April Scott; she was even found in the living room. Crime scene techs are gone, and the medical examiner just left. He put the time of death somewhere between seven and ten p.m. last night, and the cause was strangulation by pantyhose, same as in the Scott case. The victim, Julie Richards, is a forty-year-old, divorced white female with no children. She lives alone, and she was a real estate agent. Roy Harrison, the young man from her office who found her, is on his way to headquarters to give his written statement, and he's going to ask for you. If you hook him up with a steno and get him started, we'll be in before you leave and fill you in on the rest."

♦

The worst task, the most hated duty for any police officer in any police department, is the death notification, when the next of kin has to be told that a family member has been killed in a homicide, a traffic wreck, some bizarre accident, or a suicide.

A quick inquiry found that Julie Richards's mother and older sister lived together in a house about fifteen minutes from the victim. It was a modest frame ranch house in a quiet, middle-class neighborhood. Harry and Jim rang the bell, and an elderly woman opened the door. They identified themselves and asked if they could come inside. She introduced herself as Adel Sommers, and the woman behind her as her daughter.

When asked if Julie Richards was related, Ms. Sommers replied anxiously, "She's my younger daughter. What's this about?"

A few minutes later, they sat in the living room. The two women were on the couch.

Jim said, "We have some very bad news for you. It's about Julie. She was found dead this morning in her home, and it appears that she was murdered."

The women reacted as expected—shock, horror, and disbelief. They were overcome with emotion for several minutes. When they got themselves under control, they asked for details. Harry told them that they didn't have many at this time, and as they knew more, they would notify them.

"We would like to come back in a few days to learn about Julie's personal life. We will do everything we can to find the person who did this to her."

The detectives left their cards and told the grieving women to call either of them, any time of the day or night.

CHAPTER 7

Arnold was excited. He pedaled to the house that he was at three nights before, the house where a beautiful woman took her clothes off and walked around the living room for him in her underwear. It was about nine o'clock in the evening, same as the last time. He could hardly wait to get there. He was bursting with anticipation. When he finally arrived, he went to the side of the house with the adjacent vacant lot, which meant there were no nosy neighbors to see him. The living room window was on that side, towards the rear of the house. He was well hidden. He left his bicycle where he could get out in a hurry. He was ready.

The blinds were down, but open, like the last time. He looked in the window and there she was, sitting in a chair facing the window. She was wearing some sort of white night shirt.

As she stood up, Arnold said silently to himself, "Oh my god, it is so thin I can see right through it. I can see her tits and her nipples, and I can even make out the dark patch between her legs."

The blood rushed through Arnold's veins, giving him an instant erection. His heart beat faster until he could feel the pounding in his ears. As he stood there masturbating, she unbuttoned the top few buttons, slid the nightshirt off her shoulders, and let it slide to the floor. She stood there naked, looking straight at him, for less than a minute, all the time he needed.

April Scott then turned out the living room lights, left the room, and proceeded to turn out all the lights in the rest of the house, and go to bed. She thought, "I almost feel sorry for the poor, perverted bastard." Arnold sat against the side of the house for the next five minutes until he had the strength to pedal home.

When Arnold Krebbs got home, the first thing he did was turn on the TV, then pop open a bottle of beer. He sat very still in his chair thinking that she was the most beautiful woman he had ever seen, not counting the ones in Playboy or Penthouse, but this one was real, and he'd seen her in person. He couldn't decide which image he liked best—when she was standing in that sexy, see-through nightshirt, or her completely naked. He chose naked because she looked him straight in the eye the whole time he was having fantasy sex with her. She was by far his favorite. The girl on the treadmill had moved down to the number two spot.

♦

The next morning, Arnold overslept; his appointment was for 9:00 a.m. He hastily threw on his clothes, slurped what was left of a soft drink from the refrigerator, and rushed out of the door. He jumped on his bicycle and pedaled in and out of traffic, arriving with five minutes to spare. He chained and locked his bicycle to a bike rack just outside the lobby and rushed into the building. Dr. Jonas Goldsmith's office was on the eighth floor, and Arnold walked in at precisely nine o'clock. He sat in the waiting room for five minutes. When he was called in to see the doctor, Dr. Goldsmith greeted him warmly and asked him to have a seat.

"Arnold, tell me what you have been doing, or rather, what you have not been doing since we met last."

Almost a month prior, Arnold had been spying on a woman through her bedroom window when her husband came around from the rear of the house to take out the trash and caught him. The man hollered to his wife to call 911 and then proceeded to slam Arnold several times against a brick wall on the side of the house. Arnold was glad when the police arrived. Arnold Krebbs was given a thirty-day suspended sentence by the court, contingent on him reporting to a county psychologist for therapy once every two weeks, the duration of treatment to be determined by the psychologist. "Fail to comply with this court's order, Mr. Krebbs," said the judge from the bench, "and you will serve your thirty-day sentence, and if you come before me charged with the same offense, I will sentence you to one year in the county jail. Do I make myself clear, Mr. Krebbs?"

"Yes, your honor," said Arnold Krebbs, subdued.

"Dr. Goldsmith, I have not gone out since the night I got locked up. I have been working my two jobs and then going home to my apartment for the evening."

The doctor had heard the same assurances from other patients. Most of them had lied to him. He didn't see any reason for this patient to be different. "Okay. Arnold, I'm going to have someone from my staff spot check you at your apartment. You had better be home in the evenings. They won't be over every night, but more than likely two or three times a week. If you are out gallivanting, my recommendation to the court will be that you serve your thirty-day sentence in the county jail." Dr. Goldsmith looked at Arnold. "Do I make myself clear?"

Arnold replied sheepishly, "Yes, Dr. Goldsmith. I'll be there."

The doctor softened his tone. "Arnold, it's the only way to stop your roaming and trespassing. Remember, the judge said that the next time you are arrested for the same offense, he will send you away for a whole year."

On the way home, Arnold debated with himself. "Should I play it safe and go straight home after work each day, or take a chance and go back to the best one so far? I wouldn't mind watching the girl on the treadmill again, but maybe I'll try to stay home and see how often someone comes over from the shrink's office."

Chapter 8

Harry and Jim got back to the squad room late. Lieutenant McGee was waiting for them.

"I thought there was a lot of pressure coming down for one woman beaten, raped, and murdered in her home," Lieutenant McGee groaned. "If this is a serial killer, the pressure is going to be enormous when the media gets wind of it. I'll have to notify Deputy Chief Watkins first thing tomorrow morning, so tell me all you know."

"Just like Harry told you on the phone from the scene," Jim said. "It sure looks like the work of a serial killer. Everything looked the same as the Scott crime scene. However, we won't know about prints, DNA, or other evidence until we get the reports from the crime lab and the autopsy."

Harry leaned in. "The two victims lived on opposite sides of the city. Julie Richards lived in the 7th Precinct; April Scott lived in the 2nd, quite a distance apart, if that makes any difference. We don't know any more than what I told you earlier. We'll do a background on her tomorrow when the white-collar people are working. We'll also go by the real estate office tomorrow when they're open."

"By the way," said Lieutenant McGee, "we took that written statement from the Harrison kid, and from what you told me on the phone he's pretty consistent. It's in the file."

◆

The three left the office for the day, each going his own way. Harry made a call from his cell phone. "Hello, Dad, if you don't have any plans for dinner and want some company, how about meeting me at Mike's for a hamburger and a beer?"

"I'm glad you called, Harry. I was just trying to decide what to do about eating, but didn't want a big deal. That sounds good if you're through for the day. I'll meet you there in thirty minutes."

Harry was pleased. This evening would be just right—the two of them in the relaxed, friendly atmosphere of the tavern. "Okay, Dad, I'll see you there."

♦

On the way to Mike's Tavern, Harry thought back to his childhood. It was no better or worse than that of any other kid growing up in the suburb of a large city. His dad had been a cop in the city ever since Harry could remember. He still recalled his father going off to work in his uniform, so fresh, with creases sharp and neat, brass shining, and all leather equipment buffed to a rich, deep black. As a young boy, Harry would hand his dad the four belt keepers, one at a time, to be snapped around the uniform belt at his waist. After all the equipment was attached, the .38-caliber revolver was taken from the cabinet and snapped into the black leather holster. Later, when Harry was older, his dad traded in his uniform for a business suit, the apparel of a homicide detective.

Harry was an only child; his mom was at home with him until he started to school. She then took a part-time job as a receptionist in a doctor's office. She usually got home before Harry returned from school each day. There was a Plan B with a neighbor, should his mom be delayed for some reason.

Harry's dad had three hobbies: reading, chess, and playing the violin. They were a way to unwind after his eight or more hours engaged with the violence of the city, but Harry's mom was not placated by that explanation. She took it as his excuse to spend less time with her and their son. Harry remembered her complaining about the violin. She often told Harry she hated "that damn thing!"

Harry was twenty-five years old when his mom died. Then his dad expressed his regrets about all the precious time he had denied her. However, he continued to play his violin and attended the symphony whenever he could.

Harry could still hear the arguments, in an otherwise loving household, over the violin and all the time his father spent reading. It had a lasting effect on Harry's attitude toward marriage.

♦

"I don't know, Dad. It's just too perfect," Harry mused, sitting at a corner table, drinking a cold beer as he and his father waited for their hamburgers from the kitchen. He had just briefed Ben on the Julie Richards killing. "It's too well choreographed, like the killer wants to make sure we look at them as serial killings. If it's a copycat, he wants to take advantage of our thinking." The hamburgers arrived and they dug in.

"Listen, Harry, we've both worked serial killings. It all goes to motive, and it appears that rape was the motive in both the Scott and Richards cases. You'll know a hell of a lot more when you get the autopsy report and the results from the crime lab." Ben stopped, not wanting to talk to Harry as though he were a rookie, instead of an experienced homicide detective.

"On a lighter note, Harry, next month, Itzhak Perlman will appear at Symphony Hall and perform Beethoven's violin concerto with the Symphony Orchestra. I'm ordering two tickets for us. If you're still all involved in these cases, I'll get someone else to use the other ticket."

The constant grind of the job caused Harry to miss a lot of the good stuff. "Okay, Dad, I'd love to go and will if I can, so don't give that ticket away too soon." They stayed for two hours engaged in conversation, occasionally acknowledging someone waving from an adjacent table, or talking to someone coming to their table to say hello.

♦

The next morning, Harry and Jim arrived at the All-Star Real Estate office. Ms. Caroline Crawford, the broker, met them and led them straight into her private office. "You will have to excuse me, but I'm a wreck. I've been crying since I heard about Julie."

Harry nodded and said, "We're sorry that we have to be here so soon, but the sooner we can put everything together, the quicker the person who did this will be caught."

"Please detectives," agonized Ms. Crawford from behind a balled up, shredded tissue. "I want to help. Ask me anything."

"What we need from you, Ms. Crawford," Jim said, "is some background information on Julie Richards. How long had she worked here? Was she a good employee? How did she get along with others in the office? Do you know of any enemies she might have had? Any past or current clients who might have held a grudge? Can you think of anything relevant to her personal life that might have a bearing on her death?"

"All I can tell you about Julie Richards," sobbed the broker, "is that she is—oh my god, I should say was—the sweetest, kindest, most wonderful person. I can't imagine Julie having any enemies or problems with a client. She worked here for nearly ten years, and I dare say she was the most popular agent in the office; she was one of our top producers. Julie had been divorced over five years now; she never had children. She lived alone in a nice, middle-class neighborhood, and I wouldn't know if she was seeing anyone or not. She seemed to me to be very happy."

"Ms. Crawford, how about someone she might have gone to lunch with, someone she might have confided in?" asked Jim.

"Oh, dear, Julie was like a sister to everyone here. There was no one special that I know of, but I'll ask everyone in the office."

"Ms. Crawford, we are very sorry that this has happened," soothed Jim. "Should you think of anything else, we'll leave you our cards so you can get in touch with us, day or night. I want you to know we will do everything within our power to find the person who did this to Julie."

As they were about to drive out of the parking lot, Harry and Jim saw a woman hurry out of the building and motion to them.

"I might be speaking out of turn, but I thought this might be helpful. Julie asked me to have a drink with her one evening at a club not far from here—The Horizon Lounge. It seems like she went there often. Everyone knew her." The detectives thanked her.

Later that evening, at the Horizon, after identifying themselves, Harry and Jim questioned the bartender.

"Yeah, Julie was a regular here. Sometimes she drank too much. Never got out of line, but a couple of times we had to send her home in a cab."

Driving back to the office, Jim remarked to Harry, "There's nothing wrong with someone going out after work and having a few drinks—I do it all the time—but Julie Richards was not the Goody-Two-Shoes that Ms. Crawford knew."

Back at the squad room, the two detectives booted up their computers and settled down to dig into Julie Richards's life, as they had done with April Scott, previously. As always, the first inquiry was to NCIC (National Crime Information Center). The search, looking for any criminal activity, was negative, as they expected. Then, using her social security number, they used all of the resources available to them to get a snapshot of her life. There were no financial problems; the mortgage on her house was just several thousand dollars shy of being paid off. She had less than two years to go on a car payment and several credit cards with low balances. She was involved in no civil actions. Her name did appear in the marriage and divorce records: Julie

Sommers married Alan Richards 6/1/1992. Julie Richards and Alan Richards divorced 2/9/2002. They checked on Alan Richards, who had been in the United States Army since 2003 and had been stationed in South Korea for the past eight months. He had not been in the U.S. during the time of the murders.

"Okay, Harry," yawned Jim. "We've had enough. Let's call it a night."

"I've had it, too; see you in the morning, Jim."

Over the next four days and nights, they stopped by the Horizon Lounge at different times interviewing patrons, male and female. Most knew Julie, but no one could remember her huddling or leaving with a man.

♦

Lieutenant McGee appeared at their desks the moment they entered the squad room. "Conte, you and Lincoln come with me; we've been summoned to the chief's office."

On the sixth floor, a uniformed sergeant led the three into a large conference room adjacent to the chief's office. The room was crowded with the top brass of the department, the three homicide detectives were the last to enter.

Chief Robert Lansing stood and said, "Good of you to come. I know how busy you are; please take seats at the end of the table." They sat in the three empty seats and nodded to the other captains, lieutenants, and sergeants lining the walls surrounding the big conference table. There must have been twenty heavy brass, majors and above, sitting at the table.

Jim whispered, "Jesus, Harry, we're either getting the Medal of Honor, or we are about to be fucking fired."

"Okay, everyone, let's settle down and get started," said Chief Lansing. "I've been briefed by the chief of detectives. It appears likely we have a serial killer in the city. There have been two similar murders in less than two weeks. Homicide Detectives Conte and Lincoln have been assigned to both cases. At this time, I'd like them to bring us all up to speed."

Lieutenant McGee handed Jim the file and motioned for him to proceed. Conte stood and started with Jake Scott's discovery of his wife April's body. Then he moved to Julie Richards, pointing out that the second victim's murder was very similar to the first. He stressed that they hadn't learned much yet, but pointed out that when they received the autopsy report and the results from the crime lab in the Julie Richards case, they would know more.

Chief Lansing said, "Lieutenant McGee, I want you to pull Detectives Conte and Lincoln out of the case assignment queue. Do not assign them any new cases until this serial killer is caught. I want to make it clear to every sworn officer and civilian employee in this department: There is to be full and immediate cooperation with these two detectives until this is resolved. I don't want to hear that a bunch of bureaucratic mumbo-jumbo meant it took three days to get a document that they should have gotten within thirty minutes. Where it concerns this investigation, whatever they want they get, and that means right away!" The chief glared at the silent room. "I am a strong proponent of the chain-of-command; however, in this case, I'm instructing Detectives Conte and Lincoln to notify me directly if this order is not carried out. Lieutenant McGee, I want you to lean on anyone that seems to be tap-dancing around this issue. Are there any questions? No? Then let's all get back to work. Good luck, detectives. This meeting is adjourned."

As the uniforms and business suits filed out of the conference room, there was a low murmuring and a few furtive looks towards the two detectives, who were now known to all.

CHAPTER 9

Arnold Krebbs thought, "Should I stay home in the evenings to see how often the doc sends his goons over to check on me, or take a chance and do what I like doing more than anything—watch some unsuspecting woman in the privacy of her bedroom?" His mind raced. "The woman I delivered the order to today was older, maybe fifty, but very sexy. I would really like to ride back over there tonight to see if I can watch her. If not, I can always look at the girl on the treadmill."

Sitting in his broken recliner, Arnold fantasized about the best one, that gorgeous, sexy woman who put on a private show for me in her living room, twice. Arnold had an uncontrollable urge to peep into windows and watch women in various stages of undress, but he also had a phobia about going to jail and being locked in a cell. "I can't sit here every night knowing what I'm missing, but if I do go out, and they come and I'm not home, Goldsmith will call the court, and that fucking judge will send me to jail."

Arnold decided to wait and see if Dr. Goldsmith was bluffing. The first night, he satisfied himself with a stack of old Playboy magazines, waiting for someone to show up. No one did. The following day at the Sandwich Shop, he was able to curb his craving with the view from the alcove. Arnold forced himself to stay in his apartment the second evening while ogling the same Playboys, and again, no one came. On the third day, he delivered an order to a house belonging to a mother and her college-age daughter, and decided to return later that night.

It was 9:45 p.m. and dark, without a moon, time for Arnold to leave his apartment, when there was a knock on the door. It was a man who identified himself as an investigator from Dr. Goldsmith's office. "I'll report that you were home at this hour. I'll be outside watching until the early morning hours. Goodnight, Mr. Krebbs."

The next night, after he got off work and returned to the apartment, Arnold felt he had to get out. "All those women in Playboy are sexy, but they are not real." He gave it a lot of thought. "The doc said his man wouldn't be checking every night. I doubt he'll show up two nights in a row. I'll take a chance. I've got to go back to the living room woman and see what kind of show she puts on for me tonight."

It was just after nine o'clock on the night April Scott was raped and murdered. At the same time as the previous nights, he took up his position outside the living room window. The blinds were down and opened, as before; he had no trouble seeing in. He got a tingling in his groin when he saw her sitting on the couch, watching TV. This time, it looked like she was wearing a skirt and blouse. He was disappointed that she did not have on that same white, see-through nightshirt.

Arnold had not seen a man in the house the other times he'd watched her. Now a man entered the living room, but something was wrong. The man ran at her. She screamed and jumped up from the couch, but the man punched her very hard in the face and knocked her to the floor.

He straddled her and punched her face, while she attempted to protect her face and tried to fight back. When she lay on the floor, hardly moving, the man got up and came to the window, but before he closed the blind, Arnold got a close look at his face. Arnold's view of the living room was blocked, but there was a sliver of light along one side of the window, where the blind did not fit flush against it.

He looked into the room again, paralyzed with fear, but mesmerized when the man pushed her skirt all the way up, revealing her bare legs. He pulled down her panties, and when she attempted to stop him, he punched her several more times. He had something in his hand that he put on the floor, and then picked up again. The man had complete control of the woman. Her feeble efforts, pushing and tearing at his face, had no effect on him. Arnold watched the man pull down his pants and shorts with no interference from her, then slip on a condom.

Arnold had once paid to see a live sex show, but this was different. The man entered her and started driving hard, and all she could manage was to push at his face and sob. What happened next shocked Arnold. He didn't want to see more, but he stayed at the window. He watched as the man pulled out of her, then produced a long, slim object about the length of a three-cell flashlight and forced it into the woman's vagina. The woman screamed and writhed in pain then the man turned her over and shoved the same object into her rectum. He had never heard screams that pitiful, or the animal-like wails that followed.

She lay on her stomach, still screaming and crying, as he removed the object and put it into a plastic bag that he had taken from the pocket of the jacket he still wore. From another pocket, he took what looked to Arnold like a pair of pantyhose, which he wound around her throat. The way she thrashed around, Arnold knew that the man was killing her, but he was frozen at the window, staring at the horror. Some years ago, Arnold had seen a snuff film, in which the woman was raped and then killed, but this was no movie; this was real.

In a few minutes, she was still. The man turned her over on her back and arranged her. He pushed her skirt all the way back up and spread her legs wide, then ripped open her blouse and pushed her bra up over her breasts. Arnold noticed that the whole time that she was thrashing around and flailing wildly, her panties never did come completely off, but stayed wrapped around one ankle. Arnold got on his bicycle and left quietly, pedaling straight for his apartment. He had witnessed a violent rape and murder, but he could not let anyone know. Arnold would never forget the man's face and he did not want that vicious murderer coming after him.

CHAPTER 10

"These are just about the most brutal, vicious rape-murders I've seen in my twenty-three years," the medical examiner said, shaking his head slowly.

Harry and Jim were at the morgue for the autopsy of Julie Richards. "It looks the same as the Scott case," he continued. "Both women's faces were pulverized, and not just with a fist. I would say that he used something like brass knuckles. The violent penetration of the vagina and rectum was done with a foreign object. Again, as with the Scott woman, no semen was found in or on her."

When Harry and Jim returned to the squad room, the crime lab report was on the desk. "Amazing what a few words from the chief will do," commented Harry as he picked up the report.

"Yeah," agreed Jim. "They all knew he wasn't bullshitting. I've never seen one this quickly. We might not have had this report for a week or two."

"The crime lab did find evidence of microscopic particles of wood, paint, and some type of lubricant in the vagina and rectum," said Harry, reading the report. "I guess the wood and paint were from the foreign object the ME was talking about."

"Yeah, I'm convinced that we've got a serial killer working on us."

A detective two desks over motioned to Harry that he had a call on line four.

Harry picked up. "This is Lincoln. Can I help you?"

"Detective Lincoln, this is Judy Wright at the state crime lab. I'm working on some of the evidence from your serial killer cases, and I noticed something. The murder weapons, the two pairs of pantyhose? They were not worn by or removed from the victims. They were brand new; they had not been worn or washed before."

"That is important information, Judy. We assumed they belonged to the victims and that they were taken off during the attacks. I really appreciate the phone call." He hung up and told Jim. "Does that mean the killer bought them new and brought them with him to strangle

39

those women? If so, when we catch him, it will make a stronger case for the DA to convict him of pre-meditated murder."

"Yeah, but first we have to catch him, Harry," said Jim.

"The crime scene techs lifted a lot of prints from the house, so we'll be spending the next few days eliminating those prints, and then we'll see what's left."

"Well," asked Lieutenant McGee, approaching their desks. "How's the chief's new golden boys? Everyone kissing your asses?"

"Lieu, we have been getting a lot of cooperation from everyone so far, so it doesn't look like you'll have to lean on anybody, much to your chagrin."

McGee wasn't amused. Harry then told him about the call from the crime lab.

McGee said, "I know you have lots of work to do, eliminating and identifying prints—and they better not be yours, Conte. Also, the canvassing of the neighbors has to be completed. I'm assigning a couple of other detectives to handle that. You two have been hitting it pretty hard, so go home now and come in fresh in the morning. I want a briefing each day before you go home, or the next morning, if you work late the night before."

As the two walked to their cars, Harry said to Jim, "You see, the wild Irishman does have a heart after all in that barrel chest of his."

◆

The press conference was held at twelve noon the following day in the large public affairs room at police headquarters. Standing at the podium, facing the glaring lights of the TV cameras, was the police chief, Robert Lansing. Directly behind him stood Deputy Chief Glenn Watkins, Lieutenant James McGee, and Detectives James Conte and Harry Lincoln.

"As you know, we are investigating two rape-murders in the city. They appear to be linked," began Chief Lansing. "Before we get into the details of the crimes, I'd like Chief of Detectives Watkins to say a few words."

Deputy Chief Glenn Watkins stood before the bank of microphones and addressed the assembled media. "I won't take up much valuable time, but I want to stress that we are not certain these murders are connected. Be responsible and don't panic the city. We don't want to hear 'serial killer' on the six o'clock news or see it in tomorrow morning's headlines. We will keep you up to speed on the investigation, though there will be things we have to keep confidential. We don't want the killer to know what we know or what we are doing. With that said, I'll turn the podium over to homicide commander Lieutenant James McGee, who will brief you on these cases."

Lieutenant McGee proceeded to lay out most of the relevant facts of the Scott and Richards cases, skimming over the similarities, and then opened for questions. The questions came rapidly, and McGee yielded to Conte and Lincoln for the answers.

"We understand that in both of these cases, the brutality was substantially more vicious than in normal rape-murders." This inquiry came from a young male TV reporter with hundred-dollar, blow-dried hair.

Jim answered slowly, shaking his head. "All rape-murders are brutal and vicious."

A print reporter asked, "Did the victims know each other?"

"We don't believe so," said Harry.

"Detectives," called a woman reporter from another TV station. "Was there any connection between the killer and these victims?"

"That's a part of our investigation that we're still working on," Jim said.

"What about a connection between the victims?" she asked again.

Jim said, "As we've already answered, we are not aware of any connections."

From the crowd a voice cried, "Do you have any suspects at this time?"

"No, we do not," said Harry tersely.

"How about witnesses? Are there any witnesses to these murders?" shouted a male voice somewhere in the crowd.

"We haven't found any, but we're still looking," Harry answered honestly.

The woman from the TV station asked, "What about the murder weapons, the pantyhose? Were they taken off the victims by the murderer before the rapes?"

"The crime lab is working on that now and should be able to answer that for us soon."

A newspaper reporter asked, "Is the same man responsible for both of the rape-murders, or did two or more men commit each rape-murder, like a gang rape?"

"Right now, it appears as though one man committed both crimes. We believe it was the same man."

The reporter pressed, "Do you have strong evidence in these cases? Could you tell us something about it?"

"I'm afraid we can't disclose any evidence at this time. That's part of our on-going investigation." *Ask a dumb question and get the standard canned answer*. That reporter had been around a long time and knew better than to such a dumb question.

Some of the reporters were going around in circles, asking the same questions in different ways, trying to get answers. However, Conte and Lincoln had handled a few news conferences along the way.

The two detectives were losing their patience, answering the same questions repeatedly, while the rest of the brass sat back and said nothing.

The press conference went on for another twenty-five minutes, before Chief Lansing stood and said, "That's all we have at this time, and these detectives have to go to work." He thanked the media for coming and closed the conference.

Harry and Jim, feeling like wrung-out dish rags, spent the rest of the afternoon catching up on their paper work.

Harry was about to get into his car at the end of the day when his cell phone rang.

"What are you doing for dinner tonight, handsome?"

That voice always made him feel good.

"Hi, Ellen. I'm just leaving work and don't have any plans."

"Why don't you come over? I feel like cooking tonight. I've got some butter steak we could throw on the grill."

"That sounds delicious, but is that all you've got on your mind, Ellen?"

"No. I was going to ask you to pick up a bottle of red on the way."

It was just what he needed after being worn out by the media.

"Okay, I'll be there in forty-five minutes, if I can get through rush-hour traffic."

It took Harry over an hour. The freeway was backed up for several miles with stop-and-go traffic because a couple of knuckle-heads, one driving a large Hummer, the other in an equally monstrous SUV, ran each other into the guard rails, adding more stress to his day. After he got off the highway, Harry stopped at a liquor store and picked up a good Italian Chianti they both liked with steak. The moment Harry arrived and gave Ellen a hello kiss, he forgot about the freeway delay.

She always had a quiet, soothing, calming effect on him. Harry grilled the steak, and Ellen took care of the rest, resulting in a dinner that would have been the envy of a five-star restaurant.

After they finished, Harry and Ellen cleared the table, loaded the dishwasher, and cleaned up the kitchen. Then they sat in the living room, finishing the wine and relaxing to easy-listening music.

"Harry, I know you have a lot of pressure on you. Do you think one man committed both crimes? Do you think he'll do it again?"

"To be honest, Ellen, we just don't know, but if it is the same guy, we better catch him before he strikes again." She was massaging his neck and shoulders; it felt so good he did not want to move.

"Do you think I should be concerned? I have my gun, and you showed me how and when to use it, but I am still very uncomfortable being here alone."

Harry thought for a minute. "Maybe I should stay here with you until all this blows over. I could start tomorrow night. I don't have a change of clothes here and I have to be in the office real early in the morning. I'll bring my stuff over after work tomorrow, and then we can both have some peace of mind."

"Oh, Harry, I would feel so much better."

Harry wondered if he was getting too close to Ellen. That wasn't in the plan, but he'd think about that some other time. His first priority was to catch the killer who had claimed two victims.

Harry and Ellen listened to music as they relaxed on the couch until he felt a familiar stirring. He kissed her, and she responded with the intense passion that he loved about her. Buttons opened, zippers released, and a mixture of clothing trailed them into the bedroom, he removed her lacy things. Foreplay was replaced by potent emotions, resulting in a vigorous and erotic coupling. Then they both rested, Ellen feeling the afterglow, and Harry waiting until he was back at full strength. Within an hour, Harry was okay to drive home, and the wine was no longer affecting him.

Harry checked all the doors and windows to be sure the house was secure. "Listen, Ellen, when I leave, double-lock the door and don't open it to anyone that you don't know. Keep your gun with you, and should someone break in, just point and shoot as I showed you. First call 911, and then call me." They kissed tenderly at the door, and Harry left for home.

CHAPTER 11

Arnold Krebbs was an emotional, nervous wreck, his sleep interrupted by nightmares in which he could see and hear her screaming, and he had daily flashbacks while at work. He was so disturbed by what he had witnessed, that his time in the alcove of the Sandwich Shop was no longer as exciting. Every skirt he saw was hers; every face was April Scott's face. Someone left a newspaper in the kitchen next to the sink where he washed all the dishes, and there it was on the front page—not only her name, but also her photo, that beautiful face he had fantasized over for the past two weeks.

◆

"Arnold, you seem to be making good progress," Dr. Goldsmith said, pleased, at the next session as he reviewed the investigator's report. "You've been home every night that he's checked on you, even the five consecutive nights he kept coming back."

"Yes, Dr. Goldsmith. I've been trying very hard to stop what I've been doing. I don't want to go to jail."

"Well, Arnold, let's give it one more week to see if you are home when my investigator checks on you. If I get another positive report, we will terminate our sessions, and I will notify the court."

"Thank you, Dr. Goldsmith," said Arnold Krebbs, relieved.

◆

For the next several weeks, Arnold hardly went to the alcove at the Sandwich Shop. When delivering orders, he made no plans to return to spy on attractive woman customers. His fear of jail was real, and though the sessions with Dr. Goldsmith were a joke, that terrible night two weeks ago couldn't be shaken off.

Arnold was stunned the next morning when he picked up a discarded newspaper and read about the murder of Julie Richards. Her name meant nothing to him, but some of the details he read sounded familiar—the same things he witnessed with April Scott.

"Detectives Harry Lincoln and Jim Conte said, 'Yes, there are similarities in both murders, but we are not saying this is the work of a serial killer.' When asked whether they thought the killer would strike again, Detective Conte said, 'We have no reason to believe he will. We certainly hope not.'"

The article went on to say, "At this time, the police have no witnesses to either murder, but emphasize that anyone who saw or heard anything should contact the police."

Arnold didn't know what to do. He was not a model citizen, and he had broken the law when he spied on women from outside their homes. He had witnessed April Scott's murder and could identify her killer. If he went to the police and his name was made public, the man who killed April might come after him. Arnold knew how vicious and brutal the man was, and he was afraid that he, too, would be killed.

After several sleepless nights, he decided not to go to the police. He also decided to stay home after work for the time being; since the murders, the police would be more alert. He did not want to be caught sneaking around houses at night. Arnold Krebbs would keep a low profile.

◆

Detectives Lincoln and Conte projected anything but a low profile. The media hounded them, like paparazzi going after a celebrity. At lunch, reporters pushed cameras and microphones into their faces as they ate.

"Look," said Jim, trying to maintain a level of decorum. "We held a press conference to answer your questions without compromising the investigation. Following us everywhere with your cameras is interfering with this investigation, which is illegal. Let's not have an ugly incident. Just back the fuck off!"

The media could not resist the sound bite, and Jim saw himself on the eleven o'clock news with the offending word bleeped out.

◆

Harry and Jim went to the streets, into the underbelly of society, looking for informants who had been useful in the past—street people who heard things and were aware of criminal activity.

"Ham, those two women who were raped and murdered in their homes are all over the news. One was in the 7th, and the other the 2nd, so put your ear to the ground; let me know something and let me know soon, like yesterday," Harry said to one of his best informants.

Ham, a long time street hustler who heard all the rumblings, answered respectfully, "Detective Lincoln, I'll put the word out, an' if the talk is on the streets, you'll be the first to know."

"Okay, Ham. I'll be waiting to hear from you."

Most successful detectives developed informants by helping them out of minor violations, or turning a blind eye to the same. In return for a "pass," the detective got information to help solve serious crimes. The detectives had done some favors over the years, and it was time to collect the IOUs. They put out the word to others who had delivered in the past—Lincoln and Conte wanted a name.

♦

The next morning, Harry and Jim drove to the state crime lab to meet with the chief pathologist, Dr. Samuel Gordon, a veteran of several decades.

"Jim, Harry, good of you to come. I could have sent this report over to you, but I thought I'd notify you in person. Anyway, it's been too long since I've seen you both."

"Good to see you also, Doc," Jim replied. "It has been a while."

"Harry, how's your dad?"

"He's doing fine. Still playing his violin, beating me stupid over a chess board, and enjoying retirement."

"I am very pleased to hear that, Harry."

"Judy called and gave us the results of her analysis off the pantyhose used in both cases. That will give the DA a good argument for pre-meditated murder if we ever catch this guy."

"Well, here's another piece to your puzzle." Dr. Gordon opened a file on his desk and pulled out a report. "Some of the results from the murders of April Scott and Julie Richards, concerning the wood, paint, and lubricant found in them. The samples that we tested came from the same foreign object. The wood is consistent with the handle from a household broom. Garden tools such as rakes, shovels, hoes, and axes have heavier and stronger handles, and they have been eliminated.

"The paint particles are red and common to broom handles that can be found in Home Depot, Lowes, and Wal-Mart, plus other hardware stores, super markets, and other retail stores in the U.S. The lubricant is K-Y jelly, also bought everywhere."

"Thanks, Doc. We appreciate the quick analysis," Jim said, getting ready to leave.

"It's not much to go on. Sorry I couldn't be more help. You two be careful, and let me know if you need anything else."

"We will. Thanks again, and give our thanks to Ms. Wright." Harry waved as they walked to the car.

◆

The silence from the streets was deafening. There was no information concerning the murders from their most reliable informants. The detectives coaxed, cajoled, coerced, and even threatened. Harry and Jim requested that other units tighten up the streets; there would be no "business as usual." Nobody would move. Not until they had a name.

Beat cars patrolled high crime areas to give exceptional vigilance to the rougher bars. As drinkers drove away, they were stopped and given field sobriety tests. There were many DUI arrests. Vice cops cleared the streets of hookers, and neighborhood thugs were run off the street corners. The pressure was on; the underbelly could not breathe. Two weeks went by, and there was no word from Ham or anyone else.

"Ham, goddamn it, I haven't heard from you for a couple of weeks now." It was after midnight, in a vacant parking lot in a desolate part of the city.

"Detective Lincoln, I been askin' aroun'; been listening to the drum beats. With all the heat been comin' down, I woulda heard somethin' by now. I gotta tell ya, this wasn't done by no gangbanger or street thug. This is out of my jurisdiction; your killer ain't from the streets, at least not no one that I would hear about."

"Well, Ham, keep looking and listening, and if you get a nibble, I want to know about it."

◆

Harry and Jim followed up on numerous leads from the police department's tip line. These were phoned in by citizens, some anonymous, some logical and reasonable, others bizarre, but all trying to be helpful, and of course, to collect the $1,000 reward money.

They were at a standstill, past the frantic first forty-eight hours when most homicides are solved. They were at the point at which detectives keep at it until they work themselves into exhaustion. Additional leads and clues are followed up until they are eliminated. The break in the case happens when someone comes forward with the missing piece of the puzzle.

"Jim, I don't know what we can do now that we haven't already done two or three times."

"Yeah, Harry. We're stuck in the dead zone until we catch a break, and every time we enter the squad room, I expect an explosion from McGee's office."

"Well, remember what he told you about shit floating downhill, Jim. I guess we had better get ready to be the outhouse."

CHAPTER 12

Harry had been staying at Ellen's place for the past two weeks. It was different from when he saw her once each week. Missing was the anticipation, counting down the hours with the expectation of another perfect Sunday evening. Their lovemaking had always been terrific; sex with Ellen was as good as it gets. Ellen had other attributes: brainy, beautiful, successful, and damn good to him. However, too much togetherness did not work for him.

Men and women see each other as opposite parts, and when the two parts fit, it makes an exceptional whole. Men instinctively are protective of women and admirers of their beauty, enjoying private bedroom scenes of frilly, sheer nighties and lacy underwear. In time, their goddesses are more likely to be adorned in comfortable pajamas or flannel nightgowns. Harry guessed that must be what happened to married couples after a while. The freshness wore off.

However, he wasn't complaining, and until the killer was caught, they both felt better if he stayed with her. When it was all over, though, he thought it might be good to back off some. Harry would be glad to return to his loft. He loved the solitude.

◆

When they arrived at the squad room, Harry and Jim spent a couple of hours running down the leads they could on the phone. Lieutenant McGee called Jim to his office and told him to report to Deputy Chief Watkins' office.

"What's up, Lieu?" asked Jim Conte, a puzzled look on his face.

"Just go on up. He wants to speak with you," said McGee, expressionless.

"Well, Lieutenant," said Jim. "How about Harry? Is he going up with me?"

McGee answered, "No, Conte. He just wants to speak with you."

A short time before, when Lieutenant McGee had advised the chief of detectives of the sensitive situation that had developed overnight, the chief asked McGee to give him a few minutes to get one of the chaplains to his office before he sent Conte up. When Jim came out of McGee's office, he looked at Harry, shrugged his shoulders, and headed down the hallway towards the elevators.

♦

Earlier that morning, Lieutenant McGee had received a phone call from Lieutenant Otto Keehner, the day watch commander in the 5th Precinct. "Hey, Mac, I think we found another serial killer victim. Doris Conte, Detective Conte's ex-wife. We need homicide detectives here, but I didn't think it wise to put it on the air. I wouldn't think you'd want to send Conte."

"No, Otto, you're right. Thanks for the heads up. I'll send Detective Lincoln. He'll be there as soon as he can." Lieutenant McGee motioned for Harry to come to his office. "Don't sit down, Harry. Go straight to 2001 Beechwood Road in the 5th Precinct and meet the watch commander, Lieutenant Keehner. It looks like our serial killer claimed his third victim. Doris Conte, Jim's ex-wife."

Harry did sit down to digest what he had just heard. "Do you have any details? Where's Jim?"

McGee answered, "He's upstairs with Deputy Chief Watkins and the chaplain, and no, I don't have any details. That's why I want you out there as soon as you can get there."

♦

Harry headed for 2001 Beechwood Road, a house he'd been to many times, before Doris and Jim divorced. He and Ellen, Jim and Doris, other cops, and their spouses and significant others had spent some enjoyable times together there. Even Harry's dad, Ben, had been at the shindigs. *I hope it's a mistake; it's not Doris,* he thought. *If it is, I hope she was not beaten and tortured.*

Shortly after Harry arrived on Beechwood Road, he found the watch commander in the crowd. "Lieutenant Keehner? I'm Detective Lincoln, Homicide."

"Yeah, Lincoln. I recognize you from TV. Glad you got out here so quickly. Let me tell you what we have here. The victim is Doris Conte, Detective James Conte's ex-wife. She did not show up for work this morning at the beauty shop where she is a hairdresser, and she had a couple of early appointments. She didn't answer her home or cell phone when they tried to call her.

"Her co-workers called the 'in-case-of-emergency' number, which is her parents' home. Her father, George Lockwood, drove to the Conte house and found her on the living room floor. 911 received a frantic call from Mr. Lockwood. They dispatched a couple of patrol cars, the sector sergeant, fire rescue, and an ambulance. After the EMTs advised that she was dead, Sergeant Nancy Stennis got a sheet from the ambulance to cover her and kept everyone out of the house until I arrived. Crime scene techs and the medical examiner are on the way."

Yellow crime scene tape and several officers guarded the house to keep the curious at bay. "Mr. Lockwood was extremely upset and wanted to get home to his wife. He was in no shape to drive, so I had a patrol car take him. He said there was another car at home so he could return anytime to get the car he left here. Maybe you can give him and Mrs. Lockwood time to get over the shock and have his written statement taken later."

"Of course, Lieutenant. We'll have the chaplain visit and contact their minister."

"Detective Lincoln, I've been around a long time and seen a lot, but only a depraved maniac could do what he did to that woman. Get him, and get him quick. If you need anything from the 5th, let me know."

"Lieutenant, could you leave several officers here to keep people away from the house? No one goes into the house without my okay. Have an officer log in anyone that does. I'll also need a list of people who have been in the house this morning."

"Okay, Lincoln, it's done. Sergeant Stennis will stand by here. Anything else you need, check with her." With that, he left.

For the first time in his career, Harry Lincoln was reluctant to enter a crime scene. He took a deep breath as he approached the living room. She was covered with a sheet up to her neck. If Harry hadn't known it was Doris Conte, he would not have recognized her in the shattered, mangled remains of her face. He backed out of the house into the front yard and leaned against a patrol car to collect himself and wait for the crime scene techs and the medical examiner. It was one thing to deal with bloody, horribly mauled bodies, but this was different. This was personal.

The techs finished processing the crime scene according to Harry's instructions. With the arrival of the medical examiner, they both went into the living room. The sight was chilling; her skirt was up, her legs were spread, her bra was pushed over her breasts, her panties were at her feet, and there were pantyhose around her throat.

"I put the time of death between eight and eleven o'clock last night," estimated the ME. "The cause appears to be strangulation. It also looks like there was a good bit of trauma to the vagina and rectum, probably with a foreign object, but I won't be sure until I do the post-mortem, which will also determine whether any semen was left in or on her body. I'm sorry, Harry; I know she was your partner's ex-wife."

"Doris Conte was his third victim, Lieutenant. I'm convinced that we have a serial killer." Harry struggled with his emotions as he read from his notes in Lieutenant McGee's office. "I knew Doris. We socialized as a foursome before she and Jim split up. This has been a tough day for me. How's Jim?"

"We sent him home. Told him to take the next few days off."

Harry said, "Lieu, I'd rather not be there for the autopsy."

"That'll be okay, Harry. Why don't you take the rest of the afternoon, see about your partner?"

"Thanks, Lieutenant. I really appreciate that."

◆

"What about the boys?" asked Ellen speaking with Harry on the phone, after he told her about Doris, referring to the two Conte boys, both away in college.

"They are being notified by the chaplain up there. Doris's father got the call from the beauty shop and went to the house and found her."

"Oh, Harry, I'm just sick over this. I feel terrible about Doris. How is Jim taking it?" Ellen began sobbing.

"I'm on my way to meet Jim now. Don't wait on me for dinner. I'll grab something with him."

◆

They sat on a park bench overlooking the river, eating hotdogs, sodas, and large, soft, salty pretzels bought from a street vendor.

"Harry, I don't think she deserved to die the way she did, but I really don't give a shit."

"Jim, Doris was your wife for all those years; you raised two children together. You must have some feelings for her."

"Harry, after the way Doris fucked me over in the divorce, leaving me to live just above the poverty level—I have nothing but contempt for her."

"I have a feeling that McGee or Deputy Chief Watkins will pull you from the serial killer investigation because Doris was one of the victims."

"The way I see it, Harry, I am an asset to the investigation because I have no emotional attachments to the victims; I didn't know the first two and don't give a rat's ass about the third."

"Jim, when you get back to work don't be so damn flippant around the brass, and another thing—you're my partner, I've always respected you, and I like you as my friend. I'm trying to understand your feelings towards Doris, but she's dead, brutally murdered, so keep those comments to yourself, because I do give a shit!" Harry got up and left Jim sitting there.

◆

When Harry got to Ellen's later that evening, she was composed, but not very talkative. He fixed them each a glass of wine, which they sipped silently, then shortly afterwards, both went to bed. As Ellen drifted off to sleep, she sobbed softly, clinging to him.

Harry lay wide-awake staring at the ceiling, jumbled thoughts going through his head. What was it that he couldn't reconcile about Jim? All those terrible things he kept saying about Doris—was it all bluster? Could he have snapped after his traumatic, bitter divorce? It left him close to a financial ruin. Had it motivated him to strike back at her?

What about the other two victims? Was this a copycat murder to make it appear that rape was the motive? It was hard to believe Jim capable of inflicting that level of brutality on Doris or anyone. Harry finally drifted off to sleep, overwhelmed by feelings of dread.

CHAPTER 13

Arnold stayed at home, night after night, for as long as he could. Now that Dr. Goldsmith was no longer checking up on him, Arnold had to get out. He was afraid the police might catch him prowling around some house and think he was the serial killer. Even if they didn't, he remembered that vile judge's threat. However, his hunger for the sight of an undressing woman overcame his dread of going to prison.

Just after nine p.m., Arnold Krebbs got on his bicycle and began roaming different neighborhoods, looking for the familiar indicators—the lighted ground floor window with the blinds or shades askew. After a lengthy search, he found something. She was in her bedroom, getting ready to take a bath. As he watched his private striptease, masturbating in frenzy, a bright light blinded him. It was the spotlight from a patrol car. Before he could adjust his clothes, a cop shoved him up against the side of the house and handcuffed him.

Arnold Krebbs lived the horrors of jail life for the next few days until his court appearance before the same judge. Arnold had been appointed an attorney from the public defender's office, who had spent ten minutes with him before court. The arresting officer was there, along with the victimized woman. The public defender pled Arnold not guilty, and the court heard some embarrassing testimony from the victim and damaging testimony from the arresting police officer. Arnold did not testify in his defense.

The judge looked down from the bench with a scowl on his face. "Mr. Krebbs, I warned you the last time you stood before me that if you appeared here again for the same offense, I would send you away for a year. You either did not listen or didn't take me seriously. I am very serious. Arnold Krebbs, I find you guilty on all three counts of prowling, trespassing, and being a peeping Tom, and sentence you to the maximum—twelve months in the county jail—plus a $1,000 fine."

♦

Arnold was confined to a 7'x10' cell with bunk beds, a small sink, and a toilet without a seat or a lid for the next twelve months. His cellmate, Bernard Williams, who had occupied the cell for the past four months, was black, forty-one years old and serving a six-month sentence for non-payment of child support.

"The lower bunk is where I sleep. You upstairs. Try to get your fat white ass up and down without disturbin' my sleep, an' you 'n' me, we'll get along."

Arnold spent the next couple of days settling in and dealing with administrative routines, which included being assigned to the trash pick-up detail. He, Bernard and a dozen or so others were transported in a van to some road in the county to pick up trash for the day. Bernard told Arnold it was the best job in the county jail. "Look at it this way; you out of this noisy, stinkin' hole all day in the fresh air, an' there's no one fuckin' with you. You lucky, so don't fuck it up."

Arnold had heard of gang rapes of lone, defenseless inmates. Fat, out of shape Arnold Krebbs was hardly a fighter and thought he would be a prime target. He was terrified when taking a shower. One evening after dinner, before lights out, he confided his anxiety to Bernard.

"Oh, man. Arnie, that shit don't happen here in no county jail. That kinda shit go on in state prison. Most of those motherfuckers ain't seen a woman in a lot a years, an' ain't gonna see one for a lot more years. They form into gangs for protection, an' if you don't belong to one a them, you meat, Arnie. You the bitch!"

Arnold asked Bernard about the gangs. "They some mean motherfuckers, Arnie. There's the Black Brotherhood and the White Supremacists—you know, those Nazi motherfuckers, and the Latino Hombres."

"Thanks for letting me know, Bernard. I'll sleep better now. If I gotta be locked up, I'm glad I'm in here and not one of those prisons."

Arnold was used to not having a woman. What he missed was not being able to spy on women in the privacy of their bedrooms or look up their skirts and dresses. He couldn't stand the thought of doing without for a whole year. In the day room, during recreational time, the TV was tuned to the local news. One story caught Arnold's attention.

"Police say the rape and murder of the latest victim is the work of a serial killer. Three women were brutally raped and murdered in their homes, and there are similarities in the crimes. There is no connection between the victims. The latest victim, Doris Conte, is the ex-wife of

55

homicide detective James Conte, one of the detectives working the serial killings. Women in this city, especially those who live alone, are nervous. Police are asking for your help in apprehending this murderer before he claims another victim. If you know anything about these crimes, call police at the number across the bottom of your screen. The reward has been increased to $5,000 for information leading to an arrest and conviction..."

Arnold had just found his way out.

CHAPTER 14

"Jim, we are taking you off the serial killer investigation," Chief Robert Lansing told Detective James Conte in the chief's office. Present at the meeting were Deputy Chief Glenn Watkins, Lieutenant James McGee, and Detective Harry Lincoln. "Your ex-wife was one of the victims, and you might be too emotionally involved. It would be best if you were not close to it."

Lieutenant McGee said, "I have assigned Detective Liz Kovak to continue the investigation with Detective Lincoln. Conte, you will be assigned new cases and work with Detective Ronald Robinson. He's been in homicide for less than a year, so this should give him the benefit of all your years of experience. You will have a young, eager partner to do most of the running around."

♦

"Harry," said Jim as they walked down the stairs, "you could have told me this was coming. No one likes to be blindsided."

"I didn't know about it. I heard it when you did. Besides, it doesn't surprise me; I told you to stop shooting your mouth off about Doris."

"Well, Harry, the no-good bitch can't cause me any more problems."

As soon as they entered the squad room, Lieutenant McGee motioned Harry to come to his office. Detective Liz Kovak was already there. "You two know each other, so there's no need for introductions. Harry, bring Kovak up to speed and go to work."

♦

Four years prior, Harry and Liz had dated for a short time. The mutual attraction began when they were assigned as partners – Jim Conte had taken a month-long vacation – to investigate the gruesome rape and murder of a young girl. Three weeks of twelve – to fourteen – hour days passed before an arrest was made and the case cleared. During those three weeks, Harry and Liz consumed more than a few dinners and lunches, gallons of coffee, and dozens of donuts.

The break came from an informant, a street person who the put detectives onto a drifter responsible for five similar rape-murders of young girls in three other states. Harry and Liz pulled him out of bed one night at a flophouse.

The dirty, foul-smelling drifter bragged to Liz, "Yeah, I did that young piece of sweet meat and it sure was tasty, but I'll bet your juicy twat knows better moves."

Liz didn't take the bait, but Harry, who had an explosive temper, slammed him against the wall, and knocked him to the floor. Liz got between them and stopped Harry before more damage was done.

That's a side of Harry Lincoln I've not seen, thought Liz during a coffee break after booking the drifter into the city jail.

The forensic evidence matched. The drifter was subsequently tried, convicted, and sentenced to death. The other three states had to be satisfied with clearing their cases. The bastard could only be executed once.

♦

When Jim returned, he and Harry resumed working together, and Liz was assigned to someone else. The attraction that Harry and Liz had for each other grew stronger, and they started dating. They attempted to be discreet, but it wasn't long before the word got out. The looks, the whispering, and the innuendos had the greater effect on Liz. Finally, she had had enough.

"Look, Harry, you are the best guy I've dated in a very long time, but I know there's no future for us. If all the bullshit continues because of our office romance, I'll end up hating everyone in the squad. I don't want that. I hope another guy like you comes along, not a cop, someone looking for a more permanent relationship."

She and Harry stopped dating and kept their relationship at the professional level. They had maintained their friendship ever since. Now, they were partners again. This time, Liz was happily married, not to a cop, and she had a young child.

♦

Harry answered the squad room phone at his desk, "Homicide, Lincoln."

"Detective Lincoln, this is Judy Wright from the crime lab. A couple of things: first, the pantyhose used to kill Doris Conte were brand new. The other thing I thought you would want to know right away, before the report finds its way to your desk, is that Doris Conte had HIV." She paused for a reaction from Harry. There was none.

"Everything else was the same as the other two victims, except there was no lubricant found in her, and she appeared to have been beaten and tortured more severely."

"Thanks again, Judy, and yes, it would be helpful to have that information without delay. It's good to know we have a friend at the state crime lab besides Dr. Gordon. I owe you."

"Well, you could take me to dinner."

"Judy, it's not every day that I get an invitation from an intelligent, attractive woman. I'm flattered, and my ego is soaring; however, I'm currently involved with someone. One day, when I'm at the crime lab, I'd like to buy you a cup of coffee."

"Okay, Lincoln. It's a date."

Harry hung up the phone.

"Still breaking hearts, Harry?" Liz needled him.

"The only heart I'll break is Ellen's if I'm late again for dinner tonight."

Harry relayed the information about Doris Conte's HIV to Liz and then said thoughtfully, "I wonder what other surprises will be sprung on us?"

Harry dialed Jim's cell number. "Jim, I've got some disturbing news; Doris was infected with HIV. You might want to get tested right away, and notify your boys."

"Goddamn it, Harry, how many other ways will that no-good cunt fuck up my life? Okay, thanks, Harry; I'll go as soon as I can get an appointment."

They hung up, and Harry wondered if he could do or say anything that would help bring Jim out of his deep morass. Surely, he didn't mean all the things he said about Doris; however, he saw his life coming apart. Harry recalled the thoughts swirling around in his head in bed the night before.

Liz shook Harry out of his reverie. "Harry, I think I'll make a matrix and develop a compilation of what we know about all three victims, a detailed comparison. I'll take the files home with me and work on it there, away from the interruptions of the squad room."

"I don't think you should have to do that on your own time; besides, you've got your family to look after. Let's go see McGee."

"Why don't you take the files down the hall to the small conference room, Liz?" the lieutenant said. "Harry, don't let anyone know she's in there. While she's doing the matrix, Harry, why don't you follow up on some of the leads from the tip line? Who knows, maybe one of them might be the payoff."

"Dad, I guess you've heard about Doris." Harry was on the run and had just a minute to call Ben.

"Yes, Harry, it's been all over the news; it sounds like the serial killer. Have you got anything on it yet?"

"No, not much right now. The chief himself has taken Jim off the case because of Doris. He's also been shooting off his mouth too much about Doris. I suspect that was another reason he was pulled. He was becoming an embarrassment to the homicide squad and everyone up the chain," Harry quietly said. "I've got a new partner. Liz Kovak," he said with more enthusiasm. "She worked with me on the case of the drifter, who was wanted in three states for the rapes and murders of young girls. She's a good homicide cop."

"Well, good luck, Harry. Don't run yourself into the ground. Speak with you soon."

◆

The next day, Liz, Harry, and Lieutenant McGee studied the matrix, which showed the similarities and the disparities surrounding the three cases:

1) All were strangled to death with new pantyhose that had not been worn or washed. They were not worn by or removed from the victims, and had apparently been brought to the murder scenes by the killer.

2) All were home alone and found on their living room floor.

3) All were violated with a foreign object that left minute particles of wood and paint and caused massive injuries to vaginas and rectums, and traces of lubricant were found in April Scott and Julie Richards, but not in Doris Conte.

4) All were severely beaten about the face and head (possibly with brass knuckles), causing massive injury; Doris Conte was beaten more severely than the other two.

5) All were positioned the same way, and their clothing was arranged the same way.

6) None had semen in or on their bodies, suggesting that the killer did not ejaculate or used a condom.

7) Foreign pubic hair was found on April Scott and Julie Richards and in the carpet next to their bodies. Foreign pubic hair was missing on Doris Conte, which suggests she might not have been raped by a penis.

8) Panties were found on April Scott's right ankle and panties were found on the floor next to Julie Richards and Doris Conte.

9) All were white females. April Scott was 28, married; Julie Richards was 40, divorced; and Doris Conte was 45, divorced.

10) All lived in private houses in different parts of the city a considerable distance apart.

11) All had traces of skin and blood under their fingernails.

12) Unidentified fingerprints were left at all three murder scenes.

13) Doris Conte was infected with the HIV virus.

14) All three victims worked during the day at different jobs.

15) All three murders occurred about two weeks apart.

16) There was no forced entry at any of the three houses.

17) Time of deaths: April Scott died sometime Tuesday during the evening hours, Julie Richards died Wednesday between seven and ten p.m., and Doris Conte died Thursday between eight and eleven p.m.

McGee was impressed. "That certainly paints a pretty definitive comparison of the three victims."

Harry thought it put a lot about them in perspective, but he had several concerns. "We still don't know if they were connected personally or socially, and what about the killer? Was there a previous connection with his victims?"

"Well, Harry," said Liz, optimistic, "it's up to us; we have to keep hitting it until we have those answers."

"Dad," said Harry into the phone, "I hate that I missed the Itzhak Perlman concert last night, but I've been up to my ass in this serial killer investigation. If I had to give up the ticket, I'm glad it was to Ellen. When she got home, she was all excited and had to tell me all about it. It was good of you to take her."

"It's not every night I have a date with a beautiful young woman. During intermission, in the lobby, some women looked at me as if I was a cradle-robber, and I was the envy of all the men. Ellen even insisted on picking up the dinner check."

"Well, Dad, maybe next time I won't be in the middle of a major investigation, and the three of us can go."

◆

"How's the investigation going, Harry?" Ben inquired the following day while they were having lunch at Mike's Tavern.

"Well, Dad, we've done all we can do at this point. We are answering the calls coming through the tip line and waiting," Harry sighed pessimistically, "for some word from the streets. There are some unidentified prints and DNA evidence. Now all we need is a suspect, or some guy that walks in and says, 'I did it!' The prints and DNA would have to match, and a witness would be nice. Liz has been out for two days with a stomach virus, but she should be back tomorrow.

"It's Jim I'm concerned with, Dad. He's still very angry with Doris, and he keeps spouting degrading and hateful diatribes about her. He's already been removed from the investigation, but if he continues and becomes an embarrassment to the department, he'll end up being suspended."

"Harry, I called and invited him out to dinner or for drinks, but he turned me down. He doesn't want to talk about it. You talked to him and tried to help him, but if he's obsessed, there's not much anyone can do. If he doesn't stop, he'll self-destruct."

"Dad, do you think it was just a coincidence that Doris was a victim? Could you imagine that Jim…"

"No, Harry. I don't want to imagine anything like that. However, you know cops and coincidences; we don't put much stock in them."

CHAPTER 15

The mess hall was crowded and noisy during the evening meal, Arnold thought. He took a seat on the fringe of the hall, away from the throng of inmates where most of the noise and distractions were centered. After several days of contemplation, Arnold had made up his mind. He knew what he wanted to do, and how to do it, but who could he trust? He thought of cellmate Bernard Williams, but Bernard had no more contact with the outside than he did.

"It has to be one of the guards," Arnold thought, "but I don't talk to any of them except the one who drives the van for our trash gang." Arnold decided to talk to him the next day while out on the detail.

Arnold found his cellmate going through the coffee line. "Bernard, after we get through with dinner and are back in our cell, I want to tell you something very important, but you can't tell anyone."

"Listen, Arnie, this fuckin' place is a house of rumors and a vault of secrets, an' I'm the keeper of the motherfuckin' vault, so lay it on me, brother. Well, you ain't my brother, but you okay, Arnie."

Later, as soon as the cell door closed, Arnold told Bernard the dark secret that he'd kept to himself since it happened. "Tomorrow, when we're out on the road, I'm going to tell Deputy Hall that I was a witness to one of those serial killings. I actually saw one of the women get murdered. I can identify the one who did it. He'll go to the police. I'll trade the police what I know if they let me outta jail."

"Wadda ya mean, *if* they let you outta jail? Right after they kiss your white ass, they gonna take you outta here and get you a hot pastrami sandwich on rye with mustard an' a pickle, plus one cold bottle of beer to wash it down. That is one motherfuckin' get-outta-jail-free card."

◆

"Lieutenant, have someone else drive the road trash detail today and send Hall in here," said Sheriff Walter Raburn. "Also, pull Arnold

Krebbs # 40367 from the detail and hold him in his cell for the time being." Detectives Lincoln and Kovak were with the sheriff in his office at the county jail following up on a phone call from Deputy Hall. Within a few minutes, Hall came in and shook hands with both detectives.

"If you will, Deputy, go over what you told me on the phone again," Harry said.

"Well, like I said, inmate Krebbs works the detail for me each day. A real quiet guy. Doesn't talk much to anyone except Bernard Williams, his cellmate. Sometimes he'll say a few words to me. Yesterday, while the crew was spread out away from the van, he walked over to me and asked if I could get in touch with the detectives on the serial killings. When I said yes, he said to tell them that he saw one of the killings. When we came back in, I let the sheriff know about it, and he told me to call you."

Harry asked Sheriff Raburn if he would release Arnold Krebbs to his custody. "We'll bring him back as soon as we are through with him."

The sheriff gave instructions for Krebbs to be brought to the intake portal. "Now, detectives, if you both will sign the release papers."

After the papers were signed, Harry turned to Deputy Hall and told him how much they appreciated the phone call. "This might be the break we've been waiting for, and Sheriff, thank you for your cooperation." There were handshakes all around. Harry and Liz headed for police headquarters with Arnold Krebbs in the back seat of their car.

There was no conversation with Krebbs on the way. The detectives were determined that everything said to this witness was acceptable in court according to the Rules of Evidence. They didn't want to chance some obscure legal precedent being raised to keep Arnold Krebbs from testifying.

Once the three were settled in an interrogation room, the introductions were made. "Mr. Krebbs, I'm Detective Harry Lincoln, and this is my partner Detective Liz Kovak. May we call you Arnold?"

Arnold smiled. *They are kissing my ass already; I wonder when I get the pastrami sandwich?* He said, "Hey, you can call me anything you want."

"Arnold, you are a witness and not a suspect, but we are obligated to advise you of your constitutional rights. You have the right to remain silent..." Liz read the Miranda rights then asked Arnold to sign the form stating that he was advised and understood them.

"Okay, Arnold," began Harry as they sat in the room at a scarred metal table on chairs bolted to the floor. Liz had brought in three Styrofoam cups of coffee and a box of donuts. "We would like you to tell us what you know of the murders."

"Well, I seen it as it was happening; it was the first one of the three, the one named April Scott. It was tough to watch, but I watched the whole thing."

"What do you mean you watched the whole thing?" Harry asked. "How did you do that?"

"Well, I spy on women at night through their windows. That's why I'm doing time at the county jail. I had been to April Scott's house twice before. She put on shows for me. Well, this third time, I was at the window, and she was sitting in a chair, when all of a sudden this man ran into the room, hit her, and knocked her down. He came to the window to close the blinds and I got a good look at him because he was not three feet from me. He went back, sat on her, and kept hitting her in the face; I think he was using brass knucks or something. She clawed at his face, but he kept punching her."

"Arnold, did you actually see brass knuckles?" Harry asked.

"No, but every time he hit her he had this thing in his hand, and when he got ready to fu...er, rape her, he put it on the floor. I seen him put on a rubber and rape her. She was laying there moaning, but he was too strong for her."

Arnold hesitates, not sure how to continue. "Anyway, then he did something I never seen before; he had this thing, like a pipe or a flashlight, maybe six, seven inches long, and he pushed it up into, ya know, both her places. Then she started screaming and thrashing around until he took it out. Then he took some kind of pantyhose out of his jacket pocket and strangled her until she wasn't moving anymore. He killed her."

"Arnold, a lot of what you've just told us was in the papers and on the news. We'd like to ask you about a few details that weren't made public, but first, you told Deputy Hall that you could identify the man who killed her. Is that right?"

Arnold nodded and said, "That's right. I don't know who he is, but I'll never forget his face."

For the first time, Arnold looked Harry in the eye and said, "Here's the deal. You have to get me out of that jail. Free on a suspended sentence and suspend the $1,000 fine, and I mean, like, right away. If you do, then whenever you want me to come in and look at suspects, or a lineup, just let me know, and I'm there. I'll sign a paper agreeing to that. If I weasel out, you send me back to finish my sentence."

Harry and Liz looked at each other, and Harry said, "Arnold, we don't have that authority. Only the sentencing judge can do that."

"Then find somebody that can get that fucking judge to do it or the deal is off." The disappointment on Harry and Liz's faces was surpassed only by their anger.

"Okay, Arnold, one question, just to be sure that you are on the level and not conning us, that you really saw what you say you saw," said Detective Lincoln, pissed off. "What can you tell us about April Scott's panties?"

"Detective Lincoln, I remember him pulling them down, and they wrapped around one of her ankles and stayed there. I believe it was the right ankle. They were bright red."

◆

The detectives drove Arnold Krebbs back to the county jail and told him they would work on his release, but that it would likely take a few days. "Don't let it take too long. I don't want to stay in this stinking place. I also want that $5,000 reward if I identify the guy and he goes to prison."

"Listen, Krebbs, don't push it," snarled Liz. "We said we would do the best we can." They dropped him at intake and drove off.

"Harry, it galls me that a creep like Krebbs is giving us ultimatums, but if he can identify our killer, I guess I can swallow it."

Harry agreed and added, "Ellen is out of town for a couple of days, so I'm going home to eat leftovers for dinner, then kick back and read some more about the fall of the Roman Empire. When I get eye weary, I'll go to bed and get a good night's sleep."

"You know, Harry, I envy you. I'd like to spend some evenings reading, but I have my family to look after. All of that domestic stuff drains what energy I have left after a day or night at the office, so when I'm through, I just plop myself in front of the junk on TV, although I do enjoy watching baseball games. We'll get started on Krebbs's release first thing in the morning."

◆

Harry and Liz were halfway through breakfast in a rear booth at Mimi's Café. The large clock on the wall showed not quite 7:30. Liz had been unusually quiet since leaving the office and seemed distant and perplexed. "What's wrong, Liz? Trouble on the home front, or none of my business?

"No, Harry, nothing like that. I have a gnawing feeling that won't go away. It's kept me awake most of the night."

"If it's about the murders, Liz, what besides the obvious is causing you to lose sleep?"

"Arnold Krebbs! We accepted him as an eyewitness to one of the murders, but we've not eliminated him as the killer. By his own admission, he was there for the murder of April Scott, and he knows all the gory details, down to her red panties. Let's take the DNA sample that was collected after his arrest as a sex offender to the crime lab and have it compared with crime scene DNA."

"You are right, Liz. It should be done now. I'll ask McGee to have it sent to the lab right away, and then I'll call Dr. Gordon and request a rush on it."

"Okay, Harry, I feel better. That gnawing feeling has gone with the last bite of breakfast, and I'm looking forward to a good night's sleep. Now, let's see if we can get that pervert Krebbs sprung from the county jail."

◆

The receptionist said that Mr. Carlisle was on the telephone and would be with them shortly. Harry and Liz were at County District Attorney Robert J. Carlisle's office before nine o'clock to plead their case. When they were shown into the DA's office, Carlisle stood. "Harry, I haven't seen you in quite a while. How have you been?"

"Fine, Mr. Carlisle. This is my new partner, Liz Kovak."

After a handshake, Carlisle said, "Yes, I remember the fine work you and Harry did on that death penalty case this office prosecuted. I've seen a few of your cases come across my desk, and this is the first time I've had the pleasure. If you're working with Harry Lincoln, you're with one of the best. It's in his blood. As a young assistant DA, I prosecuted some high-profile cases for Harry's father, Ben Lincoln.

"Harry, when I learned about Jim's ex-wife, I wondered how it was affecting him. Is that why you and Liz are partners again?"

"Yes, Mr. Carlisle. Chief Lansing pulled Jim from the investigation. He thought, due to the circumstances, it was best."

"I understand and totally agree." After several minutes of chitchat, the DA asked, "Okay, guys, what can I do for you?"

"Well, Mr. Carlisle," answered Harry, "Liz and I are working the serial killer case. We might have caught a break, but we need your help. It appears that we found an eyewitness to one of the murders. He says he can identify the killer. He's going to give us a description and will view any suspect we develop. There's just one problem. He'll only do it if we get him out of jail and have his sentence and fine suspended."

"What's he in jail for?" asked the DA. "And what's his sentence and fine?"

Liz said, "He's a creep, a peeping Tom, and was caught several times looking into windows at night, watching women undressing. The last time, the judge sentenced him to the maximum for misdemeanors, twelve months in the county jail and a $1,000 fine."

Harry continued, "We would like you to speak to the judge and get those suspended."

The DA, dubious, asked, "How do we know he can deliver, or is he just bullshitting his way out of jail?"

Liz said, "We asked him about a fact in the case that has not been released to the public. He knew it and was very definite about it."

"Mr. Carlisle, we would like you to go to the judge, explain the circumstances, and ask him to suspend Arnold Krebbs's sentence and fine and release him from jail. Surely, he will see that catching a murderer outweighs a misdemeanor case."

"Who is the judge, Harry?"

"Judge Rosenfeld."

"Judge Aaron D. Rosenfeld! You want me to ask Judge Aaron D. Rosenfeld, that crusty old bastard, to suspend the sentence and fine and release a defendant he's sentenced to the maximum?"

"That's what we are respectfully asking," Harry answered, humble.

The DA sat still for a few minutes, deep in thought. "I will try, without a great deal of hope for success, but not entirely for either of you. I'll do it mostly out of respect for your dad, Harry, and for the many IOUs that I can never repay him."

"Mr. Carlisle, Liz and I, and my dad, are grateful to you."

CHAPTER 16

Two days later, he sat in the judge's chambers explaining his request. "Yes, your honor, I do understand that Arnold Krebbs has no respect for the law, the court, and for you in particular," Robert Carlisle said as he looked across the desk at a stone-faced Judge Rosenfeld. "But I'm convinced that if he can identify this serial killer and prevent more killings, it's a justifiable and worthwhile trade."

The judge replied, "His disrespect infuriated me, and after I warned him not to come back before me, he ignored me. When he returned, charged with the same offense, his contempt for all that I hold dear drove me to my limit. If I may use the common vernacular, I slam-dunked him. After all of my personal feelings have been expressed, I agree with your argument that one outweighs the other, and justice would be better served. I'll honor your request; have him brought before me in my courtroom."

♦

The following day, Arnold cringed as Judge Rosenfeld boomed, "Arnold Krebbs, this is the third time you have appeared before this court. It had better be the last."

Harry and Liz had picked Arnold up from the county jail earlier; they now sat in the courtroom as Arnold stood before the bench.

"The district attorney's office and the police department have recommended that your sentence and fine be suspended and that you be released from the county jail. Mr. Krebbs, make no mistake about it, if there is a next time, you will receive the maximum punishment and serve every day and pay every dollar. No more deals. I hereby suspend your sentence and fine." With the crack of the gavel, Arnold was a free man.

As they left the courthouse and drove to police headquarters, Harry said, "We're going to meet with a sketch artist; she will draw a picture of the killer as you describe him. Give us a preview. Was he white or black, young or old, fat or skinny, tall or short? Describe him to us."

"He was a white man, middle-age or older—you know, maybe fifty or sixty and kind of medium build, not tall or short or fat or skinny—you know, kind of average."

"How about his hair? Was he bald or did he have a beard?"

"No, he had a full head of close cut grey hair, and he was clean shaven."

"Okay, Arnold, we're here. Save the rest for the sketch artist."

◆

Later that evening, Harry and Ellen relaxed after a satisfying dinner. "When we questioned our witness about the age, he kept insisting that the man he saw was fifty or sixty years old. Knowing what we know about the violent nature of the three murders, we all had pictured a younger man.

"Ellen, we are putting our reputations on the line. Liz and I will be in deep shit if he is leading us down the 'yellow brick road.' The list of those we'll have to answer to is long and daunting, from our own chain of command, starting with Lieutenant McGee, all the way to District Attorney Carlisle, Judge Rosenfeld, and Sheriff Raburn."

"Harry, it's time to turn it off for the evening. Let's go to bed early, and I'll rub your back. Besides, I want to show you my new panties and bra. I'm wearing them for the first time. They're sheer, white, and lacy, just the way you like them. Then what do you say we both relax in that big Jacuzzi?"

It didn't take much to convince Harry, who felt closer and closer to Ellen as the days and nights went by. Twenty minutes later, drying off after the bath, they cooled down on the bed and Ellen rubbed his back, continuing the foreplay, leading into slow, soothing, and tender lovemaking. Within the hour, a relaxed and satisfied Harry Lincoln was sound asleep before ten o'clock.

◆

The next morning, Harry and Liz sat in the rear booth at Mimi's Cafe (most cops feel more comfortable in the rear of a restaurant, facing the door and everyone else, with no one behind them) and each ordered the sunrise special: Two eggs, choice of breakfast meat, home fries, toast, juice, and coffee. After lingering over second and third refills of coffee, they left nice tips for the attentive waitress and paid their bills.

Once in the car, they headed to Arnold's apartment. They knocked on the door and got no response, so they knocked louder, and Liz shouted, "Arnold, it's Detectives Lincoln and Kovak. Open up." In the next few minutes, they heard the padding of bare feet, and then sleepy, bleary-eyed Arnold Krebbs opened the door.

"We want you to come downtown with us and look at some pictures to see if you recognize anyone. Wash your face and brush your teeth. We'll be waiting outside at the car."

Once outside, Liz made a face and said, "Harry, did you get a peek into that pig-sty? I know I don't live in the Taj Mahal, far from it, but my God, did you see all that junk scattered around and piled up to the ceiling? I know Krebbs is a creep, but must he live like a rat in a landfill?"

Harry just shrugged. Arnold came out of the building ten minutes later.

◆

The books were big and heavy, like giant scrapbooks. They contained mug shots of known sex offenders, hundreds of them. Arnold sat at the table in the small conference room, down the hall from the squad room, and started to look through them.

"Arnold, unfortunately, the different ages are mixed together and range in age from seventeen to ninety," Harry said.

It was a slow process. At lunchtime, Harry went out and brought back Big Macs, fries, and Cokes for the three of them. By late afternoon, Arnold had looked at every mug shot in each book without identifying the killer. Harry decided they'd had enough for one day.

In the car, on the way to his house, Arnold said, "I'd like my old job back. Could we stop by the Sandwich Shop? Maybe you could speak to the boss for me."

"Arnold," Harry asked, "does he know that you've been in jail for the past several weeks or what for?"

"Well, he knows I've been in jail, but not exactly for what."

"Okay, then. Let's stop and have some coffee," Harry said, a little uneasy. "Now listen, Arnold, we'll fudge a little, but we won't lie for you."

As soon as they sat in a booth, the owner came over. "Hello, Arnold. I see you're out of jail. Who are your friends?"

Harry showed his badge and ID and introduced himself. "I'm Detective Harry Lincoln, and this is my partner Detective Liz Kovak. We are here on Arnold's behalf, to put in a good word for him."

The owner flushed and said, "Excuse me; I apologize for my bad manners. My name is Nick Polis. I own the Sandwich Shop. I guess Arnold wants his job back. Please understand that if he committed a crime serious enough to go to jail for a year, it might scare some of my customers off. Seventy percent of the lunchtime business is women from surrounding office buildings. I cannot afford to lose them."

"It concerned an incident involving trespassing and it took several weeks to get straightened out. Arnold is a free man, and needs and wants his job back. He is now assisting us in a serious and important investigation. If we solve it with his help, he might get a medal from the mayor and the police chief."

Liz gave Harry a look. He was laying it on pretty thick, but he felt all right about it.

"Well," said Polis, and right then, Harry knew he had him. "Arnold was a good and dependable worker. I've had two dish washers since that I had to let go. Okay, Arnold, you start tomorrow morning, same deal."

The detectives thanked him for his cooperation; Arnold mumbled his thanks as they left the restaurant.

When they dropped Arnold off at his building, they asked about his schedule, a time that wouldn't interfere with his job.

"The Sandwich Shop is only open for breakfast and lunch, and I get off at four p.m. It's closed Saturday and Sunday."

"Okay, Arnold, we have your phone number and will call you when we need you. When we do call, ride your bicycle down to police headquarters."

Then Harry got in Arnold's face and said in a menacing voice, "Arnold, if you get caught prowling around houses at night, peeping into windows, I will personally beat you to a bloody fucking pulp, and my partner here will stomp flat what's left of your balls. Then, when you get out of the hospital, Judge Rosenfeld will send you back to jail for a year. That's a promise; don't take it lightly. We'll be in touch."

When Harry and Liz got back to the squad room, there was a message waiting from Dr. Gordon. The crime lab had eliminated Arnold Krebbs's DNA from the crime scenes of all three victims.

♦

That night, Ben was at Ellen's having dinner with her and Harry.

"Ever since Doris' funeral," Harry said, "Jim doesn't get along with anyone; he's driving everyone away, even his partner. Young Robinson asked McGee to assign him to work with someone else. Robinson told me that at lunch, Jim will have a couple of glasses of liquor, and I believe him. I've seen Jim do it once. That's only one of the reasons Robinson wants to get away from him. Jim comes in every day, goes through the motions and goes home at the end of the watch, but doesn't talk to anyone anymore unless he has to. McGee only assigns him smoking gun cases, no 'who-done-its.' Jim Conte, one of the best homicide detectives this department has had in decades."

"I wonder what happened to make him change," Ben said. "Was it a result of their divorce? Surely he understands why he was taken off the serial killer case, and from what he's said about Doris, he can't be grieving over her."

Ellen cleared away the dishes and brewed a pot of coffee.

Ben sighed. "So, Harry, what's new with the investigation?"

Harry smiled. "Dad, we might have caught a big break. We think we have an eyewitness to one of the murders."

"How did that happen? Who is it?"

"Well, you know I'm sworn not to reveal the identity of a witness to a major crime. I can't tell Ellen or you. Our witness insists the killer is an older man—fifty or sixty years old. We need a suspect that the witness can identify."

Ben peppered Harry with questions. "How did this come about? Can you rely on this witness? Which murder was witnessed?"

Harry answered in similar fashion. "I can't tell you how it came about because that might reveal who it is. Can we rely on this witness? We don't know, but the witness said he saw the murder of April Scott."

CHAPTER 17

It had been three weeks since Doris Conte's murder. They were all waiting for the "other shoe to fall"—Detectives Harry Lincoln and Liz Kovak, Lieutenant James McGee, the entire homicide squad, the top police brass, the media, and the population, including many anxious women. Lieutenant McGee was shocked when Detective James Conte entered his office and announced, "Lieutenant, I thought I should let you know that I submitted my retirement papers this morning at city hall."

"That's awful sudden, Conte. What brought that about?"

"I'm tired of all the bullshit of late. Things are not the same as they were. It's time for me to hang it up."

"Conte, I think you're over reacting to a situation that's beyond your control."

"Anyway, it's done; it takes effect in three weeks," said Jim Conte as he left McGee's office and motioned to Robinson. They gathered car keys, radios, and briefcases, and left the squad room to investigate a domestic homicide.

◆

Later that evening, Harry knocked at Jim's apartment door. A Jim Conte that Harry hadn't known before opened it. He wore torn sweat pants and a sweatshirt frayed at the neck and both cuffs, but what really concerned Harry was Jim's look of despair and body language, which was that of an old man, bent over and shuffling around.

"Jim, I heard that you turned in your papers today. What's that all about?"

"Like I told McGee this morning, I'm tired of all the bullshit that's been going on lately, all the innuendoes. Whenever I walk into the squad room, all the conversation stops, but I know what they're saying. That I'm all washed up. I hear it, Harry. I'm not deaf, I'm not blind, and I'm not stupid. The chief body slammed me; all I get are horseshit cases with some rookie."

"Listen, Jim, you've been on this police department a lot longer than me, and you know it is one big rumor mill. Don't let the gossips cause you to make such a drastic step."

"It's not only that, Harry. Since I was pulled from the serial killings, it's true that McGee only assigns me the bullshit cases. For Christ's sake, Harry, a goddamn patrolman could do those. This kid Robinson, he's a good kid and all, but it's not the same as working with you. It's a goddamn slap in the face."

"Well, Jim, look at it from the financial reality. You are fifty years old, and your pension will be penalized two percent for every year under fifty-five that you retire. Money is tight with you; you can't afford to take a hit like that. This will all blow over. Things will settle down. I know you can make five more years."

"I've thought about the money angle, Harry. A guy with my resume should have no trouble getting on with a big company as the director of security. Harry, I know you mean well, but it's time for you and everyone else to butt out of my business. So I'd like you to leave now."

Harry paused at the apartment door. "I think you are making a big mistake. I'll see you in the morning. Goodnight, Jim."

As Harry drove back to Ellen's, he thought about Jim's situation. Harry could not resolve the logic; it did not compute.

♦

"We are all very nervous, Dad, hoping there won't be another one," Harry said on the phone. "The one thing I can't understand is that we haven't heard a word about it from any of our informants; the streets are dead silent. According to my best and most reliable informant, it's as if the murders never happened. The usual chatter rumbling at street level about so much pressure on the streets is lacking."

"Maybe your informants are not hearing anything because the killer is not from the street. Maybe no one knows him or of him," Ben said. "Another thing, Harry—as you know, there could be lots of reasons there hasn't been another murder: The killer might have moved to another state, he might be in jail or a hospital; maybe he's dead."

"Yeah, that's the talk that has been going around, but we all still have our fingers crossed. Our witness is coming down late this afternoon; we've put together a lineup that we want the witness to view. I can't identify the witness by name, but I can't help it if you happen to see that person going in and out of police headquarters." They hung up.

◆

Lieutenant McGee was on the sidewalk, in front of the headquarters building, taking another smoke break. He crumbled the empty cigarette pack and tossed it into a trash basket when Harry and Liz came out to wait for Arnold. Jim Conte and Ronald Robinson were coming in to go off-shift for the day when they spotted the three. They went over to tell McGee of the progress made in the case they were working.

About the same time, Ben Lincoln came around the side of the building from the parking lot and saw the group on the sidewalk. "Hey, what the hell is this?" he said as he approached the group. "The FOP or PBA convention?"

"Ben," said Lieutenant McGee, "what brings you down here? Slumming?"

"I was downtown running a few errands," answered Ben, "and thought I might as well get my retired officer's ID card renewed. It expires next week."

"You can forget it for today, Ben," McGee said. "The photo lab closes at four o'clock; you know civilians—banker's hours." Ben was introduced to Liz Kovak and Ronald Robinson; he knew the others.

As they were talking, Arnold rode up on his bicycle. Harry and Liz broke away from the group to meet him. They went in with him and told him to leave the bicycle in the lobby.

Lieutenant McGee said, "I have to get upstairs. They are about to hold a lineup, and I need to be there. Ben, it was good to see you. Let me know when you come in to take care of your ID. We'll go to lunch and catch up; it's been a long time."

"I'd like that," Ben said, as he waved. "I'll see you soon."

◆

There is a small auditorium within the bowels of police headquarters, a multi-functional assembly room with a stage at the front, used for meetings, lectures, briefings, and the sharing of intelligence to large groups. It is also where line-ups are held. Late on this Tuesday afternoon, it was virtually deserted except for Detectives Lincoln and Kovak, Lieutenant McGee, and several uniform cops. Also present was the star witness, Arnold Krebbs.

The line-up consisted of seven men. Four were suspects being held for other sex crimes; the other three were undercover detectives. All were white males in the same age bracket, similar in appearance.

"Now, Arnold, it's very simple. Seven men will be standing on the stage behind the glass. Each of them will be wearing a number from one through seven. You will see them, but they cannot see you. We will ask each one to step forward and turn this way and that way so you can get a good look at each of them." Harry gave the instructions he had given so many times before. "If you want to get a second look at any of them, let me know, and I'll have him come forward again and turn in any position that helps you identify him."

Arnold didn't say anything.

Harry then said into the microphone, "Okay, bring them in."

Seven men, ranging in age from their 50s to 60s were led onto the stage. They were told to face forward, and one at a time, each was told to step forward for less than a minute and then step back. Arnold showed no recognition of any of the seven.

"How about it, Arnold?" Harry asked.

Arnold Krebbs shook his head.

"Okay," barked Lieutenant McGee to the officer at the end of the stage, "you can take them back." Within five minutes, the hall was quiet again.

♦

After everyone had gone, Arnold was alone with the lieutenant and two detectives. Liz asked, "You're sure you didn't see him, the man you say killed that woman?"

"I did see him," Arnold whispered.

Lieutenant McGee exploded, "Why in hell didn't you tell us while they were still in the lineup?"

"Which one was it?" Harry asked. "What number?"

"No number. He wasn't in the lineup." Arnold started shaking. "I saw him on the street."

"What the fuck do you mean?" McGee asked, nose to nose with Arnold. "You saw him on the street? I'm a little confused."

"Hold on a second, Lieu," interrupted Harry. "Tell me, Arnold, where did you see him, and when?"

Arnold could hardly speak. After a moment or two and a few deep breaths, he said in a voice, barely audible, "I saw him today, right outside this building."

"Did you come by here earlier today?" Harry asked, confused.

"No, it was just a while ago, when I got here, and you came over to meet me."

"There was no one in front of the building when you rode up except the six of us standing on the sidewalk."

"Yes, that's where I saw him."

There was total silence in the room, as if all the air had been sucked out of it. No one moved; no one breathed. Harry felt dread curling in his chest.

After ten seconds that seemed like an hour, Lieutenant McGee said, "Listen, Krebbs, if you're fucking with us, you're playing a dangerous game. Those were all detectives you're talking about."

Liz quietly said, "Arnold, I want you to settle down, listen closely, and think before you speak. Six people were standing out on the sidewalk in front of this building this afternoon when you rode up on your bicycle. Do I have it right so far?"

"Yes, that's what I've been trying to tell them."

"Okay, Arnold, in that group of detectives, three were older with short grey hair. Did you recognize him by his face?"

Arnold composed himself. "Yes, I told you before. I'll never forget his face. The others were all wearing suits and ties. The man I'm talking about wore a dark blue windbreaker jacket and khaki pants."

Arnold Krebbs had just described Ben Lincoln.

CHAPTER 18

"**D**ad, are you home?" Harry asked, his emotions about to break the surface.

"Yes, Harry, I am."

"Just stay there, Dad. Wait for me. I'll be right over."

"You sound excited, Harry. What's up?"

"Just wait there for me, Dad." Harry left headquarters in a state of shock, not believing what he had just heard. *I hope I'm having a bad dream.*

Before Harry left, Lieutenant McGee instructed Liz Kovak to book Krebbs and hold him as a material witness. Then, the first thing in the morning, she was to collect Ben Lincoln's DNA and fingerprints from the samples kept on file of all police officers and take them to the crime lab for comparison with those found at the crime scenes.

Lieutenant McGee said gently, "This should refute Krebbs's identification and eliminate any hint of a cover-up. Harry, go home."

◆

"Do you believe him, Harry?" Ben asked when Harry told his father that Krebbs had identified him.

"Of course, I don't believe him. He's being held as a material witness, and McGee told Liz to take your DNA and fingerprint samples to the crime lab to prove that Krebbs is mistaken or a liar. He doesn't want a cover-up scandal."

"Well, don't fret about it, Harry. Why don't you go to Ellen's place, eat a good dinner, have a glass or two of wine, and calm down."

◆

The next morning, after a long sleepless night, Harry called Ben at the townhouse and got the answering machine. When he tried the cell phone, there was no answer, and his call went straight to voice mail. Harry left messages on both phones for Ben to return the calls and tried calling the rest of the day, but his calls were not answered.

The following morning, exhausted and bleary-eyed again, after calling the cell number and again getting the voicemail, Harry drove to

Ben's townhouse. The car was gone. After knocking loudly for a few minutes, he let himself in with his emergency key. Everything was as it was when he was there two days ago. Nothing was disturbed. In the corner of the living room used as a mini-office, on the small desk, was an open letter addressed to Benjamin Lincoln from a medical clinic. It concerned his treatments for the AIDS virus.

Harry was so shocked he didn't know what to think, but what he saw next shocked him even more. A piece of paper was jammed in the blades of the shredder next to the desk, part of a receipt. All that was legible was *"ntyho."*

◆

Harry couldn't think straight. AIDS? His father, Ben Lincoln, had AIDS? That couldn't be right. There had to be some mistake. However, there was no mistake about the partial receipt. *If we were sitting across from each other,* Harry thought, *at a table in Mike's Tavern, Dad would explain how these things were not as damaging as they appear.*

◆

When Harry arrived at the squad room, Lieutenant McGee motioned him into the office. "We're wanted in the chief's office. Let's go."

"Oh, Lieu, this can't be good. Tell me what's up?"

"Let's just go up where we can sit down and talk."

Chief Lansing and Deputy Chief Watkins were drinking coffee in the sitting area when they were shown in.

"Come in. Have a seat. Can I get you some coffee?"

Lieutenant McGee said he would take a cup black; Harry declined. Lansing picked up the phone and ordered another cup.

"I've got some disturbing news, Harry," Chief Lansing said as soon as they sat down, "and I wanted to tell you personally. We put a rush on those comparison tests to dispel any rumors before they got started. The tests came back positive, both the DNA and a partial fingerprint found in the living room of the Richards victim. They match your father." Harry sat and stared at him, speechless.

"The three of us have known Ben Lincoln for many years. He was an outstanding policeman. No finer man has ever worn the badge. I am shocked and find it hard to accept. There's got to be a logical explanation, but DNA and fingerprints cannot be ignored, nor can an eyewitness."

Harry wondered if it were a dream. It was surreal. Hearing them talk about his father, as if he was one of the many perpetrators, the hundreds that Harry dealt with over the years, was something he could not fathom.

"Harry," said Chief Lansing, "I'd like Ben to meet me here in my office to see if we can figure this thing out. Deputy Chief Watkins, Lieutenant McGee, Detective Kovak, and you would be here, also."

"Yes, Chief," agreed Harry. "I think that might help, but I've been trying to reach my dad by phone for two days now. I just get voice mail and no return calls. I've been to his townhouse. The car is gone, and he's not home. I've been inside, and nothing has been disturbed. I'll keep trying, and if I do reach him, I'll encourage him to have that meeting with you."

"Okay, Harry, until then I want you to take a week off, maybe two. With all the extra hours you've worked, you have enough 'comp time' coming. In the meantime, Lieutenant McGee will assign another detective to work with Kovak."

Harry left in a daze; he had the snip of a receipt and the AIDS letter with him, but made no mention of them at the meeting. *That might constitute withholding evidence and obstructing, both of which are crimes.* Harry had to speak to his dad first.

♦

Not wanting to be alone, he went to Ellen's.

"I have a real bad feeling, Ellen. It's been two days, and I haven't heard from him." For the first time in many years, Harry didn't know what to do, so he did nothing. He hardly ate and didn't sleep; he just sat and waited.

Harry jumped when his cell phone rang. He answered on the first ring, hoping to hear his father's voice.

"Hello, Harry. Lieutenant McGee. Have you heard from him?"

"No, I haven't, Lieutenant, and I've looked and inquired everywhere."

"Well, I just wanted you to know that arrest and search warrants have been issued. The search warrant is to be executed within the hour. It's best if you stay away, although I can't order you not to be there."

"Thanks, Lieu; I appreciate you letting me know. Who will conduct the search?"

"I'll be there with the search team and make sure they don't tear the place up."

"Thanks again. I won't be there." Harry hung up and sat staring at the wall, covering his face with his hands. Ellen put her arms around his shoulders and felt the sobs racking him. She didn't know what to do or say.

Within a few minutes, Harry came out of it. "Ellen, they have issued an arrest warrant for my dad and are about to search his townhouse."

♦

Harry had been to the cabin two days before, but thought he should check it again. Ben bought it seven years ago. It was a small, modest cabin up in the mountains, less than an hour's drive from the city. Ben loved the mountains, and the cabin was his getaway. It was isolated, so there were no neighbors for Harry to ask about him. Harry had no key and could not go in, but it looked desolate. Harry saw no reason to break in. There were no recent tire tracks, no fresh footprints; it did not appear that anyone had been there for the past week.

Back at Ellen's, he waited.

CHAPTER 19

"Hello, Harry," Ben said into his cell phone the day after Harry returned from the cabin.

"Dad! Where have you been? Where are you? Are you all right? I've looked all over for you."

"Slow down, Harry. Yes, I'm all right. Are you still at Ellen's? Is she there now? Is it just the two of you?"

"Yes, yes, and yes. Dad, listen to me. An arrest warrant has been issued for you, and your townhouse has already been searched."

"Yes, I figured that, but now I want you to listen to me."

"Tell me where you are, Dad, so I can meet you. We can talk there."

"Where I am is not important. What I want to say to you is very important."

"But, Dad..."

"Harry, please just listen to what I've got to say."

"Okay, Dad, but I'm worried sick for you."

"Harry, sit on the couch with Ellen, hold her hand, and listen to me."

"Dad, right now I'd rather hold your hand. Where are you?"

"Harry, just listen closely, and don't say anything.

I'm guilty, Harry! I am the serial killer!

I committed the three murders. Let's get that out of the way right now," Ben said in a clear, firm voice.

"Dad, how could you do that? I don't understand."

"Hear me out, Harry. Don't interrupt me. This is difficult enough."

"Okay, Dad, but let me meet you so we can sit down and talk. Where are you?"

"No, Harry, I don't want you to meet me. I just want you to listen. I'd give anything if I didn't have to tell you these terrible things. It all revolves around Doris Conte. Jim was bitter because she was seeing other men. Her excuse was that he was fooling around with women. The truth is they had both lost interest in each other. She came home unexpectedly one night and surprised him. Instead of spending the night with her mother, out of state, she walked in and caught him with a woman in their bed. Her attorney used that in the divorce proceedings in front of a female judge, who took just about everything from him.

That's why he despised Doris." Ben paused a moment and took a deep breath, and then continued. "Jim just despised her. I hated her!"

"Hated her? What do you mean you hated her?" Harry hadn't been this puzzled since high school algebra.

"Doris and Jim used to host get-togethers every now and then at their house. Doris and I were attracted to each other. Jim invited me because we'd worked together in the past, and I was his partner's father. There were a few other single men and women in the group, so I didn't feel like a fifth wheel. After a while, Jim and Doris started having trouble, and Jim told me about it. I knew they were headed for a divorce.

"One night, the five of us were out to dinner. I sat across from Doris. Every time I looked up, she was staring at me. When I got home, the phone rang. It was late, and I thought something might have happened to you. You and Jim had been called in from the restaurant on some emergency. It was Doris. She was seductive, wanting to know if I wore briefs or boxers. She told me she was wearing a lacey bra and matching panties, and she wanted to come over and show me. Considering how things were between her and Jim, me being a single guy, and Doris being an attractive woman, it didn't take me but a minute to agree.

"I took her up to my cabin in the mountains every chance we had, which was pretty safe because only two or three people knew about it: you, Ellen, and a local guy who occasionally did some repair work for me. She would get home very late. Sometimes she spent the night. She said it wasn't a problem because Jim was doing the same.

"Doris admitted that she had been sleeping around before she started having sex with me, and I told her that I was doing the same, so we both agreed to be tested for HIV. Mine came back negative, and she said hers did also. Doris and I then agreed to have sex exclusively with each other. I knew she and Jim were no longer having sex. When I went for my annual physical, the doctor informed me that I had the HIV virus. It was like a blow from a sledgehammer.

"I didn't understand, so I confronted Doris. I called and said, 'Doris, do you know you gave me HIV?' And she said, 'Oh, Ben, I'm so sorry. I didn't know what to do. I knew if I told you, you wouldn't see me anymore. I didn't want to lose you, but having sex with a condom would ruin it for us. I hate them; it's just not the same.'

"I exploded. I got so violently angry that flashes of bright white light blinded me. I had to sit down. Seconds passed before I could speak. 'Doris, you let me have unprotected sex knowing you had HIV? Are you fucking crazy or just plain goddamn stupid?' That was the last time I spoke to Doris. A bad situation got worse months later, when I went for my regular treatments and was advised by the doctor that the HIV had developed into full-blown AIDS."

Ben fell silent, giving Harry time to process, and then said, "I became a different person, Harry, physically and mentally. In some cases, the AIDS virus causes a neurological disorder in the brain. I wasn't good old Ben Lincoln, everyone's friend, the guy who wouldn't hurt anyone—well, except for one or two scumbags back in the day. I put on a good act for everyone, but alone my mood was black. I spent days at the cabin in seclusion, simmering. I could think of nothing but what Doris had done to me. I was enraged, Harry, overcome with hatred. I boiled over."

Ben hesitated for a few seconds, and Harry broke the silence, "Dad, please tell me where you are so I can come to meet you. We can talk so much better than on the phone."

"No, Harry, I just want you to sit there with Ellen and listen. Now comes the hard part, Harry, the part I wish you didn't have to hear. I was so enraged at Doris, I became homicidal, and I decided to kill her, but I wanted to do it in such a way that I would never be suspected. I would commit the perfect crime.

"One day, I was at the tire dealer getting new tires for my car, sitting in the lounge reading the paper. I noticed an attractive young woman. We struck up a conversation, as some people do in those situations. We introduced ourselves, and I learned that she was an assistant office manager in an advertising agency and that her husband traveled a lot. We continued to chat until my car was ready. I drove out and parked nearby until she left. I was able to follow her home without her noticing.

"A week later, I did it again, this time from my dentist's office. This woman was a little older and not as pretty. As we talked in the waiting room, she told me she was a real estate agent and that she lived alone. She went in for her appointment, and I would have been next, but she was finished and paying the cashier. I told the receptionist that I had an emergency and would call to reschedule. I got in my car and waited for her to come out, and as before, I followed the unsuspecting woman home.

"The goal was to kill Doris. If I just did that, as you and I both know, Harry, anyone connected with the victim would have to be eliminated from any forensic evidence left at the scene. The perpetrator always leaves something, so I had to create a diversion.

"That diversion would be a serial killer, but two innocent women had to die. What I regret most is that I had to do unspeakable things to them."

Ben paused and then continued. "The AIDS virus not only destroys the body physically, it also has a negative effect on the brain. I really don't understand all that psychobabble. Maybe the virus created the monster in me, maybe not. You see, Harry, Doris Conte sentenced me to a slow, terrible death. Rage was not all I felt for Doris; it was pure loathing, evil hatred. I had to kill her for what she had done to me; I wanted her to suffer. However, for the idea of a serial killer to become believable, I had to inflict the same punishment on those women as I had planned for Doris.

"I got into April Scott's house through an unlocked basement door. I used my old badge and talked my way in with Julie Richards. I called Doris and told her I wanted to come over to talk.

"My hatred, compounded by the damaging effects of the AIDS virus to my psyche, created a Jekyll and Hyde personality. I became a monster and committed atrocities against innocent women. You and I know how terrible it was, but from the beginning, the motive had to appear to be rape. I did rape the first two, but I used a condom so as not to leave semen with traceable DNA. As it turned out, I left my DNA in a few pubic hairs. My DNA was also collected from scraping skin and blood particles from under their fingernails. The first victim scratched me so badly that I stayed at the cabin until healed.

"I used a set of brass knuckles from a case I worked back in the day, but went much lighter on the first two. I got enormous satisfaction in pulverizing Doris Conte's face. I didn't rape Doris because I couldn't have forced myself to enter her if I had gotten an erection. I no longer saw her as a desirable woman, but as a slab of rotten meat. The other object of torture was a simple length of broom handle sawed off to about seven inches in length, which I jammed into their vaginas and rectums, causing enormous pain and injury. For the first two women, I coated it with lubricant, wanting to lessen their agony. Doris learned what real torture was when I pushed the dry piece of broom handle into her vagina and rectum as hard as I could.

"I drove almost fifty miles across the state line to a busy Walmart where I wouldn't be noticed or remembered, and I paid cash for three pairs of pantyhose. After I killed Doris, I went to the cabin and burned the section of broom that I used on them along with the rest of the broom. I shoveled the ashes into a plastic bag and then swept out the fireplace. I put the brass knuckles in a second plastic bag and the tube of lubricant in a third, drove about the same distance in the opposite direction, and deposited each bag in the dumpsters of three different strip malls.

"Everything went according to plan, except that some people were looking at Jim Conte because of his big mouth. Harry, I may be a monster, but I wouldn't have let Jim take the fall. I was already doomed. Then the unexpected happened. You told me about the wild card, a peeping Tom, a goddamn window peeper! Krebbs had been watching April Scott do striptease acts, and he happened to be at her window and saw me assault, rape, and murder her.

"Then I show up in front of headquarters to look at your witness, and he sees me and identifies me. 'Curiosity killed the cat?' Well, curiosity killed Ben Lincoln. I had to see your secret witness, the one who could identify me, and because of that, he did!

"Ben Lincoln, the great homicide detective. Any rookie homicide cop knows that pubic hairs are almost always left at rape scenes. I should have shaved my pubic hair. And to leave a partial print with enough points to be identified is not the act of a professional. The perfect crime? Not even close, Harry. Now I'm a suspect, and my DNA and fingerprints samples are matched against the forensic evidence taken from the murder scenes.

"I took April Scott's engagement ring to make it look like a burglary. It's in the console of the car, along with the keys to the cabin and a few manila envelopes on the seat with your name on them. They contain important papers, documents, and miscellaneous items. So there you have it, Harry. I think I covered enough for you to clear your serial killer case and not leave any loose ends."

"Dad, please, I want to come to where you are. We need to talk about this some more; let me help you figure things out."

"No, Harry, there's nothing more to figure out. It's too late now. This is a death penalty case, and there is enough evidence, and an eyewitness, to convict me. I am already doomed because of the AIDS virus. It's just a matter of time before I get sick and start to die. After

I'm convicted and sentenced to death, I'll sit on death row for years. I'll probably be dead before they can give me the needle, and dying from AIDS in a prison hospital is not something I look forward to. No, Harry, there's nothing more to figure out."

"Dad, Dad, please let me know where you are so I can see you, and we can talk."

"In a minute, Harry. First, there are a few things I want to say. I regret killing those two women, but I also deeply regret that I've tainted you. 'Hey, that's Harry Lincoln; his old man was a retired cop and a brutal serial killer.' I've disgraced myself, my badge, and the good reputation I earned and enjoyed all these years. I'm proud of you, son. You are a good cop, a good man, and the best son a father could hope for.

"I'm in the county. Call Sheriff Raburn and tell him to send a patrol car west of the city about twenty miles off State Highway 28. At the Holiday Inn Express billboard, turn right onto the dirt road. I'll be about a half-mile up that road. If there is a hell, Harry, that's where I'm going for what I did to those two women. I love you, son."

Harry heard a deep sob.

"Dad, I'm begging you, please don't."

Then Harry heard the gunshot!

Book Two

The Quest

Ingrid Hirsch finished another day's work, but it wasn't another day; it was another evening. Ingrid worked the swing shift.

On her way home, shortly after midnight, she stopped at the all-night supermarket and picked up some milk and a few other items.

There were only a few other cars in the parking lot. She was about to unlock the door of her car when she suddenly felt strong arms grab her from behind, picking her up off the ground. She tried to move, but couldn't. She tried to scream, but a coarse cloth emitting a vile odor was pressed hard over her mouth and nose.

She tried to see what was happening, but all she saw was her grocery bag falling to the ground. She did not see the milk carton rupture when it hit the ground, but she felt the cold milk splash on her ankles.

And then complete darkness!

CHAPTER 1

The desks in the homicide squad room were cluttered with the end-of-day paperwork. There were too few personnel, and each was required to do too much, in not enough time. There were papers in typewriters, on computer keyboards, over phones, some on chairs, and a few on the floor, echoing the chaos of another day in the squad room.

There was stillness now, the heavy emptiness of the middle of the night, in the same space a few work during the night, where many others do the work during daytime and evening hours.

Detectives Harry Lincoln and Jim Conte were at their desks. It was their month to work the morning watch, the long hours of the unpopular graveyard shift, when the rest of the world is sleeping. They wished they were also.

"I hate this shift, Harry," complained Jim, leaning back in his chair, eyes closed. "I can't sleep in the daytime. When I get home in the morning, I feel it's time to eat, but do I eat breakfast or dinner? Back at work again at midnight, and all I want to do is sleep."

"It's rough on me, too, Jim, but we only have to do this once a year."

"At least there's something for us to do," Jim murmured, mostly to himself. "When those punks are still out there shooting and stabbing each other, especially after the bars close, there's something for us to do, but after we do what we have to do, it tanks…" Jim said slowly, as if drifting from whatever point he was trying to make. He didn't finish his sentence; he just left it hanging. That was okay with Harry, who was not really listening.

What irked Harry Lincoln about working homicide on the morning watch was that he and the other duty roster detectives, just one pair each month, were on their own during their shift and afterwards. Most witnesses and others crucial to an investigation are usually not available after midnight, which meant staying over in the morning after eight o'clock, or coming in early in the evening. Twelve midnight to eight a.m. was a clerical reality to the pencil-pushing brass, but it was a ridiculous fantasy to those who had to do the real work.

Harry looked at his groggy partner, who seemed to be settling in for a catnap, his arms crossed, chin on chest.

The telephone rang shattered the lull that had enveloped both of them. The phone did not ring a second time. Jim grabbed the receiver immediately. "Homicide, Conte. Yeah, Sergeant, we're here, just happy to be here. What do you have?" Jim listened and scribbled some details on his note pad. "Okay, we're on the way."

"Maybe this will wake us up, Harry—keep us going for the rest of the watch. Sergeant Posey in the 4th Precinct wants us to meet him and look at a situation."

Lincoln and Conte grabbed their briefcases and radios and headed down to the detective parking lot. Everything else they might need was in the trunk of their assigned car. As they drove away from police headquarters, Jim briefed his partner on Posey's call.

"At the Good Buys 24-hour Supermarket at Oakwood and Pelham, someone reported the abduction of a female to the store's security guard. When the video from the parking lot's surveillance camera was viewed, it was clear that a woman was abducted. The security guard called 911. Sergeant Posey was among the first to arrive on the scene. It didn't take him long to determine that we should have a closer look."

Detectives Lincoln and Conte arrived within ten minutes of receiving the call, thanks to the sparse, early-morning traffic. A dozen or so people, most in police uniform, were milling about in the parking lot. Yellow crime scene tape cordoned off the object of interest—a black 4-door Honda Accord. Sergeant Posey intercepted the detectives as they approached.

"Thanks for getting here so quickly. It appears that a woman was abducted from the parking lot. This is her car; the keys are still in the door lock. She dropped that bag of groceries when she was grabbed. The man who witnessed and reported it is in the security office talking to the guard. Come inside and look at the video."

As they walked to the store, Jim radioed a request for a crime scene unit, the techs that would examine and process the area around the car to collect any evidence, physical or forensic, and take photographs and measurements.

They looked at the action on the surveillance monitor: A woman left the store carrying a small bag and walked toward the black Honda. She was about to unlock the car door when a light-colored utility van pulled alongside her. A man, his face covered with a ski mask, jumped out of the driver's seat and grabbed the woman from behind. She struggled briefly and slowly went limp; the man then tugged her into the van, closed the door, and drove away. From the grainy black-and-white video, the license tag appeared to be covered. If it weren't, enhancement of the video tape might render the tag readable.

A witness of the abduction who viewed that video tape told the detectives, "I didn't see much more than what's on the video, but when I was leaving the store with my groceries, I saw this white van pull up next to the black car, and I thought, 'The parking lot is almost empty. Why crowd the black car?' Then, this big guy, his face covered, jumped out and grabbed her. I yelled, 'Hey what are you doing? Stop!' The whole thing didn't take ten seconds."

"Did you notice the tag, see any markings or stickers? Did you notice anything about the van that might help to distinguish it?" Harry asked the witness. "Which way did they leave?"

"I'm afraid I didn't notice anything, but I did see them turn right onto Pelham Parkway. I wish I could be of more help."

As Harry scribbled the witness's contact information, he said, "We'll need a written statement from you. I'll ask Sergeant Posey to have someone bring you to the precinct. It won't take long."

"Okay, the witness is on the way to the precinct," Posey said to the detectives as he returned to the security office. "The cashier remembers the woman who bought the milk, and she pulled the sales receipt for us. She said the woman bought a small jar of instant coffee, a box of salt crackers, and half a dozen oranges. Most of that's out there on the ground next to the car. She paid in cash."

Jim and Harry interviewed the cashier, a woman in her fifties. She provided a good description of the victim. "I guess she was in her late twenties or early thirties, tall, about 5'6" or 5'7" and maybe 140 pounds. It was hard to tell because of her heavy clothing. She had short blonde hair and wore a heavy black sweater, dark pants with flat shoes, and a red wool hat and matching scarf."

The crime scene techs arrived and Harry instructed them to process the car's exterior, and to collect any evidence around it. The Honda's license tag came back registered to Ingrid Hirsch, of 1479 Starr Road, which was in the 4th Precinct. The detectives called a wrecker, and the car was taken to the secure impound lot downtown at police headquarters.

CHAPTER 2

She slowly opened her eyes. Her head was pounding. She was cold, so cold she was shivering. She could not stop shaking. She moved to pull her coat around herself, but there was no coat and no clothes, not even underwear. She was naked.

What happened? Where am I? She had no answers to the first question. She looked around and saw the answer to the second. She was alone in a small room with a concrete floor and concrete walls. No windows. One door. A dull light bulb hung from the center of the ceiling, and a plastic pail sat in one corner. There was nothing else to see. She tried to open the heavy metal door. It was locked.

Ingrid Hirsch was terribly frightened. *If this is a nightmare, please let me wake up now.* As her head continued to clear, she became aware of the unmistakable smell of excrement. It covered her buttocks and ran down the backs of her legs. Her legs were wet with urine. *My God,* she thought, *what have I done to myself?* She went to the plastic bucket, hoping for some water to clean herself. It was empty.

She went to the door and pounded on it. "Is anybody there? Please, help me. Help me!" No response. Ingrid collapsed to the floor, crying.

She shivered from bone-chilling cold, but more from not knowing why she was where she was. She lost track of time. She had no idea how long she had been locked in this room. She tried to make some sense of what had happened to her. *Why am I here? What is this awful place? Who brought me here? What do they want from me?*

The door suddenly opened. A man stepped into the room. "I see you've had an accident. You have a mess all over yourself." His face twisted up from the foul odor. "Here's a pail of water and some rags. I also brought a blanket. There's some food in this pot for you and water in the jug. Use the bucket in the corner as a toilet. I'll be back tomorrow."

"Please don't leave me here," begged Ingrid Hirsch, on her knees, trying to cover herself. "What is this place? Why am I here?"

His back was toward her as he closed the door behind him. She went to the door, but was unable to open it. Ingrid banged on the door, screaming, crying, begging, "Please, somebody, please, don't leave me in here!" There was no response.

The water from the pail was cold; nevertheless, she used it and the rags to clean herself as best she could. She wrapped the blanket tightly around herself. It was only when she was no longer shivering that Ingrid felt thirsty. She drank from the jug. As she continued to drink, her headache began to subside. She looked into the pot at the food. It was a cold, soupy mush. If Ingrid had been hungry before looking into that pot, she was no longer.

Who is that man? Is he going to rape me? Does he have me here for others to rape me, torture me, and kill me?

CHAPTER 3

Harry and Jim turned onto Starr Road and saw a row of townhouses. Unit #1479 was located mid-block. It was nearly 6:30 in the morning, not quite dawn at this time of the year. The house was dark, the driveway empty. They rang the bell twice, and then knocked several times. No response.

The detectives rang the bell at the house next door where they saw lights on inside. A young man opened the door, looking surprised at the early morning callers. "I'm Detective Lincoln and this is my partner, Detective Conte." They showed their police IDs. Pointing, Lincoln asked, "Can you tell us who lives next door?"

"Ingrid, Ingrid Hirsch. Why? Is something wrong? Is she all right?"

"What kind of car does she drive?" Harry asked. "Does she live by herself or with someone?"

"She drives a black Honda Accord. She lives alone. Would you like to come inside? My wife is upstairs getting dressed, but we have some time before we have to leave for work."

The detectives sat down in the living room with Ronald and Judy Forrest and answered the anxious couple's questions. "We are not sure she's all right." They explained the events of the night. "The more we know about Ingrid Hirsch, the quicker we might be able to help her. Where does she work and what does she do?"

"She does quality control for Airborne Panels Company. It's on the other side of the city. I'm not sure where," Ronald Forrest said. "She works the swing shift, four p.m. to midnight."

"Okay," said Jim. "We'll get out of here and let you get to work. We will be talking to you both some more, but here are our cards with our contact numbers. It would be helpful to know about Ingrid's visitors and acquaintances. We would also like to know what kinds of vehicles you've noticed in her driveway."

"One more thing," said Harry. "Who lives on the other side of Ingrid's house?"

"That's Ms. Ballard, an elderly lady. She's not home all the time," said Judy Forrest lightly. "She likes to go gambling now and then. Takes tour buses to the different casinos."

The detectives rang Ms. Ballard's doorbell several times. After no response, they left Starr Road.

"Let's call it a night," said Jim Conte, yawning. "We both need to sleep. How about we come in early tonight and go straight to Airborne Panels before their swing shift gets off?"

"Roger that!" declared Harry.

They laughed. They often joked at the way detectives said that on TV cop shows. People at home actually believed that cops use that kind of military talk.

◆

Homicide Detectives Harry Lincoln and Jim Conte were approaching their eighth year as partners. It was a perfect match. Harry was thirty-six years old. Jim was older by fifteen years, but each benefitted from the strengths and personality of the other. Many police officers, detectives, politicians, and the media regarded them as the two best homicide detectives in the department.

However, six months earlier, their partnership almost came apart as Lincoln and Conte investigated a serial killer. Three women had been raped, tortured, and murdered. A single killer was believed to be responsible. The investigation was complicated by the fact that one of the three victims was Doris Conte, Jim Conte's ex-wife.

Conte was removed from the investigation because his ex-wife was a victim, and because his many negative comments about his ex-wife became public. The divorce cost Jim just about everything he had. That left him very bitter. Rumors circulated about Jim Conte and his ex-wife's murder, and he decided to submit his retirement papers.

Then things got far worse, not for Jim Conte, but for Harry Lincoln. Harry's father, Ben Lincoln, a well-respected, retired homicide detective, was identified as the serial killer. Ben made a full confession to Harry over the phone. Harry, still on the phone with his father, heard a gunshot. Ben had shot and killed himself.

Harry Lincoln returned to duty after a two-month leave of absence. He was partnered again with Jim Conte, who had rescinded his retirement.

CHAPTER 4

The blanket was thin, but it was better than nothing against the cold. She started to feel the stirrings of hunger. She had no idea how long it had been since she had last eaten. *I am determined not to eat,* she thought, *and if that pot full of vile mush is all there is to eat, I am not going to eat it.* She drank what was left of the water. It was the best of what there was. She was thankful for it.

She tried to get a sense of time. *That man said he would be back tomorrow. Is it tomorrow now? Or is it still yesterday?*

Ingrid Hirsch sat on the concrete floor, the thin blanket wrapped tightly around her naked body, her back against the concrete wall, staring at the door, her eyes fixed on it, although her thoughts searched elsewhere. She didn't know how long she had committed her gaze to that closed and locked door. The moment she heard the click of the lock and saw the slim crack grow into the door's opening, she reacted with relief. The opened door promised, no matter how feebly, that perhaps she would be able to leave this room.

The same man entered the room. "Get up! Come with me."

Ingrid, her joints creaking, unfolded herself and shuffled behind him as he led her down a long, dark hallway, then up a flight of stairs. The moment he opened the door at the top of the stairs, she felt delicious warmth. They passed through a foyer that opened into a spacious living room. She had to squint. Her eyes had become accustomed to near darkness, relieved only by the dull light bulb overhead. The brightness of this living room demanded an adjustment.

Ingrid stood, not yet moving, staring from the entrance. She was stunned. On one side of the room was a grand piano in gleaming, highly polished mahogany. A floor-to-ceiling glass wall framed it. Across from it an oversized rock fireplace blazed, roared, and crackled, and a large, colorful oil painting above added to the warmth. Two large Persian rugs complemented seating areas on either side of the fireplace.

"We're going upstairs," the man said to her as he walked towards the open staircase in the foyer. As she climbed the stairs behind him, still clutching the blanket tightly around her, she thought, *is he going to rape me now? He looks so strong and big. I couldn't fight him off.* He opened one of the doors in the wide hallway and motioned her inside.

"Your clothes are on the bed; I had them cleaned for you. That door leads to a bathroom. You may clean up. You may shower, bathe, or both. You'll find everything you need. Take your time. When you are dressed, come downstairs to the living room." He walked out, closing the door behind him.

Ingrid stood in the middle of the large bedroom. Like the living room, everything looked very expensive: the king-sized bed with complementing furniture pieces, the large Persian rug, the crystal chandelier hanging from the ceiling, and the framed art—mostly nudes—hanging on the walls. In the bathroom was a marble Jacuzzi tub, a separate marble shower with dual showerheads, dual sinks, and a separate commode room. The bathroom was stocked with towels, washcloths, soap, shampoo, conditioner, shower cap, a sealed toothbrush, toothpaste, mouthwash, floss, deodorant, body lotion, talc powder, disposable razors, a hairbrush and comb, a hair dryer, and tampons. Ingrid, confused, nevertheless was impressed by the thoughtfulness of the inventory—everything a woman could need or want.

The hot water from the showerheads sprayed her entire body. She felt the warmth penetrate into her bones, thawing the marrow inside. She washed and conditioned her hair twice, soaped and rinsed her body four times, until her skin turned pink. She was reluctant to leave the cascading luxury.

In the bedroom, a large bath towel wrapped around her, she examined her clothes. She sniffed every article. They smelled and felt fresh and clean. She dressed. She saw her purse on the vanity; in it were her lipstick and a few other items of makeup. In a few minutes, she would be ready to go downstairs to meet with her kidnapper and hopefully get answers to many questions.

CHAPTER 5

Airborne Panels Company, Inc. was located in an industrial park on the city's east side, within the 3rd Precinct's jurisdiction. The two-story brick building was encompassed on three sides by large parking lots. The entire area was well lit by high-intensity streetlights.

It was nearly 10:30 p.m. when Harry and Jim identified themselves to the security guard in the lobby. "We would like to speak with the manager, or whoever is in charge of the company during this shift."

"Sure," replied the guard, picking up the telephone. "Mr. Hoskins, there're two detectives in the lobby asking to speak with you. No, they didn't say. Okay, I'll tell them." Hanging up the phone, he told the detectives that the shift manager, Mr. Hoskins, would meet them in the lobby shortly.

As they waited, the guard volunteered, "I guess you guys don't recognize me. I worked traffic for most of my time with the PD, rode a motorcycle. The few times our paths crossed, I was under a helmet. Anyway, I retired over a year ago after twenty-five years. Now I'm a rent-a-cop. Name is Andrews, Fred Andrews."

"I recognize the name, but your face must have been hidden under that helmet. What about you, Harry?"

"Same here. We'd like to speak to you privately, Fred. When do you get off duty?"

"My shift ends at midnight. There's an all-night diner about a mile from here on Heywood Avenue. Great pie."

"We know the place, so we know the pie. We'll meet you there," answered Jim.

Mr. Hoskins, a black man in his mid-50s, entered the lobby through an inner door. The detectives showed their identification once more and introductions were made all around.

The manager said, "Please come with me," and led the way back through the same door. "What can I do for you, gentlemen?" asked Mr. Hoskins in his private office, the door closed.

Conte took the lead. "Ingrid Hirsch. Is she an employee here?"

"Why, yes she is. It's strange that you should ask about her. I was about to call you—well, not you, personally—but the police department. She's not been to work for the past two days and hasn't called. Her supervisor tried her house and cell phones and got voicemails. We've yet to get a response from her. That is out of character for her, so I pulled her personnel file when I got in today, but I couldn't find an emergency telephone number. I also couldn't find any information about her family. Is she all right? I can't imagine Ingrid being in trouble with the police."

"No, Mr. Hoskins, she's not in trouble with us," continued Jim, "but she might be in trouble. When was she last at work?"

"That would have been Monday; she left at the end of her shift at twelve midnight."

"Mr. Hoskins," said Jim, "we are concerned that Ms. Hirsch might have been abducted early Tuesday morning shortly after she left here." He explained what was known about the incident and added, "Mr. Hoskins, we'll need to review her personnel file. There could be information that will help us in this investigation."

"Of course," said Hoskins, handing the folder to Harry. "If there's anything else you need me or the company to do, please let me know. I am so shocked; I don't know what to say."

"What type of work does she do?" asked Harry, taking notes, "and how long has she been employed here?"

"Ingrid Hirsch is a quality control specialist, an important part of our team. We have only two on each shift. She's been with the company for seven years. As you will see in her file, she's never been a problem nor had a complaint filed against her."

As Harry read the file, he asked, "It says here that Ingrid is thirty-one years old, 5'6" tall and weighs 130 pounds. Is that about right? If this is a recent photo of her, can we please get a copy?"

"Yes, that is a recent photo; we replace ID photos of all employees every other year. There are two in the file. Please take one."

"One more thing," said Jim, as they stood to leave. "Do you know of anyone in the company that she's been dating? Also, we would like to speak to her close friends or lunch-break buddies."

"I wouldn't know about any of that, but I'll check with her supervisor, who is off today. She will likely know."

"Mr. Hoskins, thanks for your cooperation," said Harry, shaking hands with the manager. "Our contact numbers are on these cards. Call either of us at any time, day or night. We'll be in touch."

♦

It was just after midnight, so the detectives had to wait for the swing shift exodus before heading to the diner. When they got there, Fred Andrews was waiting in a rear booth. As they were getting settled, Jim asked the retired cop if he missed the job.

"I don't miss all the bullshit, but I do miss belonging to the blue brotherhood. Having to be on the outside, not having the camaraderie with the other cops, that's tough. Now, whenever I walk into a precinct, I'm just Joe Shit the Rag Man."

He turned to Harry. "Detective Lincoln, I knew your father back in the day. He was one of the most respected and well-liked detectives on the force. Even us motorcycle cops, who didn't have much contact with him—except for re-routing traffic at a crime scene or maybe crowd control—he always treated us with respect. In all my years, I never heard a bad word about him. I just want to tell you that I was shocked and how very sorry I am."

Harry nodded and quietly said, "Thank you, Fred. That helps."

Over coffee and pie, they got down to business. Jim recounted the apparent abduction of Ingrid Hirsch. "Here's what we know, Fred. This big guy was driving a white utility van when he snatched her. Did you notice, or did anyone report this type of van cruising the parking lot, or a guy raising anyone's suspicion?"

"No, I'm not aware of that vehicle or any strange guy lurking about, but I'll ask around," replied Andrews. Anticipating their next question, the security guard added, "Ingrid Hirsch is a very pretty woman, and I'm sure plenty of guys have hit on her, but I haven't heard of her dating anyone from the plant."

"Well, Fred, nose around. Should you come up with anything you think we should know you know how to reach us downtown." Harry handed him a couple of his cards. "Here's our cell phone numbers, also. Call either of us at any time. Thanks for your help and the kind words. I think there's a lot of truth in what they say: 'Once a cop, always a cop.' We'll be in touch."

CHAPTER 6

*P*almer Hamilton was a very rich man. He made millions as a plaintiff's attorney, winning lucrative judgments against large corporations. Palmer Hamilton's standard fee was one-third of the total settlement. His clients were happy to pay the fee, because the settlements were nearly always seven figures, if not tens of millions of dollars. Palmer Hamilton rarely accepted criminal defense cases; he preferred to take up for the good guys rather than protect the bad guys. He did make the occasional exception, and it was not surprising that his clients, mostly entertainment celebrities and professional athletes, all had at least one thing in common—they could easily pay his enormous legal fees.

In one well-publicized case, Palmer Hamilton represented a plaintiff against a major hotel chain in the death of a six-year-old boy. The parents of the boy had occupied a suite on the hotel's eleventh floor. Another couple with a three-year-old boy was visiting. The adults were seated in the living room area, and the two boys were playing in the same room when the six-year-old fell back against the window. The window shattered, and the boy plunged eleven floors to his death. Palmer Hamilton successfully demonstrated criminal negligence on the part the hotel and the jury awarded the parents of the boy $9,000,000. Palmer Hamilton walked away with $3 million.

In one of Palmer Hamilton's criminal cases, a high-profile football player was accused of raping a young woman in his hotel suite as she delivered his room service meal. He was one of the highest paid players in the league. Palmer Hamilton paid a personal visit to the victim and talked money, big money. The following day, a $10 million account was opened in her name in an offshore bank. The DA was notified that the waitress had decided not to prosecute. Because there was no other material evidence that could prove that a crime had been committed, the case was dismissed. Palmer Hamilton was $3.5 million richer.

Palmer Hamilton liked medical malpractice cases. He represented dozens of plaintiffs against doctors and hospitals. Juries almost always awarded astronomical monetary judgments. One of the more bizarre incidents occurred at a large hospital in a major mid-western city. A local man had been diagnosed with prostate cancer. During what should have been a routine procedure, the surgeon removed the plaintiff's perfectly healthy bladder and left the cancerous prostate. Palmer Hamilton got much richer.

Despite all his wealth, Palmer Hamilton was not a happy man. Twice divorced, his problem was with women, and not only his ex-wives. A lusty, sensual man, Hamilton was searching for a woman who might not exist. She would be the link that tied together the components of Palmer Hamilton's vision of a happy life: health, wealth, and an intimate relationship with a beautiful woman. Palmer knew love was not part of the equation, but sex was. He craved sensuality, intimacy, and tenderness from a woman with physical attributes that were attractive to him. He thought he had found happiness the two times he had married, but was disappointed both times, and it cost him plenty. There was still that gnawing void he hungered to fill. He tried prostitutes, from those found in hotel lounges to a variety of high-end call girls. Most offered any sex act, however deviant, as long as they were paid. He engaged in all of it, but it was just business with them.

◆

Palmer Hamilton was a healthy forty-four-year-old man. His low-fat diet did not include junk food. He had not been in a fast food restaurant since being discharged from the army twenty years before. In his house was a fully equipped gym that he used three times a week, keeping his 6'2", 220-pound body toned and strong. Hamilton was a vain man. He was going bald by age forty, and he disliked the fringe of hair surrounding his scalp; he thought it made him look like an old man. He had been shaving his head bald for years.

Attorney Hamilton was taking a sabbatical, not accepting any new clients or cases. However, he had to make several court appearances for ongoing cases and meet with his clients when needed.

I have to have time to solve my terrible loneliness, this hole in my life, this abyss, Palmer thought as he tried to relax in his outdoor hot tub next to the swimming pool. However, he became profoundly nervous and couldn't sit still. His jumpiness kept him from relaxing and caused him to roam aimlessly throughout his spacious house. *What options do I have left?* he thought as he walked from room to room, thinking. Palmer Hamilton had built the 11,000 square foot house on a hilltop in the mountains four years ago. It was secluded, although other houses, ranging from weekend cabins to palatial estates, dotted the mountains. It was less than an hour's drive north of the city. *This place would be perfect for what I'm contemplating,* he concluded, as he reached the decision that might cost him years, maybe decades, in prison. *I must find the right woman.*

◆

Palmer Hamilton first noticed Ingrid Hirsch during jury selection; she was with Panel #4. He was immediately attracted to her. She was neither too old, nor too young. The right size, as he imagined an ideal figure hidden beneath her dark pants and blue sweater. Her blonde hair, fresh face, beautiful skin, sparkling blue eyes—she was the prettiest woman he had seen in a long time. He questioned her as he had the other prospective jurors and decided to accept her as a juror. The opposing attorney, after very little questioning, rejected her. She was sent back to where the prospective jurors were assembled, and then released by the clerk.

The judge continued the case until the next morning and adjourned for the day. Palmer went to the clerk's office and reviewed the list of those who had been called for jury duty. He found Ingrid Hirsch's name and address, 1479 Starr Road.

Two days later, he surreptitiously reconnoitered the townhouse. A black Honda Accord was parked in the driveway. He started an information sheet on Ingrid Hirsch on a yellow legal pad: her address and the make, model, and color of her car. He made a special note of the tag number, because there were many black Honda Accords.

The court case was settled before it got started; the company agreed to pay Palmer Hamilton's client a satisfying sum of money for the injury he'd sustained. Palmer's court calendar was clear, and he arranged for his colleague, Lenny Goldberg, to cover for him during his absence. Everything else could be handled by phone or email.

For the next several weeks, Palmer Hamilton maintained a quiet surveillance of Ingrid Hirsch. He followed her from place to place and updated his legal pad regularly, noting emphatically that Ingrid was a creature of habit, following well-established routines.

CHAPTER 7

Ingrid Hirsch entered the living room fearfully, not knowing what to expect. She still felt the roiling in her stomach, the furor of having been locked up in that terrible room for so long. She wanted to know why and what was going to happen to her.

Palmer was standing at the bar in the living room. "Ah, there you are. Please come in, Ingrid. Sit down. May I get you a glass of wine? Perhaps something a bit stronger? I'm having a little scotch."

"No. Is there fresh water to drink?" She sat on the couch. He brought her a glass with water and then took a seat in a large leather chair across from her.

"My name is Palmer Hamilton. I'm an attorney. This is my home. I live here alone. It's in the mountains. It's a place where I can get away from it all. I also have a condominium in the city and an office several blocks from the courthouse, where I spend a good deal of my time."

Ingrid frowned. "How did I get here and why am I here?"

"I brought you here, Ingrid. I abducted you from the parking lot of a supermarket shortly after you left work three nights ago. I rendered you unconscious with a dose of chloroform. You remained out for some time. I regret that you had to wake up in that dismal room in those deplorable conditions," Hamilton replied casually.

"Why did you do that? Why am I here? You call me by my name. Do you know me? I don't know you. I don't understand any of this. What's going to happen to me? Are you going to rape me? Kill me? Why have you brought me here?" Ingrid started to cry.

"Raping and killing you is not going to happen, I assure you. If that were what I wanted, it would have happened three days ago. Well, maybe the rape. Not the murder. Sex? Yes, I want sex, but I can get sex anywhere. Why go through all this 007 stuff just for sex? Because I want it with you. I want us to have a consensual, erotic, intimate, and tender romance. It's a bit complicated, but I'll explain. Please don't cry, Ingrid." Hamilton felt a sudden surge of sympathy. "Meanwhile, you must be very hungry. I've prepared dinner for the two of us. Please try to relax and enjoy dinner. You will not be harmed. Let's go into the dining room."

The dining room was large and formal. Like the other rooms that she had seen thus far, everything in it conveyed exquisite and expensive taste. The long table was heavy dark wood, maybe mahogany, with seating for at least twenty guests. The china cabinet covered one wall. It contained that many place settings, elegant white bone china, she guessed, accompanied by beautiful crystal stemware. The walls were mirrored, enhancing the effect of the indirect lighting. The chandelier, the largest Ingrid had ever seen in a home, had to be crystal.

Two places were set opposite each other at the table's end, nearest the kitchen. Palmer showed Ingrid to one of the places and held the chair until she was seated. He then went through a door leading to the kitchen and re-appeared with a large crystal bowl filled with salad. A pitcher of ice water was already on the table. Beside it was an ice bucket, and in it, a bottle of white wine chilling in ice.

"Ingrid, why don't you dole out some salad for us while I open and pour this wine? If you prefer, there's water in that pitcher. Please, help yourself."

"I think I'll just have water. What I want is not on this table. What I want are answers to my questions."

"I'll explain everything and answer your questions shortly. First, come and help me bring our dinner from the kitchen."

She helped bring the dinner to the table. The aroma made her stomach growl and her mouth water. She was hungry. Her anxieties were somewhat abated enough for her need to satisfy hunger. After the first few timid bites, Ingrid began wolfing down food that was delicious and carefully prepared.

"You seem to be enjoying your dinner. Please have more."

"I've had enough."

"There's a powder room off the foyer at the foot of the stairs, if you need it. Then, come and help me clean up in the kitchen. I'll brew a fresh pot of coffee that we'll take into the living room. Then, Ingrid, I'll tell you the whole story, which should answer all your questions."

CHAPTER 8

"Lieu, it's a clear case of kidnapping. It was captured on video by the parking lot surveillance camera. There is also an eyewitness to the abduction." Detectives Lincoln and Conte were in Homicide Lieutenant James McGee's office, briefing him on the events and their follow-up during the past forty-eight hours.

"We asked the photo lab to enhance the video so we could read the tag number. They blew it up, and we saw the license tag was covered with something. The witness saw the van leave the parking lot and turn north on Pelham Parkway. When we cleared the scene, we cruised up that way. It's all commercial, small businesses and light industry, everything is closed that time of the morning, except for an all-night gas station and convenience store eleven blocks from the supermarket." Harry was trying to draw a clear picture without getting mired in too many details.

"We spoke with the lone clerk at that gas station. He told us that about an hour or two before we showed up, a white utility van pulled up to the gas pump and a guy came to the window and only wanted five dollars of gas. Well, for Christ's sakes, that's less than two gallons. The clerk thought it was strange and watched him pump the five dollars in gas, then drive north on Pelham. We asked him to describe the guy. He said it was a white guy, big, over six feet, wearing heavy dark clothing and a wool cap pulled down to his eyes and over his ears. When we asked if he could identify him, he said he wasn't sure."

"Why would he stop and get so little gas?" Jim asked a silent McGee, who answered, "Maybe he was real low on gas, and that's all the cash he had. It's too bad that he wasn't dumb enough to use a credit card. On the other hand, if he were planning this, you'd think he would be sure to have plenty of gas. So maybe dumb is his middle name. Of course, it could have been random; he saw her and decided to snatch her."

"Harry and I think it might be the kind of van where the gas cap is located behind the license tag. We figure he doesn't want to drive too far and chance getting stopped for not having a tag, so as he's pumping gas he's removing the cover without anyone paying attention to what he's doing."

Harry said, "As soon as Sergeant Posey spoke with the witness, he put a lookout on all channels for that van traveling north on Pelham. How many white utility vans are going to be on that stretch of Pelham Parkway at one, two in the morning? Maybe he ducked in somewhere, hid until rush hour, and then got lost in the traffic. If he didn't hide, but kept driving, he's the luckiest bastard in this city, or all the cops were somewhere sleeping."

"The big question is whether it was a random crime of opportunity?" The answer to that question would be crucial in establishing a motive, a major hurdle for the detectives.

"We'll come in early tonight and catch the swing shift at Airborne Panels before they leave. The supervisors were going to ask around, maybe someone will be able to tell us more about Ingrid than the sketchy profile we have now." Jim read from his notebook. "Thirty-one years old, very attractive white female, lives alone in a townhouse in the 4th. She works quality control on the swing shift for Airborne Panels in the 3rd, has been there for seven years, and is well-liked by the bosses. Here's her ID photo. We caught a break with the swing shift security guard, Fred Andrews. He's a retired motorcycle cop. He's going to inquire about that van and the guy, and he's keeping his ears open for any talk concerning Ingrid Hirsch."

Harry added, "We'll pay another visit to Ingrid's neighbors, the Forrests. There's a good chance they will provide more personal information about her."

"How many cases are you currently working and what kind are they?" asked Lieutenant McGee.

"We got three shootings and one stabbing from the boys in the neighborhoods and two domestic shootings. All of them smoking gun cases," Harry summarized.

"Stay on the kidnapping. Make it your priority. The others will clear themselves. When that happens, do the paperwork when you get a break. Is there anything we can do for you during business hours?"

"Yes, Lieu, there is. We would like to get into Ingrid Hirsch's townhouse and see what we might find. Who knows? It's worth a look," answered Harry. "Maybe send someone to the courthouse and get a warrant for us. We'll check it this evening when we come in."

"I'll have Detective Delmont from the evening watch meet you there tonight with a warrant. Call and let her know what time. A woman might see something you two could miss. Okay, hot shots, get out of here, go home, and get some sleep. Bring me that big, bad-ass fucker in chains."

♦

Harry's loft was his sanctuary, where he could be alone and relax. He dragged himself in, tired after leaving police headquarters. McGee's parting words, "Bring…in chains," were echoing in his head. This case was going to take priority over everything, including his social life. *Most of the bullshit cases that I handle daily, I turn off as I walk through the door of my sanctuary,* he thought as he lay down on the bed, his mind still churning. *This one has some urgency. A woman was abducted in the middle of the night. Why? What's the motive? Was it a random attack or premeditated? Can we find her before she is harmed? Urgency!* Harry's brain dimmed as he slipped into much needed sleep.

The ringing telephone woke him. On his bedside clock, green numbers showed 7:13 p.m. Harry's first thought was that he had just gone to sleep and it couldn't already be early evening. His second thought was, don't answer it. He did because his third thought was that it might be McGee with something important. Harry answered on the fourth ring, hoarse, groggy. "Hello."

"Harry, how much longer are you going to be?" It was Ellen. "Our dinner is getting cold. If I keep re-heating it, it's going to ruin."

"Oh, Ellen, I'm so sorry. Please forgive me. Things have been crazy for the past few days. Jim and I have been working a kidnapping, staying over late in the mornings, and going in early in the evenings. I've been so damn tired that when I finally got home this morning, I fell into bed with most of my clothes still on. The next thing I know you're asking me about dinner. This morning watch has got me upside-down."

"You did want to have a home-cooked meal here tonight. You said six o'clock would be a good time. I went and shopped for your favorite foods, even got a six-pack of your favorite beer."

Ellen had put a lot effort into cooking the meal. She knew he had a lot on his mind and that handling an important case was physically exhausting for any detective, no matter how experienced. Although it made her feel a little guilty, what Ellen really wanted from Harry right now was for him to see their relationship through her eyes.

"I'm just about fed up with that police department," Ellen said. "It comes before everything and everyone else. I'll eat what I can of this dinner and trash the rest. Let's put it all on hold until you get off that damn morning watch. I hope you catch your kidnapper." She hung up.

Harry was surprised when she hung up. She was pissed, and he couldn't blame her. He had been dating Ellen Bainbridge exclusively for two years. Ellen was a beauty with a brain, a businesswoman with her own successful company. Like Harry, Ellen was career oriented. Marriage had never been in their plans. They both said so. It had been a comfortable, romantic two years, one long honeymoon, much the better because the usual trappings of a wedding did not precede it, but for the last couple of months, since her birthday, Ellen had been hinting about having children. "I'm thirty years old, Harry, I'm on the clock now, and as I get older the ticking of that clock gets louder."

It's not that I don't love Ellen, Harry thought. *I love her more than anyone. I just don't want to be married and have kids. How can I be a top homicide detective as Dad was if I'm tied down with family and social obligations?* Harry was upset with himself for missing the dinner, but it was something that would likely be repeated again and again. *She's made it clear that she wants marriage, children, and a domestic life now. This might be a good time to break it off. I was getting too close to Ellen anyway. I need to answer to no one but my chain of command, and worry about nothing but the case I'm working. Such is the life of a homicide detective, at least this one.*

Harry had to forget about Ellen for now and focus on the kidnapping case.

CHAPTER 9

They were seated in the living room. Palmer sipped his coffee, but Ingrid's coffee, barely touched, grew cold.

Palmer started slowly. "Ingrid, it's going to be difficult for me to explain my actions and answer all your questions. It will be difficult for you to listen. I had abducted you from the supermarket parking lot shortly after you left work. I brought you here unconscious, stripped you naked, and put you into that room." Palmer paused.

Ingrid stared at him, her eyes hard and flinty.

"I've had bad luck with women. My two marriages ended in divorce. I have dated different types of women over the years, lots of them. I even resorted to paying for sex with an assortment of prostitutes. Still, I have not found what I am looking for, what I truly need. That is where you come in, Ingrid; I think I might have found it with you."

Ingrid frowned, and then her face twisted in disbelief. *There is something horribly wrong here. Why me? He doesn't even know me. This man has to be unbalanced.*

"When it comes to women, the packaging is very important to me; I am always looking for attractive women. 'Attractive' means different things to different men. Thumb through any fashion magazine and see skinny female models with sunken cheeks. They look anorexic: collarbones, hipbones, backbones all protruding against the skin. Then, on the other end of the spectrum, there are the obese women. They are everywhere. Neither type is attractive to me. I reject them."

"When I think about the women I got involved with, it doesn't take long for me to see that their beauty was skin deep. Each had her own reasons for hooking up with me; most saw a rich guy. Some found me attractive; others were simply looking for a husband. I found all of them to be sexually and sensually inadequate, unsatisfying. They lacked the capacity for intimacy and romance."

Ingrid listened closely, unnerved by the formality of Palmer's language.

"I understand the enormity of what I've done. At the least, I've committed two serious crimes: kidnapping and false imprisonment, both felonies. Because of that, I cannot let you leave; all the doors and windows are locked and barred."

Ingrid felt chilled. "You are telling me that I can't leave here? Ever? You are imprisoning me? What will you do to me while I am in your prison? What do you want from me that you could not get from all those women?"

"Ingrid, I first saw you in a courtroom. You were a prospective juror. You exceeded my requirements in packaging. I thought you were the most beautiful woman I had ever seen. I wanted to know more about you. I did some snooping through public records in the courthouse. I learned you had been married and that your husband was killed in an automobile accident three years ago and you have no children. I know your parents are deceased, and you have no siblings, no other family. You appear to lead a quiet life. When you're not at work or out shopping, you stay home. You don't appear to go out socially or have company; I haven't seen any other cars in your driveway. I don't think you have a boyfriend."

"I don't have a boyfriend," Ingrid retorted. "I do remember you from that day in court. Under different circumstances, a girl would be flattered that you paid more attention to me than to the other prospective jurors, but now I am appalled and frightened. You said I couldn't leave. Does that mean I'm a prisoner here? You said you would not rape me. Has that changed?"

"No, I haven't changed my mind; I'm not going to rape you. I'd like to get to know each other and for you to be comfortable with me. Then, I'd like us to have consensual sex to see if it's at all satisfactory. If so, I'd like to build on it and see if it develops into what I've been craving all these years. I'm a very unselfish and considerate lover. The perfect result would be for you to be happy, excited, and content to be together."

"What if I don't agree to have sex with you? If I refuse, then what?"

"Well, then I'd have to take you back to the basement and lock you in that room to think about it for a few days."

Ingrid went cold with fear. *Try to stay calm, Ingrid, and appeal to him on his level.* "You're a lawyer; wouldn't imprisoning me for not having sex with you be effectively the same as the act of rape?"

"Yes, technically, it would. Threats, coercion, or intimidation amount to the same as force, but I'm hoping it won't come to that."

"I'm begging you; please don't put me in there again."

"It is all up to you, Ingrid; you may choose to live in total luxury. You have already seen your private bedroom and bathroom; I also have a master suite on the same floor. You will have the entire house to enjoy—swimming pool, hot tub, sauna, tennis court, gym, home theater, and more. Anything you want or need—clothes, toiletries, cosmetics, anything—we'll order online. Just keep a list, and I'll order everything. I'll do the grocery shopping, but we'll share the cooking. I like to cook. I hope you do, too.

"Remain here in the house for the next few days and give this some thought. You'll sleep in your bedroom. I will not bother you. You do not have to stay in your bedroom. Go anywhere in the house. Remember that all the doors and windows are locked. There are fences around the pool and tennis courts. This house is high on a mountain, away from everything and anyone. Yelling or screaming will get no response. There's no one close enough to hear. There are no telephones in the house, and I keep my cell phone with me at all times. There will be no one in the house besides the two of us. I might be gone from time to time, but not longer than a day or two."

He's telling me I'll never leave this place. Oh, God, no. Please, no. Ingrid started sobbing. "I've lived a quiet and solitary life since my husband died. It affected me mentally and emotionally. I was about to become more social with a circle of friends. If you keep me here with no outside contact, my mental and emotional state will worsen. Then I will not be the perfect woman you are looking for."

Palmer Hamilton just sat there. "Please don't cry, Ingrid. That won't change anything."

CHAPTER 10

"Gertrude Bosworth is Ingrid Hirsch's supervisor, and Alice Humphries is Ingrid's closest friend here at the plant." Mr. Hoskins introduced them to the detectives as the five sat in a small conference room adjacent to the manager's office.

Ms. Bosworth was the first to speak. "Ingrid Hirsch has been an excellent worker the entire time that I've supervised her. When her husband died, she took a month off. It was tragic. When she returned, she picked up as though she'd never been gone. I don't know anything about her personal life. Perhaps Alice can help you there."

"You will have to excuse me," started a visibly upset Alice Humphries. "I've been worried sick about Ingrid." Alice started crying. "Have you heard from her? Do you know where she is?"

"No," Harry said. "There has been no word from her or about her. As we told Mr. Hoskins, we have an eyewitness and a video of her abduction, which occurred last Monday night after she left work. Ms. Humphries, can you tell us anything about anyone she might have been dating? We need to know about any men in her life."

"Since Sam, her husband, was killed in a traffic accident three years ago, Ingrid has been quite solitary. She has not dated anyone that I know about. If she had, I would know. Ingrid and I confide in each other; we are as close as sisters. She doesn't have a boyfriend; she's told me she's not interested. I've tried to tell her that it's been three years since Sam's death and she has to get on with her life. Ingrid is a beautiful young woman. Men would stand in line just to meet her, just to go out with her, but she insists that she does not care to date. So as far as I know, there has been no man in her life."

Jim spoke up, "Do the three of you get off work at the same time and walk to the parking lot together? Have either of you noticed a white work or utility van nearby? Perhaps it seemed out of place? Maybe you noticed a big guy lurking around, someone who made you feel uncomfortable as you walked to your cars? Had Ingrid mentioned anything like this to you?"

Neither woman recalled a van or a guy. They didn't think Ingrid had, either. Both agreed that if she had noticed such a man, she would have said something.

"Detective Lincoln, Detective Conte, please find Ingrid before anyone harms her," Alice Humphries pleaded, tears in her eyes.

As Harry and Jim handed each woman his card, Jim said, "You can contact either of us at these numbers. Think about what we've discussed; ask around. Should you hear anything or remember something, please let us know. The more we know the better chance we have of finding her. We'll do our best."

On the way out, at the security desk, Fred Andrews motioned to the detectives. "I think I saw your van last Monday night. Meet me at the end of the driveway, where the south parking lot exits into Freemont Avenue. I'll be there as soon as I can."

The three had to wait until the bottleneck of employees leaving the parking lot was clear. "It was parked right over there," Andrews said pointing to the corner where Regent Street dead-ended into Freemont. "I didn't remember until this evening, but when I did my last round on Monday, I saw a white utility van on the corner facing this way. I didn't pay any attention to it, so I can't say if anyone was in it."

"Thanks, Fred. That's important," Harry said, then mused, "I guess he staked out the parking lot waiting for her to leave, and then followed her to the grocery store where he got her."

"How would he know which of the three lots she parked in," Fred wondered, "unless he's been here before? The three lots have different driveways; two exit onto Freemont a good distance apart, the other is around on Hall Street. I'll have to ask a lot more questions."

"We need to speak with the people who live in the first four houses from the corner back on both sides of Regent Street," Jim said. "It's after midnight, too late to start knocking on doors. Harry and I will come back tomorrow night around ten o'clock to see if any of those folks can tell us about that van."

"If anyone saw him in the van, maybe we can get a description of him without the ski mask. You are a big help Fred. We appreciate it." Harry said as they left. "We'll be in touch."

♦

The rest of the night was slow for Jim and Harry—just one street corner shooting. When the first patrol car arrived, the male victim was on the ground in the middle of the intersection. The shooter was standing over him, still ranting, "I told you, motherfucker, if I didn't get my fuckin' twenty back by tonight I was going to light up your sorry ass!" He then calmly turned his gun around and handed it to the police officer, butt first. The cops immediately handcuffed him.

The victim had been shot several times in the torso and writhed in pain as the ambulance, fire rescue, and several patrol cars arrived. He was stabilized, loaded into the ambulance, and taken to the hospital. The big-mouthed shooter was loaded into a patrol car for a slower ride to the same hospital and placed in a holding cell at the hospital's police detention area.

Lincoln and Conte responded to "detective radio 199" requesting a homicide unit at the hospital to investigate a shooting. When the detectives entered the trauma room, they spoke briefly with the victim, who had two gunshots to his stomach and one to the chest. The wounded man, after screaming as the trauma team inserted a chest tube, had settled down enough to be questioned by the detectives. They asked who shot him, and although he could barely speak, he was able to identify his attacker by name. The nurses then shooed Lincoln and Conte out of the room as the doctors got ready to perform another miracle.

Harry and Jim went to the detention area and met with the police officer who received the call and got the details for the report. The cop turned the gun over to the detectives and left to return to his beat. They interviewed the prisoner, and after advising him of his Miranda rights, he eagerly admitted to the shooting.

"That no good, welching bastard!" After getting a written statement from the shooter, the detectives charged him with aggravated assault; if the victim died from the incident, the charge would be upgraded to murder. The paddy wagon was called, and the latest in a long line of crime statistics was transported to the city jail.

"After we turn the gun into Property, let's grab something to eat," Harry said to Jim, and then reminded his partner of their six a.m. appointment with the Forrests. "Let's be on time. We don't want to make them late for work."

♦

"Have you found her yet?" Judy Forrest asked. The detectives were sitting with the Forrests in their living room. Dawn was just beginning to show through the large picture window.

"No, we haven't. There's not a lot to go on," Harry answered. "Could you give us some information about any activity next door?"

"There's not a lot we can tell you," said Ronald Forrest. "Judy and I are usually sleeping when Ingrid gets home from work. When we get home in the evening, Ingrid has already left. Her car is usually parked in her driveway on the weekends, her days off."

"Oh, my God, this is awful." Judy Forrest held a tissue to her eyes. "We hardly ever see her. On weekends, now and then, Ingrid and I had neighborly chats 'over the fence.' She never talked about her personal life. The only thing she told me was that she lost her husband in a traffic accident a few years before she moved here. She never has company, at least no one that I've noticed."

"I don't recall seeing any vehicle in her driveway except her Honda," Ronald added. "I wish we could be more helpful. Feel free to come back anytime. I'll be sure to call if we think of anything, or if we see any activity next door. Good luck."

"Just so you know," Harry said, "we'll be going into Ingrid's townhouse now. A judge issued a search warrant today. We might find something helpful."

Jim was on the phone with one of the maintenance crew to meet them on Starr Road. They were locksmiths and could enter the Hirsch townhouse without damaging doors or windows.

Getting into their car in the Forrests' driveway, Harry and Jim exchanged glances over the roof of the car. The look on their faces communicated without words. "Don't bet on seeing Ingrid Hirsch alive."

CHAPTER 11

It's been two days since he brought me up from the cellar. He has not molested me, he has not bothered me, and he has not said anything about sex, which is the sole reason he brought me here. How much longer before he demands a decision? Will he lock me in that room again if I refuse to submit to him? I wish I could think clearly. Should I have sex with him so he doesn't put me in that room? I haven't been with a man since Sam died, but it's not as if I was a virgin when we married. I do find him kind of attractive, but no, there's no way! If I could think clearly, I must remember that he said he couldn't let me leave. Surely, that means whether I have sex with him or not, he cannot let me leave. I wish I could think clearly. In the meantime, I'll cook dinner tonight; maybe that might appease him.

"That was the best fried chicken I've had in a long time. I normally don't eat fried foods, but I made an exception when you offered to make it. Why don't you relax in the living room while I clean up in the kitchen? I'll bring in the coffee and pie when I'm done."

Ingrid settled down onto one of the living room couches and turned on the TV.

"The police department is being tight-lipped about the details. Homicide detectives will only confirm that they are investigating the apparent abduction of a young woman from the parking lot of an all-night supermarket late Monday night/early Tuesday morning. The abductor was a large white male, who dragged her into his white utility or work van and quickly drove away. Police spokeswoman Lieutenant Nancy Ambrose asks anyone who might have seen the suspect or the van to contact police at the number on the bottom of the screen."

"That's us," said Palmer, standing in the doorway. "The police are looking. I knew they would, but they won't find us up here," he said, and then casually served coffee and pie.

"The police are very good. They do this all the time. I think they will find us," Ingrid told him. "If you let me go now, I won't say a word about it to anyone. I promise. Please, let me go. Please!"

Palmer Hamilton ignored her. "How about after we finish dessert, I boot up my computer so that you can do some online shopping?"

"The things I would order will take time to get here. I need some things right away. I went to work in what I'm wearing, and I've been living in these clothes for several days," and then, fixing a glare at Palmer's face, "except when I was downstairs without any clothes!"

"Make a list of the clothing and anything else that you need immediately. I'll go to town first thing in the morning. I should be back by midday. Meanwhile, you can make lunch for us. I'd like tuna salad, the way my mother used to make it. I have her old recipe, which I'll leave for you. You'll find everything you need in the fridge and pantry. I'll stop by the bakery on my way back and pick up a loaf of fresh pumpernickel bread."

"I have accounts at Neiman-Marcus, Lord & Taylor, and Saks. That should get you started. Excuse me, I'll be right back." When Palmer returned with his laptop computer, he sat across from her and logged in his password. He then handed the laptop to Ingrid, who was still seated on the sofa. Palmer showed her how to get the department store websites. "Here you go. Select anything you need. There's no hurry. Take as long as you like, and when you're finished, let me know, and I'll take care of the rest."

It was the first time Ingrid had shopped online. Moreover, she had never shopped at any of these stores. They were too expensive for her, a working girl. *I don't think I want to do this, but after what he's done to me, after all he's put me through, I should get everything I want. No, that's what I should feel. The more I let him obligate me, the more he will expect from me. I wish I could think clearly.* Nevertheless, after shopping online for two hours, she handed the laptop back to Palmer, with a long list specifying in more detail than perhaps necessary, all the items she needed immediately.

"I put a rush on these orders, so you should have them by the day after tomorrow. I have a commercial mailbox in town and anything that I order for this address is delivered there, including U.S. Mail. No one comes to this house."

"Another thing, Ingrid," Palmer said as he again gave her the laptop. "This is the website of a fine art gallery in the city. Browse through it and pick out any wall art that you like. We'll replace those nude paintings in your bedroom."

"I'll be glad to do that. Looking at those nudes is intimidating. I see flaws when I look in the mirror; those nudes have no flaws."

"Ingrid, a painting is just that—a painting. I imagine plenty of women have been intimidated by being in the same room with you."

Wanting to change the subject, she asked, "Is that grand piano just for show or do you play? If you do, would you play something?"

"I'd be happy to. How about *Rhapsody in Blue*?" He went to the piano and started to play without the benefit of sheet music. It was one of her favorites. He played it well, she thought.

"Thank you, that was wonderful. I'm very tired. I would like to go to bed now. Good night," Ingrid said casually, leaving the room.

"Good night," answered Palmer, still seated at the piano.

♦

As she slipped into bed, she thought of her husband. She had not forgotten that night three years ago. She opened the door to a police officer. "Sam Hirsch was killed in a traffic accident."

Two days later, she read the shocking details on the accident report. He was on his way home from the airport after a business trip when he was hit head-on by a huge pickup truck, one of those monster things with gargantuan tires. The front bumper slid over the hood of Sam's car and smashed through the windshield, taking Sam's head off. The driver was drunk and crossed over the centerline. He had three prior convictions for DUI and driving with a suspended license. The driver was subsequently tried and convicted of vehicular homicide. *He'll be in prison for twenty-five years, but Sam will always be gone.*

Whenever facing a dilemma, she turned to her husband. *Oh, Sam, I don't know what to do.* She had to resolve this dilemma on her own. *I don't want to be locked in that horrible room. Even if I do consent to sex with him, I don't think he will ever let me leave this place.* She trembled. There was another thorn to this dilemma that she hadn't considered.

What if after we have sex, he finds that, like all those other women, I don't satisfy him? What happens to me then? Well, Ingrid, stop being the helpless, defenseless female. You're neither helpless nor defenseless. If it's sex he wants, then give it to him, but on your terms. It could be the way out of here. You might even enjoy it; after all, he's not exactly Quasimodo. So stop crying and start thinking.

CHAPTER 12

For the second night following the abduction, the two detectives reported in early. At eight p.m., they were back out on Regent Street across from the Airborne plant, knocking on doors. Harry and Jim had no luck until they were at the second house from the corner across the street from where the van had been parked. After identifying themselves to Mr. Carl Harding, a retired plumber, they explained the reason for the inquiry.

"Yes, I do recall seeing a white utility van Monday night. It was parked across the street at the corner. I remember thinking that it wasn't a great place for it to be because it's a no-parking zone. The buses have a hard time making the turn if anyone's parked there.

"Are you sure it was Monday night?" Jim asked. "Did you see anyone with it?"

"Yeah, I'd been watching the football game on TV and I took my dog out after the game was over. My dog piddles around without leaving my front yard while I wait on my porch until he's done his business. While I sat on the porch, I saw a guy get out of the driver's door and walk around to the rear of the van. He didn't open the rear door, but he bent down doing something for a couple of minutes."

"What did he look like? Could you see what he was doing?"

"There's a street light on the corner, but no, I don't know what he was doing. When he got back in, the van's interior light came on. He took off his cap, and I saw he was completely bald, but he wasn't moving like an old man. He was a big guy."

"Is there anything else you can tell us about him or the van? Anything unusual that might be helpful?"

"I guess there is one thing. When the shift at the plant was over and the parking lot was emptying, he took off with a jackrabbit start and bullied his way into the traffic leaving the lot. He almost hit two cars, got in line, and kept on going."

"Thank you, Mr. Harding. You've been very helpful," said Harry, "and we might want to come back to talk some more, but should you think of anything else, our contact numbers are on these cards. Call either of us at any time. Another thing, one of the swing shift security guards at the plant is a retired police officer. He is assisting us with this investigation. His name is Fred Andrews; he might come by to speak with you, also. Thanks again. We'll be in touch."

Harry and Jim went into the plant lobby before leaving. They told Fred about the van almost hitting two cars on Monday night. Fred said he would ask around.

◆

"I think I'll go ahead and draw up a case matrix with everything we know at this point, which is not a helluva lot," Harry said as he and Jim, back in the squad room, settled down at their desks.

"The years are taking their toll on me, Harry. I forget shit more than I used to. I used to keep everything about a case in my head. Now, I depend more and more on our matrix chart, where everything we learn about a case is posted, but the best part about the chart is that the bosses don't bother us at home. They just stare at the wall," Jim said while booting up his computer. "I'll search in the sex-offender's files to see if there's anything on the big bald-headed bad guy or the white utility van."

Despite all the work they had done already, it was just shortly after midnight, the official start of their shift. With nothing more to do in the office, the detectives got out on the street to nose around. Harry decided to look up Ham, one of his informants; maybe he could come up with some useful information. They found Ham with a small group of neighborhood night owls at his usual hangout. As they waited for the traffic light, Harry made eye contact with his informant. The light changed, and Harry continued on to where they always met, a dark, desolate parking lot two miles away.

Within a short time, a car drove up, Ham got out of it and immediately climbed into the back seat of the detective's car.

"Detective Lincoln, Detective Conte, y'all haven't been around in a while. I bet you gonna aks me about the lady what got kidnapped from the grocery store in the 4th."

"That's right, Ham," answered Harry. "What have you heard? What can you tell us?"

"Nothin', Detective Lincoln. Big white guy, white utility van. Got that from the TV news. A little buzz on the street, but everybody aksin' everybody else. Nobody seem to know shit about it. My guess is this guy ain't from the streets."

Harry said, "She was snatched in the 4th, lives in the 4th and works at a big plant in the 3rd. Right after he got her, he stopped at an all-night gas station on Pelham Parkway about a dozen blocks north of the grocery store, where he put five bucks worth of gas in the van. Nose around and let me know if you hear anything. The bad guy is completely bald, if that helps." Harry let Ham out, and then each car drove out of the lot in a different direction.

Harry's cell phone rang. "Detective Lincoln, this is Fred Andrews. I spoke with a couple of guys who remembered that van almost hitting them coming out of the parking lot on Monday night. One of them was going to report it, but the tag was covered. He said the van fell in behind a black Honda. I guess that was Ingrid's car."

♦

They waited for Lieutenant McGee, who usually arrived at the office each morning by 6:45. Jim had brewed several fresh pots of coffee in the squad room for the day watch detectives who would arrive soon. When McGee settled behind his desk with a steaming mug of Jim's strong coffee and his morning Danish from the nearby bakery, Harry and Jim joined him for the morning briefing. There was little to tell. They had gone into the kidnap victim's townhouse. Everything appeared to be neat, clean, and normal, but there were no leads to follow. Nevertheless, they brought him up to date on what they had learned during the night.

Harry's matrix was sparse. Jim's database search had not returned any encouraging leads on known sex-offenders or utility vans. McGee listened quietly, without his usual bluster. "Okay, guys," he said. "You've had a long night. Go home and get some sleep. If there's anything the day watch can follow-up on, let me know."

♦

Harry had been home long enough to take off his jacket and tie when his cell phone rang.

"Detective Lincoln, this is Ronald Forrest. I hope this is not a bad time."

"No, Mr. Forrest, this is a good time," lied the detective. One of the first things he had learned was that anytime was a good time to get information on a case. "What's up?" asked Harry as he unsnapped his holster and gun.

"Well, I'm almost embarrassed to tell you," continued Ingrid's neighbor, "but when I woke up this morning, my brain kicked in. That

white utility van, the one you are looking for, I think I might have seen it. I don't know if you noticed, but at the end of our street is a vacant service station. A van has been parked there for long stretches from time to time over the last few weeks, in a direct line of sight to Ingrid's townhouse. When the van wasn't there, a black Mercedes was—an S600. It didn't dawn on me until a short time ago."

"Mr. Forrest, how can you be sure it was that model? Did you see anyone with the van or the Mercedes?"

"Detective Lincoln, I work at a Mercedes dealer. I'm sure. No, I didn't notice anyone in or near them because at that time, the old gas station was of no interest to me. I did notice the Mercedes because you don't see that model every day. I wish I had been more alert and put it all together sooner. I guess that's why you solve crime and I sell cars."

"It would be very helpful if you could get us a photo of a car like that, a black one," replied Harry. "We will come by tonight to pick it up on our way in, if that's okay. What time do you go to bed?"

"We're normally up 'til about eleven o'clock", answered Forrest.

CHAPTER 13

Ingrid awoke. It was almost eight o'clock in the morning. She went in to shower, locking the bathroom door, despite knowing that the bedroom door was locked. She could not help feeling vulnerable.

Dressed for the day, Ingrid ventured into the kitchen and fixed herself a light breakfast. The house was quiet. Ingrid assumed that Palmer had already left for town. On the counter, she found the tuna fish salad recipe, hand-written on a single sheet of lined notebook paper, yellowed with age, curled, and frayed along the edges. She easily found everything she needed; she had no trouble following the recipe. Lunch would be ready for Palmer by the time he got back.

While waiting for Palmer to return, Ingrid wandered through the huge, modern house. She roamed from room to room, upstairs and downstairs, inside and outside, looking for a door, a window, a shaft, anything that would let her slip away. She was amazed to discover that there was much more of the house than she had already seen. Everything was clean and orderly, in its proper place, and expensive. There was fine artwork everywhere; there were paintings on the walls, sculptures here and there, and breathtaking pieces of blown-glass art.

Palmer's spacious office was furnished and decorated elaborately and tastefully. There was a large home theater with reclining leather seats, a vast, fully stocked bar with tables and chairs, even booths. There were pool tables and Ping-Pong tables. Ingrid was surprised to find a two-lane bowling alley. Outside were the swimming pool and hot tub, and the tennis, volleyball, and basketball courts.

Under normal circumstances, it would have been impressive, but Ingrid had only one thing on her mind—escape.

I must find a way out. I have to get out before he rapes me and locks me back in that terrible room. Even if he simply lavishes me with expensive things, I'll still be unable to leave, and I'll be his sex slave. While he's gone, I have to try to find a way out.

Every window was barred. Although she moved freely throughout most of the house, she found three doors that were locked. Hopefully, they represented a way out. *The next time he leaves, I'll watch him move through the house and see how he gets to his car.*

An unlocked door in the rear of the house led to the large, fenced area enclosing the swimming pool, tennis, and basketball courts. The fourteen-foot fences were covered with a metal mesh. She would keep looking whenever she got a chance. There had to be a way out.

Ingrid sat in the living room. *He should be back soon; he said he'd be back for lunch. There has to be a way to escape!*

She heard the unmistakable sound of an automatic garage door opening followed by the low rumble of an automobile engine. The garage door closed, and then there was a brief silence, interrupted by the soft closing of a car door.

Palmer is home, Ingrid thought. *There's a garage somewhere underneath here—and a garage door!*

He entered the living room carrying packages. "Here, Ingrid. Take this; it's bread and pastries from the bakery. The rest is your stuff. I'll take your things upstairs and put them on your bed."

When Palmer came back downstairs, he went into the kitchen where Ingrid had started preparing their lunch. "I'm making myself a glass of iced tea. Can I fix one for you, also?"

They ate at the breakfast bar. Palmer devoured the sandwiches, one after the other, pausing in between to compliment Ingrid on the tuna salad. "As good as my mother used to make. Thank you."

He looked at her for a few seconds. For some reason, she did not feel intimidated. "Why don't you go upstairs and make sure I got everything you asked for, and that the sizes are right. When you come back down, I'll be in my office. Come right in."

After sorting through the many boxes and bags, Ingrid found that Palmer had gotten her twice as much as she had asked for on her list. She had asked for a 3-pack of white cotton panties, but he had added another, a second pack in pastel colors. *A woman can always use underwear,* she thought, *but I ordered very expensive lingerie, not only underwear, but also nightgowns, pajamas, and robes.* She'd had only one pair of inexpensive jeans on her shopping list; there were three new pairs on the bed. In a couple of days, she would receive two pairs of expensive designer jeans from Neiman-Marcus and two more from Lord & Taylor.

Ingrid went downstairs and knocked softly on the office door. Palmer was sitting at the desk, talking on his cell phone. He motioned her to come in and sit down. "I know it's a lucrative case, but I'm taking a sabbatical for an indefinite period. Why don't you give Jerry Kravitz a call? He's very good with that kind of case. No, no, I'll let you know when I'm ready to go back to work. Thanks for calling, Lenny."

"How'd I do? Did I get the things you wanted? The right sizes?"

"Yes, but too much of everything. Take some back the next time you go into town."

Ingrid replied without looking at Palmer. She was contemplating the wall of framed certificates, awards, and photos—the sort of documents that some professionals liked to display. Palmer wanted to see what she was looking at, to explain what it meant to him, but there wasn't room to move past her. He reached for her, and his hand barely brushed over the back of her shoulder, merely to suggest she move forward a bit so he could step past her.

It was the first time in three years that a man had come that close to touching her. Even after she and Sam were married, she often thought about the first time he touched her in a way that showed he cared for her.

She moved slightly back into him. He put his arms around her. She turned to face him. They embraced for no more than five seconds, but Ingrid found herself clinging to him and reluctantly letting go when he stepped back. Her arousal was like a lightning bolt shooting through her. In those few seconds, the desire and emotions she had suppressed for so long returned. She had missed being held like that by a strong man with a hard body, and she hadn't known it until now

"That was nice, Ingrid," said Palmer, leaning on the front of this desk. "It was a start; we'll go slowly, very slowly."

"I want to believe you, Palmer," replied Ingrid. "However, I can't forget that you locked me in that dungeon. Naked! Cold! Scared! Filthy! I didn't know why I was there or when, if ever, I would be released! I want to be free, not the captive you want me to be!"

CHAPTER 14

Handing the photo of the car to the detectives, Ronald Forrest said, "This model S600 has had the same body style for the past two years. They are expensive, so you are not likely to see one every day."

"How many Mercedes dealers are there in the city?"

"There are two in the city and two more in the metro area," Mr. Forrest answered. "There are three within a two hundred-mile radius of here. There are also used car dealers, but I wouldn't think this model would show up there. There are also private sales."

"Could you supply us with the names and addresses of those who bought black S600s from your dealership?" Jim asked, even though it was a low percentage lead.

"Sure I can do that, it's not confidential or privileged information."

Judy Forrest spoke for the first time while she wiped her eyes with a tissue. "It's been almost a week now; I can't stop thinking about what that poor girl could be suffering, if she hasn't been killed by now." She left the room crying uncontrollably as Harry and Jim stood to leave.

Outside in the clear, cold night, the bright moon lit up the street. It was almost midnight. "I'm sorry that our visit caused your wife distress," Harry said softly to Ronald Forrest as he and Jim got into their car. "Please call us as soon as you have those names or anything else you think might be helpful."

They drove to the corner and into the abandoned gas station. "This is a perfect spot for surveillance of the Hirsch townhouse," Jim said. "We'll have to knock on some doors here in the next few evenings. Maybe someone saw our guy hanging around in the van. Surely, they would have noticed that Mercedes lurking. You don't even have to know it's a Mercedes to recognize that it's a helluva special car. Who the hell would have forgotten it if they had seen it here?"

"Let's go back to the office and get statements from those two guys Fred Andrews is sending in from Airborne," said Harry.

Neither man's statement contained much more than they had already told Andrews, but their observations were now documented in the official case file.

They left the office, drove downtown, and went into The Night Owl, a strip club owned by Moe Graddis, a long-time informant for Jim Conte. Jim got right to the point after the three exchanged hellos.

"Moe, you heard about the girl who was snatched from the grocery store parking lot a few nights ago? It's been all over the news."

"Yeah, I heard about that, but there's been no talk that I know of," Moe said. Two girls were on stage above them, dancing and gyrating around the poles, each wearing just a couple of small tattoos. Harry and Jim had been in so many titty bars when they worked vice that they hadn't noticed the dancers.

Several years back, Jim had been instrumental in saving Moe's liquor license. Since then, Moe had been repaying Jim with information about an assortment of crimes. "Moe, all we have to go on is a big, bald-headed white male, a white utility van, and a black, top-of-the-line Mercedes. Put out your feelers. We need this guy quick, before it turns into a homicide, if it hasn't already. I'll be listening for your call."

◆

Back in the squad room, they updated the case file with the new information and added the Mercedes to the matrix. They booted up their computers and tried several other searches. The police radio kept up a continuous babble in the background, largely ignored by the two. Jim and Harry were engrossed in their computer searches when the quiet of the squad room was pierced by the radio transmission of their call numbers. "Detective Radio 199 calling Homicide 134 or 136." As with cops everywhere, their radio numbers stood apart from the chatter and got their immediate attention.

"134, go ahead 199," Harry answered, looking at Jim, thinking that this close to the end of the watch was a hell of a time to catch a homicide.

"199 to 134 meet the Sector Sergeant in Primrose Cemetery on Fowler Avenue in the 1st Precinct on a Signal 50/48."

"We copy, 134 and 136 on the way." Jim looked at Harry. "Person shot/person dead. Maybe it's a smoking gun domestic case, and we'll just have the usual paperwork."

They arrived at the dark cemetery within twenty minutes. They left the car, saw the lights and activity across the cemetery, and met a uniformed sergeant. "I'm Sergeant Ortiz. I'm glad to see you guys."

"I'm Detective Jim Conte, and this is my partner Harry Lincoln. Let's see what you've got here."

She lay on a gravel footpath amongst the graves, a white female— very naked, very dead. It looked to Harry and Jim like she'd taken four gunshot wounds: one to the buttocks, two in her back, and a contact wound to the base of the skull. They first thought she might be Ingrid Hirsch, until they noticed her long dark hair.

"I don't think it's her. Ingrid has short blond hair," reflected Harry. "When the medical examiner gets here and turns her over, we'll look at her eye color."

"The guard was making his rounds and found her lying in the path just like you see her," Ortiz told the detectives. "We're holding on to the guard so you can talk with him before he leaves the scene." Sergeant Ortiz motioned for Jim and Harry to follow him.

"Jim, you go with Sergeant Ortiz," Harry said, walking the other way. "I'll get a sheet from the car to cover the body and call McGee."

At the car, Harry used his cell phone to call the lieutenant, who was already at the office, and advised him of the situation. "Lieu, it looks bad. It's a nude white female with four gunshot wounds. We don't think it's our kidnap victim, the hair is all wrong. When the medical examiner arrives, we'll check her eye color to make sure. A security guard found her, and there were apparently no witnesses. It doesn't look good. It could easily turn into a media circus."

"Listen, Harry, I want you and Conte to stay with the kidnapping. I'm sending the first of the Day Watch to come in this morning your way. Just stand by and turn everything over to these guys when they show up. Then you come in and give me a briefing on the kidnapped girl. By the way, Hotshot, while you and your partner were out on the town during the night, the coffee leftover from the evening watch turned into cold, bitter shit. I had to brew a fresh pot, and by the time it was ready, my warm Danish was cold."

♦

"Sergeant Ortiz," Harry said as he and Jim covered the victim with the sheet, "day watch homicide detectives are coming out to handle this case. We'll stay until they arrive. There's not much we can do anyway until the medical examiner gets here."

Ortiz nodded. "That's fine. It's watch change for us, too, so I'll request a day watch crew relieve me and my guys. One good thing about a crime scene in a cemetery—there's no crowd control problems. Don't forget we're still holding onto the security guard for one of you homicide guys to talk to."

The medical examiner arrived, made some notes, and then turned the slain girl onto her back. It was not Ingrid Hirsch. The detectives saw the victim's eyes staring lifelessly toward the stars. They were brown.

CHAPTER 15

The ceiling fan hummed softly overhead. She watched it spinning slowly. Glancing at the clock on the night table, she saw she had been in bed awake for almost two hours.

Palmer wanted to have consensual sex with her; he thought she was the special woman he'd been looking for. *Why would he think I might be that woman? Be honest, Ingrid. If it comes to that, what then? If I do manage to please and satisfy him, and I am the one he's been searching for, he won't let me leave this place, in any way, at any time. Worse, what if I'm not that woman? If I'm just another disappointment, what will happen to me? If he lets me leave, he knows I'll go to the police. Or would I? Oh, I'm so confused. Turn over, and go to sleep, Ingrid.*

Palmer Hamilton was also having difficulty falling asleep. He was unable to erase the good feeling he got earlier in the day during their spontaneous hug. *Of all the women I've hugged over the years, she felt so different. It was like holding a cloud, soft and light, yet not fragile. It's how I want a woman to feel. I was surprised and delighted when she pushed herself against me. I stepped back just in time. I can't help but think sex will come soon.*

♦

Breakfast was ready when Ingrid walked into the kitchen. "Good morning, Ingrid," Palmer said as he put food on the table. "Did you sleep well?"

"I did, "she replied, taking her seat at the table, adding pointedly, "When I finally got to sleep."

"I hope you like it," said Palmer, sitting down next to Ingrid. "Please eat while it's hot. I'll be going into the city today to take care of some business that I can't handle on the phone or computer. On the way back, I'll pick up the things you ordered online. They should be there."

♦

At the Hamilton Law Office, Palmer collected his messages from Martha, his secretary of eight years. Martha was a thirty-five-year-old widow who had lost her husband to cancer two years earlier. She ran Palmer's office and managed two junior staffers. She was very efficient and fiercely loyal. He walked past her desk and said, "No calls," without greeting her.

Palmer closed the door to his private office and sat down at his desk. He needed some uninterrupted time to review important papers from Dr. Edmond Beecher's office. Beecher was a prominent psychiatrist and had appeared as an expert witness for Palmer nearly a year ago.

♦

By the time Palmer Hamilton emerged from his office, Martha and the other staff had gone home for the day. After locking up the office, Palmer got in his car to drive back to the mountains. As he drove, the attorney reflected on the material he had spent all day studying and on his feelings about the episode with Ingrid Hirsch.

On the positive side, he thought, *she seems to have softened toward me. That hug was a real indication. Sex can't be far off, and I'm betting my freedom that she is the one I've been wanting. That bet covers my hope that she will want to stay with me, too.*

However, I can't undo the terrible things I've done to her or the fear and anguish that I've caused her. I'm not a brutal guy. I'm not a monster. The kidnapping had been hard on Palmer. He had hated shoving her into the van after knocking her out with the chloroform; he had hated even more locking her into that freezing cold basement without any clothes. He had almost cried as he listened to her pounding on the door, calling and begging for someone to help her. Palmer Hamilton was most upset by Ingrid's pitiful wails coming from the other side of that basement door. He had to resist the temptation to throw open the door, carry her up into the warm house, and gently put her into a bathtub of warm water. He had initially planned to leave Ingrid in the room for five days, but after two days, he couldn't take it any longer and let her out. *I was almost as grateful as she was. Still, I couldn't blame her if she despised me for what I've put her through. Does she? What should I make of her sexual response to me yesterday? Was it a ploy to make me drop my guard so she might escape from here? What would I be willing to resort to if my freedom depended on it? I've learned to read what other people are thinking and feeling, but I'm having a difficult time reading Ingrid Hirsch.*

Chapter 16

Harry and Jim had worked their normal shift the previous night and, after a quick breakfast, were back on the streets, knocking on doors. They started at the far end of Starr Road just after eight o'clock that morning. There was no response at the first two houses. People were probably at work.

"I'll be so damn glad to get off this fucking morning watch," complained a tired and irritable Jim Conte. "At least we'll be in sync again with the rest of the world and won't have to put in these long-ass days just to interview people." It was the same song that Jim Conte sang to whoever would listen. At the third house, Harvey Sooner greeted them and invited them in.

Harvey Sooner spoke deliberately and sat very still as he talked. "I had major surgery a couple of months ago, and I sit out on this screened-in porch quite a bit. I like to breathe the fresh, cold air," he said to the detectives as they settled into comfortable patio chairs facing Mr. Sooner.

"I've been on a medical leave of absence for a few weeks. I work for Afta Labs as a chemist."

The detectives glanced at each other. Where they sat on the porch was in a direct line-of-sight to the old gas station on the corner.

"My dad had major surgery several years ago," said Harry. "It took a few months for him to recover. As soon as he did, got back in the groove at work and was fine. You look like you are about ready to get back to work."

"Yes, I should be okay to return in a week or two. I guess you guys are here about the woman down the street who was kidnapped. It's been on the news."

"Yes, we are," Jim answered. "Have you seen or heard or noticed anything unusual or different in the neighborhood for the past few weeks? More specifically, here on the street?"

Mr. Sooner said, remembering, "A man used to sit in that abandoned gas station across the street, sometimes for hours. He used to show up in two different cars, well actually a van and a car. I thought he might be another private investigator, like the last time."

"He might be another private investigator like the last time?" Jim asked.

"Yes, about a year ago, I noticed a car parked in the gas station with a man sitting in it for several hours. I thought it strange, this being a quiet residential street, so I called 911. It turned out to be a surveillance deal, a private investigator in some child custody case. It never amounted to much."

"Mr. Sooner, you said this man showed up sometimes in a van and sometimes in a car," Harry said. "Can you describe those vehicles?"

"The van was a commercial type, no windows on the side, plain white, without any markings. The car was a late-model black Mercedes. I don't know the model, but it looked to be expensive. I figured this PI was using two different vehicles to cover his surveillance. I saw him parked there at different times, sometimes in the middle of the day, and other times very late at night, after midnight."

Interrupting him, Jim asked, "Don't you ever sleep?"

"My sleep habits have been pretty erratic since the surgery. I've sat back here quite a bit lately."

"Did the man you saw match the description that has been in the news? Can you add anything to it?"

"Yes, that sounds like the man I saw," said Sooner. "He's definitely bald, and yet he doesn't appear to be old. Sometimes he got out of the vehicles to stretch his legs. He seemed to be in pretty good shape."

Harry asked, "Did you chance to see a tag number on either vehicle?"

Mr. Sooner hesitated before he answered. "I'm not certain, but I think I saw the letters LAW on the Mercedes tag. It could have been part of a vanity tag. I'm pretty sure there were more letters or numbers, but I can't tell you what they were. The tag was white with dark letters."

"Do you think it was this state tag?"

"Yeah, I'd say so."

"Do you know Ingrid Hirsch, or do you know anything about her?"

"Don't know her or anything about her."

The three headed for the front door. "Thanks for your help, Mr. Sooner," said Harry as he handed him a business card. "Please call us if you think of the rest of that tag number or anything else that might be helpful."

◆

Later, at the Department of Motor Vehicles, the detectives questioned a DMV supervisor about the license plates.

"Mr. Elrod," began Harry, "how many prestige plates have been issued that included the letters LAW?"

"If you give me a moment, I can bring that information up for you on our system right now," replied the supervisor as he punched keys on his computer. "It's amazing what you can do these days with a few clicks of the mouse. Here we go. There are one hundred and eighty-seven throughout the state that include the letters LAW."

"One hundred eighty-seven," Jim blurted. "Holy shit, Harry! How the hell can we check out all of those?"

Frank Elrod interjected, "Excuse me, detectives, but if you are intending to trace a car, I have more bad news for you. Our regular tags have three letters and three numbers. Some have four numbers. L, A, W are the prefix letters on probably 10,000 or more license tags that have been issued statewide."

Jim was stunned. "How many states are like ours have black or dark letters on a white background?"

"About half of them; I can send you a complete list, if that will help you."

"Yes, that would be helpful," said Harry.

The detectives thanked Mr. Elrod and left the building without the high hopes they were feeling when they entered. "It's almost eleven o'clock. I'll call McGee before he goes out to lunch."

Harry explained to the lieutenant where they were and why they were late getting off. "Listen, Lieu, Jim and I are both beat. Why don't we keep the car? I'll drop Jim off at his place and go home. We'll both be back tonight at the regular time."

"Okay, Harry, and make it the regular time. Don't come in early."

"Thanks, Lieu."

◆

Harry was exhausted. He just wanted to collapse into bed and pull the covers over his head, but he hadn't eaten since when? He could not remember eating during the night or morning. He scoffed several bowls of cereal. He was so hungry, and he did not want to think about the kidnapping while he ate.

He was so tired. He did not want to think about Ellen, but he did. *The last time we spoke, she wanted to put everything on hold until this case was over, but then it will be the next case and the case after that. That will continue until the day I retire. It's been a week, and we haven't spoken. That hasn't happened in the two years we've been dating. Don't do it, Harry. Don't call her. Face it; it's not going to work, not if Ellen wants to marry and have kids, not if you want to remain a homicide detective. When this case is over, have an honest talk with her, explain the reasons why both of you would be unhappy, and try to make a clean break.* Breaking up with Ellen would be difficult, and he would miss her. He would never stop loving her. Ellen had set the bar high. He might never find another woman as good. Harry mused, *I'd like to play the field and not be committed exclusively to one. I'll have to explain everything to Ellen soon, but first I need to find Ingrid Hirsch.*

Harry didn't want to think anymore, about anything, anyone. He placed the empty cereal bowl in the sink, left his clothes where they hit the floor, got into bed, and was asleep within a few minutes.

CHAPTER 17

"**H**ere's the stuff you ordered online. I'll take them right up to your room." He handed her a small white box tied with a string. "Dessert. I sure hope you like lemon meringue pie." Then Palmer went downstairs and returned with another armload of packages, which he also brought up to her room.

"Why don't you go up and put on one of your new outfits, then come down and knock my eyes out? I'm going to open a bottle of wine. Would you like a glass before dinner?"

"Wine sounds good. I'll go up and see what I can put together. "Don't count on me knocking your eyes out. I'll do my best to look presentable."

As she emptied the many bags and boxes that covered her bed, Ingrid thought, *All these beautiful clothes, and look at the prices, Ingrid.* As a working girl who shopped at modestly priced department stores, it was overwhelming. She did not understand why she should have these clothes but, *after what he's done to me, I shouldn't feel the least bit bad. I deserve all this, and that's that, Ingrid!*

She had taken a shower earlier in the day and now wedged herself into a new pair of skin-tight designer jeans; she had never owned a pair. There was so much to choose from, but she didn't want to take too much time. Eventually, Ingrid decided on a light blue cashmere sweater and a pair of plain black leather flats to go with the jeans. She quickly applied her new makeup and fixed her hair. As she left the bedroom, Ingrid felt confident that she was more than presentable.

Ingrid entered the kitchen, put on an apron to protect her new clothes, and began to prepare dinner. She was glad that she chose flats instead of heels. However, she did want to look nice for Palmer. From his reaction, she believed she succeeded.

A short time later, having finished their dessert, Ingrid sat across the room from Palmer. The fireplace was as hot, as was his stare. *He is devouring me with his eyes. Look hard, Mr. Palmer Hamilton. Maybe*

I am that special woman you've been searching for. I'm going to make you believe it. In the meantime, Ingrid, the next time he leaves the house, go over every inch of this place to find a way out.

"Palmer, will you play something for me on the piano? I really liked when you played 'Rhapsody in Blue.'"

As he played, she thought, *Okay, Ingrid, this is becoming awkward. It looks like Palmer is a man of his word and isn't going to force anything. He said we would go slowly; however, if I don't give him some encouragement, it's not going to happen tonight.*

Ingrid did not want "it" to happen tonight, but she did want to see whether she would be the one to affect if it would happen and when. When the Gershwin piece ended, Ingrid stood and applauded. She sauntered to the piano and stood next to Palmer, who was still seated on the bench.

"Palmer, please do something else for me. Kiss me. You said we would go slowly. Let's start here. Then see what tomorrow brings."

He got up from the bench slowly, and the fragrance of her new perfume enhanced what he was feeling. They kissed gently, neither knowing what would happen next. It was no longer simple. There was passion between them. Ingrid held him tightly. *Oh, my,* she thought as she felt his arousal. *Don't get too worked up, Ingrid. The longer you let this continue, the more difficult it will be to stop, and the more difficult it will be for him to walk away.*

She ended their long kiss, pulled away, and held him at arm's length. "I said let's see what tomorrow brings. I think we both know what tomorrow will bring, so let's make it special. Let's make tomorrow evening our first official date. Let's dress for dinner, as if we were going out. After dinner, let's go dancing. Don't worry. We can do it all right here. Just one request: Ask someone else to cook dinner for us so that we don't have to waste any time in the kitchen."

Palmer was stunned. "It all sounds terrific, better than terrific. I'll take care of dinner. You can choose the music."

"Okay, then it's a date." Ingrid gave Palmer a quick peck on the cheek and said, "I think I should go upstairs and get some beauty sleep. I want to look my best for you tomorrow. Good night."

Palmer knew that sleep would not come easy for him. "Sweet dreams, Ingrid."

CHAPTER 18

The detectives were happy to comply with Lieutenant McGee's instructions. It was midnight when Lincoln and Conte dragged themselves back into the squad room. It promised to be another eight monotonous hours of trying to uncover a vital clue in the case.

Harry and Jim were frustrated and embarrassed. They were the two most experienced detectives in the squad, with the best 'cleared by arrest' record that the department had produced in a long time. Yet, in this case, they had not even been able to establish a motive.

"Jim, we don't know much about what actually happened, but we can be sure of one thing—it wasn't a random act. The big baldheaded guy had been planning it for a while, but why?"

Harry was sure that the kidnapper had snatched Ingrid Hirsch to rape her. What he couldn't explain to himself or his partner was why someone would go through all of that surveillance; it didn't make sense. "Maybe he killed her after he raped her, and we just haven't found the body yet. Couldn't have been ransom; she has no family, and her husband's been dead for several years. Maybe another man was involved, a love triangle? Everyone who knew her said the same thing: there are no men in her life, she doesn't date, and she has no visitors. She's got no more money than she needs to pay the expenses of a working woman."

Jim pondered all that and shrugged his shoulders.

Harry updated the case matrix with what they had learned about the tag ID. He and Jim had agreed not to give this information to the media. The benefit of using the media to procure leads was outweighed by the risk of driving the suspect deeper under cover. They could always release the tag information later if they thought it would help the investigation.

"It's time to hit the streets, Harry. This place is spooky with no one around. I can feel the ghosts." Then, as if he had forgotten, Jim said, "Oh, yeah, I called Jasmine, and she's available. Let's pay her a visit."

"Getting a little horny in your old age, Jim?" laughed Harry as they gathered their notes and equipment and left the empty squad room.

"Partner, you don't know the half of it, but the last thing I need is to get involved with a princess of the oldest profession."

Jasmine Bell, a twenty-eight-year-old call girl, was the offspring of a Swedish father and a Singaporean mother. Jasmine was an independent contractor—no pimp, no madam, no agency, no manager, no one. She was her own boss. She had built a successful business with an impressive list of clients—politicians, corporate executives, judges, lawyers, professional athletes, and others who could afford her services. She lived in an expensive midtown condominium, but she never met her clients there. Jasmine made house calls for single men; she met the married ones at hotels.

Two years earlier, a client at a downtown hotel had beaten Jasmine badly. Harry and Jim had responded to the aggravated assault call. Their first meeting with Jasmine Bell had been in the emergency room of the hospital where she was being treated. When detectives questioned the classy prostitute about the incident, they found her answers suspiciously vague. They guessed the reason.

"Listen, Ms. Bell," Jim said in a clear, firm voice, "we are here to help you, but you've got to level with us. We need you to tell us who did this to you, no matter who he is. My partner and I are homicide detectives, not vice, and we don't care why you were in that hotel room, okay? We want to catch the S.O.B. who beat you and arrest the bastard."

She told them everything, including the man's identity. He had been a first-time client and was arrested by the pair of detectives a few days later. Bell's attacker was tried, convicted, and sentenced to ten years in prison. Jasmine had been surprised that it had gone that far. She hadn't believed she would get any justice. Lincoln and Conte had supported her throughout her ordeal, and they had pushed the prosecutor every time he wavered.

Jasmine was thankful. Immediately after the trial, she gave them information about a large-scale burglary ring. She also told them who the "fence" was. Harry and Jim turned it over to burglary squad detectives, who took the gang and their fence off the streets, recovering hundreds of stolen items and returning them to the victims.

Since then, Jasmine had helped the detectives clear other major felonies. They hoped she could help them again. They arrived at her condo, and despite the late hour, were invited in. Many men would have loved to know it existed. Harry explained that they were looking for the man who had abducted a woman a week ago from a grocery store parking lot. "It's been all over the news, Jasmine. Have you heard anything?"

"I guess you mean the big, baldheaded guy," she replied. She was dressed modestly in jeans and a sweatshirt. "I don't have a client who looks exactly like that, but shaved heads are in style now. I'll keep my eyes and ears open, particularly my ears. Many guys like pillow talk. They like to brag, you know? Me, I just listen and learn, and when I learn, you'll learn. Maybe that'll help you catch your kidnapper. As long as you're here, how about some coffee?"

"Sure, thanks. We could use a cup. The bald guy drives a black Mercedes, a very expensive one, with the letters LAW in the tag. If you happen to see a black Mercedes with those tag letters, try to get the full tag number. You've got our cell numbers; please call either of us anytime, okay?"

◆

Driving away from the condominium, Harry said, mostly to himself, "That's a beautiful woman. More than beautiful, she is exotic. If she were in a different line of work, I would love to wine and dine her."

"Harry, are you telling me that if Jasmine were in a different line of work, you would cheat on Ellen? You, Harry Lincoln, the pure and the faithful?"

"Ellen and I are about to go our separate ways, Jim. She's been pressing me about marriage and kids, and I don't want that. I'm trying to work out the best way to handle the breakup and still remain friends."

"Sorry, partner," said Jim. "I didn't know."

"Don't worry about it. I'll figure it out. Anyway, let's head for the south side and find Ham to update him on the Mercedes tag."

They saw the informant sitting alone in his car, which was parked on the curb. They drove by slowly. Shortly afterwards, Ham pulled up alongside of their car at their usual rendezvous. As he rolled down his window, Harry asked, "The woman that was kidnapped, Ham. What have you heard?"

"Nothing, Detective Lincoln, not even a whisper. I seen lotsa' bald guys, big and small, white and black, lotsa dudes shavin' their heads, but not one driving no white work van."

"Okay, Ham, here's an update. He's also driving a late model black Mercedes, a top-of-the-line S600. The tag will have the letters LAW; it might be a prestige tag. Get the word out to the guys that work in the parking garages downtown and midtown. Please call either of us immediately if you get anything; you've got our cell numbers."

◆

Back in the squad room, near the end of the watch, Harry was on the computer updating the case file. Jim was on the phone with Moe at the Night Owl.

"You've heard nothing on either vehicle, Moe? Here's an update on the Mercedes. We have a partial on the tag: LAW and unknown numbers or letters. It might be a prestige tag. Okay, Moe, you know what to do. Call me right away if you get something. This is important, man, my number one priority, so don't let me down."

◆

"Is that fresh coffee I smell?" McGee barked as he came through the door, striding toward his office. "At least you two deadbeats accomplished something in eight hours. I brought Danish, so grab us some coffee and get your butts in here."

The briefing was just that—brief. There wasn't much for the detectives to tell their boss except that they had put the word out to three of their best informants. Lincoln and Conte hoped that might lead to information on the black Mercedes; they did not want to go public with sensitive street intelligence. Lieutenant McGee supported his detectives' decision to withhold the tag information from the media; he agreed that using informants was a good alternative at this stage.

"Oh, yeah," McGee said, still chewing on his breakfast, "this should make your day. The fuckin' media's demanding a press conference on the kidnapping. Airborne Panels contacted them earlier today wanting to know why we haven't found Ingrid Hirsch yet. That's like throwing a barrel of chicken parts to a pack of hungry wolves. The chief wants to meet ASAP to discuss the press conference. He wants to know how we're going to handle it. The two of you have been invited. You're the guests of honor. I'll let you know when it's gonna happen. Now go home and get some sleep; you both look like shit."

CHAPTER 19

Palmer got up early and left the house before six a.m. He had an urgent meeting with a client whose latest appeal was coming up soon, to be heard before the State Supreme Court. The meeting was set for ten a.m. He wanted to prepare for the meeting in his office, after eating breakfast.

Palmer sat alone in his usual booth at Mimi's Café. It was two blocks from the courthouse, and it was popular with members of the legal community. The restaurant did a brisk business, and this was the peak time for the breakfast crowd, which included judges, prosecutors, police officers, and lawyers. Two booths were filled with uniform cops and plainclothes detectives. Not one gave Palmer a second look; most knew who he was and saw him there most mornings. He was a fixture; he belonged.

Palmer's mind wandered as he ate his omelet. He was oblivious to those around him and unconcerned that someone might realize he fit the description of the wanted man. All Palmer Hamilton could think about were the events of the previous night and his date with Ingrid later that evening. As he left the restaurant and walked the short distance to his office, he promised himself to focus on his client and not to be distracted by his forthcoming dinner date. One quick phone call to the restaurateur would ensure that everything went as planned.

◆

"Good morning, Harold," he said into the phone. "Palmer Hamilton here. I wasn't sure you would be in this early."

"Good morning to you, my friend," replied the restaurateur. "I just got back from the markets. I haven't seen you for quite some time. I've missed you."

"I've been very busy lately; don't take it personally. Did you get my message about the catering for tonight?"

"Yes, I did, Palmer. It'll be ready for you to pick up at 5:30, just like you said."

"Thanks, Harold. Any chance you could pack it all up in those little warmer ovens? I'll return them to you next time I'm in town."

"Yes, of course, my friend. Anything for my best customer."

♦

Early that morning, Ingrid heard noises. She glanced at her bedside clock; it was 5:42 a.m. It was still dark outside. When she realized that the noise was Palmer moving about, she rolled over in bed and pulled the blankets up over her shoulders. She could not go back to sleep. She was thinking, not only of later this evening, but also of her search for a way out once Palmer left the house.

The house was quiet; Palmer was ready to leave. Ingrid got out of bed. She padded barefooted after him, slipping into an alcove to watch as he went through one of the locked doors to a garage. She was about to leave the alcove to see if he had locked it behind him, when the door opened, and Palmer walked back in. Ingrid ducked behind some luggage and lay flat on the cold floor. Palmer must have forgotten something, she guessed, as she lay quietly, hardly breathing.

She silently prayed that he would not look in her bedroom. Palmer returned a few minutes later and again went through the door. She heard the garage door, then a car starting. She followed the sound of the car backing out, and then heard the garage door come down. Palmer was gone, so she left her hiding place. She was not surprised to find the door to the garage locked.

Ingrid checked the two other doors. They were still securely locked. She looked for tools; anything to force open the doors. There was nothing. She searched every nook of the house and found nowhere to squeeze out. She now knew the one door led to the garage, but it was locked.

She would have to concentrate on tonight.

♦

Back in her bedroom, Ingrid inspected all her new clothes and accessories and took a long, leisurely look. She hung dresses, blouses, and sweaters around the room so she could see them all. She arranged skirts, pants, and lingerie on the bed, shoes on the floor, accessories on the chair, and jewelry on the vanity.

Ingrid was amazed that most of the clothes fit her perfectly, given that she had ordered everything online. She modeled each article before the full-length mirror. Hoping to look sexy and classy, she decided on a cranberry-red sheath dress with a suggestive neckline and modest hem two-inches above the knee. Matching the shoes was easy; choosing the lingerie thrilled her in a way no other lingerie had ever excited her. It had been a long time since Ingrid Hirsch had worn special lingerie for a man. She had never owned anything as elegant as what she was now going to choose.

Ingrid did not keep track of how long she spent on her private fashion show, mixing and matching different outfits with her new clothes. She went downstairs to the kitchen for a quick lunch, and then searched once more for a way out. *If I could only get through those locked doors,* she thought. *The one leading to the garage would do it.* The second search was no more fruitful than the first one.

Think, Ingrid, think. Be smart. Switch your efforts to Palmer Hamilton. Enchant him. Bewitch him, then who knows what.

Palmer had said he would be home by seven o'clock with dinner. It was now three o'clock. She started to get ready. She wanted to do everything slowly and luxuriously, beginning with a warm bath. After toweling off, there were fingernails and toenails to be painted in a deep rich red to match her dress. She had plenty of time for her nails to dry before fixing her hair. She used very little makeup. She applied her perfume lightly and strategically.

It was 6:30 when Ingrid slipped into her dress and shoes and added a string of pearls to complete the ensemble. Ingrid inspected the finished product in the wrap-around mirror. She was pleased. She felt good. *I'll knock your eyes out tonight, Palmer Hamilton.*

Just after seven o'clock, Ingrid heard Palmer come into the house. From the sounds, she could tell that he was organizing their dinner in the kitchen. She decided to give him a few minutes to finish before she made her appearance. Palmer walked into the foyer and watched her descend the spiral staircase. As they stood on the black and white marble squares, she said, "My, don't you look handsome for someone who's been working all day."

"Well, I shaved, showered, and changed into fresh clothes before I left the city." Palmer kissed her lightly on the cheek, then held her at arm's length and turned her completely around. "Ingrid, I'm weak in the knees looking at you. Let's go into the living room before I fall down."

As they sat across from each other, Palmer, overwhelmed, said, "Ingrid, you look sensational, absolutely beautiful!"

Ingrid enjoyed the repartee and played along, "Am I supposed to say, 'Shucks I just threw on this old dress,' and then blush beet red?" They laughed. As they sipped their wine, Palmer gave her a preview of the meal that Harold had prepared. Eventually, they made their way to the dining room. Both anticipated the date, but neither seemed to be in a hurry.

The dinners were as good as Harold had promised. "Palmer, that was the best take-out meal I've ever had."

Palmer laughed and said, "I'm glad you liked it, but Harold prefers 'catered.' He disdains the term 'take-out'; says it gives him indigestion."

Motioning to the living room, Palmer continued, "Make yourself comfortable while I clear the table. We'll leave the cleanup for tomorrow."

Ingrid had chosen mellow music. They listened without saying much. The sexual tension in the room built. Palmer had hardly taken his eyes off Ingrid since he first saw her on the staircase. He got up, walked over to her, and asked her to dance.

As they glided across the hardwood, Ingrid realized that Palmer was a very good dancer. She clung to him. It didn't take much more to arouse him. They stopped dancing, kissed tenderly, and then climbed the stairs arm in arm, into his bedroom.

Palmer felt awkward while standing. His erection dominated his presence, so he sat down on the bed. She stood before him. He wrapped his arms around her legs and ran his hands under her dress, slowly up her legs, then over the smoothness of her panties. She parted her legs slightly, just enough as he felt the silken wetness ; she was ready. The line had been crossed. They were about to become lovers. They slowly undressed each other. When all that remained on Ingrid's body was her lingerie, Palmer paused, to retain the image of what he was seeing, to take a picture with his mind.

They hastily pulled the bedding down, and lay naked on the sheets. There was passion from one to the other, but Palmer needed to control it. He had to slow things down early for her to trust him fully later. Ingrid's capacity for passion and sex had been buried with Sam. Palmer helped her rediscover it. He tore open the condom and offered it to her to put it on him. She did. When they merged, it was soft, warm, tender. She felt him go deeper. She made sounds she hadn't heard coming from herself in years. Palmer set the rhythm, and the tempo built as the minutes ticked away; then a powerful crescendo led to an electrifying simultaneous climax for both of them.

They breathed hard, lying on their backs, hearts pumping. They were quiet. A few minutes later, heart rates back to normal, Ingrid turned to him and quietly said, "Palmer, I'd like to sleep here with you tonight."

"Yes. Absolutely. You will."

After she returned from the bathroom, she climbed into bed, kissed him good night, and turned around, her back to him. They lay together, pressed tightly against each other, his arm wrapped around her.

"This was one of the most pleasurable nights I can remember. Thank you."

"It was exciting and wonderful for me too, Ingrid. I will never forget it."

She mumbled something, and he could tell by her breathing that she was drifting off to sleep. As Palmer lay there, he thought back to the abduction and the awful two days that followed. He was ashamed of himself. He was also in love. He would always remember the sight of Ingrid in her red dress as she descended the stairs. Could he have finally found his ideal woman?

CHAPTER 20

Harry saw it—a black Mercedes with a bald man driving. He made a quick U-turn and caught up to it. There it was: "LAW" on the tag, and the chrome "S600" proudly displayed on the trunk over the tail light. He turned on the blue lights and siren, and the Mercedes pulled to the curb and stopped. The bald man got out and just there, hands on his hips, and laughed. A white utility van approached from the opposite direction and stopped. The driver, a baldheaded man, got out, looked at Harry, and laughed. Then several more black Mercedes and white utility vans stopped, their baldheaded men laughing, louder and louder and louder…

Harry sat up in bed sweating and trembling; the telephone was ringing. He reached for it on the bedside table and pushed the green call button, but he could not speak yet.

"Hello, Harry?" said the caller. "Harry Lincoln, are you there? Why the hell don't you answer, goddammit?"

It was McGee, Harry realized, and found his voice. "Is something wrong, Lieutenant? Sorry, I was asleep."

Lieutenant McGee turned off the bluster. "Harry, I hate to have to call, but it's important. The chief wants a meeting today about how to handle the press conference, and he wants you and Conte there. The meeting's set for one o'clock, right after lunch, so you had better hustle on down here. I called Conte. He's on the way."

A few minutes after one o'clock, Lieutenant McGee and Detectives Lincoln and Conte entered Police Chief Robert Lansing's office.

The chief wasted no time. "I apologize for disrupting your sleep," he said to the bleary-eyed detectives, "but, this couldn't wait any longer. Lieutenant McGee informed me of the extra hours you both have been working since you started investigating this case. It's bad enough working the morning watch, I know. I just want you both to know that I recognize and appreciate the extra time and effort you've had to put in."

Deputy Chief Glenn Watkins and Sergeant Martin Bowser of Public Affairs were also there. "I'd like to echo the remarks made by the chief," said Watkins, with well-practiced diplomacy.

"All right, let's get to it," Chief Lansing said. "Up till now, we've withheld details on the tag. It's been worth the risk, but now we're getting a lot of pressure from the media. We need to give them something to calm them down."

Deputy Chief Watkins said, "Lincoln, Conte, what are your thoughts?"

Harry shrugged. "Well, chief, it's hard to say. We don't believe it was a random kidnapping, but we haven't established a motive. We assume it was rape, but we don't know what to think beyond that, and it's hard to say if she's still alive or not."

Jim added, "Lincoln and I have given the car tag information to three of our best informants, but we haven't heard anything yet. It's only been a few days."

Sergeant Bowser said, "Chief, if the girl gets killed and it gets out that we've withheld information, well, it's going to be a PR nightmare."

"Okay," said Lansing. "Let's release the tag information to the media at the press conference tomorrow; it's scheduled for eleven a.m. Lieutenant McGee, give Lincoln and Conte the night off, with the understanding that they'll be on-call for anything connected with the kidnapping case. Have a pair of your day watch detectives cover the morning watch tonight for everything else. I'll see you all tomorrow at 10:45 a.m., here in my office. We'll go to the press conference together. Thanks for coming in."

♦

"Okay, you heard the boss. We release the tag information tomorrow at the press conference." The three, now seated in Lieutenant McGee's office discussed the fate of Ingrid Hirsch. "We all know it's a crap shoot, but with a full week sneaking up on us, it's better that the media hears it from us than from someone else." McGee continued, "and the victim, what's happened to her?"

"Although we don't know the motive, I've believed from the beginning that he snatched her to rape her." Jim had been adamant, "but did he kill her after he raped her? Or, was it such good stuff that he's keeping her to get some more?"

"What do you think, Harry?" McGee asked. "I'm inclined to think that he killed her."

"Well, my guess is as good as either of yours," Harry ventured. "I'm just hoping she's still alive."

"All this guessing and wishing isn't getting us any closer to identifying the bald guy and finding her alive," McGee said. "Maybe the big break will happen tonight, and you'll have to come in anyway. I'll notify the communications supervisor that you both will be off from the morning watch tonight, but that he is to call you if anything develops on the case. Now you two get out of here."

♦

Harry was almost home when his cell phone rang. It was Ellen.

"Hello, Harry. Did I wake you?"

"No, McGee already did that. I'm in the car on my way home now."

"Harry, I cut you off the other night, and I feel awful about it," said Ellen. "If you don't have plans, meet me at the Downtown Diner for an early dinner, say about five. I'm buying."

"The Diner at five. I'll be there."

Harry parked the car, went up to his loft. He shaved, showered, and put on a fresh pair of jeans with a long-sleeved sport shirt. He popped a cold Harp and settled into his recliner. *This is going to be painful,* he thought. *It would be a helluva lot easier if she was still pissed at me, but she didn't sound pissed.* Ellen's talk of marriage and kids was serious. He needed to sort out all of the personal stuff with Ellen, but the kidnapping case had gotten in the way.

He had decided to wait until the case was resolved to discuss their relationship, but it seemed that Ellen was doing what she had decided for herself. *I guess it will have to be now,* he mused, draining the last of his beer. *I just hope I can find a way to tell her it's over and somehow still be friends.*

♦

Harry got to the diner a little early and took a booth at the rear. Ellen walked in five minutes later. *God, she is a looker,* Harry thought as soon as he saw her.

"Hello, Harry. Been waiting long?"

"No, about five minutes, Ellen. You look lovely; you always do."

"You look pretty dashing yourself," she replied as she slid into the booth across from Harry. They made casual conversation while waiting for their food to arrive. Harry felt his anxiety build as he anticipated saying what he had silently rehearsed before she arrived.

Not long after their meals were served, Ellen took the lead. "Harry, the last time we spoke I was abrupt, and I want to apologize, but that's not the reason I asked you to meet me. I love you to death, Harry Lincoln. The last two years have been the happiest of my life, but things between us are about to change. I've developed strong maternal feelings, and I'm not getting any younger. You've told me several times that domestic life, marriage and children are not for you. Those things would have a negative impact on your career. For a long time, I felt the same about myself, but not anymore."

Ellen paused and took a deep breath. "Harry, I've met someone. He is a new client. We have not been out socially. It's been all business. I'm attracted to him, and I know he is interested. This is awkward for me, but I wanted to tell you in person before going on a date with him. I very much want us to stay friends, Harry. You have been a big part of my life. Now stop gawking and eat your hamburger."

Harry smiled. "This is incredible, Ellen. Ever since you phoned earlier, I've had pangs of conscience, concerned that I might hurt you because I wanted to call things off. I've been struggling to find the right words to say the same thing that you just did, but from my point of view. Yes, I'll always be your friend, and I'll always be there for you if you need me." Then he winked. "That doesn't mean I won't be jealous of any man with you on his arm."

♦

The following day at police headquarters, during intense questioning from the media, an aggressive female reporter from the local news team asked for the third time, "When was the lead on the license plate learned and how was it developed?"

"I've told you that this latest development is protected under investigative confidentiality," Jim snapped back.

The press conference had been going on for only twenty minutes. Tempers were beginning to flare. Chief Robert Lansing and Deputy Chief Glenn Watkins had opened with the formalities. Lieutenant McGee made a few comments, and then the spotlight was on Detectives Harry Lincoln and James Conte.

"So, what you are telling us, Detective Lincoln," said a reporter from the city's largest newspaper, "is that you don't know where she is, have no idea whether she's dead or alive, don't know the identity of the kidnapper, and you don't know his motive. What *do* you know?"

Harry took a deep breath. He'd dealt with this asshole before, but was not going to be goaded into unprofessional conduct. "We know that it was not a random act. He targeted and followed her for several weeks. We have a very good description of him from several witnesses; he's also on video. We know of two different vehicles that he's been seen in, and we have a partial tag number for one of them. We have not heard from the kidnapper or received any ransom demands. This is a high priority case that we are working 24/7. The investigation includes members of the fugitive squad and other detectives, uniformed police officers, superior officers, and office and civilian personnel. The Metro PDs have been notified and the State has the lookout. Now, if you and your colleagues will do your jobs and get the information about the partial tag on that black Mercedes out to the public, there will be many more people looking for it. Hopefully, someone will spot it and report it. Then, we can conduct a rescue operation and get her back safely, if she's still alive."

Public Affairs Sergeant Bowser moved to the podium, "No more questions, ladies and gentlemen. That concludes this press conference. Thank you for coming."

CHAPTER 21

Palmer had been awake for a while. Ingrid was sound asleep. Everything was quiet. A full moon, shining through sheer curtains that covered the large window, illuminated the bedroom.

Staring out the window, Palmer thought, *Is my search over? Is she the one? If so, what happens now? I certainly can't keep her locked up and never let her out. Is this all an act? Is she biding her time, waiting for me to lower my guard? She would not be the first woman who out-smarted a man using sex when it meant survival. If so, she's one hell of an actress.* He could not accept that, did not want to accept that, not after tonight.

Palmer couldn't concentrate any longer; he was too emotionally exhausted to think. His breathing slowed, and he succumbed to sleep.

◆

He awoke to a sun-brightened room, and the light brightened his outlook, as well. Ingrid was still asleep next to him, lying on her back. He looked at her face in its natural, vulnerable state—no make-up, no posing, no smiling—so goddamn beautiful. He lay quietly, not wanting to wake her, happy to gaze at her, to drink her in. He finally got up and went in to take a shower, confident that the next few days would offer some answers and solutions.

Ingrid suddenly opened her eyes and looked around the room. It felt strange, and for a moment, she forgot where she was. She remembered as Palmer came out of the bathroom with a towel wrapped around his waist. "Good morning, Ingrid. You slept well, didn't you?"

"Good morning. Yes, I did. The best night's sleep I've had in a long time. I see you've showered; I'd like to go to my bathroom and do the same."

"I'll throw on some clothes, and then go downstairs and get breakfast started," said a smiling Palmer Hamilton.

CHAPTER 22

O nce again, it was just the two of them in the eerie quiet of the deserted squad room. "We've only one more week working upside down in the purgatory of this damn morning watch. Then, Harry, we're back to a normal life, where lunch is at twelve noon, instead of four a.m." Jim was pacing. "You know, Harry; I bitch about working the morning watch for all the obvious reasons. Then, I bitch when I'm on the day watch because I feel crowded. There is too much brass around, and I'm always glancing behind me, thinking one of them is crawling up my ass trying to catch me doing something wrong. When I work the evening watch, I bitch because it gets so goddamn busy that there's not even a break to get a cup of coffee, much less to eat a meal. There were times we've been called to the ER on a shooting or stabbing at the beginning of the watch and couldn't leave the hospital until the end of the watch because they kept coming in shot or stabbed.

"I've made up my mind, Harry. When this case is over, I'm going to pull the plug. I know I put in my retirement papers during our last big case, but that was different. My ex had fucked me up again, the pressure was too much, and I lost my perspective. This time, I'm going about it in a calmer, more rational way. Two companies, an armored car service and a bank, have offered me head of security positions, and a large law firm offered me a job as their lead investigator. All I have to do is choose. The law firm pays the best. My condition with each is that I cannot start until this kidnapping case is over. I've given this police department thirty years of my life, Harry; it's time."

"I can't say that I'm surprised, Jim. Your anxiety has been obvious to me for some time now, and I think I understand. My dad told me that a police officer knows when it's time to go, and when they do, it's very emotional and painful. I think you'll be happier once you do and settle into your new career, whichever one you decide on. I'm glad you're sticking with me until we get our bad guy and find Ingrid Hirsch."

The squad room phone rang. Harry answered. It was the detective radio dispatcher; homicide detectives were needed at the hospital on a serious aggravated assault. "Okay, Jim, put that retirement on hold and let's go to work."

The victim was blood, bone, and gore from the neck up. The trauma team worked with furious intensity, and Harry thought, *I've seen these ER doctors perform miracles before, but I doubt they will this time. I think this will end up another homicide.* Harry and Jim left the room and headed to the police detention area to find the officer who answered the call.

"He is part of a construction crew working on one of the new skyscrapers going up downtown," the cop read from his notes. "They got off work earlier this evening and went to shoot dice at a vacant lot nearby. The way I got it from a couple of witnesses, two guys had some kind of beef with him about the game, and when almost everyone was gone, they worked him over pretty good with a tire iron. Those two over there are the witnesses. Good luck!" The cop dashed for the exit as if he was answering an emergency call.

The witnesses couldn't add much more than the name of the victim, the names of those who attacked him, and the building where they were working.

"You know, Harry, it gets me. That cop couldn't wait to get the hell out of here. Why the fuck couldn't he have gotten the victim's name and the names of the perpetrators? He certainly had the time, waiting for us. He didn't even know which building the crew was from. What was his big goddamn hurry? The donut shop is still going to be there."

They were about to leave the hospital when an EMT crew rushed a gurney from an ambulance to the ER. Harry and Jim followed them into another trauma room. It was a man, the victim of a stabbing. The nurses cut away his clothes and asked them to hold him down until the doctors could insert a chest tube. When he stopped hollering, the twenty-year-old victim said he was stabbed by another guy in a fight over a woman. The doctor told the detectives the guy would make it. Harry and Jim got all the information, but before they left the hospital, they checked and found the doctors still working on the victim with the bashed-in head. He was alive. It was not a homicide. Not yet.

As they had done for the last couple of nights, they rode the city streets looking for the black Mercedes with the LAW license plate.

They checked private driveways, empty parking lots, and large parking decks, stopping at the IHOP only once to eat. Then there was work to be done at the office before they went home.

When they got back to the squad room, Lieutenant McGee was already in his office, although it was just past five a.m. Harry and Jim advised him of the two latest victims at the hospital and that the odds were that the one probably would not make it.

"If that one becomes a homicide, Lieu, do you want us to work it, since the kidnapping has hit a lull?" Harry asked, feeling a little guilty about the lack of progress in the case.

"No, I'll turn them over to the day watch; I want you two to stay with your kidnapping."

Harry and Jim spent some time on the squad room computers, finishing the rundown of prestige tags with the letters "LAW." Of the one-hundred-eighty-seven, they found that twenty-nine were issued to Mercedes; of those twenty-nine, only six were black, and they were less expensive models. Four of them were SUVs.

"Well, Harry, I guess we can now start on the ten thousand-plus regular tags with the 'LAW' prefix," an exasperated Jim exclaimed in his most sarcastic voice.

"We'll just have to hope someone spots it and reports it," answered Harry.

"Lincoln, Conte," called McGee from his office. "Run over to the hospital and handle a gunshot that just came in."

At the ER, the detectives followed the sounds of shouting from one of the trauma rooms, where they found a young black male lying on the table, very much alive. He was shot multiple times in his arms, legs, and torso. The detectives didn't have to ask many questions; he told the trauma team all about it. "The motherfucker was my homeboy, my man, until he shot me for nothin'."

"Okay," Jim said trying to calm the victim. He identified himself and Harry as homicide detectives. "Who shot you?"

"Who, me?"

"No, the doctor over there who is trying to save your life. Of course you! Tell us what happened," answered Detective Conte, who had gotten the same answer to that simple question a dozen or more times in the past.

"My man, Tyrone, that's who shot me for nothin'. Tyrone Washington. We was just hangin' out on the street talkin' shit when the dude gets on my ass about some bitch I don't even know. Before I know it, he pulls his piece an' the dude shot lots a times."

The doctor gave them a silent high sign, indicating that the victim would likely live. They left the trauma room and tracked down the responding officer, who was in the nurse's lounge flirting with a pretty nurse. When they got the officer's attention, he gave them the information needed for the report. "Let's get the hell out of here, Harry,"

After the morning briefing with Lieutenant McGee, they left police headquarters and went home. Harry jumped into the shower, then his pajamas, and slid into bed. He could not sleep, disturbed over the probable outcome of the case. *Is Ingrid Hirsch still alive, or has he already killed her? In the past, it has always been solve the case, identify the bad guy, find him, and arrest him. This is different; there is urgency here. Solve the case, identify the bad guy, find him, and arrest him* before *he kills her. If she is still alive, find her. Come on, Harry. You and Jim are hotshot homicide detectives; do some of your hotshot stuff!* Slowly, sleep came.

CHAPTER 23

They sat in the sunroom having a second cup of coffee and a pastry.

"Ingrid," said Palmer, "I want to believe my long, frustrating search is finally over. I told you before that I'm betting my freedom, my life, on the premise that you will eventually care for me as I do you. I think my feeling is love, but I've never known true love. If, however, what you showed me last night was to survive, to catch me at a weak moment, to escape from me, then I lose.

"Something has been on my mind, and I've agonized over it. I've been tormented whenever I think about it. I would do anything to undo what I've put you through, to make it go away. I'll try to explain. When I first saw you that day in the courtroom and interviewed you as a prospective juror, I had to have you. I thought—at least, I hoped—you might be the one. I wanted to approach you and introduce myself, but I didn't, for fear of rejection. I could not chance being stopped cold by, 'No, thanks, I'm not interested.' As attractive as you are, I presumed men attempted to meet you all the time.

"Then I remembered a conversation I had almost a year ago with a psychiatrist concerning hostages and kidnap victims. He explained a psychological phenomenon called 'transference,' commonly known as 'Stockholm Syndrome.' Victims are initially subjected to fear and harsh treatment and conditions. When those conditions improve, the victim is so grateful that he or she develops positive feelings toward their kidnapper. That's why I did what I did, and when I brought you up into the house, I thought I saw transference occurring. Last night had to be more than just positive feelings toward me. I'm hoping it's gone beyond that and that your feelings are genuine.

"Ingrid, I want you to know how very sorry I am, and I deeply apologize to you from the bottom of my soul. Please, please, forgive me!"

"My feelings and actions have been genuine, Palmer. I'm not dwelling on the hell of those first couple of days—what you did to me. I've forgiven you. That psychological stuff might have had some bearing on my feelings earlier because I was frightened and confused. My strong good feelings could go very deep. Being kept here against my will, not able to leave, has left me angry and resentful, but I'm ready to put those feelings in the past."

"I have more business in the city today. It should take a few hours. Before I leave, I'll disarm the security system that locks all the doors and windows; it's all computer operated. I'll be driving my Mercedes. There is another car in the garage, a white BMW convertible. Here are the keys. The gas tank is full. The road from the house will lead to the main road. Turn right, and take it south. When you come to the interstate, take it south. Within an hour, you'll be in the city. Take this cell phone, so when you get to the city you can call 911 for any help or protection you want. My cell phone number is in the phone I'm giving you, should you feel the need to call me.

"Ingrid, you are free to come and go as you please. The car is at your disposal. If you are here when I return, I'll know that you chose to stay of your own free will. We'll take it slowly and see where it goes. Dress for going out tonight, and we'll go to Harold's for dinner and dancing." Palmer looked silently at her for a few seconds and then said, "Goodbye for now, Ingrid. I hope to see you here later."

◆

That evening, Palmer opened the automatic garage door, and there it was. The BMW looked like it hadn't been moved. He entered the house and saw her in the living room, sitting by the fireplace. She got up to greet him. Ingrid wore a blue dress and looked as gorgeous as she did in red the night before. He was ecstatic.

"Ingrid, I don't know whether to laugh or cry. You've made me so happy. I didn't expect to find you here, but you are. You have made this the best day of my life."

"Palmer, I felt the same emotion today as I got ready for our first night out together. I want people to think, 'Who is that attractive woman on Palmer Hamilton's arm? Such a handsome couple.' I'm looking forward to it and returning later tonight to share your bed again."

"I'll need about thirty minutes to shave, shower, and get dressed then we'll head downtown."

CHAPTER 24

It was eight p.m., four hours before Harry had to report at midnight. He relaxed in his recliner, reading, *Hitler's Willing Executioners*, by Daniel Goldhagen, a documentary of the Nazi atrocities in Europe during the Second World War. Books were Harry's most satisfying relaxation; all types filled the bookcases that covered one entire wall of the loft. He always had one on the small table next to his chair.

His phone rang. Harry pounced on it, answering before the second ring. "Detective Lincoln, it's Ham. I'm lookin' right now at that car you been lookin' for."

"What do you mean you're looking at it? Is anyone in it? Is it moving? Where are you?"

"No, Detective Lincoln, no one's with it. It's parked in the valet parkin' lot at a restaurant right downtown. The one at Burnside and Jerome. Ya know—Harold's Restaurant an' dance place. It's one sweet ride, man—a black Mercedes S600 with the tag LAW dash 7-2-8-7. One a my homies is a valet at that restaurant, an' when it came in, my man parked it an' dropped a dime to my new cell phone."

"Okay, Ham, stay there and watch it. I'm going to get a beat car over there right now. When it shows, you can take off. If the Mercedes leaves before the patrol car gets there, I want you to follow that fuckin' Mercedes and call me to let me know which way it's headed so I can get a couple of patrol cars to intercept it. I'll get with you in a few days. Thanks! Thanks!

Harry called the 5th Precinct, which covered downtown. He told Lieutenant Morgan, the watch commander, that a marked car was needed and why. Harry said he and his partner were on their way and would relieve his car as soon as they arrived. Harry's next call was to Jim then he was out of the door.

The patrol car was parked across the street from the restaurant parking lot. The officer inside was intently observing the Mercedes. Harry, wearing jeans and a sweatshirt covered with a leather jacket,

162

pulled up in his personal car and identified himself. He was about to relieve the officer when Lieutenant Morgan arrived. Then Jim arrived. The four stood behind their cars, four pairs of eyes watching the Mercedes.

"I think it might be best if my officer stays," the lieutenant told Harry and Jim. "When your man shows up and you approach him for the arrest, you'll have a uniform with you." To the cop he added, "I'll notify communications that you are out of service, so no calls. Stay with these detectives until you are relieved."

"Thanks, Lieutenant," said Harry.

Jim looked at Harry. "I'll go a few blocks to the office to bring back our city car. I should only be a few minutes."

CHAPTER 25

Ingrid settled into the luxurious feeling of sitting in an upscale restaurant with a man who would provide her with a future she could never have imagined for herself.

A portly, swarthy man, dressed in white, with thick black hair and a two-day growth of facial stubble approached their table and sat across from Ingrid.

"Ingrid, I'd like you to meet Harold Dietz, the owner and award-winning chef of this wonderful restaurant."

"I'm pleased to meet you, Mr. Dietz. I had one of your catered meals last night and found it prepared to perfection. It was the kind of dinner I've always dreamed about."

"You are very kind, Ingrid. You are one of the most beautiful women to brighten my restaurant since I've been here. Palmer, you are a lucky man. I envy you. Ingrid, please call me Harold."

"Harold," said Palmer as he studied the menu, "what would you recommend for dinner?"

Harold offered suggestions among the specials for dinner and wine. They left it up to him to fulfill Palmer's preference for meat and Ingrid's for fish, as well as the wine, since Harold made it clear that it would be complimentary.

"I will prepare your dinners personally. I'm delighted to meet you, Ingrid, and glad you are both here. Enjoy!"

As she sipped her second glass of a very good French Remoissenet, Ingrid felt the warmth deep inside and a pleasant glow in her head. The music from the adjacent dance floor seemed distant, so it did not interfere with their table conversation. The small band played soft, slow dance music. The low buzz from the other tables, the soft clinking of dishes and silverware, the intimate talk with Palmer, all created a wonderful, distinct atmosphere.

They were glad they accepted Harold's dinner recommendations. Later, on the dance floor, Palmer's thoughts were filled with how much

164

he loved holding her as they danced. She was soft, yet firm; light, but not fragile, and she was smooth as they danced.

It was late when they left the restaurant. Palmer gave the claim ticket to the valet. Both were anxious to get home and fall into each other's arms.

CHAPTER 26

"Hey, Detective Lincoln," the patrol officer said as he emerged from his car. "Lieutenant Morgan just radioed me that because it's almost watch change, he's arranged through the morning watch lieutenant to have one of his cars relieve me."

Twenty minutes later, a patrol car turned into the lot with the headlights off. It pulled up next to the group and took the place of the first car. The detectives had a short conversation with the relief cop and found him fully briefed. A reply came in on the tag request for registration.

"Palmer Hamilton. Palmer Hamilton?" spouted an incredulous Jim Conte. "Jesus, Harry, I can't fucking believe it. Palmer Hamilton! There's got to be some kind of fuck up down at the DMV."

"Yeah, Jim. It's hard to believe. We'll find out what's what when he approaches his car. It shouldn't be too much longer; most of the patrons have left the restaurant."

They saw a valet get into the Mercedes and drive it toward the restaurant entrance. Harry and Jim followed the Mercedes in their unmarked detective car, the patrol car right behind them. Palmer Hamilton was standing there with a woman; they recognized him right away.

"Palmer Hamilton, I'm Detective Lincoln and this is Detective Conte." They showed their IDs. "We need to talk to you about a kidnapping. You will have to come with us to police headquarters. Ma'am, I'd like to have your name."

"My name is Ingrid Hirsch."

Harry's knees almost buckled with relief as he and Jim exchanged glances.

Palmer said, "This is an unfortunate misunderstanding. Ms. Hirsch will not press charges. Ask her."

"What Mr. Hamilton said is correct. You're making a terrible mistake. I will not press charges."

Jim put in a call to the 5th, requesting a female officer to transport Ingrid to the homicide office downtown. "Mr. Hamilton, before anything more is said, I have to advise you of your constitutional rights."

Hamilton interrupted, "I know my rights better than you, so you don't have to bother."

"I must, so please indulge me. You have a right to remain silent…"

When he finished reading the Miranda warnings, Harry asked if Palmer understood those rights. Palmer sarcastically affirmed that he did.

"If you are going to take me downtown, I'd like to leave my car with the owner of the restaurant, instead of having it impounded." He turned to the valet. "Go inside and have Mr. Dietz come out right away." In a few minutes, a concerned Harold Dietz took charge of the Mercedes. Palmer told him not to worry; it was an innocent misunderstanding that he would explain in a day or two.

The female officer arrived and asked Ingrid to get into the patrol car with her. Ingrid did as requested. Palmer was searched, handcuffed, and placed in the back seat of the detective car. The other patrol car was relieved. Palmer and Ingrid were transported to the homicide office.

"Lieutenant," Harry said softly into the phone, away from the others. "I'm sorry to wake you in the middle of the night, but I thought you'd want to know right away. Yes, I know it's a little past two o'clock in the morning, Lieu. And why are you saying all those nasty words with your wife sleeping beside you? Take it easy, Lieu. I'm making jokes because I have great news; Ingrid Hirsch is alive and well! You told Jim and me to bring you the kidnapper in chains. Will handcuffs do? They are sitting in the squad room at this moment."

Harry heard McGee struggling to get dressed; each article of clothing was laced with bad words, then worse words as he asked a lot of questions before Harry could answer one.

"Lieu, slow down and let me give you the part that's going to turn this whole thing into a media circus. The kidnapper is Palmer Hamilton!"

"Hamilton? Palmer Hamilton, the attorney? Oh, Christ, I'll be down as soon as I can." On the drive downtown, Lieutenant McGee called and notified the chief of detectives. "No, chief, I don't have any other details; I'm on the way down now, and I'll brief you when you get in."

"Lenny, wake up. It's Palmer," Hamilton said into the phone. "If this wasn't an emergency, I wouldn't be calling you. I need you to come to police headquarters as soon as you can. I'm being detained here on a felony charge. No, I'm not kidding. I'll explain when you get here. Third floor, homicide squad."

"You can wait for your attorney in this room. Do you need to use the restroom before I lock you in?" Jim asked. Palmer declined and took a seat in the spartan interrogation room to wait for Lenny Goldberg, hoping he would get there quickly.

Jim put in a call to the district attorney's after hours number, requesting the on-call assistant DA meet him and his partner at the homicide office. Then, he called down to the lobby. "In a short time, Mr. Leonard Goldberg will arrive. Make sure he finds his way up to the homicide office. Lieutenant McGee will also be coming in, so wake up and put your tie back on. One of the on-call assistant DAs will also be looking for us. If any of the media show up, they're not to get past the front door, and don't listen to any of their first amendment bullshit. This building might suddenly get very busy. "

Seated at one end of the long conference room table, Harry and Jim had their first opportunity to speak with Ingrid Hirsch since they arrived.

"Ms. Hirsch," Harry began, "we are so glad and relieved to see that you are all right. Detective Conte and I have agonized over your safety and well-being from the beginning. Is there anything you need right now? Restroom, coffee, water?"

"I could use a restroom," said Ingrid nervously.

"I could also use a restroom," said the female cop. "Come on. I'll show you where it is."

In the bathroom, as the two women washed their hands, Officer Gayle Larkin commented, "A lot of cops are familiar with Palmer Hamilton. They have been cross-examined by him. He's quite the hunk, and rich, too."

♦

Lieutenant McGee arrived. He did not interrupt the group in the conference room. Doing so would have violated the "Golden Rule" among detectives: Never break the rhythm of an interview. He busied himself by scrubbing the nasty coffee pots and brewing some fresh. He would wait for a complete briefing.

♦

"But, Ms. Hirsch," Harry pleaded. "We must get a written statement from you. You are the victim of a serious crime. Victims give statements so that we know exactly what happened." Assistant DA Harper had joined the others in the conference room.

"I am not the victim of a crime. I told you that you are mistaken. I'll not give you that statement until I speak with Mr. Hamilton."

Assistant DA Phillip Harper had been sitting silently since his arrival, until now. "Ms. Hirsch, please don't force these detectives to hold you as a material witness."

"I will not say anything or sign any statement that might cause trouble for Palmer. He did nothing wrong."

Harry, Jim, and Phillip Harper left Ingrid in the conference room. They met Lenny Goldberg, who was coming out of the interrogation room. "What charges are you using to hold Mr. Hamilton? Clearly, the kidnapping charge is a result of a misunderstanding."

The ADA answered, "We are charging him with kidnapping and false imprisonment. We will set up a bond hearing sometime this morning. We will not oppose releasing him on a signature bond, although the judge will have to grant it."

"That's fair enough. What about Ms. Hirsch?" Lenny Goldberg inquired.

"She declined to give a statement. She's free to go. You can give her a ride home, or I can call a patrol car," said Harry Lincoln.

"I'll take her with me. We'll return later for the bond hearing. I'll check with the court clerk for the time."

CHAPTER 27

The meeting started at precisely nine a.m. The participants included County District Attorney Robert J. Carlisle, Assistant DA Phillip Harper, Chief Investigator Charlie Cooke, and Senior Administrator Gloria Dempsey. Representing the police department were Homicide Commander Lieutenant James McGee and Homicide Detectives Harry Lincoln and James Conte. The morning sun, coming through the windows of the small conference room, felt good on this bitterly cold, winter day. The adjacent room was the private office of DA Carlisle. The sign on the door read "HIMSELF."

"Okay, folks, let's settle down," the District Attorney called. "Lieutenant McGee, get us started."

"I think the facts can best be laid out by the two closest to the case. Detectives Lincoln and Conte have been assigned to it from the start, but I will say this is a strange case. Harry, go ahead and start, Jim fill in as necessary."

The detectives began with the abduction, the witness, and the video surveillance camera. Next, they explained how the investigation proceeded, that they had learned that the victim was stalked daily for three weeks at her home as well as her place of employment. The detectives next explained that Palmer Hamilton's vehicles were identified as the vehicles that harbored the stalker, and that the partial tag was ultimately what led them to the vehicle. "The Mercedes S660," continued Harry, "was located, and we were notified through a confidential informant."

Jim explained that they learned, just minutes before the arrest, that the car was registered to Palmer Hamilton, the prominent attorney. He stressed that he and Harry were relieved when the woman with Hamilton identified herself as Ingrid Hirsch.

Harry said, "Jim and I identified ourselves and informed Mr. Hamilton that he had to come downtown with us to talk about a kidnapping. He insisted there was no kidnapping, that it was an

170

unfortunate misunderstanding. He said Ms. Hirsch would not press charges, and she said that it was all a terrible mistake, which is why she would not press charges."

Phillip Harper said, "It's bad enough that our defendant is Palmer Hamilton, but he's retained Lenny Goldberg, one of the best criminal defense attorneys in the state. Mr. Hamilton was granted a signature bond, which we didn't oppose, a few hours later. Hamilton had nothing to say and entered a plea of not guilty to the judge at his bond hearing."

Jim then informed the group of Hirsch's refusal to make a statement, written or oral. "For almost a week, Harry and I worked fourteen- and sixteen-hour days. We beat ourselves up worrying that we hadn't found her before he killed her, and then she turned on us."

District Attorney Carlisle said, "Charlie, I want you to set up a meeting with Dr. Ruetger, the psychologist," the DA instructed his investigator. "Maybe he can shed some light on her reluctance. People, this case is thin. We lack the evidence we need to bring it to trial. We need more if we want a bill of indictment from a grand jury. Let's meet again in a few days, maybe Dr. Ruetger will be able to join us then. Thank you all for coming."

♦

"I've found three places, Harry." Jim had been on one of the squad room computers for over an hour, trying to locate residential or office properties owned by or rented to Palmer Hamilton. "He rents office space in the Champaign Building downtown, 334 Myrtle Avenue, four blocks from the courthouse. He owns a condo a little further up in midtown, in the high rent district. 1711 Centre Street, the penthouse. I guess that's his residence. Then he owns a house up in the mountains, valued at well over four million dollars. No weekend get-a-way cabin."

"Let's get search warrants for all three places, Jim. The probable cause in our affidavits will be slim, and we are dealing with two high-powered attorneys. We'll need to do everything by the book, no cutting corners. Let's take it to a judge and see what happens."

♦

"So, detectives, why do you think a crime was committed at any of these locations?" Superior Court Judge Cynthia Haynes asked Harry and Jim as the three sat in her chambers.

"Well, Your Honor, these are two of our suspect's residences—a condo in the city and a house in the mountains about an hour's drive north of the city. The third is his law office, four blocks from here. We will be looking for fingerprint or DNA evidence to show that the victim was in any of these locations. We will be looking for restraints and chemicals, such as chloroform, that would render a person unconscious. We will be looking for the white utility van used in the abduction, which was seen on video and described by multiple witnesses. We will be looking for computers that can be analyzed at the state crime lab. We will be looking for the victim's clothing or other personal items."

"My judgment tells me these warrants may be problematic should they be subjected to constitutional scrutiny. Your probable cause is shaky. However, since neither of you have let me down in the past, I'm inclined to approve your search warrants. Don't make me regret it."

CHAPTER 28

Palmer and Ingrid left downtown, to distance themselves from the courthouse and police headquarters. After a quick call to Harold at his home, Palmer asked Lenny to drive him and Ingrid to the restaurant to retrieve the Mercedes. The three then met at the diner near his condo in midtown.

"Palmer, did you actually tell those detectives when they first approached you that it was a misunderstanding?" Lenny asked, pouring Ingrid a second cup of coffee. "Did you say she would not press charges? Ingrid, you also said you would not press charges?"

"They caught me off-guard, Lenny. The toothpaste was already out of the tube," mumbled Palmer as he devoured an order of bacon and eggs.

"You are the local media's 'Crime of the Week' bad boy, and Ingrid is the damsel in distress. Those statements will be hard for the public to understand, and as you well know, the public are your peers, and they will be the jury that judges you. Those statements will be difficult to overcome at trial. Let's leave it there for now. Let's meet in two days at my office. Palmer, please transfer a $25,000 retainer into my account. I can't represent you both in this case. I will arrange for Jerry Kravitz to represent Ingrid. Ingrid, when you see Mr. Kravitz, pay him a retainer of one dollar."

◆

The drive to the mountains was silent, except for music from satellite radio. In the house, Palmer and Ingrid moved in slow motion. The long sleepless night, coupled with the stress of the past sixteen hours, had worn them down. They slept a long time, and were astonished at how long they slept. They showered, dressed, and had coffee silently, until Palmer said, "Ingrid we have to talk about what happened last night. We must give a reasonable explanation of our activities during the past week. We must provide a sufficiently reasonable explanation that everyone will believe. Whatever plan we devise will only work if you don't want me punished for what I've put you through."

"I will support any explanation one-hundred percent. If you haven't thought of anything yet, maybe I can help. I'm not a lawyer, but I might have an idea. It may be bizarre, but here's what I'm thinking..."

She explained her plan, looking at Palmer for his approval.

"Why, that's brilliant, Ingrid, absolutely brilliant, and so damn simple! We'll run it by Lenny to see what he thinks."

Ingrid was thrilled that she had thought of it. She felt that her plan would convince Palmer of her loyalty to him.

The last log added to the fire was a glowing ember, and it was time to go to bed. "Palmer, let's talk more about this tomorrow. Right now, I'd like to go upstairs to your bedroom."

It was a kaleidoscope of color and fabric as clothing was hastily removed and tossed aside. Last, Palmer slid her panties down slowly and deliberately, revealing the ultimate prize. They were in no hurry as they each explored and caressed the naked body of the other, not only the obvious, but also the hidden places. A half hour of kissing and murmuring, looking and admiring, touching and feeling went by. When they merged, it was a soft, warm, smooth connection, driven hard and deep by the foreplay that preceded it. The passion was fierce, and the rhythm synchronized with their vocal duet of pleasure. Time stood still, until with a roar and a scream, their emotions were released!

Exhausted, they slept.

CHAPTER 29

"**M**r. Hamilton," cried Martha, "they took your things. They just came in and took them. I tried to stop them, but…"

"Wait a minute, calm down, Martha," said Palmer, confused and not fully awake, into his cell phone. "Who took what things?"

"Two detectives had a search warrant, Mr. Hamilton. They took the laptop in your office and some of the files and other papers. They left a copy of the warrant with me."

"It's all right, Martha. I want you and the others to take the rest of the day off. Leave the copy of the warrant on my desk, lock up the office, and go home." Palmer called Lenny Goldberg and told him what had happened. Lenny told him to come in the following morning with Ingrid and the copy of the warrant.

"What is it, Palmer?" said Ingrid, trying to wake up. "Is something wrong?"

Palmer told her what he knew as he got out of bed. "Get up, Ingrid, and get dressed. If they searched my office, my condo will be next. I guess they know about this place and will show up here with a warrant. I'm going to have to check the house for anything that could be used as evidence. Check your bedroom, and remove the tags from your new clothes. It has to appear that you've been living here on weekends for almost a year."

"Palmer, why did the police have a search warrant for your office this morning?"

"I would think it concerns the kidnapping case, Ingrid. I can't imagine what kind of incriminating evidence they would be looking for in my office. I don't want to talk about that now. This might not be the right time. We're both on edge, but you have given me my life back. What I found in you means more to me than money, and I want to give so very much to you. Within a week or so, you'll have a duplicate of my credit cards with your name on it; go shopping. You can live here, or at the condo in the city, or continue to live at your townhouse. If you want a home somewhere else, we can buy or build one. You might want to keep working; that's your decision, but if not, we can travel the world: London, Paris, Rome, Venice, Tokyo, Hong Kong, Singapore, Australia, or New Zealand. I know I'm getting carried away, but you get the idea."

The doorbell rang. They looked at each other. "That must be our friendly detectives with a search warrant, sooner than I thought." The bell rang again then there was a loud pounding on the door.

Palmer opened the door to six people.

"Good morning, Mr. Hamilton. I'm Sheriff Roger Anderson, and this is Deputy Nancy Adams. These two detectives have a search warrant for these premises. These two crime scene techs drove their special van up from the city."

"Let me see the warrant."

"Mr. Hamilton," suggested the sheriff. "Why don't we all go inside and sit down while you look over the warrant? Who else is in the house now besides you?"

"Only Ms. Hirsch," answered Palmer, annoyed, as he let them in. "Looking at this affidavit, it seems like you're fishing and made the trip for nothing. Help yourselves, but don't trash my house."

"If memory serves me, you had this house built about four years ago," the sheriff said as he and his deputy sat with Palmer and Ingrid.

"Yes, it's a place to get away from the pressures and problems of the big city. Ingrid and I love to come up here for the peace and quiet."

Sheriff Anderson talked about how the people up there were peaceful and friendly, "unlike most city folks." He said he wouldn't trade his little mountain paradise for any big city in the world. The four continued the polite conversation, mostly talking about nothing at all, until Lincoln and Conte came back into the living room.

"Mr. Hamilton," Conte asked, "do you have any other computers besides this laptop? We have to take it until the hard drive can be analyzed, and the van in the basement garage has to be impounded for processing. Sheriff Anderson, can you call a wrecker for the van and have it brought to a secure lot?"

"Detective Conte, that's the only other computer I have; you took the one from my office this morning." Palmer Hamilton was livid. "The removal of those computers will result in a loss of business. I can't run my practice without them, so tell your bosses that I'll be filing suit against the city for damages."

"We'll try to have them back in a day or two," answered Jim.

On the drive back to the city, Harry and Jim congratulated each other for surviving their month on the morning watch. "To celebrate our return to the day watch," smiled Jim, "there is a nine a.m. strategy meeting at the DA's office."

CHAPTER 30

"Coffee is on the side table," said Robert Carlisle as he greeted the people filing into the conference room. "For those of you who have not met," continued the DA, "let me introduce to you psychologist Dr. Erwin Ruetger. Doctor, thank you for joining us on such short notice." Greetings were exchanged.

"I discussed this case with Dr. Ruetger briefly on the phone yesterday. I told him of Ingrid Hirsch's initial statement to the detectives that she would not press charges. At the homicide office, she refused to make any statement, written or oral, until she could speak with Mr. Hamilton. I'd like for the detectives to continue."

Lieutenant McGee nodded to Harry, who then addressed the psychologist. "Dr. Ruetger, this is not the normal reaction of a kidnap victim. We know she was kidnapped; we have it on video, and there is an eyewitness. We have evidence that ties Palmer Hamilton to the crime. Why would she view us with such hostility and defend him?"

Jim spoke up before Dr. Ruetger had a chance to respond. "For Christ's sake, doctor, they were having dinner at a restaurant, all lovey-dovey!"

Dr. Ruetger explained the facts of the much-publicized Patty Hearst kidnapping case. "The young woman was abducted from her home in California by a domestic terror gang engaged in a series of bank robberies. She was locked in a closet and subjected to sexual, physical, and psychological abuse for a long time. When her harsh treatment ended, she was so grateful that she accompanied the gang as they robbed banks. Was Patty Hearst a victim or just another gang member? This psychological phenomenon, called 'transference,' affected Patty Hearst, causing her to commit those crimes.

"Another famous case involved the hostages in Stockholm, Sweden, during a bank robbery. The police responded quickly, causing the robbers to take hostages and barricade themselves in the bank vault. After six days inside the vault, the robbers surrendered. When the police entered the vault, they were met with hostility from the hostages, who stood between police and the hostage takers. One of the women became engaged to one of the hostage-takers while he was serving his sentence in prison. Transference is now commonly referred to as 'Stockholm Syndrome.' I suspect that it is what you are dealing with in this case."

"Whether it was transference or not, the fact remains that a felony, possibly more than one, has been committed." The district attorney looked at everyone sitting around the table and continued, "It is not up to Ingrid Hirsch whether this case gets prosecuted or not. It will be the State versus Palmer Hamilton."

CHAPTER 31

Three blocks from the district attorney's office, another meeting was taking place at Leonard Goldberg's law office.

"We are here, Ingrid, just the three of us. Anything said between us is privileged information. Nothing gets repeated to anyone unless I say so. So let's be honest; give me all the facts, as you both know them. Let's not have any surprises later."

"After they took my office computer early this morning, Lenny, they had another search warrant for my house in the mountains. They took my other computer, which just about shuts me down, and they impounded my van. I warned them about legal action against the city, which I'd like you to handle.

The hard truth is that I did kidnap Ingrid," Palmer said, looking at Ingrid. "It was a violent, physical abduction, and she was a helpless victim."

Palmer told the whole story, beginning with the search for his perfect woman. He explained that he first noticed Ingrid in court, and described the weeks of watching and following her, culminating in the abduction. He described the two terrible days she spent in the basement and his reasons for subjecting her to it. He said he made her more comfortable and less fearful by bringing her into the house, but told her he could not let her leave. He said things slowly changed for the better over the next few days, buoyed by a mutual attraction, and said that they then acted on that attraction. He said she was given a chance to leave, but she chose to stay. Then he described being out together in public and being approached and detained by the detectives.

"The only statement we made was that it was a misunderstanding, and that Ingrid would not press charges. This was said before they read us Miranda. Nothing was signed by either of us."

"Lenny," said Ingrid, "I want to put this whole episode to rest and remain with Palmer, whom I've grown deeply fond of over the past few days."

"That's very good to hear, Ingrid, but we will be dealing with Robert J. Carlisle, who is known for his inflexibility. I don't think he'll care about anything except that a crime was committed in his county."

"What if we convinced Mr. Carlisle no crime was committed, Lenny?" asked a confident Palmer Hamilton.

"How in the hell would we do that, Palmer?"

Palmer proceeded to reveal how they would do that, and that it was Ingrid who suggested it.

"The first time I saw Ingrid was several weeks ago in court. That will be privileged information. Those detectives and the DA's office will hear a different story.

"We were downtown—I was returning to my office after meeting with a client, Ingrid headed to a shop for new drapery material. Suddenly, there was a thunderstorm with heavy rains and strong winds. We both ducked under the same cafe awning along the avenue, but we were getting wet, so we went inside for shelter and wound up sharing the only vacant table in the cafe. That was how it started, ten months ago.

"Sam had been dead just over two years when we started dating, and Ingrid had some guilt about it, but the attraction was so great, she continued to see me. She met me at my condo before going out for the evening. She spent weekends at my house in the mountains. She never allowed me to come to her townhouse because of the neighbors. She told her friends at work that she had no interest in men since Sam died.

"I wanted Ingrid to quit her job and move in with me. She worried about what co-workers, friends, and neighbors would think, and she wanted to maintain her independence. We gradually became bored. One evening, we decided to do something to re-kindle how we felt about each other at the start.

"I would kidnap her!

She would be detained in the mountain house and be my prisoner. After playing out the fantasy, the sizzle was back. We went into the city to celebrate, and that's when the detectives detained us.

"Well, Lenny, what do you think? It's plausible, and who's to say it didn't happen that way? There are no witnesses. Ingrid will back it up."

"It's not what I think Palmer; it's what District Attorney Robert J. Carlisle thinks and believes. I'll talk with him as soon as I can get an appointment."

CHAPTER 32

Two days later, there was a follow-up meeting at the district attorney's office. Leonard Goldberg sat at the conference table, facing DA Carlisle, Assistant DA Harper, and Detectives Lincoln and Conte.

"It's as Mr. Hamilton said when he was approached the other night at the restaurant," Lenny Goldberg explained. "It was a terrible misunderstanding that started with some play-acting. I've taken affidavits from each of them and brought copies for you."

"Why would Mr. Hamilton tell the detectives that Ms. Hirsch would not press charges when they wanted to talk to him about a kidnapping? I'll answer my own question, Lenny. Because he committed a crime and Ms. Hirsch changed her mind, or he was able to change it for her."

"He meant to say was that there was nothing to press charges for, here she is, ask her yourself."

"Bullshit, Lenny," exclaimed the DA. "Hamilton meant exactly what he said. She would not press charges for the crime he committed against her. That crime was kidnapping."

"That's not what we are saying," Lenny said as he stood. "If you insist on taking this further, Robert, your office will suffer a tremendous embarrassment. I represent Palmer Hamilton. Jerry Kravitz represents Ms. Hirsch. Both have been instructed not to say anything or answer any questions. See you in court!"

♦

After Lenny Goldberg's departure, they sat, stunned and silent, until Carlisle spoke. "I'd like to have reactions to Goldberg's comments. I say this is some horseshit fairy tale to confuse the issue and cover up his crime."

Harry nodded. "I have to agree with Mr. Carlisle. My larger concern is Ingrid Hirsch. My gut tells me the kidnapping was not play-acting; it was a crime, but why is she hostile to us? Why is she defending him? Other kidnap victims, once rescued and safely away from the kidnaper, are anxious to help put their attackers away. Maybe we should look more closely at Dr. Ruetger's theory of transference and how it might have affected Ingrid Hirsch."

"I don't know about all that hocus-pocus stuff, Harry," Jim said, "and I think what Goldberg said about play-acting is believable. Who's to say it isn't? We don't have evidence to say it isn't."

"It might come down to proving it to a jury beyond a reasonable doubt," Assistant DA Harper reminded them. "My first concern is whether a grand jury would indict on what we have so far. If we go to a courtroom, present it to a jury, and Lenny Goldberg brings up that scenario, we might very well be laughed out of the courtroom."

Carlisle sat for a moment and looked at the others. "I will certainly consider what you've said at decision time. If it does go to trial, Palmer Hamilton will probably take the stand and testify in his own defense. He will be very convincing. The key is Ingrid Hirsch and how she holds up under cross, but we need more evidence, so Harry and Jim, I'm counting on you to come through as you have so many times in the past."

♦

At the mountain home, the somber mood did not change. Palmer had just spoken with Lenny about his meeting with the DA and was relaying the details to Ingrid. "Lenny is optimistic about the play-acting story. The only one who spoke up was Mr. Carlisle, and he maintained his negative stance, but Lenny read the body language of the others and they were not in total agreement with the DA."

"But, Palmer, if Mr. Carlisle insists on a trial, I'll be called as a witness, and I've never testified in court before. I'll stick to the story that we've given in our affidavits, even though I'll be committing perjury, a felony for which I could go to prison. I'll do it for you, Palmer, for us, but I'm scared of what an experienced and vicious prosecutor might do when he or she cross-examines me."

"Ingrid, please don't worry about it because there isn't likely to be a trial. Lenny and I don't believe there is enough evidence to present at a trial. Don't forget the burden of proof is with the prosecution to establish guilt beyond a reasonable doubt. If there is a trial, Ingrid, you will be so well prepared that you will feel confident. You will be testifying about your own brain-child, the thing that's going to get us out of this mess."

CHAPTER 33

Detective James Conte arrived early one morning at the city personnel office to submit his retirement papers for the second time in the past few months. He had quite a bit of compensatory time coming from the long hours worked on the Hirsch case. He took a couple of those days to give it a lot of thought. He had to make the decision sooner or later. He would miss Harry and some of the others. He wouldn't miss the bullshit and the dirty politics. He notified the law firm that he would start as their investigator on the first of next month.

In Jim's absence, Harry continued to look for evidence that the DA could take to the grand jury. Palmer Hamilton was at his condo when Harry and the techs executed the fourth search warrant. There was nothing of significance found in either of Hamilton's residences, his office, or his van. He brought the matrix up to date, and studied and analyzed it, but nothing jumped out at him. He met with Lieutenant McGee, looking for a fresh approach, had meetings with ADA Harper, and spent time at the State Crime Lab reviewing everything they had on the case.

"Detective Harry Lincoln!" Judy Wright, one of the technical analysts said. "How about I buy you a cup of our famous crime lab coffee? It just happens to be time for my break."

"Sure, Judy, I could use a cup. Let's go." Harry noticed her for the first time and thought, *Pretty girl. There could be a nice figure under those baggy clothes. Smart, too. Helped me with quite a few 'who-done-its.'*

"I see you are still working that kidnapping case. Everything from your search warrants came across my desk. Sorry, Harry, but we drew a blank. Take those laptops with you when you leave so they can be returned. And..."

"Oh, shit, the laptops, of course! Let me have them quickly, Judy. I have to go. Sorry about the coffee; I'll explain later."

Harry practically ran from the building to his car and headed downtown to the district attorney's office. On the way, he called ADA Harper's cell phone.

"Phil, are you in your office? Wait for me. I'll be there in fifteen minutes. This is very important. I'll explain when I get there. If Mr. Carlisle is in, tell him he might want to hear this, also."

♦

In the district attorney's private office, Harry Lincoln said, "Mr. Carlisle, at our last couple of meetings, you didn't think much of Lenny Goldberg's 'play-acting' story. I seem to recall you using the Latin legal phrase 'horseshit' to describe it. I felt the same. I have with me Palmer Hamilton's laptop computers, seized when executing our search warrants. The night we detained Hamilton, after he made his call to Goldberg, we took his cell phone while he was in the interview room. I made a note of his number and his phone company's provider. I need you to issue subpoenas to his internet provider for all e-mails incoming and outgoing for the past year. Also, subpoena the phone company for all calls incoming and outgoing for that same period. If there are no e-mails or phone calls between Palmer Hamilton and Ingrid Hirsch for the past year, as hot and heavy as they've said their romance was, they were lying. If there are neither e-mails nor phone calls, it should prove he kidnapped her. On the other hand, if they did e-mail or call during that period, it proves their case, and what's the other Latin legal phase? We're up 'shit creek.'"

The silence in the room was stark, as if the air had been sucked out. An animated Robert Carlisle broke it. He promptly said, "Phil, draw up those subpoenas now and get them in the works right away. Harry, we'll have to wait and see if you've come through again."

♦

"Hi, Judy, it's Harry Lincoln. I'm calling to apologize for my rudeness earlier today. Do you have a minute?"

"For you, Harry Lincoln, I've got two minutes. What happened? Was it a family emergency or something like that?"

"No, but it's too complicated to explain over the phone. Judy, I'm sorry to be so blunt. Are you married? Do you have a boyfriend?"

"No, to both questions, but if this is an interrogation you haven't advised me of my rights."

"Judy, if you are not busy tonight, I'd like to take you to dinner to make up for running out on you today. I'll explain then."

"Okay, Harry, it's a date. Pick me up at my place, the Midtown Manor Apartments, at about seven o'clock; I'll be in the lobby."

♦

At Garibaldi's Italian Restaurant, Harry went over details of the case with Judy including his anticipation of the phone and e-mail records. Judy wondered how the victim of a violent abduction could be in love with her kidnapper within a week. They talked of Jim Conte's upcoming retirement and who might replace him as Harry's new partner. The conversation turned personal as they caught up with each other's lives. Harry explained about the breakup with Ellen. The evening passed pleasantly and too quickly for both of them.

As Harry left her outside the door of apartment 12 C, Judy thanked him for dinner, reached up, and kissed his cheek.

Chapter 34

District Attorney Robert J. Carlisle presided over the meeting. On one side of the gleaming solid oak table sat Palmer Hamilton and Ingrid Hirsch. Between them sat Leonard Goldberg and Jerry Kravitz. Looking at them from the other side were DA Carlisle, Assistant DA Phillip Harper, Lieutenant James McGee, and Detectives Harry Lincoln and Jim Conte. At the end of the table sat a court stenographer, her hands poised, ready to start recording.

"As we all know by now," DA Carlisle said, "Palmer Hamilton's phone and e-mail records show no communication between him and Ingrid Hirsch during the past twelve months. This makes it clear that their story is highly unlikely. So here's the deal I'm willing to offer you, Mr. Hamilton. In exchange for a guilty plea to the lesser charges of obstruction and lying to police, you will serve ten months in a minimum-security prison, be placed on unsupervised probation for five years, and have your license to practice law suspended for five years. The State Bar Association concurs." The DA got no reaction from Palmer Hamilton. "If you would rather roll the dice, Mr. Hamilton, we will go to trial for kidnapping, false imprisonment, and possibly rape by threat or intimidation. I will ask for twenty-five years to life, and you will never again practice law."

Robert Carlisle looked at Ingrid. "Ms. Hirsch, your role in all this is more complicated. Are you a victim or a conspirator? I've had several talks with Dr. Erwin Ruetger. He advised me to consider you a victim, due to strong psychological forces that might have contributed to your conduct. You also committed obstruction and lied to police, but I'm inclined to follow Dr. Ruetger's advice and let you skate. You will not be prosecuted. If we do go to trial, and if, from the witness stand, under oath, you support Mr. Hamilton in this fairy tale, that is perjury and you will go to prison."

Palmer, Ingrid, Lenny, and Jerry went into an adjoining room for a private conference to discuss the terms of the plea offer. "Listen,

Palmer, I'm strongly advising you to jump on the offer. Ten months in a minimum camp isn't so bad, and we'll try to get you somewhere close, so Ingrid can visit. Then, you both will resume your lives. Most importantly, Palmer, you can continue your law practice."

"I agree with Lenny," said Jerry Kravitz. "It's a sweetheart deal, and you are lucky to get the offer."

After looking at Ingrid, Palmer slowly nodded assent to Lenny.

When they returned to the conference room, Lenny Goldberg announced, "Mr. Carlisle, my client accepts your offer."

"Okay, everyone," announced ADA Harper. "Superior Court, tomorrow morning, nine o'clock sharp."

♦

That evening, after a light dinner at a small café in midtown, Palmer and Ingrid returned to his condo a few blocks away. Their mood was heavy.

"I want you to be independent while I'm gone," said Palmer, "so I've opened a $500,000 money market account in your name at my bank. Just go in and sign the paper work. I've also transferred $50,000 into your checking account. You have my credit cards in your name. Lenny will pay my bills as they come in. He'll also pay Martha her salary each week. I've told her to keep the office open; she's a single mom. I know she needs the money. The other two will take a leave of absence. If you need anything at all before I get back, call Lenny; he will arrange it. The title and registration to the BMW convertible have been signed over to you. It's less than a year old and has hardly been driven. It's yours; here are the keys. Here are the keys to everything—the condo, the house, and my other car—all yours to use until I return. Go back to work if you like, but you don't have to. Contact Detective Lincoln to get your car back. I'd like you to visit me often. Lenny will know where I am. The judge ordered that it would be nearby. I've fallen in love with you. We'll look to the future when I get out. Now let's go to bed and make love with enough passion to last us for the next ten months!"

CHAPTER 35

"All rise," called the court clerk as the judge stepped up to the bench. "Superior Court is now in session, the Honorable Cynthia Haynes presiding."

The announcement hushed the courtroom. It was a place of ruined lives and anguished survivors; distraught families visited daily. Its walls were imbedded with tragedy. Beyond the rail, alone among the spectators, stood a solemn Ingrid Hirsch. Watching. Listening.

"Please be seated," said Judge Haynes to the muted assembly. "The first item on this morning's docket is the *State vs. Palmer Hamilton*. I understand the defendant wishes to enter a plea, and that Mr. Leonard Goldberg represents the defendant, with District Attorney Robert Carlisle prosecuting for the State. Before we proceed, I'd like to say to Mr. Hamilton that I am shocked and saddened to see you stand before me as a defendant." The words from the bench were not stern, but spoken softly by a stunned and sympathetic Judge Cynthia Haynes.

"Mr. Hamilton, has District Attorney Carlisle explained all the options of this plea to your satisfaction? Has he also discussed the alternatives with you and your defense counsel?"

"Yes, Your Honor, he has," Palmer answered, humbled and embarrassed.

"Palmer Hamilton, how do you plead to the charges of obstruction of an officer and lying to police?" asked Judge Haynes.

"Guilty, Your Honor."

"Palmer Hamilton, under the terms of this plea agreement, I accept your guilty plea and sentence you to ten months confinement in a minimum security facility of the state prison system, commencing immediately, to be followed by five years of unsupervised probation. You will surrender your license to practice law for a period of five years. Is there anything you wish to say?"

"If it pleases the Court, I ask to be placed in a facility close to the city to make it convenient for visitors."

190

"So ordered!" With the crack of a gavel, Palmer Hamilton was led from the courtroom in handcuffs. Before passing through the door leading to his captivity, Palmer Hamilton turned and smiled at Ingrid. She smiled back.

♦

Descending the courthouse steps, Ingrid underwent an immediate metamorphosis. The pathetic smile of the grief-stricken lover transformed into a satisfied smirk. In the parking lot, Ingrid sat a moment in her new BMW. She then headed for the bank.

CHAPTER 36

It was Saturday night and the large private room at Mike's Tavern, the place where most cops and firefighters had their retirement parties, was packed. This night belonged to Jim Conte as he celebrated retirement and experienced the bittersweet emotions veteran police officers feel when they leave the circle of blue. It's hard to turn the page after thirty years; it takes time.

Jim was working the room, greeting everyone, shaking hands, and thanking the attendees for celebrating with him. Chief Lansing and Deputy Chief Watkins put in an appearance to wish Jim well, but they didn't stay long.

Harry was also enjoying talking with friends, including civilians he hadn't seen for a while. He saw Judy Wright standing near the bar, talking with a robbery detective. It was the second time Harry had seen her in a dress. The other night at dinner, she was wearing a loose-fitting dress. This dress was tighter. It showed off her figure, especially highlighting a great pair of legs. She saw him staring, excused herself, and came over to him. "Well, Detective Harry Lincoln, do I pass inspection?"

"You look terrific, Judy. I'm glad you're here. I have a hamburger coming to go with this beer. Let's grab a couple of seats at that table over there. Can I order something for you to eat?"

"No, Harry, I'm fine with this glass of wine, but I'll sit with you while you eat your hamburger. What a nice turnout for Jim. I had a pleasant conversation with him before, and I've enjoyed seeing some of the detectives that come to the lab."

The waitress brought his food to the table. It was difficult to eat because so many stopped by to greet them. He had just washed down the last bite with a long pull of beer when he felt a tap on his shoulder.

"Hello, Harry," said Ellen. She was with a man he did not recognize. "I'd like you to meet George Summerville." They shook hands, and then Harry introduced Judy.

"I saw you sitting here with this attractive woman," Ellen said, "and I thought, 'Harry still has good taste in women.'" They all laughed as Ellen and her companion sat down. She said she had not been able to get through the crowd to say hello to Jim and wish him well. After a few minutes of conversation, she said, "Come on, George, the herd is thinning out."

Ellen stood and said her goodbyes, and then George and Ellen left.

That was classy of Ellen to come over, thought Harry, *but I've always known Ellen had a lot of class.*

◆

It was getting late, close to midnight, and many had already left. "Listen, Harry," said Judy, standing, "I guess you'll want to stay with Jim until everyone's gone. I'm going to head home and put on a fresh pot of coffee to go with some cheesecake that's in the fridge. You remember apartment 12 C?"

Harry nodded.

"This time, come in."

◆

The room had emptied, the last person had shaken Jim's hand, wishing him well, and he and Harry walked to the parking lot. They stood near their cars for a few minutes, just the two of them.

"You know, Harry, on my last day as a cop, we were in the courtroom, standing together, sending another one to the slammer. It's strange the way the timing works out. Harry, you are the best partner I've had, and I'll never forget the years we worked together and all the shit we've been through. I better stop talking now, before I start slobbering."

"I feel the same way, Jim. If I couldn't work with my dad, you were the partner I always wanted. We have been through a lot and done pretty well over the years. So cheer up, partner, you're retiring, not dying. I'll just leave it at that. Thanks. Thanks for the memories."

Harry drove out of the parking lot, headed to the Midtown Manor Apartments, 12-C.

EPILOGUE

Palmer Hamilton waited and waited, as he had waited every visiting day for the past three months. He had not seen Ingrid or received any mail from her. When he called her cell phone, she did not answer. He called Lenny Goldberg daily, and Lenny always accepted the collect calls. "Where is she Lenny? Why doesn't she visit me? What happened to her? Lenny, please find out."

The next visiting day, Lenny sat with Palmer at a small table in the prison's day room. "Ingrid's gone, Palmer. She's probably left the city. She quit her job and sold her townhouse and her Honda. She closed out both of her accounts at the bank and maxed out your credit cards." Lenny told Palmer he would try to get back to visit when he could. He shook Palmer's lifeless hand. "Goodbye, Palmer."

Palmer had to endure seven more long, lonely months without her. Then what? The crippling thought and unanswered question rattled around in his head, and a dejected Palmer Hamilton shuffled back to his cell.

BOOK THREE

STREET THUGS

CHAPTER 1

"**C**heck it out, dog—white and blonde," he said to the other young black man in the car. "Good lookin' tits, an' a ass that belong on a black sista."

The supermarket parking lot was almost full. Shoppers came and went, and the two gangbangers watched and waited, looking for some action. They had not been waiting long when the Singers, an attractive young couple, emerged from the store pushing a grocery basket and stopped at the rear of a grey car. After loading the trunk of their car, Roy and Lillian Singer got in and headed for home.

They were followed.

Jamal "Cellblock" Eaves, a thirty-year-old career criminal and ex-con had earned his name the hard way, with half of his life lived behind bars. Bernard "Bad Dog" Jackson called himself that because it made him sound like "the baddest motherfucker on the block." Eaves and Jackson, natives of Detroit, Michigan, had been cellmates for several years. They spent their time outside prison walls terrorizing innocent people with random acts of murder, rape, and robbery. Detroit police had finally identified the two in the wake of a heinous, violent crime spree and posted statewide lookouts. The fugitives felt law enforcement breathing down their necks, about to put them back in prison. In a bank parking lot, they robbed a man of several hundred dollars, which he had just withdrawn from an ATM. They shot and killed him, took his black 2001 Ford Taurus, and left the state.

"Where we gonna go, blood? We gotta get away from here, an' fast."

"I know just the place, dog. When my old man got outta the federal pen, he got hisself a place where we can hole up until the heat go out. An 'it's' near a thousand mile from here."

That was two months ago.

◆

Reggis Eaves, Jamal's father, was also an ex-con, a serial pedophile who transported children across state lines and spent

196

twenty years in federal prison in Marion, Illinois. Upon his release, he came to the city and through the federal rehabilitation program found employment as a maintenance man/janitor/super in an older, six-story apartment building. The policy of the government-assisted residence was "adults only," and the socio-economics of the area were marginal, at best. He lived rent-free in a basement apartment with an adjoining shop in which to do repairs and maintenance for the building. Next to the shop was a separate parking area for him to use. After settling in, he had contacted his son to let him know where he was living.

◆

The thugs followed the couple a short distance and parked. They watched Roy Singer close the lid of the trunk and bring the last bag of groceries into the modest apartment. Lillian was in the kitchen putting them away. The two men pushed in behind Roy. They hit him in the head with a gun, knocking him to the floor.

Lillian screamed. She was slapped so hard she fell next to Roy. "Now shut the fuck up, an' if you scream again, I'm gonna shoot him," said Cellblock Eaves.

"Get the fuck up an' stand over there by that couch an' start strippin', bitch," Eaves yelled.

Roy, still dazed, staggered to his feet. "Hey, wait a minute, what the hell are you doing in here?"

Jackson hit him in the head again, and Roy fell down, almost unconscious.

Lillian got up slowly, stumbled into the living room, and stood near the couch.

"Let's go, bitch. Start takin' 'em off, or I shoot your boyfriend in the balls, an' I come over there an' take 'em off of you."

"Please, don't hurt him anymore," pleaded Lillian. Frightened, she shed her jeans and blouse, and stood quivering in her panties and bra.

Cellblock hit Roy once more in the head with the gun. Red blood began to pool on the floor between the kitchen and living room.

Sobbing, Lillian closed her eyes as she removed her underwear.

"Oh, don't she look fine?" leered Jackson as he ran his hand over her naked body, pulling her toward him, probing her until she almost fainted.

"Hey, Dog, get somethin' to tie this cracker up with while I check the whore out," Cellblock said as he squeezed her breasts and forced his hand between her legs. "I'm gonna tell you one time. Me an' my homey gonna fuck you, an' you gonna like it so much, you gonna beg us to fuck you some more. An' when I fuck you, you gonna say you ain't never had a white boy make you feel so good, an' your boyfriend gonna watch the whole show. An' if you don't, I'm gonna shoot him in the head. You got that, bitch?"

She looked at him and nodded slightly. She stood naked and watched them hog-tie and gag Roy. He was coming out of his daze.

They took turns raping her on the floor and couch, and then bent her over the arm of the couch, anally raping her so brutally that blood flowed. She screamed; she couldn't help it. The final degradation was forcing her to perform oral sex on their filthy, bloody penises. The stench of their body odor caused her to gag some more. When she could no longer hold it, Lillian vomited.

When they were finished with her, they tied her with stockings found in a dresser drawer. They ransacked the apartment and piled up at the door the items they could sell: TVs, computers, cell phones, jewelry, and clothing. They took the money and credit cards from his wallet and her purse.

Lillian heard them discussing which would shoot the white boy. Cellblock made the stronger case.

"Listen, Dog, the only thing I like better than fuckin' white girls is killin' white boys."

"But," Lillian cried, as she lay on the floor next to her husband, "you said if I did what you wanted, you would not kill him."

Eaves placed the barrel of his gun against Roy Singer's right eye. He pulled the trigger, splattering Lillian with blood, brains, and bone. As he closed the door, Cellblock looked at her with a satisfied smirk.

"I lied, bitch!"

CHAPTER 2

The homicide squad room was a cacophony of telephones ringing, computer keyboards and typewriters clicking, laughter, and a friendly argument about the best hitter in the history of Major League Baseball: Babe Ruth, Lou Gehrig, Joe DiMaggio, Ted Williams, Stan Musial, Hank Aaron, Willie Mays, Ty Cobb, Pete Rose, Mickey Mantle, Roberto Clemente, and the list went on. The raucous laughter continued around the room as other issues were debated.

"What the hell is this, a goddamn fraternity house?" Homicide Lieutenant James McGee stormed out of his office. "How about solving some crime, like you're paid to do? Put the bastards in jail. Clear some of those files you've got on your desks. Maybe I should get some new blood in here? There are a bunch of eager beavers in uniform who would sell their souls to be where you clowns are, getting your salaries. The laughter died down. They went quietly to their desks without making eye contact with McGee.

"Bloomfield and Harrington, you're up next—a homicide and rape, the murder scene is in Apartment 106 in the Valley View Apartments on Jefferson Boulevard in the Second Precinct; the rape victim is at the hospital. Meet Sergeant Foster at the scene and work from there. Your rape victim has been hysterical. She was given something to calm her down at the hospital, so you'll have to wait until tomorrow to talk with her." Lieutenant McGee left it with the evening watch detectives and headed for home, his twelve-hour day over.

♦

The lieutenant's thoughts turned to Detective Harry Lincoln, who had been working solo for the past week since his longtime partner, Jim Conte, retired. Lieutenant McGee was looking for a replacement, but didn't want to break up any of the current partners within the squad. Harry Lincoln was an outstanding homicide detective with good instincts. He was very capable, and he had a strong sense of mission.

If Lincoln has a weakness, the lieutenant thought, *it's his emotions. I've known him to be out of control before, but his partner stopped him in each case before he crossed the line.* McGee was looking for the right one. During the drive home, he considered which detective and qualities would make the best fit with Lincoln.

Detective Liz Kovak put in a transfer request last month to return to the homicide squad from the gang unit where she worked the past year. Lincoln and Kovak were partners for a few months when Conte was on a leave-of-absence. They proved a damn good fit. Why not again? I remember the gossip circulating about the two of them, particularly the probable reason she transferred out. I'll talk with her about this before I recommend her transfer to work with Lincoln.

♦

Harry had finished dinner, the rest of the chili he'd made the night before, and had just settled down with a book chronicling the Korean War, *The Coldest Winter*, reputed to be the most comprehensive book on the topic. He hadn't read one page when his cell phone rang.

"Harry, did I disturb you? It's Lieutenant McGee."

"Lieu, when you are concerned about disturbing me, I get very suspicious. What's going on that I don't want to know about?"

"Liz Kovak."

"Liz? What's happened? Is she okay?"

"Slow down, Harry. Nothing's wrong. She's fine. She recently put in a request for transfer back to homicide. I was thinking of putting her with you. How do you feel about that?"

"I'm fine with it, Lieutenant, but do you recall why she wanted out of homicide?"

"Yes, I remember. I'll see that it doesn't happen again. I'll take care of it. See you when you get back after your off days, Harry."

♦

Lieutenant McGee asked Liz Kovak to meet at the Downtown Diner for breakfast. He asked her about working with Harry if her transfer request was approved. Liz was excited and assured him that there could be no better partner than Harry Lincoln.

"Listen, Kovak," said McGee, "can you work alongside the same people who caused you to leave before, without it affecting your performance?"

"Yes, Lieutenant. I've given it a lot of thought and concluded that should it happen again, I will address it immediately and directly to the person with the big mouth."

"You will have my support. I'll be glad to have you back. I know Lincoln feels the same. I am recommending the transfer and sending it up the chain."

They left the diner, McGee headed for headquarters. Liz drove across town to the mini-precinct that housed the gang unit.

♦

Lieutenant McGee held the day watch over and, along with the evening watch detectives, directed the squad to the lineup room, the auditorium-like room where lineups and large briefings were conducted. The lieutenant stood on the small stage and addressed the twenty homicide detectives.

"Detective Liz Kovak has put in a transfer request to return to homicide, and I've recommended its approval to the boss. She transferred out after a bunch of talk, smirks, and innuendos about her and Lincoln. She didn't want to end up hating everyone in Homicide. She wants to return, and I'm glad to get someone of her caliber to fill the vacancy left by Jim Conte. Lincoln and Kovak will be partners. Liz Kovak is a happily married woman with a young child, and Harry Lincoln respects that. I want all of you to remember that before you go flapping your jaws.

"Now, I'm only going to say this one time. Each of you is supposed to be a professional, not someone who gets his kicks from spreading rumors. If you don't already know it, a rumor is unfounded; it has no basis in fact. So, if I hear the first hint of what went on last time, get your uniform out of the closet, because you will be working a patrol car on the morning watch, handling automobile wrecks on cold, rainy nights, breaking up bar fights, fighting wild-ass drunks and enraged drunken husbands after they've beaten the shit out of their wives. If you think I'm bull-shitting, try me!"

He dismissed the squad.

CHAPTER 3

"Glad to have you back, Liz," said a happy Harry Lincoln, giving her a hug as the three stood in McGee's office, "and Lieu, thanks for assigning her as my partner."

"I hate to break up this little homecoming," said Lieutenant McGee, "but it's time to go to work. A man and woman were kidnapped late last night from Madison Park. She's at the hospital; the man is missing. Go to the hospital and start there."

♦

"She had multiple cuts, abrasions, and contusions all over her body," said the ER doctor. "There were burns on her breasts and abdomen that might have been made by lit cigarettes. The major trauma was to her vagina and rectum, apparently from sexual assault."

Lincoln and Kovak thanked the doctor for his report and retrieved a copy of the admission sheet. They already had the incident report from the responding police officer, documenting the names of the victims and a vague narrative of what had occurred.

Lisa Daniels, a twenty-six- year-old white female, was mildly sedated and had been admitted to the hospital from the ER. Harry and Liz were in her room, at her bedside. They found her awake and alert enough to relate the events of the night before.

Liz identified herself and Harry. "Can you tell us what happened last night?" Liz asked as she held the hand of the traumatized woman.

"They hurt me so bad," she sobbed. "Those vicious goddamn animals hurt me so bad." She cried while Liz and Harry sat quietly, then suddenly she stopped and looked at them. "Edmond. Where's Edmond? Is he all right?"

"What's Edmond's full name, Lisa?" Harry asked.

"It's Franklin, Edmond Franklin," said Lisa, sobbing. "Did they hurt him some more? Where is he?"

"We haven't heard from him yet," Harry answered. "We don't know if he's all right or not."

"They were going to shoot him if I didn't do and say all those awful things. Please find him and bring him here so I can see that he's all right."

"That's what we are going to do," Liz assured her, "but tell us from the beginning, as best you can, what happened, so we'll know where to start looking."

"Edmond, my boyfriend, and I work at the same place and get off at midnight. We took my car and drove to the park, which is not far from there. We were sitting in the car, just talking, when these two black guys started knocking on the windows, one on each side. They had guns and said if we didn't open the doors, they would shoot us through the windows. I tried to leave, but the car wouldn't start. I must have flooded it in my panic. We unlocked the doors, and they took us to their car and made me get in the back seat. One of them got in with me. They told Edmond to get behind the wheel, and the other one sat in the front seat beside him.

The one with me told me to take off my pants and panties. When I hesitated, he slapped me hard in my face, so I did. He told me to open my legs, but I didn't do it quick enough, so he slapped me again. Edmond hollered for him to stop it and the other one hit him in the head with a gun. The one with me put his gun between my legs. I could feel it right against me. He told Edmond to drive the car, saying the other one would tell him where to go. He warned Edmond that if he tried anything while driving, he would shoot me there, where the gun was.

It seemed like we drove for less than ten minutes, and when we got out of the car it was a dark, rundown area, desolate, no lights anywhere. They took us into an abandoned house. There was trash all over the place. One room had a smelly mattress on the floor. They made me take off the rest of my clothes and lie down on it, and the guy that was in the car with me raped me. Then the other one did the same."

She started to cry again. Liz handed her some tissues. "Take a break and try to relax a little," she told the sobbing victim. "Can you remember if they called each other by name?"

"All I heard was 'man,' 'bro,' 'dude,' 'blood,' 'dog,' and 'home.' That's all I can remember. The whole time they were cursing and talking filthy and nasty either to Edmond and me or to each other. I just can't repeat some of the things they said or the words they used."

"If you are feeling better tomorrow," Harry suggested, "you can write down on paper everything they said, just the way they said it, and then we'll type it into our computer for the file. The more we know, the quicker we can identify them. If you are okay now, tell us the rest of what happened."

"Yes,I would rather write those nasty things than say them," she said with relief. "After they raped me, I thought they were through with me. I was wrong. The first one told me to turn around and kneel on my knees and rest on my elbows, and that's when I felt the worst pain I've ever had in my life. I screamed. He hit me. I couldn't help it. I screamed again. He hit me harder. I kept screaming because he was pushing himself harder and harder into my backside. The other animal then hurt me the same way. It was so bad. I wanted to die.

"They made Edmond watch everything. He hollered and pleaded for them to stop. Every time he said something, they hit him in the head with a gun. His head was all bloody. One of them took Edmond outside, and that's the last time I saw him. I'm so worried about him. Please, find him." She started to cry again. "I thought the worst was over, but then I was told to turn over onto my back, and that I was going to give them oral sex. They weren't telling me what to do the way I'm telling you the story; it was filthy, slimy, disgusting. I was told to think about that while they took a smoke break. A few minutes later, when I told them I couldn't do that, they burned my breasts with their cigarettes. Screaming and begging did no good; they burned my stomach until I couldn't stand it anymore, and I did what they wanted. Each of them had blood and I don't even want to know what else on their penises. They both needed baths; they stunk so bad that I kept gagging, but they wouldn't stop until they were finished.

"Suddenly, it was quiet. No one was there. I put on what clothes I could find and pulled myself out of the door and through the front yard. When I reached the sidewalk, they caught me, dragged me back into the house, and raped me all over again. One of them had what looked like a garden clippers and told me if I didn't 'move my ass like I was lovin' it,' he was going to cut off my nipples. I begged him not to do that. I tried my best to satisfy him.

"I don't know how long I was there. The house got quiet and I thought I was alone, but this time I didn't bother with clothes. I dragged myself out of the house. I had to get away. I dragged myself into the middle of the street, hoping to see a car, someone to help me. It was so desolate; there was no traffic. Then I saw headlights. It was a police car. It stopped. A female officer got out. I was hysterical. She saw that I was bleeding. She put me in the car and got a blanket out of the trunk to cover me. She asked what had happened, and I told her that I had been raped, and I pointed to the house. The officer got on her radio and gave an address. Two police cars came. Three officers went into the house, but the men were gone. A sergeant came and asked me some questions. He told the female officer to take me to the hospital. The doctor said I would probably stay for a few days. Please, find Edmond and bring him here to the hospital, please."

"We'll do our best, Lisa," Liz assured her. "In the meantime, let the doctors and nurses fix up your wounds and take away some of the hurt. Detective Lincoln and I will stop in to see you until you go home, and then we'll get that written statement from you. Here are our cards. Call us anytime, day or night, if you think of anything we should know. The more we know the better chance there is of catching those animals. Feel better and get well, Lisa."

Edmond Franklin's body was found the next day in a ditch, next to an over-grown vacant lot, three blocks from the abandoned house. He was shot twice in the back of the head.

CHAPTER 4

"Hey, Blood, we runnin' low on Ben Franklins, so we betta make a quick withdrawal pretty soon," urged Bad Dog Jackson.

Cellblock Eaves was staring off at nothing after dipping into the meth.

"The little we got from those two at the park wasn't shit, man, an' it's about gone now, but the pussy was pretty good, an' how 'bout that nice, round, shiny, white ass?"

"I don't know, Dog, I liked that little blond bitch we fucked at that apartment. She had such good stuff that we shoulda taken her with us and kept her ass. There are plenty more of them white bitches aroun', an' I'm gettin' as many as I can."

What about hittin' the Jew store again for some green?" Bad Dog suggested. "That was easy as shit, man." They had been in and out of the store a few times before they robbed it the first time.

"Okay with me, Dog," muttered Cellblock through a fog. "I don't like the old Jew, anyhow, or his fat, loudmouth, bitch wife. They always watchin' us when we in the store, think we gonna steal a piece a bubble gum or somethin'."

The little mom and pop grocery store had been on the same corner of Griffin and Wells Streets for over fifty years. It served the neighborhood, whose demographics had changed several times. Joseph and Frieda Rothstein, both in their late 70s, had owned and run the store since it opened. They lived in a modest apartment above it. Their children, grown with families of their own, lived in the suburbs and had urged their parents several times to close the store and retire. Their concern was that the neighborhood had changed dramatically in the last few years and become too dangerous. The store had been robbed at gunpoint twice and burglarized three times. The argument from the elder Rothsteins was that if they left, the store would close up, and where would the neighbors without cars go for a carton of milk, a loaf of bread, a dozen eggs, and a pound of butter? Joseph and Frieda Rothstein remained to serve the neighborhood.

It was 9:45 p.m., just before closing, when the most money would be in the cash register. The Rothsteins did not believe they should give the banks a percentage of their small profit to honor credit cards. Cash was the only currency. Cellblock and Bad Dog entered the store, but this time they didn't bother covering their faces. "I hope you got enough fuckin' money in that register to die over, old man," said Cellblock, holding the gun six inches from Joseph Rothstein's face.

"Get the hell out of my store, you hoodlum," yelled Mr. Rothstein before he was shot twice in the face.

Frieda Rothstein came shrieking from the back room. "Joseph, Joseph!" She fell to her knees over her husband's body. "Oh, my God, oh no," she screamed.

"Shut the fuck up, you fat Jew bitch," Cellblock shot Mrs. Rothstein, and Bad Dog emptied the cash register of $327.

They heard movement and saw a shadow down one of the aisles. They went to check and found an elderly black woman cowering beside the cold drink case. She looked at them and whispered, "Please, don't shoot me."

Cellblock smiled before he shot her, and then Bad Dog said, "Come on, blood, let's get the fuck outta here."

A customer came into the store for some milk just before closing. She had to concentrate to get her trembling finger to dial 9 – 1 – 1. Three patrol cars and a sergeant responded, along with an ambulance and fire rescue. The next call was a request for homicide detectives. Evening watch detectives, Fisher and Briscoe, arrived. With the help of the sector sergeant and several officers from the 4th Precinct, the detectives established the bounds of the crime scene to see what could be learned from it. Fisher put in a call for a crime scene unit and additional detective teams to canvass the neighborhood for witnesses as they waited for the medical examiner.

♦

The following morning, Harry and Liz went to the hospital. Lisa Daniels was still there.

"It will be a few more days," Lisa said. "It all depends on my healing progress and pain management. I'm hooked up to a morphine pump to control the pain. After you left yesterday, a nurse brought me a notebook and a pen, and I've written everything they did to me, including all the nasty, filthy words they used. Take it with you. What about Edmond? Have you found him? Is he all right?"

Liz took her hand and looked at her. "We've got some very bad news, Lisa. Edmond is dead. He was found a few blocks from the house. He had been shot."

It wasn't a scream. It started as a shivering whimper, became a wail, and evolved into the kind of a howl that comes from suffering the greatest possible loss. Liz sat on the bed and held Lisa to comfort her and keep her from dislodging the tubes and wires attached to her.

"Why did they have to kill him?" she moaned. "They already had his wallet, money, and credit cards, and they took his watch and ring. I did everything they wanted. Oh, my God. Why did they have to kill him? How do you know it was Edmond? He didn't have his wallet."

"It was him, Lisa; he had his company photo ID badge tied to one of the belt loops on his pants. They didn't have to kill him," Liz said, knowing that words could not comfort. "They are a couple of no-good, vicious animals. We will find them and see that they are punished." They stayed with her and talked until she calmed down. "Lisa, is anyone coming to visit you?"

"Yes, I called my sister. She should be here soon. Don't feel like you have to stay with me. I'd rather you be out looking for those bastards."

"There will be a police officer sitting outside your door," Harry said. "No one will come into the room unless you give the okay. We'll be back to see you, check on your progress, and give you any updates."

As they left the hospital, Liz said, "I feel so much better now that Lieutenant McGee got the bosses to authorize a cop outside of Lisa's room 24/7."

"Let's find Ham. The two we want are street thugs, gangbangers. Ham might be able to get a line on them for us."

On the way, Harry asked Liz why she decided to transfer back to homicide.

"Well, Harry, there were several reasons. I really liked working homicide, and when I heard that Jim was going to retire, I knew you would need a new partner. I hoped McGee would remember that we worked well together. He told me so when he asked me about us being partners again. He also told me there would be no more gossiping about us from the rest of the squad."

"McGee put the fear of God in them, or so I've been told. I don't think we'll hear any more of that. You and I are going to be fine, but you said there were several reasons for the transfer."

"Well, Harry, working homicide we have to deal with scum, like looking for those filthy bastards who attacked the couple in the park, but we also get to interact with decent people. Working the gang unit, everyone you come in contact with is scum. It's like working vice; you feel filthy and dirty all the time. It was time for me to get out of that environment. No matter how hard I scrubbed, I never felt clean."

"There he is. He's seen us. Let's drive to the parking lot. He'll be along soon." Harry thought about his relationship with Ham. Both thought it was a good deal. Ham was a street hustler, but as long as no one got hurt, and nothing was stolen, Harry looked out for him. In return, Ham heard things, things that helped Harry clear major felonies.

"Hello, Ham. I want you to meet my new partner, Detective Kovak," Harry said as Ham climbed into the back seat.

"I remember you, Detective Kovak. You worked with Detective Lincoln once before."

"Ham," Harry said, getting to the point, "over in the 7th, a couple were kidnapped from Madison Park last night and taken to an abandoned house. She was raped, and her boyfriend was murdered. Two black thugs. Nose around and let me know as soon as you hear something." As Ham got into his car, Harry said, "And, Ham, that Mercedes a couple of weeks ago—I won't forget that."

They felt better knowing the word was getting out at street level through one of Harry's best CIs.

CHAPTER 5

It was their third date. Judy suggested they go to Sophia's on 43rd Street, a late nineteenth-century mansion converted about forty years before into a restaurant. It was a local favorite and a tourist destination. Harry enjoyed his meal and wondered why he had not been there before. He was a stay at home guy. There were many different great restaurants he had heard about, but never tried.

Something had been on Harry's mind. Now, while sharing a generous slice of German chocolate cake and sipping after-dinner coffee, he thought it would be the right time. "There's something you should know, Judy, something I want to tell you before more time slips away. We became lovers on the night of Jim's retirement party. I'm glad we did, but I'm not looking for a long-term, committed relationship. I want to be free to date others. I hope you will want to do the same, but honestly, I don't consider the other night a one-night stand. I think much more of you, and I'd like us to continue to date as often as we both see fit. I'm hoping you feel the same."

"I didn't see that coming, Harry. I am not sure how I should feel about it. I wanted us to date for quite some time, but I knew you were taken. That changed the other night. It was wonderful, and I'm glad to be here with you tonight. I just haven't had time to think beyond. Give me some time. In the meantime, Harry, let's get out of here and go to your place."

♦

"This is it, Judy, my sanctuary—the place I hide from the world. You are one of the very few who has been here. I like it that way."

"It's lovely, Harry, just enough of a woman's touch to warm it up. I guess that woman was Ellen."

"Yes. She thought it had as much warmth and charm as a medieval castle. She helped me with some decorating ideas and brought in a few things. Now I guess you could say it's charming," Harry said with a grin.

"It is quite charming. I've always been curious about lofts. I can see why you feel so comfortable here, but some might not like all this openness. Now, if you'll excuse me, Harry, I need a few minutes in the bathroom."

"It's right there, through the bedroom."

As she left the living room, Harry thought that Judy was the right woman at the right time.

"Harry," he heard her call from the bathroom. "Will you come in here?"

Opening the door, he saw a very naked and soaking wet Judy Wright standing under the shower. "Come join me, Harry. I need someone to scrub my back."

With the delicious, warm, soapy water came a deeper intimacy than the first time at her apartment, when they had too hurriedly fallen into bed. The shower was so pleasurable, they were reluctant to get out and dry off, but after wrapping each other in soft bath towels, they drifted into the bedroom, where Harry and Judy took their time. They connected smoothly, warmly, and deeply, until they fit together like two pieces of a jigsaw puzzle. The tempo increased, and the pressure mounted, until release surged through them both.

After a while, as their breathing returned to normal and they again felt in control, Judy said, "You are a wonderful lover, Harry. I always imagined you would be. Now, I need to tell you something. Harry, I'm all woman; you should know that by now. But I'm not like most women, who cling after making love, who want to cuddle and plead or cajole their lovers to spend the night with them. I'm different, Harry; I guess I think more like a man sometimes. I realize it's after two in the morning, and please don't misconstrue this as a rejection, but I'd like a lift home so I can sleep in my own bed for the rest of the night. These past few hours have been wonderful, and I hope we can do it again very soon."

After driving Judy home, seeing her to the door of apartment 12C, and returning to the loft, Harry changed into pajamas and climbed into bed. Her scent still lingered on the pillows and sheets; it was pleasant.

Yes, he thought, *the loft is my sanctuary, the place I can escape the madness and violence that is part of the world in which I chose to live. It is where I fit best. However, it is more than making a living; it is a calling. We are the front line of a lawful, orderly, and sane society, and we stand firm against the flotsam and jetsam, the dregs among us. The flaws in society must be controlled, repelled, and defeated—to* quote Malcolm X—*"By any means that are necessary."* Because there are bullies, brutes, and thugs, our world needs troops like Lieutenant McGee, Jim Conte, Liz Kovak and the rest of us who wear the badge. I wouldn't want to do anything else, but from time to time, I need to decompress, to forget for a while, so when I walk through that loft door into my sanctuary, I leave all the garbage outside.

Harry thought about all of that before drifting off to sleep. His last pleasant thoughts were of the two recent women in his life. *Ellen always kept me on an even keel with the intimacy I needed to maintain my stability and keep me sane. Judy is very much like Ellen—brainy, attractive, and giving.*

CHAPTER 6

"**B**loomfield, Harrington. Lincoln, Kovak," bellowed Lieutenant McGee from his office doorway. "Conference room, five minutes!"

It was just before eight a.m., when the squad room was all about coffee and donuts. Day watch detectives reporting for duty were at their desks, having a second jolt of caffeine and gooey, fat-laden donuts. The four grabbed up their morning sustenance and case files and went into the quiet room, away from the noisy, hustle-bustle of the squad room.

"I've noticed two active cases with similarities," Lieutenant McGee said as he walked into the conference room. "Bloomfield and Harrington, your home invasion case resulted into a sexual assault on a woman and the murder of her husband. Lincoln and Kovak are investigating a kidnapping of a woman and her boyfriend, which also resulted in a brutal sexual assault on her and the murder of the boyfriend. Tell me about it."

Harrington said, "Well, Lieu, the medical examiner recovered a bullet from Roy Singer's head. We took it to the state crime lab for ballistics tests. The wife is staying with her parents. She is still under moderate sedation, so traumatized that she can't talk about it. We're going back this morning to see if she is ready to give a statement. The only thing we got from her two days ago was 'two black men.'"

"Take Delmont with you. Maybe a woman can coax the gory details from your victim. And," said McGee, "when they start talking, you two leave them alone for a while."

"In our case, Lieutenant," reported Kovak, "after two black males took the couple from the park, they were taken to an abandoned house, where Lisa Daniels was raped and sodomized. Edmond Franklin's body was found the next day in a vacant lot three blocks from the abandoned house. He was shot twice in the head. Those bullets were recovered and taken to the state crime lab. Lisa was traumatized, but she gave us a hand-written statement, which we've typed into the computer for the file. She's still in the hospital being treated for her injuries. Lisa Daniels is the only one in our case who can identify the perps, and Harry and I feel better that you've had a uniform outside of her room."

"Our victim, Lillian Singer, should be able to ID the two, but she's not the only witness," Bloomfield added optimistically. "During our canvass, a neighbor saw two black males leaving the Singers' apartment. She saw them load two flat screen TVs and two laptop computers into the Singers' car, and a bunch of smaller items wrapped in two blankets into an older model car, and drive away. We got a pretty detailed statement from her."

Harrington saw the look the lieutenant was giving his partner. He answered the obvious question before a red-faced McGee asked it. "Lieu," said Harrington, "we asked that witness why she didn't call 911 when the two were emptying out the Singers' apartment, and she said she 'never got involved.' I guess when we showed up at her door, she had no choice."

Bloomfield said, "Ms. Singer will not be returning to that apartment. We assured her we would keep her new location confidential."

"Okay," Lieutenant McGee said, "I want you four to stay coordinated. Each new report, every piece of paper that is generated concerning those two mutts, I want you to make two copies, one for each file. The five of us will meet as time and the situation dictates. Now, let's go to work."

◆

Harry and Liz went to the hospital to look in on Lisa Daniels and see if she remembered anything of significance.

She sounded very bitter. "I'll never forget those faces as long as I live. Show me their photos or put them in a lineup; I can identify them."

"We are counting on you to do that when we catch up with them, and we will." Harry looked at Lisa and tried to imagine the pain she had endured, both physical and mental. "You can help us now by making a list of the jewelry they took from you—your watch, rings, bracelets, necklace, earrings, and anything that can be easily identified as yours, as well as anything you know Edmond had, such as the watch and ring."

"Lisa," asked Liz, "when you are released from the hospital, will you be staying with someone for a while?"

"Yes, I'll be staying with my sister. I'll let you know her address. I've got your cell phone number."

♦

On their way out of the hospital, Harry's cell phone rang; it was Lieutenant McGee. "Harry, are you still close to the hospital?"

"Yes, Lieu, we are just about to leave. What's up?"

"Meet with a traffic sergeant in the ER. She said there was something strange about a traffic fatality. She wanted homicide to have a look."

A nurse directed Harry and Liz to a trauma room already crowded with two police uniforms, two nurses, and a young intern doctor. A sheet covered a body on the table.

"We believe this is a homicide, rather than a traffic fatality," Sergeant Jane Griffin told the two detectives. "By the way, what the hell is wrong with your lieutenant? I'd hardly started talking when he grumbled that he would send someone over and 'we'll see about that.'"

"He gets a little cranky every so often. He doesn't mean any disrespect. Tell us what you've got here," Liz said.

"I answered a call on a single vehicle wreck with injuries," said the second cop, reading from his accident report. "This car was eastbound on Merrick Avenue, a four-lane surface street, when it jumped the curb and traveled several hundred feet on the sidewalk, missing pedestrians, but taking down eleven parking meters, a mail box, a light pole, and a fire hydrant before coming to a stop. The car sustained major damage. The driver, a seventy-three-year-old white male, Bernard Rosen, was bleeding around his head and face and unresponsive. The witnesses we talked with saw the car barrel down the sidewalk, smashing everything in its path. When they got to the car, they saw the driver was elderly and not moving. They assumed he'd had a heart attack or seizure of some kind.

One of the witnesses recognized him as the owner of a small business about a half dozen blocks from the crash site. I've listed it here in the accident report. Here's a copy."

Sergeant Griffin interjected, "Fire Rescue showed up at the scene and brought him here. The docs tried to revive him, but they found a bullet hole in the left side of his head. We'll have to wait for the autopsy to know the official cause of death, but I thought homicide should be notified."

"Okay," said Harry, "have your officer file his accident report. We have a copy with names, places, times, and vital statistics. We'll start the homicide investigation. Then, when the autopsy report and the death certificate are released, we'll both be covered."

♦

Harry and Liz arrived at the Rosen Metal Plating Company on Smith Street, which was really more of an alley that dead-ended into Merrick Avenue. They spoke with Joseph Bleaker, a short man in his mid-fifties, who met them at the door.

"Is it true that Mr. Rosen was shot, that he didn't have a stroke?"

"That's what we're trying to determine. Tell us what you know about his movements this morning."

"This is a small company. We have twenty, twenty-five people employed here, depending on our workload. Mr. Rosen is the owner, and I'm kind of a foreman. When he left this morning, he said he would be back later this afternoon. He didn't say where he was going, I didn't ask. Mr. Rosen is, I mean was, a flashy old guy. He drove a new Lexus LS 460, and he wore expensive clothes, a Rolex watch, and a diamond ring. I warned him that this was not the neighborhood to attract attention to those kinds of things. He was old school. He didn't like credit cards and carried a lot of cash, several hundred dollars in his pocket held with a large paper clip."

They confirmed with Mr. Bleaker that Bernard Rosen was wearing his watch and ring that morning when he left. Bleaker also said his boss had peeled off a fifty-dollar bill from a roll and given it to him for the coffee and donut fund. He saw the large roll go back into Mr. Rosen's pocket.

After checking at the property section, Harry and Liz determined that Mr. Rosen's watch, ring, and cash had not been turned in with his personal property.

"So if he was shot in the head," Liz said, "the motive is pretty clear."

CHAPTER 7

"**D**etective Kovak, this is Lisa Daniels. Is this a bad time to call, or do you have a minute to talk?"

"No, Lisa, this is a perfect time. Harry and I are in the car on the way to get a bite of lunch. What's up?"

"I've been released from the hospital. I'm with Jessica, my sister. Could you and Detective Lincoln come by her house for a cup of coffee after your lunch? I'd like to talk to you about something."

♦

1926 Walton Avenue was a modest, gray frame house in a blue-collar neighborhood.

"I'm so glad you could come," Lisa said, as she greeted them at the door. It was the first time the detectives had seen Lisa smile. "Detectives Liz Kovak and Harry Lincoln, this is my sister, Jessica Daniels."

After the introductions, they went into a small, but comfortable living room. Jessica brought in coffee and apricot-filled pastries. Then the four engaged in small talk.

"I'm glad to meet you both," Jessica said, "and I want to thank you for the kindness you showed Lisa after her ordeal. She will be staying with me for a while. When she's ready, she'll find a place of her own. They got her purse and her driver's license, so she can't go back to her apartment."

During a lull in the conversation, Liz said, "On the phone, you said there was something you wanted to talk to us about?"

"I wanted you to know where I was and to give you the phone number here. Jessica and I wanted to tell you how much we appreciate what you've done for me."

"It's the least we could do after all you've been through," Liz said, "but more important now is finding those animals and making sure they never hurt or kill anyone else. Harry and I need to get back on the street to do that."

"Lisa," Harry said, "we have other people, like us, also looking for them. You just need to get to feeling better. We have the house phone number, and we'll stay in touch. Jessica, thanks for having us over. Those apricot things were very good."

♦

"Those apricot things?" Liz laughed as they drove back to headquarters. "Come on, Harry, you were looking at Jessica like you were about to eat her up, instead of the pastries. In case you missed it, she loved it. Lisa could have told us where she was staying over the phone. Lisa was playing matchmaker and doing a damn good job. Making sure we had Jessica's phone number? Give me a break."

"Jessica is a very attractive woman, but I saw her as the sister of a victim. For me, it was all professional."

"Don't bullshit me, Harry," Liz said, still laughing. They were cruising the streets of a high-crime area. Liz stopped teasing, put her game face back on, and made a call. "Mule, do you know who this is? Is this a good time to meet?"

"I know who you are, and I can meet you in the bowling alley parking lot, out away from the building. Fifteen minutes."

"I saved his sixteen-year-old son from going to juvenile. He was caught up in a sting with a bunch of gang members," Liz told Harry. "I knew the kid didn't belong and wasn't involved in the gang's activities. He was just hanging around, acting out a fantasy. I pulled him out of the crowd. I made a lot of noise about his age and going to juvenile. I took him home and turned him over to his father, who beat the living hell out of him before I could leave. The father, Mule, is sort of a Godfather-type in his neighborhood and a few surrounding ones. He's very low-key and doesn't hang out on the street corner playing tough guy with the rest of the boys. He has a history of violence, but never hurt an innocent person. The thugs give him a wide berth. They show him respect because they fear him. He will not allow his son to be one of the thugs. He insists on his son getting a good education and makes him do homework and get passing grades. He said he owed me and to let him know when he could pay it. I thought this would be a good time to cash in that chip."

♦

"Mule, this is my partner, Detective Harry Lincoln," Liz said as the three sat in the car away from the bowling alley. "You might be able to help us."

"Detective Kovak, I owe you one, and I know it. Tell me what you want me to do, and I'll do it if I can."

Liz told him of the kidnapping from Madison Park by two black men and of the subsequent rape in an abandoned house. "The woman was able to escape after several hours, but the body of the man was found the next day in a vacant lot three blocks from the house. He had been shot in the head. Just a week before that, there was a home invasion in the 2nd Precinct by two black males that resulted in the woman being raped and her husband shot and killed. It could be the same two."

"Detective Kovak, give me your card, and I'll do what I can. If I know something, I will call you." Mule got out of the back seat and the detectives drove away from the bowling alley.

"Ham," said Harry into the phone, "can you talk now?"

"Yeah, it's cool." Ham had finally gotten a cell phone.

"I want to give you something else. The two from Madison Park may have been involved in a home invasion in the 2nd about a week ago. Same deal—woman raped, the husband shot and killed. They also cleaned out their apartment: TVs, computers, and all the rest. Closer to you, in the 3rd, on Smith Street and Merrick Avenue, a man who just left his business was shot and killed while in his car with the motor running. The car jumped the sidewalk and did a lot of damage. His Rolex watch, diamond ring, and several hundred dollars in cash were taken. As always, call me anytime.

"Your aunt's assistance got snarled in red tape because she couldn't fill out the forms properly. None of those damn clerks would help her. I spoke with a supervisor who was very understanding and had some common sense. Bring your aunt down to the same office. Ask for Ms. Brownstone. She'll straighten it out."

"Thanks, Detective Lincoln. I owe you one."

"No Ham we're even. Remember the Mercedes last month? Now go and find those two bad dudes."

Harry broke the connection, glad he could do something for the guy who had come through.

"Okay, Harry," said Liz as they headed toward police headquarters, "let's report to Lieutenant McGee so I can get home and feed my family."

They drove in silence, Liz thinking of groceries, Harry thinking about Jessica Daniels.

CHAPTER 8

Cellblock and Bad Dog cruised the posh neighborhoods of the city's north side. The houses were huge, each in a different style; an English Tudor mansion stood here, and a few acres away was an ultra-modern structure resembling a design by Frank Lloyd Wright. Large manicured lawns with neatly trimmed shrubs and magnificent old oak and maple trees, stood sentry over the tidy estates.

Eaves and Jackson, looking for the big score, knew that rich white people who lived in that neighborhood had expensive items that could be sold for a lot of cash. They wanted the bonus of raping and degrading a white woman.

"Yo, wake the fuck up, fool," hollered Cellblock, annoyed. "You been smokin' too much of that shit. You missin' some great ass. I'll turn around so you can peep the white bitch at the mailbox. She plantin' flowers and shit; check it out when she bend over."

By the time they were able to turn around and come back, the woman was halfway up the driveway, walking toward her house. They watched her disappear into an open garage on the side of the house.

Sue Darlington had been working in the yard for almost three hours, trimming shrubs and nursing her flowerbeds. She enjoyed gardening; it got her out into the fresh air and provided the exercise she needed. After taking care of the flowers around the mailbox, her last chore, Sue returned to the house and headed for the shower. *I'll get a refreshing shower before the girls get home from school.* However, Sue Darlington made a costly mistake. She left the overhead garage door up and the door into the house unlocked.

There was a Lexus in the double garage. Eaves and Jackson drove in and parked next to it. It appeared that there was no one home except the woman seen outside a few moments earlier. Upstairs, Eaves and Jackson followed sounds coming from a large bedroom. Once in it, they saw a closed door; it was not hard to imagine that behind it was a bathroom. They quietly, carefully opened it. She was behind the shower door, singing under the cascading water, the outline of her body and her movements distorted by the frosted glass.

She was unaware of their presence. They were quiet and still, watching. The water stopped, the glass door opened, and one foot stepped onto the bathmat. She raised her eyes, which filled with shock, disbelief, fright, and then horror. Cellblock Eaves stepped to her and delivered a punch to the center of her face. Sue fell hard into the shower stall. He grabbed her by the hair and dragged her, wet and bleeding, across the tiles of the bathroom floor. In the bedroom, they picked her up and threw her onto the king-sized bed.

"Turn around, bitch, an' bury your ugly, bloody face in the pillow, an' stick that ass up in the air for me," Cellblock ordered.

They viciously raped and sodomized her.

By the time Jackson had his turn, Sue was surprised she hadn't passed out. When they were through with her, what would they do then? *Will they kill me?* Through all the pain and fear, there was the cold terror that it wouldn't be long before the girls, Ashley and Karen, came home from school. *"Oh, God",* Sue prayed. *"Please don't let that happen. Let them finish with me and leave before my children get home."*

After what seemed like an eternity of excruciating pain, degradation, and horror, the men finally lost interest in her. Cellblock and Bad Dog started looking for things to take with them, things they could turn on the street for quick cash. The TVs, laptop computers, and cell phones were the first items collected. Sue's purse, wallet, credit cards, and cash were taken next.

"We want all your jewelry an' watches an' shit. An' we want all the money you rich folk keep stashed in the house, an' if you don't give it up right now, we gonna tear this house up till we find it."

She gave it up, all of it, all the jewelry and cash that was in the house. She told them the keys to her Lexus were in a bowl on the kitchen counter. *"They can have it all",* Sue thought, *"I just want them to leave before the girls get home."*

She was sitting on the edge of the bed when Eaves stood in front of her telling her how much he hated rich white people. He smacked her across the face so hard she fell to the floor. They left, but not before he kicked and stomped her several times. It all went dark; Sue Darlington was unconscious.

♦

"911; what is your emergency?"

"Please help us. My mom is on the floor naked, and there's blood."

The 911 operator recognized the voice of a young girl. "Listen, honey, I'm sending help to you right now at 2146 Grand Terrace. Is that where you are?"

"Yes! Please hurry! My mom is hurt! She won't answer us!"

"Stay on the phone with me. Don't hang up. An ambulance and police are on the way. They should be there in a few minutes. If there is a gate to your house, make sure it's open, and unlock the door so they can get in. Everything is going to be all right as soon as they get there. How old are you, hon? Who else is in the house with you?"

"I'm twelve! My sister is nine! Please tell them to hurry! She's not moving!"

♦

EMTs stabilized Sue Darlington. She was transported by ambulance to the hospital. She awoke and was treated in the ER for her injuries. Twelve-year-old Ashley Darlington called her father at his downtown office and told him what had happened. "Can you come home right away, Daddy? There's a lady policeman staying with us until you get here."

Jake Darlington immediately left the office and rushed home. Entering the foyer, his daughters, crying, ran to him.

"How is she? What happened to her?" Jake asked the officer as he hugged and tried to comfort his daughters.

"She was still out when she left here in the ambulance. Her injuries didn't appear to be life threatening. I don't know any of the details. The detectives should be at the hospital and be able to fill you in. I'll remain here to secure your house until the detectives and crime scene people arrive to process the house for evidence. No one except those authorized will enter or disturb anything while you are at the hospital with your wife. I tried to calm the children as much as I could. They were pretty shaken."

"Thank you, Officer Borden," Jake said, reading her nametag as they walked to the front door. Jake called his mother to let her know he was dropping the girls off, that something had happened to Sue, and that he needed to get to the hospital right away.

♦

"She's just been admitted. She was raped," the ER doctor told Jake Darlington after he showed his ID to prove he was her husband. "We just sent her to the third floor; you can get her room number from the nurse's station. We did the required rape kit for the police investigation, and we treated her for injuries to her face and ribs. She also has some cuts, abrasions, and contusions. She's had a pretty rough time, but there is nothing life threatening. Your wife is going to be all right. She will probably be here a few days."

Jake pushed open the door and quietly entered the room. Sue was staring at the ceiling until he approached her.

"The girls, Jake, the girls," Sue begged. "Are they all right?" She was sobbing, not waiting for him to answer. "Please tell me they didn't hurt the girls!"

"Ashley and Karen are not hurt. They are upset, but not hurt. I dropped them at Mom and Dad's on my way here. When they got home from school, whoever was at the house was already gone."

"Thank God. Oh, thank God. I was so terrified they would still be there when the girls came home. Oh, Jake, what those filthy beasts did to me. They hurt me so bad! I can't stop thinking about it. My mind keeps playing it over and over."

Sue was still crying when a nurse appeared to introduce a sedative into the IV. Sue drifted into merciful, if temporary, sleep.

♦

"Lincoln and Kovak," Lieutenant McGee hollered, over the noise of the squad room. It was during watch change, when most of the day watch detectives were getting ready to leave for the day. The evening watch men and women were drifting in, taking coffee or soft drinks to their desks, going through their messages. The laughter and boisterous talking quieted down to murmurs.

McGee continued, "Go to the hospital and find Ms. Sue Darlington; she was raped during a home invasion in the 8th. She's been admitted. These could be the same two perps from the Madison Park kidnapping/ rape/homicide in the 7th. Bloomfield, Harrington, it could be connected to your home invasion/rape/homicide in the 2nd. I want you to go to 2146 Grand Terrace, runs off Tremont Avenue, in the 8th and work the crime scene. Eighth precinct cops are standing by and have secured the scene."

Harry and Liz found Sue Darlington under heavy sedation. Jake Darlington was with her. He told them his wife was not able to be interviewed in her present condition.

"We are very sorry about what happened to your wife. We have committed a lot of resources to identifying and finding the perpetrators. We have reason to believe they were involved in similar unsolved crimes."

Liz saw Sue Darlington's eyes look toward Harry as he talked to her husband. Liz took her hand, and when their eyes met, she said, "We will find them. They will be punished for what they did to you and to others. We'll leave you now so you can get some rest. Maybe tomorrow you'll feel more like talking with us. See you then."

Still looking at Liz, Sue Darlington nodded slowly.

CHAPTER 9

The following morning, eight people gathered around the table in the small conference room adjacent to the homicide squad room. Lieutenant McGee had called the meeting to "coordinate and communicate" whatever could be related to the recent kidnappings, home invasions, rapes, and homicides. With Lieutenant McGee were Detectives Lincoln and Kovak, Bloomfield and Harrington, and Delmont and Robinson. The eighth was Judy Wright from the state crime lab.

"Let's get started," McGee said, wrapping his knuckles on the table for the chitchat to stop. "It's apparent, at least to me, that there are enough similarities in these cases to consider them as possibly being connected. I'm forming a small task force to investigate these crimes, and you're looking at it." The lieutenant gave them a minute for his announcement to sink in.

"Lincoln and Kovak have two of the cases; the second occurred just yesterday. Bloomfield and Harrington are working the other case, with some assistance from Sandra Delmont. The first of the victims in these three cases was so traumatized that she would open up only to a woman, so I sent Delmont with them. We all know how important it is to get every detail, such as the language used by her attackers and the names they might have used to address each other. It enables us to establish a profile. Because of the nature of these cases, I'm glad to have two woman detectives on our task force.

Yesterday, Bloomfield and Harrington worked the crime scene for Lincoln and Kovak, so you are already acting together. Robinson, don't feel like you're the odd man out. You're not. The two bad guys are black, and again, as we all know, there are street blacks who know things, but will only talk to a black detective, so I want you to get down and dirty. The six of you will work these cases and others like them, should they occur. I'll work out the logistics so the rest of the squad handles everything else that we do to earn our daily bread.

Let me know of other cases you are working that will interfere with our task force, and I'll re-assign them.

"To complete the task force, we have Ms. Judy Wright, from the state crime lab. She has assisted in clearing many of your cases. Her boss, Dr. Gordon, has loaned her to our task force. She will be the 'clearing house' for anything that needs to be done: fingerprints, DNA, ballistics—whatever the crime lab does. She will cut through the red tape and give top priority to anything that could be connected to these cases, with Dr. Gordon's blessing. Ms. Wright, we are glad to have you on our task force.

"We'll meet here twice a week at this time. The next meeting will be the day after tomorrow. We'll go over all the details of the cases. Now, let's go to work and get more details that could be helpful."

"It's time for lunch, Judy," said Harry, as McGee's new task force filed out of the conference room. "Liz and I are headed for Mike's Tavern. Why don't you come with us before going back to the crime lab?"

"Why don't you and Judy go on," Liz suggested, after the two women made eye contact. "I have some exchanges to make at the mall, and I'll grab something at the food court. I'll take our car, Harry, and you ride with Judy. We'll hook up after lunch."

♦

Mike's Tavern was busy with the lunchtime crowd. Harry and Judy found a corner table at a sunlit window. "Dad and I came here quite a bit. I miss him so very much." Tears welled in Harry's eyes.

Judy wanted to hold and comfort him, but that was not a good thing to do in the crowded restaurant. "I know you do, Harry. I liked him for the short time that I knew him. I had just started at the crime lab. Anyone who spoke of Detective Ben Lincoln, from Dr. Gordon on down, spoke with affection and respect," Judy said, holding his hand in both of hers.

"Sometimes, when I think about him, my emotions get the better of me. On occasion, I get confused about my feelings. Am I angry? Am I sympathetic and understanding, or do I feel cheated that he's not here for me? Now, let's talk about you and me."

As the waiter set down their lunch, Judy thought, *Well, that sounds ominous. He's not about to get down on one knee here amidst the lunchtime crowd at Mike's Tavern and give you a diamond ring, Judy.*

It's more likely you are about to be dumped. Remember, you told him you were not like other women, so if he does dump you, don't get all weepy.

"Judy, I just want to reinforce what I said after our first time together. I don't want to commit to one woman, any woman. I want to feel free to date any woman who interests me, and want anyone that I do date to understand that, and for them to feel the same and to do the same. I want them to know there is no future with me. It wouldn't be fair of me to do otherwise."

Harry stopped talking briefly, although he had more on his mind, and began to eat his fish-and-chips. Judy relaxed and started on her lunch.

After a few bites, Harry started talking again. "Judy, I practice safe sex; I use protection for us both, but that's not enough, so due to HIV and AIDS, and all the other diseases, I get myself tested on a regular basis. If you date other men, it would be good for you to do the same, and to insist they use protection. I may be crossing a line here, suggesting you do this, but I enjoy being with you and want to continue to see you. When we are together, I want our minds to be in the moment, not on those other concerns."

Harry waited for the barrage of indignant words. After a long silence, Judy was still smiling, so he continued. "If you are free tomorrow night, I'd like us to have dinner at a restaurant of your choice and spend the rest of the evening together at 'your place or mine,' that tired old cliché."

"I'd love to, Harry," Judy said, still smiling. "Let's meet at Ralph's Steak House in midtown. Ralph's are the best steaks in the city, but it's kind of pricey, so let's go Dutch. I'll try to get seven o'clock reservations; if not, I'll let you know." After a pause, she continued, "And for dessert, I'd prefer your place and that wonderful shower. In my apartment, I have to climb into the bathtub to get a shower. Anyway, I'll have my car and follow you home after dinner so you won't have to get out of your nice, warm bed in the middle of the night to take me home like last time."

After Judy left for the crime lab, Liz picked Harry up at Mike's Tavern, and they headed to the hospital. They found Sue Darlington in a deep sleep, her husband still at her bedside.

"She cried most of the night. When I tried to talk to her, she started screaming and became hysterical," Jake explained. "She was given sedatives twice until she calmed down and went to sleep. I don't know when she'll wake up, and I don't know if she will be able to talk to you."

"You have our cards, Mr. Darlington," Harry reminded him. "Call either of us when she's ready. Keep in mind that the sooner we get details about the attack, the sooner we will be able to track down the ones we need to put away."

CHAPTER 10

Police dispatcher: "Car 1127, at the Greenfield Apartments, 2804 Seneca Avenue, Apartment 3D-Delta; Signal 39 [the radio code for 'Information for an Officer']. The woman there has information on a shooting."

Car 1127: "I copy. Signal 39 at the Greenfield Apartments on Seneca, Apartment 3D-Delta."

◆

"Yo, blood, you sounded just like a bitch," Bad Dog told his smirking partner.

"Yeah, Dog," Cellblock bragged. "I fooled the shit out of that 911 chump on the telephone; I hope that bitch po-lice get the call. This be her beat."

Officer Niki Reston, working her regular Car 1127 on the morning watch got the call at 3:51 a.m. Officer Reston parked at Building Three and locked her patrol car. Walking up the stairs to apartment 3D, she radioed the dispatcher that she had arrived on call. She knocked on the door. It opened, and she was immediately pulled into the dark room. Before she had time to react, she was hit across her face and knocked to the floor, stunned.

"Get her gun, quick, an' the radio, too. See if she don't have another gun aroun' her ankles, an' turn her over so I can put these motherfuckin' handcuffs on behind her back," ordered Cellblock. "Now tape her mouth with the duct tape. Don' cover her nose. I don' want her to die before I can get some of that pussy."

Niki Reston regained her senses to a pounding pain in her nose and mouth. As her head cleared, she realized she was on a hard, cold floor with two men over her, pulling at her clothes, grabbing and groping at her. Her leather Sam Browne belt that held her equipment came off first. Niki tried to fight, but her hands were held together behind her. She couldn't scream through the tape over her mouth.

"Shit, man. I can't get her shirt off 'cause of those motherfuckin' handcuffs. Take the key, bro, and get them off. An' this fuckin' bullet proof vest got to come over her head, an' that tee shirt."

As Niki rubbed her wrists after the tightness of the handcuffs, Eaves slapped her hard across the face. "That's just a sample of how I'm gonna put the hurt on you, girl, if you start fighting. Now let's see what you got," he said, leering as her bra was removed. "Look at them fine tits, Dog. Now, get them pants an' panties off an' put them handcuffs back on her."

Officer Niki Reston was naked and helpless. In the darkness, she saw it was a vacant apartment, and the only illumination came from an outside street light.

"Too bad you a po-lice, brown-skin girl, 'cause you look fine. You got some good-looking stuff out that motherfuckin' uniform. You look lots better than those white bitches, an' I know you got lots more rhythm in your black ass." Cellblock showed her the garden clippers he held in his hand. "If you don't move that ass when I want you to, I'm gonna cut off them pretty nipples of yours."

He forced open her legs and lay between them. "Just wait your turn, Dog. I'm gonna fire her up, an' then you can have her."

Her mouth was so tightly taped she could hardly breath, talk, beg, or scream. After both had violently raped her, Cellblock turned her over and sodomized her, the same as he had the others. "This sista's got a bitchin' ass on her, but the front door was better. Get some of that black ass, bro, but slam it fast."

They had to get out quickly. They did not have time for more fun. Before they left, Cellblock said, "Nigga bitch, you a fuckin' pol-ice, so I gotta fuck you up."

Then to her horror, he cut off both nipples. Her eyes did the screaming that was prevented by the tape across her mouth. He kept smiling as he forced her gun up between her legs. Inserted it. Pulled the trigger.

♦

Police dispatcher: "1127."
Long pause and no response.
"Calling car 1127."
(Still no response)
The sector sergeant monitoring the radio transmission asked how long 1127 had been out on the call and the location. Given that

information, he was also advised that a neighbor had called about hearing a gunshot.

"Send cars to that location right away. I'm on my way, also."

Police dispatcher: "Cars in the area of Greenfield Apartments, 2804 Seneca Avenue, possible Signal 63 [Officer needs help], gunshots reported. Car 1127 is at that location. Check in apartment 3D-Delta."

Officer Niki Reston was found a few minutes later, dead in a pool of blood on the wooden floor of the vacant apartment. Her mouth was taped, her hands were cuffed, and most of the blood came from between her legs. There was blood on her breasts where her nipples had been cut off. The first two cops to arrive stood frozen over her and stared at their mutilated colleague. A female officer, who got there seconds later, ran back down to her patrol car and returned with a blanket. She covered Niki Reston's nude body to preserve a measure of dignity before the rest of the responders arrived.

Homicide detectives Brown and Cohen, working the monthly morning watch, arrived shortly afterwards. The neighbor who had called in the gunshot also said he heard noises on the stairs. When he looked out, he told the detectives, he saw two black males running to a dark car. It drove away at a high rate of speed, south on Seneca Avenue. The detectives supervised the gathering of evidence by the crime scene techs. When the medical examiner finished and ordered the body removed to the county morgue, Brown and Cohen returned to headquarters.

♦

"When Delmont and Robinson get in," McGee said, "turn everything, and I mean every small detail you've got on Officer Reston's homicide, over to them. They will be assigned that case. Then, you two get home and get some sleep."

As the day watch detectives arrived for duty, the buzz over morning coffee was shock and anger about the grisly murder of Officer Reston.

"Brown and Cohen handled the scene on the morning watch and interviewed a witness," McGee said to the somber day watch detectives. "We think it's the same two perps who committed the recent rash of violent crimes. Our task force will handle it. There will be a meeting at watch change this afternoon. I want you all to be there."

♦

Twenty homicide detectives assembled in the lineup room, everyone talking about the brutal murder of one of their own. Lieutenant McGee stood before them.

"As you all know, there has been a series of violent crimes. Rape and robbery was the apparent motive, resulting in at least three homicides. The same two black males probably committed them. I've created an in-house task force to handle only these crimes. Delmont and Robinson of the task force will take the lead in the investigation of Officer Reston's murder. I expect any leads you develop to be passed on to them. That goes for the other cases, too. No one will work from the office today. All of you hit the streets. Go find your snitches and put the fear of God in them."

♦

The church was packed with people, many standing along the walls, and there was a large somber crowd outside. After the service, the mourners lined up for the ride to the cemetery. The funeral procession was three miles long. It was made up mostly of city and metro area patrol cars and many others, representing law enforcement agencies from other states. Twenty city police motorcycles and motorcycle units from surrounding departments led it. To the rear of the hearse carrying the body of Officer Niki Reston and the three limos transporting the immediate family, were the sedate, black city vehicles of the mayor, the police chief, and all the dignitaries who chose to attend. In line also were numerous private vehicles that followed.

En route to the cemetery, the major intersections on the surface streets were controlled by motor units. On the freeway, state police units blocked the entrance ramps and conducted a rolling roadblock at the rear of the procession. At the cemetery, all the honors due an officer killed in-the-line-of duty were conducted—the sorrowful sounds from a lone bag-piper, mournful "Taps" played by a trumpeter, a twenty-one gun salute, and a helicopter fly-over in the missing member formation. The United States flag that covered the casket was then folded and presented to Niki Reston's husband Alfred by the chief of police. Huddled closely and crying softly, were their two young children.

CHAPTER 11

The cops were pissed. No, they were enraged, and not just in the 7th Precinct, where Officer Niki Reston was assigned. Every cop, at every level, in every precinct and mini-precinct throughout the department felt it. Their rage intensified as the gruesome details emerged. Every cop in the city, every rank—female and male, black and white—and with the media and public looked to the Homicide Squad. Within the squad, the focus was on the task force.

The meeting was tense. Lieutenant McGee, his anger clearly in his face, was demanding. "We are going to catch those vicious, goddamn brutal, savage animals. I expect you all to work as long as there is a lead to follow, a snitch to lean on, or a witness to interview. If your workload gets too heavy, I'll expand the task force, but goddamn it, I can't deplete the squad too much because the everyday shit that we handle is not going to stop. Eight-hour days will become twelve- and fourteen-hour days and nights. Forget about off days! If we have to, we'll set up cots in the office and bring in food. That's the way you'll live until those bastards are in chains."

Judy Wright said, "Since Dr. Gordon insisted that these cases take top priority, the DNA analysis has been completed. Lieutenant, we can now be certain that the same two men were involved in the four rapes, according to the DNA taken from those victims. Two sets of fingerprints were found at each of the crime scenes. They have been entered into the FBI's database for identification. Also, the results of the voice analysis test determined the 911 call in Officer Reston's murder was made by a male, not a female. Ballistic tests show that Roy Singer and Edmond Franklin were shot with the same Smith and Wesson 9mm semi-automatic pistol. Officer Reston was shot and killed with her department issued Smith and Wesson .40 caliber semi-automatic service weapon. The weapon is missing, but the bullet was matched to the sample round fired and kept on file for every weapon issued by the department."

"Good work, Judy," McGee said, addressing her by her first name, which surprised her. "Now we know for certain that these vicious crimes were committed by the same men, and we have indisputable evidence to back it up. Bloomfield, draw up the master matrix. Yours is the most comprehensive, concise, complete, and readable. Funnel any information that needs to be entered on Bloomfield's matrix to him for listing. Because these crimes are connected, each pair of you will be working on every case. That means when any report or follow-up narrative is generated, it is to be distributed to all members of this task force. There will be no secrets and no turf guarding within the task force. If I find this order has been violated, it will not be pleasant for the guilty party. Any questions?"

The lieutenant looked around the room. None offered questions or comments.

"Go home now and make arrangements with your families. Be sure they know and understand your absence from time to time. Report back here tomorrow at the same time. Play time is over!"

♦

She sat in the reception area at the restaurant. Judy was early and had decided to wait for him there, rather than at the bar. She would have liked to relax with a glass of wine before Harry's arrival, but did not want to attract unwanted attention.

Judy thought about his frank conversation with her yesterday during lunch. She wasn't sure how she felt about it. She certainly understood and agreed with his wanting to protect himself and the women he'd be intimate with from HIV, AIDS, and other STDs.

Harry Lincoln is a remarkable man, she thought, *but I've always known that. So perk up, Judy, and cherish the times together, however brief that might be. He made it clear that there was no future with him, and I told him that I was not a clinging woman. Like he said, enjoy the moment.*

Harry walked into the restaurant, saw her sitting there, and thought that every time he saw her recently, she seemed more and more attractive—her wit, her candor, her smile, and her figure, not shown through her work attire.

"Hello, Harry, if this is your first time eating one of Ralph's steaks, I bet you'll be back."

"I have heard about these steaks, and I'm glad you suggested it. I'm very pleased to be here with you," Harry said.

"A couple of things have been on my mind," Judy said, after they were seated and sipping on glasses of wine. "There is no one I'd rather be with until the wee hours of the morning than you, Harry Lincoln. However, with us working closely on the task force, it will become obvious, and I don't want tongues to start wagging. Liz knows, Harry. Women have radar about these things that sometimes men are oblivious to, and I started to feel awkward this afternoon."

"What's your point? It's no secret," Harry said. "We are two unattached adults who can do whatever personal thing we want."

"You are right, Harry, but I think it would be best to keep us on a professional basis until the task force business is over and we go back to our regular routines. So since we are here, and we will be together after dinner, let's make this entire night special."

The evening was very special, and it lasted until well after midnight. When there was no more left to give to each other, Judy slipped quietly out of Harry's bed and showered. Harry was half-awake when she came back into the bedroom and dressed. He had watched when she took them off, and he watched her now when she put the same clothes back on. She bent and kissed him tenderly as he lay there.

"Goodnight, Harry. I had a wonderful time. Thank you for making me feel special." Without another word, Judy left, closing the door quietly behind her.

◆

They gathered for the ten a.m. task force meeting. Liz leaned over and whispered, "You look like shit, Harry, and Judy looks even worse. What have you done to that poor girl?"

"Thanks for the compliment, Liz, but do I detect a bit of envy?"

Liz just smiled. McGee entered, and the room became quiet.

"Okay, listen up. The chief has called for a meeting with our task force. Be in the chief's conference room in fifteen minutes with your case files. Finish whatever you are chewing and leave your coffee mugs on your desks."

◆

Police Chief Robert Lansing, sitting at the head of the large conference table, addressed Deputy Chief Glenn Watkins, the nine police precinct commanders, the special operations commander and Lieutenant McGee and his task force. Judy Wright was the only civilian present.

"I want to thank each of you for being here this morning, I know how busy you all are. First, I want to acknowledge Ms. Judy Wright, one of the top analysts from the state crime lab. Ms. Wright, we are fortunate and thankful to have you working with the task force. I spoke with Dr. Gordon this morning and expressed my gratitude to him for the good work you've already done as a member of this team. Let's get right to it. Lieutenant McGee, please bring us up to date."

"In the past week, there have been three homicides and four rapes. One was a 7th Precinct police officer. Her rape and murder occurred while she was on duty. In two other cases, a female was raped and the male with her was murdered. In one case, the victim was a husband; in the other case, it was a boyfriend. We now have evidence that the same two black males committed all of these crimes. Two of the three female victims can identify them; the third hasn't been able to talk yet. A 9mm semi-automatic was the murder weapon in two of the homicides; it has not been found. Officer Reston was killed with her service weapon; it is missing. There will be sketches of both suspects made today from descriptions provided by two of the rape victims. They will be distributed throughout the department. I would like any information and all leads to be forwarded to the task force. That's all I have at this time, Chief."

"Thank you, Lieutenant McGee, and his request is a direct order from me. All leads and information will be forwarded to the task force. The media has had extensive coverage of Officer Reston's murder, but they do not know that we have two suspects, or that the same two suspects committed the other three cases. We have to decide whether it's in the interest of the task force to give out these details. What's your feeling on it, lieutenant?"

"If the sketch goes department-wide, chief, the media will get wind of it anyway," McGee answered. "Why don't we give it to them in connection with Officer Reston's murder and let everyone see what her killers look like. When they ask who provided the descriptions needed to make the sketches, tell them witness identities are confidential. Let's not connect the other incidents with her homicide yet."

"Okay, we'll go with that for now," the chief decided. "Deputy Chief Watkins and I will handle the media when the sketch is ready. After that, refer all comment requests to Sergeant Bowser in Public Affairs. We are not ready to go public with the task force. Lieutenant McGee, brief Chief of Detectives Watkins daily. That will do it for now. Thank you all."

236

CHAPTER 12

At the hospital, Harry and Liz found Sue Darlington propped up in bed, talking with her husband. They shook hands with Jake Darlington, who introduced the detectives to his wife.

"We're glad to find you a little better," Harry said. "We hope you feel well enough to tell us what happened."

Sue Darlington looked from one to the other and said, "Detective Liz Kovak, is it? Can you and I talk privately?"

Liz and Harry exchanged glances. Harry said, "Mr. Darlington, let's go down to the cafeteria and grab some coffee."

"What is going to happen now, Ms. Darlington," Liz began, "is that I'll be taking notes as you talk. After you finish, I'll ask you some questions. It's very important for you to tell me, however embarrassing you think it is what they said, and how they said it. I also need to know what they made you do, what they did to you, and how they did it. You may not think so, but you have to believe that anything like that could help us catch and convict them.

"When I return to my office, I'll type it all into the computer and bring a hard copy back for your review and signature, which will become your official statement and part of the case file. Criminals, in this case rapists, say and do the same things each time; we call that their MO, or modus operandi, which means, 'the way they do things.' It may be a way to identify them, hunt them down, and arrest them. It also makes a stronger case for the district attorney's office when it comes time to prosecute. Tomorrow, a police sketch artist will be here for you to help her draw a likeness of those two."

Sue drank some water, took a couple of deep breaths, and with downcast eyes started talking. "I came out of my shower. There they were. In my bathroom. Watching me. Then everything happened so fast, like fast-forwarding something on TV. I was hit hard in my face. They broke my nose. I slipped on the wet tile floor, fell, and hit my mouth—on one of the faucets, I suppose. I broke two of my teeth.

Next thing I know, I'm being dragged across the floor by my hair. They pulled me into my bedroom and threw me on my bed. The pain in my face was awful. My face was bloody, and I was still wet from the shower. I remember shaking uncontrollably. The one that seemed to be the leader kept telling the other one about the basement. And the main floor. And the front door. And the back door. And the penthouse.

"Detective Kovak, that whole time I was worried for my two girls. I knew they would be home from school soon. What would those two animals do to my daughters? I wanted them to do whatever they were going to do to me then leave. Leave before my girls got home.

"The leader, the one that did the most, said the most. He kept slapping me. Calling me a white bitch. A white whore. Said he was going to show me that black was beautiful. Made me turn around and kneel on the bed. He raped me like I was a dog."

Sue Darlington began to cry. She couldn't continue. Liz said she should take a break. "You're doing just fine. You're telling it like it should be told."

In a few minutes, Sue Darlington was composed and ready to continue her statement. "When he was finished in my vagina, he pushed himself into my rectum. Very hard. Very deep. It hurt so much I screamed. He shouted, 'Shut the fuck up, you motherfucking whore,' and he punched me in the back of my head. I kept screaming. He kept pushing into me. He kept punching my head and back. Then he turned me over on my back. Told me to take him in my mouth."

Liz interrupted, "Is that the way he said it? 'Take me in your mouth'?"

"No, that's not the way he said it."

"Just take your time. Don't be embarrassed. I've dealt with scum like them many times and have heard it all before."

"He said, 'Lick my shit off my sweet dick.' Then he said to suck his big, black dick like a lollypop. He said, 'If I feel any teeth scraping, I'm gonna knock every motherfuckin' tooth out your motherfuckin' mouth.' I knew then what he meant by the front door, the back door, the main floor, the basement, and the penthouse. The other one did those same things to me.

"When they finally lost interest in me, they began looking for things to steal. I told them where all the valuables were so they would hurry and leave. I gave them the keys to my car. Before they left, the first one knocked me to the floor and started kicking me. I must have passed out. I don't remember anything after that. I think I woke up in the ambulance; I'm not sure. When I woke, despite what happened to me, I was consumed with anguish about my daughters. Would they get home before those vicious animals left? I am glad that didn't happen. I can easily deal with my pain. I just thank God that didn't happen."

The two women looked at each other, a silent understanding between them.

Sue broke the silence. "They hurt me something awful—my nose, mouth, ribs, and kidneys. I have a punctured lung and many minor injuries, but in time, all will heal. What will not go away is my shame. I've been abused, humiliated, and degraded. I am soiled forever. I am dirty, so dirty that my husband won't want to touch me again. I am so ashamed!"

"No, Sue. You have no reason to be ashamed. They came into your home and attacked you. When the safety of your children was at stake, your maternal instincts kicked in. You did what you had to do. You did it for your children. You did what you had to do so that the rapists would leave before the children came home. If your husband truly loves you, and he does, if staying at your bedside for the three days and nights is any indication, I'm sure his love is strong enough to feel even closer to you now."

Liz embraced Sue. She stopped crying. By the time Harry and Jake returned, the women were chatting about mundane things. "I've taken Ms. Darlington's statement. Let's get back to the office, and I'll get it on the computer," Liz said to Harry, who had already asked Mr. Darlington to list all of the stolen items, especially those with serial numbers.

"We'll come by tomorrow to pick up that list," Harry said. "Hope you are feeling better, Ms. Darlington."

On the way back to police headquarters, Liz told Harry of Sue Darlington's ordeal. "They gave her a rough time. The docs will put her back together and her wounds will heal. Unfortunately, the psychological scars are going to be with her for a long time."

"Yeah, Liz, but at least they didn't murder her. Niki Reston is dead! She can't come back from that. Maybe she could have come back from psychological scars."

◆

Both stolen cars were recovered the following day. The Singers' Toyota was found parked near one of the low-income city housing projects. The Darlington's Lexus was found stripped of its sound system and GPS on a dirt road several miles outside of the city.

The sketch of the two suspects made from Sue Darlington's description matched the sketches drawn from descriptions provided by the two other rape victims.

CHAPTER 13

Liz's cell phone rang in her purse. Liz answered on the third ring.

"Detective Kovak, this is Mule. I might have something for you. Can you meet me at the same place as last time?"

"Yes, Mule, my partner and I will be there in fifteen, twenty minutes."

Liz stuck her head into Lieutenant McGee's office and told him of the phone call and meeting. "Lieu, this could be important information from a strong street boss, a neighborhood powerhouse. We think this could be important enough to hold up the task force meeting until we get back. We'll try to be quick."

They pulled up alongside Mule in the bowling alley parking lot, driver-side to driver-side, so they could talk without getting out of their cars.

"Hey, Mule," Liz said. "We bugged out of a meeting with the boss to come over. What's up?"

"The little grocery store at Griffin and Wells in the 4th, the one that was robbed the other night and three people were killed. The old man that owned the store and his wife, who worked there with him, were gunned down. Those two people did a lot for the folk who live in the neighborhood. They made sure nobody went hungry, especially older folk. An old black lady was in the store when it was robbed. They shot her, too. Someone was looking out of their window across the street and saw two black dudes in dark clothing run out of the store, down Griffin, jump into a black car, and haul ass." After a pause, Mule said, "You asked about two blacks doing a lot of bad shit all over the city, so I thought you might want to know about that."

"We certainly do want to know. It's vague, but it will help. Now we can zero in on the same two black males," Liz agreed. "Thanks, Mule. If you hear anything else about those two, please call me. We've got to bug out, back to the boss's meeting."

◆

"So," grumbled Lieutenant McGee, "tell me what you learned while we were waiting for you to return."

"A witness saw two black males run from the triple homicide at that small Mom and Pop in the 4th," Liz said. "It could be the same two who are responsible for all our cases."

Detective Ronald Robinson said. "That's interesting, Liz, because last night I got information on the homicide you and Harry have on Merrick Avenue. I was told the driver was shot on Smith Street before he turned onto Merrick, where he jumped the curb and did all that damage on the sidewalk. When the car was stopped for the stop sign on Smith, two black males were seen scuffling with the driver."

"That gives us a reference point, Ron, just like Liz's info on the grocery store," Harry said, asking if he got a description of the two.

"I'm afraid it's kind of lean. You know, —two black males in their 20s, average size, dark clothing, baggy pants, hooded sweatshirts with the hoods up. My snitch said they could not be identified."

"Okay," McGee interrupted, "let's get this right; first we need to know if the homicides were committed by the same two the task force is investigating. We know that the same 9mm semi-automatic was the murder weapon in both homicides. Officer Reston was killed with her.40 caliber semi-automatic. In the two cases that gave us this information, there were slugs recovered from the victims."

McGee then turned to Judy Wright. "Judy, I'd like you to follow up with the ballistics people at the crime lab and do a comparison. See if the slugs from the grocery store and the driver of the car match our cases. Try to get the results for us at our next meeting, if you can."

The lieutenant sat, deep in thought, for another minute. Then he said, "The chief talked about having a press conference about those two. He understands that there is a serious public safety problem and that the public should be told these crimes are connected. He believes that people should be aware of the threat and take precautions. We are checking two additional cases—four more homicides. If ballistics gives us a match, he will want to go public.

"I've thought about requesting help from the Special Operations Section, in particular, from their decoy squad. However, these two perps are hitting all over the map. If we do get a ballistics match, we'll know that rape is not their only motive. It would be difficult, if not impossible, for the SOS people to know where to set up a decoy operation."

McGee paused and then added, "Bloomfield, when Judy comes back with the ballistics results, be sure to have your matrix up to date. I'll let you all know about the press conference. He'll want the task force there. Okay, that's it for now. Let's go to work."

"Harry, I've gotten a call from Amy's pre-school. She's not feeling well. She threw up her snack. I'm taking the afternoon off. McGee approved it. See you tomorrow."

♦

Harry sat in the car and thought about Jessica Daniels. He also thought about Lisa and thought this might be a good time to check on her.

"Hello, this is Harry Lincoln. Is this Lisa or Jessica?"

"Hi, Detective Harry Lincoln. This is Jessica. Hold on a minute, and I'll get Lisa for you."

"Hello, Detective Lincoln, it's good to hear from you. How are you and Detective Kovak?"

"We are fine thanks. I was about to have some lunch. I thought I would call to see how you were getting along."

"I'm doing all right, I guess. Slow, but sure, and still having nightmares. Jess and I were getting ready to have lunch also. Why don't you and Detective Kovak come over and eat with us? She made a big pot of split pea soup that she serves over rice with large chunks of ham."

"Liz had to take the afternoon off. Her daughter wasn't feeling well, and Liz went to pick her up from school. You make it sound inviting. I like split pea and could use a hot bowl of soup. I can be there in fifteen, twenty minutes."

"Lunch will be ready when you get here."

Lisa hung up and exchanged looks with Jessica—looks they both understood.

♦

The following morning at the task force meeting, Harry casually mentioned his lunch the previous day with the Daniel sisters. Liz gave Harry some tongue-in-cheek grief about it. "You just happened to 'check on' Lisa Daniels yesterday when I was off. Well, I'm glad I wasn't there to see you and Jessica making goo-goo eyes at each other." Liz laughed and gently punched Harry's arm.

Lieutenant McGee called the group to order and asked Judy Wright to give her report. "The ballistics comparisons were completed last night," she began. "They proved that all of the homicides, with the exception of Officer Reston, were killed with the same 9mm semi-automatic pistol. That includes Roy Singer, Edmond Franklin, and the three from the grocery store—Mr. and Mrs. Rothstein and the customer, Ms. Hattie Mayes—and the driver of the car that wrecked on Merrick, Bernard Rosen."

"Okay, now we know that rape is not the only motive of those bastards," McGee said. "There will be a press conference at two o'clock this afternoon. We have been directed to be there. We'll meet in the chief's office precisely thirty minutes before. Bloomfield, bring your matrix. The chief and chief of detectives will want to have a look. I'll see you all then. Don't be late."

CHAPTER 14

Members of the news media were gathered in the public affairs room. It was a noisy gathering until the principals entered. Then the shouting, gabbing, and laughing in the room stopped. Chief Robert Lansing led the group to seats across the front, facing the room. Deputy Chief Glenn Watkins and Lieutenant James McGee with the task force followed him.

Public affairs Sergeant Martin Bowser opened the press conference, yielding the podium to Chief Lansing.

"In the last couple of weeks, we have experienced a rash of violent crimes. Of course, all crimes in which people are injured are violent. These have been particularly vicious. They have included homicide, rape, home invasion, kidnapping, and armed robbery." The chief paused and said, "We have recently developed evidence that these crimes were committed by the same two individuals. We believe these individuals raped and murdered police officer Niki Reston. Deputy Chief Watkins and I want the public to be aware of this and take precautions. The victims have been chosen in a variety of ways, and the attacks have occurred in different locations in the city. A task force has been created from within the homicide squad to investigate these crimes. Homicide lieutenant James McGee will give you details and then take questions."

Lieutenant McGee faced the crowd and began. "We are looking to identify two black males on a deadly crime spree. We have committed the resources of the entire police department to this effort. The tip of the spear is the newly created task force behind me. They are homicide detectives with a senior analyst from the state crime lab. This task force will be responsible for the investigation and arrest of the suspects. We have DNA evidence from the rape victims that belongs to the same two men, and we have fingerprints, which are currently being run through the FBI database. We have ballistics comparison results that show that all of the homicide victims were killed with the same gun, except for Officer Reston, who was killed with her service weapon.

Three witnesses can identify the two suspects. They have looked through countless mug shots and have assisted the police sketch artist with drawings, which have been given to each of you as you came in. We ask that you show these drawings on TV and in the newspaper. Put the drawings on your websites so that people who get their news online will see them. Additionally, you have been provided with copies of reports of the crimes that we have outlined. I'll take a couple of questions."

"Lieutenant McGee," asked a TV reporter. "Have these crimes been committed in the same manner? Have they established a pattern?"

"No," answered McGee. "Two started as home invasions, one as a kidnapping, and two as armed robberies."

"Have there been any particular times of the day or night, or days of the week?" asked another newspaperman. "What about different areas of the city?"

"No, they happened all over the city, at different times of the day and on different days of the week. All of that information is contained in the incident reports, which you were given on your way in. I'll take one more question."

"If these crimes continue, will the task force be expanded?" a veteran TV reporter asked.

"That decision will be made by the chief, when and if the time comes."

Sergeant Bowser stepped to the podium and signaled a close to the press conference.

♦

Detectives Robinson, Delmont, Bloomfield, and Harrington went back to Seneca Avenue to canvass the apartment complex where Officer Reston was killed. They would expand their inquiries to the surrounding area. Lincoln and Kovak spent the rest of the afternoon in the squad room on their computers. Harry entered all of the victims' statements into one file, and Liz checked all 9 mm semi-automatics stolen in the past twelve months. Halfway through the statements, Harry got up, went to the lieutenant's office, and although the door was open, knocked on the door facing. McGee was concentrating on piles of paper work scattered among books and manuals stacked on his desk. Without looking up, he grunted, "Come in."

Harry stepped in and closed the door behind him.

"Is there a problem, Lincoln?" McGee asked.

"No, Lieu, not a problem," Harry answered. "I need some personal and professional advice. I'm thinking about something, but I don't want to get myself in a jam, or cause you and the department any embarrassment."

"Sounds kinda serious," said McGee, now paying attention. "I'm listening, Harry. What's on your mind?"

"Lisa Daniels, the rape victim who was kidnapped from Madison Park with Edmond Franklin. She was the one sexually assaulted in an abandoned house. He was murdered."

"Of course, I recall, Harry. What do you want to tell me or ask me?"

"Well, Lieu, when Lisa was released from the hospital, she went to stay with her sister, Jessica Daniels. One day last week, Liz got a call from Lisa, and we went by to check on her. Yesterday, Liz had to take the afternoon off to be with her sick kid. The Daniels sisters invited me to the house for lunch. I enjoyed it. Here's the punch line. I'd like to take the sister, Jessica, out to dinner. You know, on a date."

"When it comes to affairs of the heart, Harry, I'm not the guy to ask. However, the way I see it, if she's not a married woman and you're not attached to anyone, then it's no one's business. Except you are investigating a major crime spree with multiple felonies, and the sister is one of the victims. Before you know it, some enterprising reporter will sniff it out and makes something out of nothing, which will become a juicy sidebar to the main story."

Harry saw the look on McGee's face. It was the same kind of look his dad had just before telling Harry something he didn't want to hear.

"Will you get in a jam? Maybe. Will the police department be embarrassed? Probably. Will I be embarrassed? I don't embarrass too easily. You're not doing anything wrong. The problem will surely evolve from how it's perceived. The media pumps it up like a huge goddamn blimp, and the public eats that shit up. What am I saying to you? What's my advice to you? Leave this one alone for the time being, Harry. You can have half the single women in this town and some of the married ones, too. Wait until this case is over. When those two animals are in chains, then take her out and celebrate."

Harry left the lieutenant's office knowing McGee was right. It was just common sense.

CHAPTER 15

Annette Jenkins and Penny Bosworth got off the elevator on the fourth level of the parking garage. They were both feeling the effects of the wine they had consumed that evening. It was after one o'clock in the morning, some seventeen hours since Annette had parked her Toyota Camry in one of the few parking spaces left during the morning rush. The two women car-pooled to work, alternating cars every other day. Annette and Penny had decided to stay downtown after work to have some dinner and visit several of the clubs within walking distance of their office building.

"It's kind of creepy here with no one around," Annette commented as they looked for Annette's car. "I know we parked on this level, but those two are the only cars I see. Maybe I parked around that bend." They walked around the bend. There it was. Leaning against it were two black men dressed in an exaggerated "gangsta" look, emulating rappers.

The women turned and ran, but in their strappy heels, they only made it to the third level when Jamal Eaves and Bernard Jackson caught them. They each took a woman and slammed her against the wall. Both women screamed and the men punched them.

"Shut the fuck up. Jus' shut the fuck up," Cellblock yelled at them. "You can scream all night long. Ain't no one gonna hear you up here. We don't wanna hear no more screamin'. We just wanna hear you beggin', an' I mean beggin' to be our bitches."

Annette began to protest and was slapped so hard, she fell down in a sitting position. Her head hit the concrete wall she was sitting against.

Cellblock got up close to her face. "You got somethin' else you wanna say, bitch?"

Both women sat and silently cried.

Cellblock grabbed Annette by her hair. Bad Dog had Penny the same way. They dragged and pulled both women, stumbling, up the ramp to the next level, to a small box truck across from Annette's Camry, where they were picked up and thrown into the cargo area.

"Okay, Dog," leered Cellblock. "There's plenty room in here for us all. Let's do some bad shit now."

♦

Several hours later, when people started to arrive for work and parking spaces were filling up in the garage, a car pulled in beside the truck and two men got out. They heard pounding and cries for help coming from the truck. The rear overhead door was latched from the outside. The men slid it open. Inside, they saw two hysterical, bloody, disheveled women. One of the men called 911, and requested an ambulance and police.

Lieutenant McGee stepped out of his office and called into the squad room. "Lincoln, Kovak, Robinson, Delmont."

When the four detectives had gathered in the office, McGee gave them a few sketchy details about the victims from the downtown parking deck.

"Get over to the ER. Find out what you can. It appears that the same two mutts were at it again last night."

♦

The four detectives sat in Dr. David Deutch's office. He was the chief ER physician in the city's largest trauma one hospital. After they identified themselves as homicide detectives, the doctor said, "Those two women who were just admitted sustained multiple injuries due to physical and sexual abuse," Dr. Deutch said. "Annette Jenkins, age twenty-five, has a slight concussion, a broken nose, both eyes swollen closed, and various cuts, abrasions, and contusions. The trauma to her vagina and rectum was considerable. The injuries to Penny Bosworth, age twenty-three, were only slightly different. She had a broken jaw, a fractured cheekbone, one eye swollen closed, and various cuts, abrasions, and contusions. She had the same trauma to her vagina and rectum. When they arrived, both were hysterical, and they had to be sedated, but they were able to tell the trauma team they had been attacked by two men. Could it be the same two men who have been raping and murdering for the past two weeks?"

"We believe so, doctor," said Harry. "That's why the four of us are here. We are part of the task force to identify and arrest those two before they can do any more damage."

"If I can do anything to help, let me know," said Dr. Deutch. "The women are under heavy sedation. I doubt you'll be able to talk to them until tomorrow. However, they will be here for the next few days."

After thanking the doctor and leaving the hospital, the four detectives split up. Harry Lincoln and Liz Kovak went to interview the men who released the victims from the truck. Sandra Delmont and Ronald Robinson went to run down the details of the truck, which after a quick online inquiry, was confirmed stolen.

Wyatt and Hines, Inc., an engineering firm located on the twenty-eighth floor of the building, above the parking garage, was where the attacks took place. James Cerbone and Joseph Pfeiger, the electrical engineers who rescued the women, were called to Mr. Wyatt's office. After the introductions were made, the engineers accompanied Harry and Liz to a conference room.

Liz said, "It's our understanding that you gentlemen found those women in the truck this morning and called 911. Tell us what happened."

"It was just luck," said Mr. Cerbone. "Joe and I ride together to work each day and park in the building's parking deck. This morning, we drove up to the fourth level and saw a space next to a truck. Joe even commented that we'd never seen a truck up here."

"The truck was parked to our right," said Mr. Pfeiger. "I was in the passenger's seat. When I opened my door, I heard pounding and screaming coming from the truck. Jim got out and heard it, too. It was a box truck, with a rear door that slides up. The latch was closed, but it had no lock. When we slid the door up, these two women jumped out. We each caught one. They were beaten up and bloody. Jim called 911. An ambulance, a fire rescue unit, and the cops responded quickly."

"Sometimes a job site can get pretty dirty," Jim Cerbone told the detectives. "So, we always keep a clean shirt in the office. This morning, when we got blood on us, we were able to change our shirts and forego our ties for the day."

When the men asked how the women were and what had happened, Harry said they were doing all right, although they were still in the hospital. They wouldn't know what had happened until tomorrow, when the women were well enough to talk.

As the detectives left, Joe asked if this was connected to the sketches in the morning paper. Liz nodded as she stepped into the elevator.

When Delmont and Robinson returned to the office, they had information for Bloomfield's matrix. The truck was stolen the day before from the parking garage of a builder's supply company on the other side of the city. The crime scene techs processed the truck's cargo area, collecting blood and hair samples and dozens of fingerprints. Prints were also lifted from the truck's cab.

◆

The following morning, Detectives Liz Kovak and Sandra Delmont knocked on Annette Jenkins' hospital room door and walked in. A man and woman sat at her bedside. Annette's parents and the detectives were introduced. Annette looked frightful. Her face was orange and purple, swollen as round as a full moon, her nose was covered with bandages and her blackened eyes looked out of tiny slits. Patches of skin had been ripped from her hands and arms.

"Annette," said Liz softly, "I'm Detective Liz Kovak, and this is my partner, Detective Sandra Delmont. Do you feel well enough to tell us what happened?"

Annette Jenkins nodded her head and said, "Yes," in a voice stronger and clearer than her condition and appearance suggested. Turning to her parents, she said, "Mom, Dad, please."

Sandra stepped to the door and opened it. "Mr. and Mrs. Jenkins," she said by the open door, "why don't you go down to the cafeteria and have some coffee, so we can speak privately with your daughter?"

"Annette," Liz said with a soothing voice, "we've spoken with your doctors, and have been told that all of your injuries, as painful as they are, will heal. Tell us what happened the other night and how it happened. Please be detailed. Try to remember exactly what they said and how they said it. We need to know what they did to you, what they made you do, and what they made you say. We know it's embarrassing, but Sandra and I have heard it all before. The more you tell us, the better chance we have of catching them before they can do the same thing to some other woman."

Annette first asked, "Is Penny all right? Where is she?"

Liz told her that Penny was also in the hospital, recovering from her injuries. "The doctors say that you both will heal nicely."

Annette told the detectives, "We ate dinner and then went to a club nearby. They required ID, and Penny had left her purse in the trunk of my car, so we went back to get it. The parking garage was still about half full, with people and cars coming and going. If the truck was there then, I didn't notice it."

She then recounted returning to the deserted parking garage later that night and seeing the two men at the car. "We started running down the ramp, but they caught us. That's when they beat us and dragged us back up to the truck." Annette stopped talking and started shaking with uncontrollable sobs. They called a nurse, who injected something through the IV. "That will calm and relax her."

In a few minutes, Annette was able to continue. "The four of us were in the back of the truck, and it was like a horror movie. The one that was doing most of the talking, the same one that punched me and pulled me by my hair on the ramp told the other one, 'You take the blond bitch. This is my bitch,' and that's when he told me to take off all my clothes. When I hesitated, he punched me in my face. 'I said take off your motherfuckin' clothes, you worthless white whore.' I don't know which was worse, the punches or the cold fear, the stark terror. When I was naked, he took my breast in one hand. In his other hand, he held a pair of garden shears. He put my nipple between the blades. He told me that if I didn't do what he said, he would cut off my nipples. I could feel the sharp, cold blades. I cried and begged him not to do it, and I promised I would do what he said.

"He stood over me and said, 'Who is the master, and who is the slave?' He made me tell him that he was the master and I was the slave. He said, 'You gonna come off some of that pussy,' then dropped his pants and shorts, got between my legs, and raped me. He kept saying, 'How do it feel, slave girl, to hafta spread your white legs for your master?'"

Annette paused. Tears rolled down her swollen, greenish-yellow cheeks.

Liz gave her some water and hugged her to comfort her. "Keep going, if you can. We need to get it all."

"I heard Penny scream. When I glanced over, I saw she was on her stomach. The other guy straddled her back. I knew what he was doing because Penny kept screaming and screaming. The one that had just raped me told me to turn over on my stomach and get up on my knees with my elbows on the floor. He got behind me and said, 'Put that nice, shiny, white ass up here for me, slave girl. Your master's gonna show you who's the boss.' After slapping my buttocks five or six times, he pushed himself into my behind. The pain was so awful that I screamed, and as he kept thrusting, I couldn't stop screaming. I must have fainted, because the next thing I knew, Penny was hugging and rocking me, and both of us were still in the back of the truck. The two brutes were gone.

"After a long time, we heard cars and people talking. We started screaming and banging on the sides of the truck. The back door slid open, and two men were there. They caught us when we jumped down. The police came and an ambulance brought us here to the hospital." She started to cry again.

Liz said, "Okay, Annette, you did great. That's enough for today. We'll stop by tomorrow to see how you are doing."

Penny Bosworth didn't look much better when Liz and Sandra entered her room. They identified themselves as detectives investigating her case. Penny stared at them with her good eye, the one not swollen shut. She could not say a word, because her broken jaw was wired shut.

"We want to introduce ourselves and see how you are doing. We would like to know what happened, and whatever you can tell us about the two men who did this to you and Annette. We know you can't talk because of your jaw, but I see you have a couple of note pads and pens on your table. I guess you'll have to talk in writing until your jaw gets better."

Penny picked up a note pad and printed, "HOW'S ANNETTE?"

The detectives smiled, and Sandra answered that she seemed to be doing okay. "We were in to see her earlier. She told us what occurred the other night. Later today, or tomorrow, write out the course of events starting when you got to work Thursday, until you arrived at the hospital yesterday morning. Penny, write it just the way they said it, what they did to you, and what they made you do or say. We know it will be very graphic, and you wouldn't normally talk like that, but we need it just as it happened. Don't leave what you have written where it can be seen by anyone who visits you. Let's keep it private and confidential."

Penny Bosworth nodded her head and smiled as best she could as Liz and Sandra left the room.

CHAPTER 16

Deputy Chief Glenn Watkins was at the meeting. The task force detectives glanced at one another, surprised at his presence.

"I'd like to qualify my questions and remarks by making it clear that I am familiar with each of you. I know you are competent, conscientious, hard-working men and women." Chief Watkins paused, looking from one to the other, then continued. "What I don't understand is why we have not identified these two murdering rapists yet. They've left their DNA, fingerprints, and other forensic evidence at the crime scenes. We have five eyewitnesses—the rape victims all say they will be able to identify them—and each gave similar sketches that have been on every media outlet in the city. Lieutenant McGee, please help me to understand."

"What we know, Chief," answered the lieutenant, "is that the same two black males are responsible for the crimes. We believe they are street thugs, gangbangers in their early twenties to mid-thirties, but are they our street thugs, or are they from somewhere else? Yes, we have DNA evidence that matches from all five rape victims, but it doesn't match the DNA samples taken from every inmate as they enter our state prison system. We feel certain these two have been in prison before, so why can't we get a DNA match? One theory is that they served time in another state.

"We've sent inquiries to law enforcement agencies across the country, complete with the sketches of the rapists and a summary of the crimes that have been committed here. We have requested identification, if available, of anyone who resembles either one of the two, and notification of similar crimes in their jurisdiction. We've taken hundreds of fingerprints at the crime scenes, and prints that we could not identify were sent to the FBI database. That could take weeks or months; it depends on how backed up they are. Unofficially, Chief, if a request to the FBI is not from the NYPD or LAPD, it goes to the bottom of the stack."

Chief Watkins gave McGee a look that said, "Let's not start a war with the Bureau."

Lieutenant McGee continued, "We are looking for the 9mm semi-automatic pistol used in six of the homicides, and the .40 caliber semi-automatic service weapon that killed Officer Reston. We have had dozens of calls on the sketches, which we've run down as they came in. So far, they've been false alarms. The word is out to our most reliable informants, who know the streets and who's doing what on their turf. There have been sightings of an older model black car, but that information is vague. The make is unknown and no one has seen a tag."

"Okay, Lieutenant. That gives me a good snapshot of the situation. I feel bad for the victims and the terrible abuses they have suffered. This task force has the highest priority in the department. I know each of you is highly motivated. Thank you all for your hard work. I appreciate the briefing, Lieu. Whatever you need let me know."

◆

It was quiet on the hospital's third-floor recovery unit. When they entered the room, Annette was staring at the ceiling, her swollen eyes a collage of purple, black, yellow, and green. She was alone. Her mother had just left.

"Annette," said Liz softly, "this is my other partner, Detective Harry Lincoln. We came by to see how you are getting along."

"The pain is still there. They give me medication for it. The worst part is the dreams. This morning, I woke up screaming and they had to give me something through my IV to calm me down. I'm afraid to go to sleep; I'm terrified that I will not be able to stop thinking about the horrible things he did to me. I awoke this morning, hysterical, thinking that he had just cut off my nipples."

Harry, sitting in a chair next to the bed said, "Liz and I, and others, are working very hard to find out who they are and arrest them. When we do, Annette, I promise you they will be severely punished."

Liz said, "Do you have someone besides your parents, to stay here with you? Knowing you are not alone should help with the nightmares."

"Yes, my mom is arranging that today. Thank you for your kindness and all that you are doing on our behalf. Detective Lincoln, I want them more than severely punished. I want them dead!"

◆

Three doors down the hallway, Detectives Sandra Delmont and Ronald Robinson went to visit Penny Bosworth.

"Penny," Sandra said as they entered the room. "This is one of my partners, Detective Ronald Robinson."

Penny came awake out of a troubled sleep. Her swollen, multi-colored face, her jaw hideously wired, turned towards the door, and she stared, horrified, through one opened eye at Detective Robinson. Penny tried to scream, but it sounded more like the muted cry of a wounded animal.

"Penny, it's all right," said Sandra, sitting on the bed, holding her hand. "That's Detective Robinson. We have different partners from time to time, all working together as one unit."

"Ms. Bosworth," said Robinson's calm, mellow voice from across the room. "Please don't confuse me with those two animals. I am black, and I am ashamed of what they have done to you and others. I assure you that I will work as hard as my colleagues to hunt down that scum."

Sandra told Penny that Annette's parents were setting up a schedule for family members, or close friends, to be in the room with her all the time. Sandra suggested that her family do the same. Penny wrote on her pad that her mother planned to start this evening after dinner. She then tore some pages out of the notebook that contained her statement, which she had written that morning, and wrote, *"I hope this will be all right. I've never made a statement about a crime before."*

Penny then scribbled on a clean sheet and handed it to Ron. *"Detective Robinson, when you and Detective Delmont came into the room, I was having a nightmare. He was hurting me again, over and over. I'm sorry if I offended you."*

"You did not offend me. I understand completely," Robinson said. "Tomorrow, we, or other members of the task force, will be here to show you some mug shots. If we are not back tomorrow, you can be sure we'll see you again soon."

Bloomfield and Harrington returned to the Valley View Apartments, to re-interview the neighbor who reported seeing two black males leaving the scene of Lillian's rape and Roy Singer's murder. She saw the Singers' car and an older model black car being loaded with items stolen from the apartment. When questioned further about a tag on the older black car, she recalled the tag was plain white with blue lettering, as opposed to the familiar black lettering on a white background of her own license tag. That was the only time the car was sighted in the daylight, and there was bright sunshine that day. The witness was sure about the blue lettering.

Nearly half of the states' license plates have blue lettering on white backgrounds, but it was a lead, however anemic, for Bloomfield to add to his matrix.

CHAPTER 17

Lieutenant McGee started the task force meeting. "We've gotten a response from the Detroit Police Department. The DPD has identified them as Jamal Eaves, aka Cellblock, age thirty; and Bernard Jackson, aka Bad Dog, age twenty-six. I have a stack of information sheets up here on the table with their physical descriptions, mug shots, and other stats. Be sure each of you gets copies of everything here."

There was a buzz around the room as the sheets were studied. Liz was amazed at how similar the DPD photos were to their own sketches.

"Our sketch artist should get a raise," answered Harry, "or at the very least a bonus."

McGee rapped his knuckles on the table to get everyone's attention. "If you read about the crimes they've committed in Detroit, it's a good bet these are the two we want. This morning, I spoke to my counterpart, the DPD homicide lieutenant. After we compared notes, she and I are convinced these are our guys. She said they came very close to catching up with them, but were a day late. They are believed to be driving a stolen, black 2001 Ford Taurus that was taken in a robbery/homicide. The plate number is on the handouts. Bloomfield and Harrington, your witness is correct, the Michigan plates have blue letters on a white background. The word was that they left Detroit, but no one knew where. We know where they went."

Robinson said, "With a name like "Cellblock," I guess he's done time in prison?"

"That's right. Detroit cops are getting us prison records from the Michigan State Board of Corrections for each of them. Bloomfield, update your matrix. We now have their names. Soon we'll get the meat. We know who they are. We don't know where they are. Your job is to find out." Lieutenant McGee looked around the table. "I guess all of your friends are impressed with you because you are homicide detectives. It has a ring to it. 'Homicide Detective.' It conjures up images of Sherlock Holmes, using your brains, skill, and simple deduction to solve crime, like on those dumb TV cop shows. Most cases you investigate are smoking gun cases that don't need solving. They just need you to put it all together, find and gather witnesses, take statements, talk to people, arrest the dumb son-of-bitch who pulled the trigger in front of all those witnesses, and then do the paperwork. You don't even have to collect evidence, tag-n-bag, or take photos. The crime scene people do that. So, how about the who-done-its? Do you solve them like Sherlock Holmes? Like TV detectives? No! You are real detectives; you rely on your informants. The most successful detectives are those with the best informants. These horrific crimes are going to be solved at street level, so get down into the gutter and put the fear of God in your snitches."

The room was silent. No one moved while McGee drank some water. "One more thing," he said. "I'm meeting with Chief Watkins this afternoon to ask that the fugitive squad be attached to the task force. Now that the suspects are identified, with photos and descriptions, they can help us search. The fugitive guys are down in the gutter every day. They hunt two-legged animals that need to be caged, and they are good. No turf guarding. No pissing contests. The only thing that matters is Eaves and Jackson in chains before they claim another victim."

◆

The six detectives and Judy Wright went for lunch at Mike's Tavern. They sat at one of the long tables in the rear of the dining room.

"Boy, I sure didn't see that coming—the lecture about Sherlock Holmes," Bloomfield said.

Liz said thoughtfully, "I think it's his frustration with these cases coming one after the other. We haven't been able to stop them. Until today, we didn't even know who was responsible."

"Liz is right," Harry agreed. "McGee has been around a long time. He has seen just about everything, but these guys have taken it to a different level—the brutality, the viciousness, the savage nature of the rapes, and the casual way they murder. That has to be stopped. McGee is most likely getting heat from above, so he lashed out at us."

"Well," said Harrington, "he's under a lot of pressure. I can't blame him for the way he feels."

Bloomfield answered with a smirk, "Yeah, you Irish guys always stick together."

Ronald Robinson quietly said, "I don't think I'm Sherlock Holmes. He was a white guy."

They all laughed and started eating.

◆

"This is what they look like, Ham," Harry said, pointing to the black-and-white mug shots. "Their names and all the other stats are right there. I am giving you a handful of these to hand out where it will do the most good. This is big stuff, Ham. Go the extra mile for me on this one."

While Harry talked with Ham, Liz called Mule and arranged to meet him in the bowling alley parking lot.

Twenty minutes after leaving Ham, they pulled up next to a grey 5 series BMW. Mule was behind the wheel.

"Thanks for meeting us on such short notice," Liz said, talking car-to-car. "I can't emphasize enough how important this is. Here are mug shots and more information on those two murdering rapists. They come out of Detroit. We want them. Big time!"

"Detective Kovak, I would do what I could for you, anyway, because low-down thugs like these don't need to be on the streets, but this is personal. I knew Niki Reston pretty well. I liked her. She always treated me right. From what I heard, she was okay with everyone I knew. She was tough, but she was fair, and she was straight up, man! She was straight up! The best!"

Mule paused as if he had more to say. Liz and Harry were silent.

"One night, late, I saw a patrol car parked at the all-night diner on Maxwell Avenue, and through the window I saw her sitting alone. I went in and asked if I could sit with her and drink some coffee. She'd been in the 7th long enough to know who and what I am. She was friendly. We had a nice conversation. I asked her for a favor. I asked that if she saw my son out at night with the gangbangers, to snatch him up before he did something he shouldn't do, and to bring him home so I could give him a good ass-kicking." He paused again. "I went to Niki Reston's funeral. That's the first time I've cried since I'm grown. Afterward, I heard from a friend who works in the ME's office about some of the stuff those two did to her. I choked with rage. I still feel that rage. I'm glad you brought me their names and pictures. Detective Kovak, Detective Lincoln, I'm going to give these sheets to my people. We're going to start looking."

CHAPTER 18

The task force and the fugitive squad hit the streets. The manhunt was massive. Homicide detectives and detectives in other squads called in all IOUs. Cops in every precinct in the city, especially the 7th, skipped their second and third coffee and donut breaks. Morning watch cops no longer found places to hide and snooze when they should be working. Instead, they intruded into the darkest corners of their beats. Every cop wanted to find Eaves and Jackson for what they had done to one of their own. This groundswell reached the surrounding suburban police and sheriff's departments.

It wasn't only law enforcement. The street people, people close to Ham and the far-reaching tentacles of the community czar, Mule, turned the groundswell into an urban avalanche. The media, with its campaign of public awareness, brought the images of Eaves and Jackson, and the details of their terrible crimes into every household. This posse, populated with a diverse people, assisted by modern communications technology, formed around two wanted posters. It engulfed the city.

♦

Despite all that, the two most wanted fugitives in the city remained invisible. Eaves and Jackson blended into the cityscape, un-noticed. The building's basement apartment, where the super lived, was a perfect hideout. The super was Jamal's father, Reggis. The basement's separate entrance and parking area prevented contact with the building's tenants.

As for Reggis Eaves, he knew what his son had been doing. Everyone in the city knew. He didn't stay quiet out of father-son loyalty, but from the effects of twenty years of the golden rule among convicts and ex-cons: "Keep your mouth shut!" Of course, a little green after a score was a soothing balm; the few bucks Cellblock threw the old man for rent kept him happy and mute.

"We gettin' low on funds, blood. We gonna need some coin pretty soon," said Bernard Jackson, looking worriedly at the dirty few bills he pulled from his pocket. "It's time we did some more business, an' I'm thinkin' maybe we should hit one of the fast food places just before closin', when them cash registers be full."

"Yeah, I been thinkin' the same thing," answered Cellblock. "'Cept I ain't fuckin' with no punk-ass joints no more. I got a plan been in my head for 'bout a week now. Gonna put us in the big time. Leave them mom 'n' pop grocery stores and gas stations to the two-bit chumps. You see what I'm sayin', home?"

"No, man. What are you sayin'? We gonna rob a bank or somethin'?"

"This is better than a bank. I'm talkin' about a damn armored truck. When you rob a bank, ya gotta go in an' get the money. When you rob one of those armored trucks, they bring it out an' hand it to ya on the sidewalk," Cellblock said with a satisfied smirk.

"You fuckin' crazy, blood? There be two, maybe three motherfuckers with guns on them trucks," said Bad Dog. "This ain't the same as knockin' off the old Jew and his wife. An' beside, what if there's some kinda alarm in them trucks? Pol-ice be all over the motherfuckin' place. No, man, you been smokin' too much a that shit."

"Hold on, dog, 'fore you go walkin' away from a score like we never had before. Me an' you, we done a lot a time behind the walls because we was stupid, man, just like those other chumps doin' time. Ya gotta' have a plan, an' like I already tol' you, I been workin' on this plan, but if it gonna work, my old man got to be involved. My plan call for three of us to pull it off, but I ain't tol' him yet, an' he better not come off all high 'n' mighty on me, tell me he some kind a model citizen an' don't do shit like that no more. 'Cause, if he do, I'll tell you right now, brother man, I'll cap his black ass, just like any other nigga. Come on. Let's take a walk, an' I'll 'splain my plan to you."

♦

The emergency 911 system was swamped. Hundreds of calls came in every hour, reporting sightings all over the city. Communications operators and dispatchers were placed on twelve-hour shifts. Each sighting required a physical response by police, which quickly caused an overload, resulting in delayed response times to high priority calls. That was unacceptable. Within forty-eight hours, Chief Lansing ordered the entire police department to an emergency schedule of twelve-hour shifts.

It was no longer business as usual on the streets. The illicit markets were non-existent for thieves, hustlers, whores, and their pimps. Illegal goods and services no longer passed, unencumbered, from one to another. Drugs, sex, stolen items, and other illegal commodities no longer fit the basic law of economics—supply and demand. Sellers needed buyers; buyers needed sellers. There was none of either. The city's underbelly wasn't functioning.

Why not?

Jamal "Cellblock" Eaves and Bernard "Bad Dog" Jackson.

The police were everywhere, day and night. Cops in uniform, detectives in suits, more cops and detectives in street clothes—all upset the natural order of homo sapien vermin infested gutters and sewers in the city. Eaves and Jackson had been identified. Now they had to be found. The pressure was enormous. The twelve-hour shifts began to take its toll on the cops, but there was little bitching. They were motivated with a desire for payback for Officer Niki Reston.

Task force detectives worked fourteen- and sometime sixteen-hour days and nights. Others also worked extended shifts, disrupting family life and causing friction at home.

This was precisely the reason Harry Lincoln rejected marriage. Harry's concentration was on this crime spree, and he didn't have the distraction of domestic pressure. He brought copies of the victim's statements taken back to his loft. He was at the point of exhaustion, but he still analyzed the statements once again, before having to rest until again reporting for duty.

On the drive back to headquarters later that day, after a few hours of much-needed sleep, Harry couldn't shake the feeling that his reaction to this investigation was different. Reading and re-reading those statements lit a fire in his belly that he hadn't felt before. *What was the word Mule used when talking about Niki Reston's murder?* Harry thought. *Rage! That's what I feel when I think of what those two did to their victims. A smoldering rage!*

CHAPTER 19

"That's the place, dog."

Eaves pointed across the street to a storefront with a large yellow sign over the window. "CHECKS CASHED" written in large black letters.

"Armored truck come every Friday an' bring thousands of dollars in cash. When the chumps get off work, they go in an' cash their paychecks."

"How you know all that shit, man?" asked a surprised and skeptical Jackson.

"While you been smokin' that shit an' sleepin' all motherfuckin' day, I'm out checkin' out our next score. Now, let me show you somethin'." They walked through an alley two doors from the check-cashing store, and then into an old shed leading to an abandoned building cluttered with discarded junk. They left the building through a far door to a second alley, which put them on the street a half block from the basement entrance to the old man's apartment. "That the way we go after we rip off the truck. Ain't that easy?"

Eaves and Jackson walked back around to the check-cashing store and stood across the street from it. "I been watchin' the last two Friday mornin'. Armored truck come at ten o'clock, an' two guards get out, both carryin' a canvas bag full a money. When they on the sidewalk, 'fore they go in the store, that when we cap 'em. We each grab a bag, then duck aroun' the alley like I already show you. Now, here's where my ol' man come in…"

They went back to the apartment and sat down with Reggis. Jamal told him the plan. "Now here's what you gonna do, Pop. That cart of yours in the maintenance room, the one you use to tote supplies an' shit into the building, is how we get the bags of money in here. You take the cart, go to the hardware store, an' get shit you need for the building here. Then on the way back, you go down the alley into that empty building an' wait for us. We gonna put the bags a money an'

264

the guns in the bottom of the cart under the stuff you jus' got from the store. Then, you go out that far door into the alley that bring you out to your street, an' you push your cart like you always do, an' go in the side door to this building."

"Are you fuckin' crazy, Jamal? You an' him gonna rob an armored truck not three blocks from here, shoot two guards on the sidewalk in broad daylight, an' then put that money an' your guns on me? The guns you jus' shot them guards with? You might be crazy, but I'm not. No, leave me out of that shit."

"Let me tell you somethin', old man," said the younger Eaves. "You gonna do what I tol' you, but you don't have to worry none about going back to prison, 'cause if you fuck it up, I'll light up your black ass, an' don't think I won't. We gonna do it Friday, two days from now." He turned to Jackson. "Come on, dog. Let's get outta here."

♦

On Thursday, the elder Eaves made his weekly visit to the senior center, a place to have a bit of social contact with people much like him, to mingle and talk. He looked forward to these hours, a bright spot in his otherwise dreary and lonely life. He remembered a guy telling him of an unofficial neighborhood organizer, a man who solved problems and fixed things without going to the police or other government agency. He sat with that same guy again, and after a brief conversation, Reggis Eaves had a phone number.

"I have information, and I was told to call this number. I know where the men from Detroit who killed that cop are. I don't want to get involved with the pol-ice."

Mule sat up straight and listened intently. This was not the first call he'd gotten since the media blitz, but they all resulted in false alarms. "I won't ask who you are unless you want to tell me, but I'll listen to see if I'm interested in what you've got."

Reggis explain the situation without revealing his connection to the two. He gave the address of the building where they were hiding, and told Mule they were in the maintenance man's basement apartment. "The building super has nothing to do with them and does not want any trouble because of them. They plan to rob an armored truck tomorrow morning at ten in front of that check-cashing place on Cypress Avenue, three blocks from the building."

♦

Later that evening, as Cellblock Eaves and Bad Dog Jackson drove the Taurus into the secluded parking area under the building, they were surrounded by six men with guns and immediately disarmed.

"Hey, my brothers," said a surprised Cellblock. "What's goin' on?"

"Just shut the fuck up and get in," was the only reply. Two SUVs, Eaves in one, Jackson in the other, left the building and blended into the normal street traffic.

The elder Eaves sat alone in his basement apartment contemplating what he had done. After serving years in prison, the convicts' golden rule was ingrained. "You don't snitch!" Reggis Eaves didn't ever want to go back to prison, and that's where he would end up if he went along with Jamal's reckless plan. However, he could not go to the police. They were still the enemy. *Anyway,* he thought, *it's done, and now I have to live the rest of my life knowing that I ratted out my own son.*

♦

On Friday morning at ten o'clock, the armored truck pulled to the curb in front of the check-cashing store. Two guards got out with guns drawn, each carrying a canvas bag of money. The third guard stayed in the truck, watching. The guards went into the store, got a signed receipt from the manager, and returned to the truck. It drove off, as usual, to the next stop.

CHAPTER 20

It was just after dinner. Liz Kovak had given her daughter a bath and was now reading a bedtime story, one of the few times during this investigation she had been able to do that. Her husband was cleaning up the kitchen when her cell phone rang. It was Mule.

"Detective Kovak, do you know the old tool and die factory that closed up a few years ago? The one by that abandoned industrial area in the Sixth Precinct."

"Yes, Mule, I know where it is."

"I got an anonymous call that those two you been looking for are in that old building."

"You mean the ones who killed Officer Reston?"

"Yeah, and you don't need to bring no SWAT team with you. Maybe just an ambulance. I hear they in pretty bad shape. You go ahead and see if they are the right ones. I'll be in touch."

◆

"Harry, meet me at the office right away," said an excited Liz Kovak as she gathered what she needed and rushed to her car. She told him of the phone call from Mule as she moved. Her next call was to Lieutenant McGee.

"Okay, Kovak, I'll meet you and Lincoln at the old factory," said the lieutenant. Then he added, "I'll have a couple of patrol cars and a sergeant dispatched; they'll get there quicker than we can. I'm also having the others meet us there."

When Liz and Harry arrived, the activity was inside the huge brick building. Several patrol cars illuminated the darkened factory with headlights and spotlights. Cops with flashlights circled two men lying on the floor who moaned feebly and screaming intermittently. There was lots of blood and trauma, which made identification difficult. The only thing that was certain was that these two damaged creatures were black males.

"Let's hope these are our cop killers," the patrol sergeant said, acknowledging the detectives. "I've got two ambulances on the way, and I have requested a generator truck with auxiliary lights."

"Thanks, sergeant," Harry said. "This place will get crowded pretty soon. We'll need some officers to secure the entry points. No one gets in unless okayed by the task force detectives."

Lieutenant McGee arrived a few minutes after the ambulances and saw the injured men being attended to by EMTs, who stabilized them before they were loaded into the ambulances.

"Sergeant, I'd like one of your cars to follow the ambulances to the hospital. I'll have some cops from the 5th relieve your guys."

"Sure, Lieutenant. Over there, on that old workbench, we found a couple of semi-automatic handguns. The clips are missing, so we don't know if the chambers are clear. We didn't want to touch them."

McGee thanked him and started issuing orders. "Kovak, Lincoln, go to the hospital and stick with those mutts. Find out what you can. Bloomfield, Harrington, Delmont, Robinson—the four of you stay here and work this scene. Send for crime scene techs. I'm going to the hospital."

◆

"We snuck a quick peek into the trauma rooms they are being treated," Harry told Lieutenant McGee. "We saw them momentarily. Lieu, we've never seen anyone mangled that badly and live, both of them. We went through the clothing that the docs cut off them. Neither had any identification."

"They were beyond communicating," Liz added, "so we haven't learned anything else. As soon as the trauma teams finish their work, we'll get some techs here to print them and collect DNA. Lieutenant, I saw a man hit by a train several years ago when I worked uniform. He didn't look any worse, and he was dead."

"I've spoken with the watch lieutenant here in the 5th. He's detailed a couple of uniforms to stay with each 24/7," McGee informed the two detectives. "There's nothing more for us to do here right now. Let's go to the office, and you can get started on the report. Kovak, be sure to make a separate written statement concerning that phone call from your C.I. Make it short and sweet, but very, very accurate, because it will be read, re-read, reviewed, and turned upside-down and inside-out before this is all over."

The two handguns found in the factory, a Smith and Wesson 9 mm semi-automatic and the .40 caliber semi-automatic issued to Officer Niki Reston, were taken to the state crime lab for Judy Wright's expedited attention, along with the DNA samples taken from both men at the hospital. Their fingerprints were sent to the Detroit Police Department for identification. Within a few days, there was no doubt they had caught the two most wanted men in the city.

CHAPTER 21

The large assembly room in the basement of police headquarters, known by most detectives as the lineup room, was almost full. The media had clamored for a press conference, which had to be held in the larger room because it was more than just a local story. It had gained national, even international, interest. Reporters from TV, radio, newspapers, and several national magazines, as well as major wire services were there.

A hush fell over the room as Police Chief Robert Lansing led a group onto the stage, where they took seats. Public Affairs Sergeant Bowser stepped to the podium and introduced Chief Lansing, who replaced Bowser.

"Good afternoon, ladies and gentlemen of the press," began the chief. "I want to welcome you and thank you for coming. These past few weeks have been tragic for some of our citizens and tense for the rest. I know I speak for every member of our police department when I say we are relieved and thankful that this nightmare has ended with the arrests of these individuals. The men and women behind me have worked very hard and put in long hours to end these vicious murders and assaults. I'd like to ask Deputy Chief Glenn Watkins to say a few words."

"Thank you, Chief," began the chief of detectives. "These are brutal cases of murder, rape, kidnapping, home invasion, and armed robbery. The perpetrators of these heinous crimes were located using information provided by a confidential informant. Relationships between confidential informants and detectives are developed and nurtured in various ways, resulting in this case with two very bad men removed from the streets. They will brutalize no one else. We are still investigating how they were located, and recording the nature of their injuries, which were extensive. Here now to give you details of those injuries and to answer some of your questions is homicide commander, Lieutenant James McGee."

Lieutenant McGee dispensed with the niceties and got right to it. "Jamal 'Cellblock' Eaves and Bernard 'Bad Dog' Jackson have been positively identified through fingerprints and DNA evidence. The handguns found with them were run through ballistics and proved to be the weapons used in seven homicides being investigated, including the rape and murder of Officer Niki Reston. Five other rape victims have identified them in photo lineups, using mug shots from the Detroit PD. They recently committed similar crimes in Detroit, Michigan, before arriving in our city."

McGee pulled another sheet of paper from the file. "Now to their injuries, which Deputy Chief Watkins described as 'extensive.' He was correct. The two men we recovered from the abandoned tool and die factory were barely alive. There are strong indications that they were systematically tortured."

"Hey, lieutenant," shouted a young man standing five or six rows back. He identified himself as a reporter from the *Detroit Free Press*. "How about giving us a rundown of those injuries?"

"Okay, hot shot, I was about to do just that. You interrupted me before I had a chance," answered McGee, red-faced, trying to stay in control. "That rude shit may be okay in Detroit. Here a speaker is given the courtesy of being allowed to finish his statement. Then it's opened for questions. How about sitting back down and keeping your mouth shut until then?"

McGee then addressed the press corps, who listened in stunned silence as he listed in graphic detail the physical damage done to both subjects. "They were castrated, had their testicles surgically removed. Surgically removed might be a stretch. It was a crude job, done by amateurs. Their shinbones and kneecaps were shattered, most likely with an iron bar found at the scene. They sustained cracked ribs and ruptured spleens. Their thumbs were cut off with garden shears, also found at the warehouse. The rest of their fingers were broken, their front teeth, uppers and lowers, were knocked out, their jaws were broken, their noses smashed, and they suffered severe facial bruising. A length of metal pipe was removed from deep in their rectums. When the EMTs got there, they were able to slow down the blood loss and stabilize them enough to keep them from going into shock. The ER trauma docs kept them alive until they got to the operating room. I'll take some questions now."

There was quiet following McGee's invitation for questions. Although the room was filled with reporters who had covered violent crimes in the past, the magnitude of this was at a different level.

"Who would have done such horrible things to them? Why?" asked a young female TV reporter in the front row.

"That's the focus of our investigation now," answered Lieutenant McGee. "When we find out, we'll pass it on to the media."

"Deputy Chief Watkins said they were located through a confidential informant," shouted a newspaper reporter from the back of the room. "Who is this informant?"

"If I announced a name, that person would no longer be confidential, or a source of critical information," the lieutenant snapped. "Don't you get that? It should be simple to understand."

"Where are they now, and what is their prognosis?" asked an older TV reporter, a man McGee recognized from one of the major networks.

"They were brought to the main trauma-one hospital in the city and are being treated in a sealed-off section of the ICU. Their condition is critical. They are pumped full of antibiotics and pain medication. They are under police guard 24/7. Access to them is restricted to authorized medical personnel. We don't know when their condition will allow us to question them."

Ten minutes later, after Lieutenant McGee had fielded a dozen more questions, Chief Lansing nodded to Sergeant Bowser, who went to the podium and closed the press conference. As the principals walked off the stage toward a back room, a barrage of questions followed them.

Lieutenant McGee called an impromptu meeting of the task force. There were things that needed to be said. Back in the small conference room adjacent to the homicide squad room, McGee cleared his throat and began. "Those two mutts are off the streets, and they will never brutalize another victim. Our job is done, or is it? If they live, they'll more than likely get the needle, or spend the rest of their miserable lives in prison."

The lieutenant paused and looked around the table. "We are all relieved that it's over and we can go back to our normal routines, but we have two unanswered questions. How were they located? Who tortured and nearly killed them?"

Robinson said, "Who would care? They certainly got what they deserved, didn't they?"

272

"Yes, I suppose they did, and all of you probably agree, but that's not up to us. We can't just say 'chalk it up' or 'fuck 'em, they got what they deserved.' We have an obligation to get answers to those questions." McGee looked at Liz. "Kovak, your CI is the key to those answers. So get together and press a little."

He turned back to the group. "You have worked long and hard. You'll have to wait until those two are able to talk before the case files are closed. Let's all go home and have a normal dinner, spend time with the families, and get a good night's sleep."

EPILOGUE

*I*t was more than a dozen years ago, and Homicide Detective Ben Lincoln had not yet retired. The younger Lincoln was working a patrol car in uniform assigned to the morning watch.

"When you get off duty, change clothes and drive down to the river, pier twenty-eight; I want you to meet someone," Ben told Harry.

◆

"Lucas Muline, this is my son, Harry."

They shook hands. Lucas was a nicely dressed black man somewhere between his age and his dad's.

"Good to meet you, Lucas."

"Pleased to meet you, Harry. Everyone calls me Mule."

"Mule and I respect each other and have formed a strong bond through the years," Ben said. "He is not exactly a pillar of the community, you know. Hardly the sterling citizen. Nevertheless, he has done a lot of good for people living in different parts of the city. Between us, we've managed to cool down the fervor of racist cops and rescue folks from over-zealous types. He knows the criminal element in the city. He knows the individuals that comprise the criminal element. If it were not for his information, some of my cases would not have been cleared."

Harry wondered why his dad was telling him this after all this time and what it had to do with him.

"Harry, I've seen the results of the detective test you took several months ago. You are number one on the list. You should get your gold shield soon, and you have a good chance of being assigned to homicide. When that happens, it would be good for you to develop a relationship with Mule. Believe me when I tell you that he will be invaluable to you."

Mule said, "Harry, there are several ground rules that I insist on. We must always be straight with each other—no lies, no tap dancing, no bullshit. No one is to know we know each other personally, and that

274

means no one—partners, buddies, wives, girlfriends—no one. When we are in someone's presence, I will address you as Detective Lincoln. You will address me by the name that person calls me. Your father and I have had these same three understandings for many years and it has worked well. It will work as well for us when you get to be a detective."

◆

Harry had cleared some major cases because of crucial information supplied by Mule. Then Liz stumbled into the mix by saving Mule's teenage son from a trip to juvenile detention. Since then, Mule felt he owed her and had become Liz's CI. Harry stayed in the background when the three of them were together for the first time. He did as he was supposed to do, by agreement. He acknowledged Mule, saying he was pleased to meet him, when Liz introduced them.

Harry was relaxing, listening to Beethoven's violin concerto piped in over the loft's sound system. He was listening, but thinking about the last couple of days. *Mule asked me to meet him at the old tool and die factory. To come alone. He didn't say why. I didn't ask, but I knew it must be important, or he wouldn't have insisted I come alone. I made some bullshit excuse to Liz about a personal matter and drove to meet Mule at the factory. That's when I saw the two who had been terrorizing the city. They were on their backs tied to tables, surrounded by six formidable men. The two were talking street jive to the men. The six men ignored them.*

Mule informed me that he was about to administer payback, some street justice for what they had done to Officer Niki Reston. He reminded me of my desire, my craving for my own payback, to physically hurt them for what they had done to those innocent women. He told me to what the extent they would suffer punishment. He offered me the first crack. I thought of their cruelty, their brutality. I could not forget what those animals had done to Niki. That fire in my belly became an inferno. I picked up a pair of brass knuckles from a nearby table and struck each as hard as I could repeatedly in the face, breaking noses, knocking out teeth, and injuring eyes. It was the first time I ever hit someone who was helpless and could not fight back. They begged and screamed. I wondered if the women they hurt begged and screamed the same way. Did Niki Reston beg them not to torture and mutilate her before they killed her? I became enraged. I grabbed an iron pipe, yelling and cursing at them. I smashed their kneecaps and shinbones until I was soaked in my own sweat. I had to stop. I'm still a cop. I've heard it a hundred times: 'You are not judge, jury, nor executioner.' I walked away and went home, where I stayed until Liz called later that evening.

Did the punishment fit the crime? A couple of other phrases go through my mind as I sit here listening to classical music. I am held to a higher standard and have tarnished my badge. It means everything to me. I have violated my oath as a police officer. Those words are a declaration of honor. I have committed a crime, a felony, and concealed another. I've put people in jail for the same thing.

Can I tell myself that I'm only human? That the things I did happen to others who had the same feelings I did? Will I feel guilt when I arrest someone for committing a crime? Will I get over it? I fervently hope so. I want to believe that these concerns and the questions they raise will be resolved with the passage of time. Okay, Harry, enough! Stop beating yourself up and get on with your life.

♦

He picked up the phone and with the rich violin music in the background said, "Hello, Jessica. Harry Lincoln. Would you like to have dinner with me? I know a great place for steaks."